Printed in Canada

Library of Congress Cataloging-in-Publication Data on file.

ISBN: 979-8-89778-911-5

Also by **LISA K. STEPHENSON**

The Snows of Khione: Book 1

Green Trees

The Yellow Brownstone

Even My Hair Is Mad

Late Bloomer

To Korri,

The best fur baby a gal could ask for.

Dear Janelle Banks,

You tuck him away in the quiet corners of your heart, not because your love isn't real, but because the world isn't ready for just how real it is.

ASIAS BRANDS

New York

The Artist:
Late Bloomer
Part II

CHAPTER I.

WELCOME HOME

It was a city still healing—its rhythm returning, but not quite the same. Midtown buzzed with a cautious kind of energy, like an old engine trying to restart after too long in the cold. The sidewalks were busy again, but the hustle had dulled; masks still dangled from wrists or tucked into coat pockets like faded memories of what once was.

Glass towers loomed high, catching reflections of taxis, corner vendors, and men in suits who looked more tired than ambitious—a new type of look for New York City residents. Skyscrapers didn't shimmer quite the same. Some offices remained half-empty, their floors dark, desks abandoned. Coffee shops reopened with hand sanitizer by the register, and doormen at luxury buildings greeted residents with nods instead of smiles.

The scent of street food mixed with the metallic tang of subway grates, and the air, though heavy with smog and ambition, carried an edge of uncertainty. People had returned, yes, but something had shifted. The grind was still alive, but it had softened. Priorities changed. Eyes lingered longer on sunrises between buildings. Quiet moments held more weight.

For Nelly, Midtown was no longer just the place she worked—it was the space between who she was and who she wanted to become. A place where dreams either cracked under pressure or found a way to survive. But it was the belligerent horn honking, the greasy croissant with melted cheese and bacon, the bitter black coffee, and the return to normalcy that she missed most. From the seventeenth floor of a slowly fading legacy, Janelle 'Nelly' Banks stared out of her office window, watching the city breathe below her—alive, relentless, and completely unaware of her longing. Just one moment of stillness.

But reality comes quickly. The shrill ring of her desk phone breaks the silence.

"Hey, I need the piece on *Eleven*," her senior editor snaps—a voice like sharp glass: strict, firm, and once essential. Now, with magazine subscriptions becoming harder to justify and digital content stealing the spotlight, her authority feels more like a ghost of power past.

The days drag. The fear of unemployment hangs in the air like smoke—unseen by most, but suffocating for those who know it's coming.

"Yes, of course. I'm emailing it now," Nelly stammers, already clicking through tabs, masking her quiet panic.

The open office layout was still a novelty—trendy, exposed, and supposedly "collaborative." Cubicles had become relics of a more private time, replaced with glass dividers and shared desks that encouraged forced interaction. Past issues of She's Single lined the ornate walls like trophies from a war no one could quite explain. The plush carpet, once pristine, now held layers of dust and city grime as heels, boots, and sneakers stomped across it once again with newsroom urgency—journalists, photographers, and graphic designers moving like everything was breaking news and every headline might be the one to go viral.

But everyone knew the truth: it was all just another desperate spring to stay relevant. A race against the scroll. The articles—bold fonts and pastel layouts—screamed from the pages with curated empowerment: *"How to Make Him See You as the Woman of His Dreams"* or *"Why Choosing You is the New Choosing Him."* It was glossy, it was loud, and if you squinted hard enough, maybe even convincing. But to Nelly, it felt like a performance. Cheesy at best. Desperate at worst.

Still, she stayed. Not for the clickbait headlines or the Instagrammable cover stories, but for the few pieces she could still carve out with integrity—investigative features that made her feel more like she was saying something real. Her friends didn't mind being characters in her stories. In fact, they loved it. But while the office buzzed with faux purpose and modern feminism, Nelly's quiet rebellion lived elsewhere—downstairs, on the ground floor, where an empty storefront sat like a blank canvas. Every lunch break, she'd pass by and stare into it. No customers. No lights. Just potential. A gallery in waiting. A quiet dream in a city that never shuts up. The blaring horn shattered the silent moment like glass.

"Get the fuck out of the road!" the cab driver shouted, his voice thick with irritation and Manhattan impatience. Nelly blinked out of the trance, still rooted to the sidewalk, her gaze fixed on the empty storefront window. The glass reflected pieces of her dreams she hadn't spoken aloud, the version of herself that maybe only existed in moments like this, just outside of reach.

"Hey!"

This time, the voice came from behind. Nelly jumped, her heart skipping a beat—caught in the collision of a honking cab and the sudden presence of Emily's voice. In a flustered rush, her lunch slipped from her fingers, the neatly wrapped sandwich tumbling to the pavement with a soft plop. No saving it now.

"Oh no," Nelly muttered, staring down at the mess of bread in disappointment.

Emily Harrington rushed to her side, her heels clicking as the two women stepped up from the busy street back onto the safety of the curb. "I'm so sorry! I didn't mean to scare you," Emily said, her voice softer now, touched with guilt. Emily was striking in a way that made people turn around and then pretend they hadn't. Big, bright eyes that seemed to hold light, long wavy hair cascading in soft curls down her back, and lips glossed with just the right shade of pink to look effortlessly perfect. Her honey-beige skin caught the sunlight, smooth and dewy—except for the faint strawberry marks dotting her legs, exposed beneath the hem of her spring dress. Even her imperfections were enviable.

Emily looked at Nelly with a playful scowl. "Why'd you even buy lunch? I told you I was coming to your office today to get you so we could eat together." Nelly sighed, still staring at the sandwich like it had taken the hit for her.

"I wasn't sure if you were still coming. You ignored my text," Nelly said.

"I'm sorry," Emily smiled, slipping her arm through Nelly's. "Come on. Let's go somewhere and get you a proper meal, honey." And just like that, the chaos of the city faded again—replaced by the easy rhythm of two friends walking side by side, one trying to keep her dreams intact, the other just trying to feed her.

A few minutes later, the ladies arrived at a Tavern not too far from their offices. As they stepped inside, they were instantly wrapped in the warm hue of conversation and clinking silverware. The restaurant was intimate but alive, a cozy blend of rustic charm and artistic flair. Wooden beams stretched across the ceiling like the ribs of a well-worn ship, grounding the space in something old, while the vivid, abstract murals lining the upper walls breathed in something undeniably modern—bold florals, saturated hues, and chaotic brushstrokes that somehow worked together in perfect harmony.

A long, granite-topped bar wrapped the left side of the room, polished and gleaming, set with copper lamps and neatly folded white napkins, every glass in its place. Behind it, bottles of wine lined the shelves like quiet sentinels, watching the lunch-hour crowd.

At the center, round tables filled the floor with a subtle elegance—no tablecloths, just warm wood and soft candlelight. It was the kind of place where people lingered, where meals turned into stories and wine turned into secrets. A grand arrangement of bare winter branches rose from the planter in the middle of the room, unexpected but striking—like a centerpiece of stillness in an otherwise vibrant space. Nelly took it all in, her eyes scanning the art, the plates, the soft glows of conversations.

"You seem surprised to be here," Emily teased. She was always at home in places like this, leaning toward her with a grin. "Better than a deli sandwich, huh?" she said, guiding them toward an empty table. The hostess acknowledged her as a regular.

"I can't afford a place like this. I'm barely making rent on the loft," Nelly smiled. The tension from earlier slowly unraveled from her shoulders. "But yeah, this is much better." Taking a seat and removing her cardigan, Nelly snuggled into her chair, taking a long look at the menu.

"So, what's the status on the gallery?" Emily asked, her tone light, but her eyes full of genuine concern as she leaned slightly across the table. Nelly let out a quiet sigh, her fingers absently tracing the edge of the table.

"There is no status," she said flatly. "My parents won't loan me the startup money, and I can barely save a dime. The magazine doesn't pay that good, and the pandemic sure didn't help anything."

Frustration curled in her voice like smoke. "I'm turning thirty in a few months, and it's like...my life feels stagnant. Like I'm not progressing, you know?"

Emily leaned back, her expression softening. "I told you I'd lend you the money. You can take your time paying it back, and even if you can't, that's okay." Before Nelly could respond, the waitress appeared quietly beside them, placing down small glasses of water with delicate precision. Nelly waited until she walked away, then shook her head.

"I can't take money from you guys. I know you and Lisa both offered, but it would feel weird. Money can ruin friendships—and that's not a risk I'm willing to take. But please know, I appreciate you both so much for even offering."

Emily sighed, drawing a long breath as she reached for the menu. "Well...have you considered working with other galleries? Maybe they can get your work in a show, sell a few paintings—and hey, you never know."

"I have," Nelly replied quickly, her voice sharper now. "But so many galleries are focused on artists with these huge social media followings. I don't have that. I don't come with a pre-existing audience. It's not even about the art anymore, it's—" she cut herself off with a scoff, "—how many followers do you have? Like, who gives a fuck?"

The energy between them simmered at that moment—frustration, ambition, resignation. But before it could settle, the waitress returned, pad in hand, ready to take their orders.

"I'll have the beet and goat cheese salad with grilled shrimp," Emily said, barely glancing at the menu. Just as Nelly uttered, "I'll have the same—" Emily's phone buzzed on the table. She glanced down and immediately rolled her eyes.

"My boss," she muttered, silencing it for a moment before picking it up. "Let me guess—you want an update on Sundwall." As Emily stepped away from the table to take the call, Nelly stared past her, the restaurant suddenly too warm, too loud. Her dreams felt like they were on the other side of a thick pane of glass—close enough to see, but too far to touch.

Emily clutched her phone tightly, her heels clicking anxiously against the pavement as she paced just outside the restaurant's entrance. Her jaw clenched; her brows furrowed in frustration. "I need more time to work my contact," she hissed into the receiver, lowering her voice just enough not to draw attention. "The leads you gave me were dead, and there's no reporter in the city who has any real update on him. They know he's in Manhattan, but have no clue where—and even if I did know, I can't just pop up at his house. That's not how this works."

Her boss's voice crackled through the phone, smooth but cutting. "Emily, I hired you because you're ruthless and tough. You sign the hard folks. You get the job done. Bringing Nathan to us was a masterstroke. But now we need Sundwall. He's architect gold—and I'm hearing whispers he's sinking serious cash into tech. We need in on those dividends before someone else gets to him."

Emily took a steadying breath and looked around. The spring breeze brushed through her waves as she watched pedestrians move about casually—some carrying shopping bags, others locked in conversation, laughing, distracted. It felt unfair how normal the world looked while her job teetered at the edge of pressure and performance. Every few seconds, she'd glance back through the glass to see Nelly, now idly scrolling her phone, completely unaware of the high-stakes conversation happening just outside.

"Listen," Emily said, at last, her tone cooler now, more composed. "Relax. I'll see what I can do. I'll find out what functions he might be attending. If he's here on business, he's not going to stay hidden forever. But placing this entirely on my shoulders? That's a little cruel. It's not like I know anything about him outside of the drama the papers wrote up. You're asking me to chase a ghost."

"A rich ghost," her boss replied dryly. "And believe me, if I didn't have faith in you, I wouldn't be calling. This is what you do, Emily. This is your alley. You haven't failed me yet." And he was right.

After laying her Grand Aunt, Vernette Robinson, to rest beneath the heavy, humid skies of South Carolina, Emily returned briefly to San Francisco. Just long enough to pack up what was left of a chapter she'd already outgrown. Her relationship with the reporter, Washington Clarke, though strained and awkward at first, had matured into something grounded in mutual respect. They didn't particularly like each other—too many differences, too much history—but Emily appreciated the care he took in sharing their family story with the world. It was honest. Tasteful. And in a strange way, healing.

They didn't keep in touch much after that. Not even when Emily finally made the leap and relocated to New York City, settling into a cutting-edge, glass-walled apartment on the Upper East Side. She had bigger things on her mind. The wealth management firm snapped her up almost instantly, dazzled by her promise to deliver Nathanial Ramirez—a multimillionaire and, more importantly, her ex-Elliott's most valuable client. San Francisco wasn't used to handling such wealth, and so, it was her final move in a long game of quiet revenge. Poaching him was personal, but also smart business. And it paid off.

Now, Emily was the firm's top earner. The most respected advisor in the building. And with that title came weight, expectation, pressure, and high-stakes deals that couldn't afford a single misstep. What once felt like ambition now felt like survival. Each win only raised the bar higher. Each client, a new mountain to scale. She rubbed her temples before slipping her phone back into her pant pocket. The conversation was over.

After lunch, Emily and Nelly parted ways—Emily back to her Upper East Side office, and Nelly back to Midtown, where her unfinished article and a cover shoot awaited. But no amount of caffeine or deadline pressure could snap her out of the fog that had settled over her. She moved through the rest of the day like a shadow of herself—present in body, but somewhere far away in spirit. Each keystroke felt heavy. With each passing hour, a slow crawl.

By the time the clock finally struck five, Nelly did not even bother saying goodbye to her coworkers. She gathered her things quietly, called a taxi, and sank into the backseat, eyes fixed on the blur of city life outside the window. All she wanted was to go home—to disappear into her loft, her sanctuary.

The 2,000-square-foot space in the Meatpacking District was a hidden gem. A true steal, especially in New York terms. It had once belonged to an elderly man who, by some twist of fate, Nelly had helped carry groceries for one chilly Saturday morning two years ago when she worked at a shop nearby. The gesture led to a friendship, and eventually, a rare opportunity: when he decided to move down south to be closer to his family, he offered Nelly the space at a fraction of its value, agreeing to rent it to her until his grandkids were old enough to decide what to do with it.

Tucked inside a quiet two-unit building, Nelly's loft is a peaceful, serene, sun-drenched haven that mirrors her creative, yet often introspective nature. The space feels like a breath of fresh air, with its soaring ceilings, vast industrial windows, and a careful blend of soft pastel tones and bold artistic expression.

The main living area is open and airy, with whitewashed floors that enhance the flood of natural light. The loft's charm lies in its curated minimalism—lush greenery in ceramic pots, sculptural furniture pieces, and its mid-century design give the space personality without overwhelming it. A long blue bench sits beneath a row of windows, offering a perfect perch for reflection or casual reading.

In the dining area, a mint-painted accent wall is adorned with a large, modern portrait, signaling Nelly's love for contemporary art. Nearby, the compact yet contemporary kitchen is outfitted with open shelving filled with colorful books and delicate ceramics—useful but also stylish.

The true heart of her loft, however, reveals just how much art is woven into Nelly's life. On one level, a soaring bookshelf stretches floor to ceiling, accessed by a sliding wooden ladder. Tucked among the novels and design volumes are her own works—bold abstract paintings hang prominently throughout the space, while a few framed prints near the staircase and in the adjacent hall suggest a rotation of ongoing pieces.

The blue bench in the sitting area, the thoughtful placement of mirrors, and even the moody lavender-and-sage-tones of her bedroom, all hint at an artist's eye—someone who understands balance, texture, and how space itself can evoke emotion. It's clear that Nelly doesn't just live here—she creates, contemplates, and dreams here.

As twilight settled over the city, Nelly slipped into a linen dress that fluttered gently against her skin, its airy fabric whispering across the wooden floors of her home. With a steady hand, she popped open a bottle of red wine, the cork releasing with a soft pop that echoed pleasantly in the spacious room. The crackle of a vinyl record followed soon after, filling the space with a mellow, nostalgic hum. The aroma of aged grape and aged jazz mingled as she stood before her canvas, brush in hand, clearing her thoughts as she would clean a surface—readying herself to begin again.

Then came a thud.

It wasn't unusual to hear the occasional creak or bang in this old building—its bones had stories older than hers—but this noise was different. Louder, closer. And it didn't stop at one. A second thud followed, then a third, heavier, sharper, unsettling. She hesitated, wine glass suspended in the air, the brush paused mid-stroke. Curiosity pricked at her. With a sharp exhale, she moved purposefully across the loft and into the dimly lit foyer, her bare feet silent on the cool floorboards. Leaning forward, she pressed one eye to the peephole, expecting nothing more than the usual stillness. But the hall was eerily empty. Just grey walls. The old wooden elevator. Silence.

And then—an eye.

It blinked.

Nelly recoiled instinctively, her heart leaping into her throat. A single knock rang out on her door. Not loud. Not hurried. Just…certain.

She stared at the door, her breath shallow, the soft sound of the record continuing in the background like a heartbeat, slow and steady.

"Who is it?" she asked nervously, her voice barely audible.

"Um, your upstairs neighbor," came a polite voice from the other side. Nelly hesitated, then unlatched the door. As it creaked open, she was met not with some gruff stranger, but him—Kenneth Sundwall. Tall, impossibly handsome, with warm eyes that seemed to apologize before his mouth even moved.

"Hey there," he said with an easy smile, the kind that made her knees loosen slightly. "Just wanted to apologize for the noise. I've been moving back in over the past few weeks, but today's the day all the heavy stuff's coming in. I heard the music and figured I should let you know—didn't want to throw off your vibe."

Nelly blinked, a little stunned. She licked her lips unconsciously, a flicker of nervous innocence in the gesture. He was too perfect—like someone you'd see in an ad for cologne or impossible love.

"Um, it's fine," she managed, tucking a loose curl behind her ear. "I was wondering what that was. I haven't heard any noise like that since I moved in, so…thanks for the heads-up. Welcome home, I guess."

Before she could say more, Kenneth stepped slightly backward—and just then, *she* walked in.

CHAPTER 2.

MARS

"Baby, I'm hungry," she said. Her voice was the kind that didn't just speak—it lingered. It wrapped around every word like velvet smoke and whispered secrets. There was something magnetic in it, a sultry hush that pulled you closer and made you lean in without even realizing it. Every syllable felt like it was dipped in honey, with subtle gravel that gave it an edge—confident, low, and utterly captivating. She didn't need to say much. The sound alone made people want to listen.

Mars stood behind him like a vision sculpted from moonlight—impossibly seductive. Her skin, smooth and rich like melted onyx, was draped in a cascading white dress that hugged her hips before spilling to the floor in a trail of pure grace; she was a portrait of sensual sophistication. Her back was bare, long, and graceful as if designed to be admired. A wide-brimmed hat with bold black and white rings framed her soft features that hid beneath. One hand grazed his shoulder, fingers delicate and adorned in gold.

He scoffed—pleasantly, almost in disbelief—as if he couldn't quite wrap his head around the fact that she was standing there. A glimmer of pride flickered in his eyes, as though her mere presence elevated him, like he'd won a prize no one else even knew was in the running. It was as if he were under her spell, entranced by her elegance, surprised that she was here…and not just here, but with him.

"Right, of course," he murmured, catching himself. "I think they're about done now, so I'll order us some dinner." His voice was low, grounded, steady—but there was warmth behind it. With a smooth turn, he leaned in and pressed a light kiss to her cheek, his hands finding the curve of her waist, pulling her flush against him. She moved like a secret—like a woman born of the shadows, someone you only meet once in a lifetime and never forget.

Nelly watched, her eyes locking with Mars's for just a second, before the two disappeared up the hallway stairs, swallowed by the shifting light and the noise of movers hauling the last bits of furniture. But as the sun sank behind the city skyline and the clamor of boots and boxes faded into silence, Nelly found herself alone again. She entered her bedroom, slipping into something soft, her body winding down for rest—until, almost on cue, the quiet shattered.

The unmistakable rhythm of lovemaking thudded above her. Sharp. Loud. Persistent. Her jaw fell open, eyes wide in disbelief. Upstairs, Kenneth moved with a tenderness that made every motion feel deliberate, like he was tracing poetry across Mars' skin. Their measure was slow, almost hypnotic, a dance that echoed through the walls with a steady pulse. She lay down, trying to ignore it, but still, her breath catching with each creak and muffled moan, her body responding as though it were her being touched, cherished. She squeezed her eyes shut, trying to fight against the tempting sounds of their gyrating—but it only teased her, slipping into her thoughts like silk against bare skin.

It had been so long since she had felt that kind of passion. The edges of her mind blurred, Kenneth's name lingering somewhere between fantasy and ache. She bit her lip, heat blooming in her chest as her own breathing quickened. Her fingers rotated quickly along her clitoris in unison to their throbbing, and when she finally gave in to the vision, the sensation washed over her like a tide—her body trembling softly, secretly, as upstairs the rhythm continued.

By morning, Nelly felt a curious kind of release—an airy lightness in her limbs, as though some hidden tension had melted from her body overnight. She thought only painting could bring her this kind of calm. But she was wrong. Whatever last night had stirred within her, it had left her softer…maybe even a little happier, though her eyes still carried the fatigue of a restless night.

Hoping to beat the traffic, she scheduled her Uber and moved with intention. But as she stepped out the door, locking it behind her, she felt it—eyes. Watching. Pinning her gently in place. She turned subtly toward the top of the stairs, her gaze lifting. It was Mars.

Effortlessly poised, Mars descended like she owned the building, and maybe, in some ways, she did.

Nelly's instincts teetered between avoidance and acknowledgment, but politeness won. "Good morning," she said softly, fumbling with the lock on her door. Nelly had the kind of beauty that didn't beg for attention—it simply *was*. Her skin a golden brown, and her eyes, soft and warm, seemed to hold a quiet kind of intelligence, the kind that made you feel like she was always a step ahead—just too polite to say so.

A small, delicate nose ring hugged the curve of her nostril, adding an understated edge to her otherwise tender look. Her full lips, naturally tinted with a soft rose hue, carried a story even when she wasn't speaking. She wore her hair in a neat, practical bun, a style that framed her high cheekbones and long neck perfectly.

Dressed in a sleeveless black mock-neck top that hugged her frame, she was a modest girl. Everything from the curve of her collarbone to the stillness in her expression spoke of a softness that had not yet been hardened.

"Good morning," Mars replied, her tone velvety, unbothered. "Off to work?" She wore a large sunhat, shielding her expression, her dark hair pulled into a tidy bun. A pair of wide-legged dress pants flowed around her heels, paired with a cream silk blouse and a modest clutch—elegant, yet guarded.

"Yes," Nelly answered, a light stammer betraying her nerves. Mars looked over with the faintest smile.

"I see," she said, then added with a natural polish, "Well, allow me and my driver to take you."

Nelly's eyes widened, caught off guard. "Oh no, no—that's not needed at all, actually," she stammered. "I already called my cab, and they'll charge me a fee if I cancel. But I appreciate it, though." She tried to sound composed, but her words came out tangled, uncertain.

Mars tilted her head, unfazed. "My car is just outside," she said smoothly. "Let's go." And with that, there was no room for protest.

Nelly sat poised but on edge, doing her best to seem cool as the black Cadillac Escalade glided down the street. The moment she canceled her ride, her phone lit up with a five-dollar cancellation fee. A small price to pay for the discomfort already simmering in the air.

She thought she masked her expression well, but Mars, ever perceptive, caught the flicker of disappointment in her eyes. Without a word, the woman reached into her clutch, retrieved a crisp hundred-dollar bill, and offered it to Nelly with polished grace.

"For your cancellation," she said, her tone light, almost amused. Nelly hesitated, her pride nearly rejecting it—but eventually, she took it, fingers brushing awkwardly as the bill passed between them.

"Um…thank you."

"Where is your work?"

"Midtown," Nelly replied cautiously. "The Sky Building."

Mars gave a slight nod and turned to her driver. "Midtown. The Sky Building, please." And just like that, the SUV melted into traffic, the hum of the road their only company—until Mars broke the silence.

"So," she said, glancing over with keen interest, "how long have you been living in New York? You seem really timid for a city like this."

Nelly chuckled, smoothing the fabric of her pants. "Born and raised, actually. East Harlem. My dad's a dentist, and my mom teaches Spanish at a local high school." Mars nodded, lips pursed with a hint of surprise.

"Oh, interesting. And how long have you been at that loft?"

Nelly relaxed slightly, her voice warming. "Uh, a little under two years. Luck really—"

But Mars cut in, her tone shifting, deliberate.

"Oh, so you wouldn't know anything about Kenneth and his wife?" The question hit like a slap dressed in silk. She froze—her throat tightened. The memory of the night before echoed in her bones; the rhythm above her, the sounds, the aching pulse between her legs. Now, here was Mars, casually tossing Kenneth's wife into the air like a dagger made of glass. Nelly blinked, caught between guilt and the chill of confusion.

"No," she finally whispered, eyes on the passing skyline. "I wouldn't. I—I don't even know his name."

Before she could gather the remainder of her thoughts or find the right words to smooth over the uneasy silence, the car rolled to a graceful stop in front of her office building. The looming glass façade of the Sky Building stared back at her like a mirror, catching her reflection—composed on the outside, unraveling within.

She turned slightly, lips parted to offer a polite thank you, but Mars cut in, voice commanding.

"Have a good day. I'm Mars, by the way," she said with a sly, close-lipped smile that gave nothing away.

"Oh…yes, um—I'm Janelle. But my friends call me Nelly or Nelle sometimes. Thanks for the ride."

"You're welcome, Janelle."

Something about the way she said her full name— firm, final—sent a tiny chill down her spine. With an awkward laugh and a glance toward the building's entrance, she fumbled with the door and stepped out, flats against the rocks on concrete as the city's noise swallowed her whole. She shut the door behind her with a thud that seemed too loud, too certain.

Standing still for a second, she blinked into the chaos of morning traffic, heart thudding faster than it should have. Then, with trembling fingers, she pulled out her phone, opened her group chat with Emily and Lisa, and typed: *"I need to talk to you guys!"*

She hit send—fast. The message was short, but everything in her body screamed that it wasn't just a chat she needed. It was backup. Clarity. An explanation for why her morning ride felt more like a scene from a thriller than a casual neighborly gesture.

The group chat had been nonstop all week, but neither Emily nor Lisa wanted to dive into that conversation over the phone. This was tea best served hot and in person. So, a girls' night was officially scheduled: Friday, 6 PM sharp, at Emily's place. Emily made it clear— she needed all the details, and Janelle was more than ready to spill every last drop.

But as the days dragged on, so did the relentless sounds of love—or lust—banging through the ceiling. Kenneth and Mars were like teenage jackrabbits, insatiable and entirely oblivious to the existence of the outside world. Morning, night, and even mid-afternoon, when Nelly wasn't home, still, the walls told stories. By the fourth night, Nelle had almost grown numb to it. Instead of fighting the chaos, she simply adapted, shifting her easel and paints to the living room, far from the room beneath their feverish escapades. Art was her escape, her refuge, but even that was starting to wear thin.

So, by Friday morning, she made an executive decision as she packed: this wouldn't just be a girls' night. No—this was going to be a girls' weekend. She packed her things and texted Emily, *"Hope you've got enough wine and patience—I'm staying the whole damn weekend."*

As the clock struck five, Nelly stepped off the curb with a soft click of heels and raised her hand for a yellow cab. The city pulsed around her—frenzied, familiar—and yet the spring night felt unusually gentle as if New York had taken a deep breath and decided to play nice for once. The air held that perfect in-between warmth, kissed by jasmine and the faint trace of street vendors shutting down for the evening. She leaned into the cab's open window, her voice smooth, decisive. "Upper East Side, please." It was the kind of night made for rooftop cocktails and candlelit risotto, for laughter spilling out of a good bar, or for walking just a little too far in heels that didn't quite hurt yet. Something was bound to happen. Nights like this always held a hint of promise, and Nelly wasn't about to waste it.

Emily's apartment sat five floors above a tree-lined stretch of East 75th, quiet enough to hear the rustle of sycamore leaves in spring. The building was prewar, dignified in its architecture, with a doorman who never forgot a face. Inside, her space felt like the inside of a whispered secret—understated and eerily calm. No kids. No husband. It was just her and the Bombay cat, Midnight.

The master bedroom was all soft creams and blush undertones, a palette chosen not for show but for serenity. A velvet armchair curved in the corner like it had been waiting for someone to curl into it with a book and a glass of Sancerre. The light, when it hit just right in the early afternoon, cast golden slants across the room, illuminating the textures—woven throws, tufted headboard, the subtle sheen of silk pillows that looked untouched but often weren't.

Down the hall, the drawing room opened wide and gracious, like a breath held in and then released. It was equal parts gallery and living space. White walls framed with delicate trim bore abstract art in quiet colors—a Rothko knockoff beside the real Cy Twombly sketch she rarely mentioned. A curved white sofa wrapped around a coffee table made of thick-cut-out marble, the kind that couldn't be bought impulsively. Atop it is a copy of Washington's novel, *Green Trees*. Nothing about the room begged for attention, but everything held it.

Fresh flowers—peonies when in season, otherwise cream roses—were always in bloom, placed in a handblown vase found at her aunt Vern's cottage. The round dining table, simple and sculptural, stood in front of the wide French windows that opened just enough to let in the city's hush.

There was a kind of woman you expected to live here—stylish, connected, possibly cold. Emily was none of those things, not entirely. The space wasn't designed to impress; it was a reflection of who she was when no one was looking. A woman who liked silence. A woman who lit candles in the middle of the afternoon. A woman who left one chair always turned slightly toward the window, as if waiting for someone who might never come.

Once inside, the girls wasted no time slipping into comfort. Emily, ever the hostess, showed Janelle to the guest room—fluffy robes, fresh towels, and a candle already lit on the dresser—before placing a dinner order for the nearby steakhouse they all loved. Within an hour, the warm scent of truffle fries and garlic butter began to fill the space. Laughter echoed through the apartment as the two curled up on the couch, swapping stories and watching reruns of their favorite shows, the kind they could quote line-for-line.

By the time Lisa arrived, the energy only intensified. Thirty-two, fiercely stylish and known as the mouthpiece behind some of the city's most celebrated brands, Lisa had a presence that always turned heads—even in sneakers and sweats. She greeted them with loud hugs and the same dramatic flair she was famous for, handing off a bottle of top-shelf tequila and a box of delicate macaroons—Emily's favorite.

As the evening wore on, the city outside softened, trees rustling a lullaby through the windows. The girls were nestled in the heart of the living room, a tangle of throw blankets and tired limbs. The TV murmured in the background, forgotten, as their laughter gave way to quiet confessions and warm silence. For once, the world outside felt far away—and that was exactly what they needed.

"Alright now, so catch me up," Lisa said, already elbow-deep in a carton of fries from her meal Emily had kept warm in the oven. Her perfectly manicured fingers glistened with salt and oil.

"Girl, we were waiting on you!" Emily crackled, tossing a throw pillow at her with mock frustration.

Lisa laughed, but Nelly was already leaning forward, eyes wide and wild like she'd been holding this story in all week. "Lisa, girl…I'm living downstairs from the kinkiest couple from hell," she started, waving her tequila glass for emphasis. "And it's so confusing because—Mars—that's her name…she's so fascinating to look at. I'm talking dipped in chocolate royalty—she's bad! Like, the kind of woman who steps into a room and makes everything else disappear. But how can I respect someone who's knowingly sleeping with a married man? It just goes to show—some of these women might look like they got it all on the outside, but their morals? Dead and buried. Straight up!"

"Mars?" Lisa blinked, sitting up straighter. "Is she from Seattle?"

"I don't even know, girl," Nelly groaned, slumping back against the cushions. "She barely talked about herself. I told Emily—she dropped me off at work Monday morning in this black Escalade, barely said two words about her life. Only wanted to know if I knew Kenneth's wife—the married man she's fucking above my damn head every night!" She threw her hands in the air, took another messy sip of tequila, and let her words slur slightly. "It was weird. Like…calculated weird."

Emily's head snapped to Lisa, the two of them exchanging a look that had its own silent language.

"Alright now, you ain't said nothing about his name being Kenneth. Is his last name…Sundwall?" Emily asked slowly.

But Nelly was somewhere between tipsy and not caring. She waved the question off like an annoying mosquito. "Girl, I don't know. Probably. Who else got that kind of stamina?"

Lisa let out a low whistle and set her drink down.

"Damn," she muttered. "This just got messy."

But Emily wasn't letting it drop—not now. Not when her firm's quarterly bonus and her own long-awaited raise were hanging in the balance. This wasn't just tea anymore. This was strategy. This was money.

"Nelly, honey, I need you to focus. I know you're a lightweight, but please," Emily said, leaning in, her voice urgent but calm. "Do you remember seeing that man's name anywhere? A mailbox, a slip of paper, anything at all?" Her wide eyes searched Nelly's face like they were scanning for clues.

Nelly blinked slowly, tequila still buzzing in her bloodstream. "No," she said, shaking her head. "She only ever said his first name. That was it."

Emily sighed and stood up, running both hands through her curls before pacing the living room like a woman possessed. "Lisa, let's think. You mentioned Mars being from Seattle, right?"

Lisa tilted her head. "Well, I don't know for sure. I just—listen, I know of a Mars Taylor in Seattle through her husband. He owns this crazy house in the Hamptons. Our office went there last year for a party. It's just…not that many people walking around with a name like Mars, you know?"

Emily paused mid-step; her lips pursed in thought. "Kenneth Sundwall is definitely back in the city. We know that. But the odds of him shacking up in some loft in the Meatpacking District? I mean, sure, it's luxe, but Kenneth

Sundwall could buy a penthouse overlooking Central Park. Why hide out in the Meatpacking area?"

"Maybe that's the point," Nelly said softly, curling into the couch. "Maybe he doesn't want anyone to find him. He is, after all, cheating on his wife."

Just then, Emily's face lit up. She grabbed her phone with a sense of purpose, fingers already moving. "Lemme call Plum."

Lisa raised an eyebrow. "TMZ's Plum?"

"The very one. Plum knows everything that happens east of SoHo and north of Delancey," Emily said, already dialing. "If anyone can confirm if Mars and Kenneth are the same Mars and Kenneth, we think they are, then…it's him."

The room fell silent as the phone rang. Nelly sat up a little straighter—she loved watching her friends in girl-boss mode; they inspired her. Even Lisa paused mid-sip. Whatever Emily was about to find out could turn this from messy to explosive. And they were all here for it.

The phone rang, cutting through the background noise of the television. Everyone stiffened, the volume quickly lowered as they leaned in, waiting for the answer. After the fourth ring, a gruff voice came through the receiver. "Em. What's going on, doll?"

"Plum! Honeyyyyy. Has TMZ heard anything lately about Sundwall? Any coverage? He's back in the city, and I need to find him."

Plum's voice remained casual, a touch of indifference in his tone. "He's been around…parties and such. Tossing money at his problems and that, Taylor. The usual."

"No tech investments?" Emily pressed, her voice steady with determination.

"You know I can't give that away without something in return. Information like that is very useful to someone like you," Plum responded, a playful edge creeping into his words.

Emily didn't miss a beat. "Oh, come on, Plum. What about his wife? Could the Taylor woman be Mars? Isn't she married?" she asked, her eyes on Lisa. "Look, I have a story that could be worth your while. I'm going to need time to get some evidence, but once I do, you'll be the first to know."

Plum's interest seemed to fizzle. "I mean, it's 2022, and to be fair, he's very public with Mars, doesn't seem to me like they're hiding anything. As far as his wife or her husband, whatever is going on between them, I doubt anyone cares. At least not front-page news or breaking. When they vanished from the island, so did the public's interest."

"Plum, please! I just need a solid location. A party or something where I can run into him," Emily begged, her voice tinged with urgency.

Plum's voice dipped, growing even more nonchalant. "Emily, I wish I could help. I really do."

"Why not just find his office and schedule a meeting with him that way? Maybe even get his number?" Nelly asked innocently.

Emily shook her head, frustration creeping into her words. "I wish it were that easy. Men like him don't meet in offices. Deals are done in the crowd, on golf courses, lounges. They need to know you run in the same circles if you want to get your hooks on their wallets. They don't just trust anybody."

Just then, Lisa chimed in, "Oh, so very true."

Plum, now curious, asked, "Hold on, is that Lisa?"

"Yep!" Emily said, casually sipping her tequila as she leaned back, the glass glinting in the dim light.

"Ohhh, doll, please put me on speaker! Your BFF might be able to save you, Em," Plum teased, his voice oozing with playful sarcasm. Emily grinned, her eyes flicking to the others in the room.

"You're already on speaker."

Plum's voice perked up from the other side, "Lisa, your guy. We have a story pending legal right now. Set to break top of next week."

Lisa's eyes widened, a flash of disbelief crossing her face. "What guy? And why the fuck wouldn't you call me before you thought to run it, Plum?"

"I did. I called your office, your cell—kept getting your voicemail," Plum replied, a hint of annoyance in his tone. "I know you thought I was calling for a story, but it was actually because I got one."

"Listen, don't start," Lisa shot back, irritation evident. "What's the story and who?"

"Richardson…from Hollywood's golden boy to golden showers in red rooms and yacht parties," Plum said, his voice thick with intrigue. Lisa's jaw dropped. Emily tossed the phone to her. Both of the girls watched in silence as the blood seemed to drain from Lisa's face, her expression going ashen. Plum's voice came through the phone, calm and unyielding. "Not only that, doll, but a wedding in Vegas to NikkiThaThickest. Caucasian

Pornhub star. He's been on a roll this month. I wonder what his Black Female fan base is going to think of him now. My guys got the certificate and everything. Better hope she's not pregnant."

Lisa lowered her tequila slowly, the glass trembling in her hand. She didn't look up, her voice barely audible. "Plum, I am at your mercy. Please, don't have TMZ run that story next week. Roddy just signed a multimillion-dollar contract with ASIAS Films and brand deals…he'll be ruined if this gets out. You're gonna fuck up my money!"

Plum's tone remained cold, as though he had heard it all before. "Nothing I can do, hun! Unless you have something better for me. Breaking news. I'll shelf it if you or Emily can give me something better than this. Otherwise…my hands are tied." The line went silent, the weight of the situation settling heavily in the air. Lisa's appetite seemed to vanish, her shoulder sagging under the pressure. She stood, her body tense as she prepared to leave, the room feeling a little colder with each passing moment.

CHAPTER 3.

FRIEND OR FAVOR

It was Monday morning, and as Nelly got herself ready for work, she heard footsteps from the apartment above—only this time, it wasn't the sharp click of heels. It was the slow, unmistakable drag of slippers. She paused for a moment, curiosity piqued. A part of her hoped Mars had finally left, and with that, maybe—just maybe—she could better help to identify this Kenneth, the elusive man Emily had been obsessively trying to locate.

As she stepped into the hallway and moved toward the front door to wait for her Uber, a door creaked open above. And there he was.

Kenneth.

Shirtless, wearing pajama pants and slippers, he looked like he'd stepped out of a fitness commercial. His chest was carved with definition, like a man who never skipped a single gym day—arms thick, legs muscular beneath the fabric. But it wasn't just the physique that caught her off guard. It was the noticeable dick print through his pajamas that made her spin away, flustered.

He tossed a bag of trash down the chute before catching her stare. Before she could chicken out, the words left her mouth:

"What's your last name?"

Bold. Reckless. But necessary—for Emily's sake, or so she told herself. Kenneth laughed, clearly amused.

"Wow, what happened to a regular, 'My name is…what's yours?' The city's losing its manners. Maybe I should lead by example." He offered a charming smirk. "Good morning, lovely lady. My name is Kenneth. What's yours?"

Nelly blushed so hard she had to turn away…again, fanning her cheeks like she was back in high school. Glancing down at her phone—Uber, three minutes away—she steadied herself.

"Janelle, but my friends call me Nelly…or Nelle for short," she said, smiling now.

He nodded. "Oh, okay, have a good day, alright?"

She grinned. "Okay, Mr. Kenneth No-Last-Name."

He stopped, clearly caught off guard, then turned back with a playful grin. "Okay, Ms. Janelle—but my friends call me Nelly or Nelle for short."

They both laughed. The moment was fleeting, light, unexpected—but it lingered with her that morning, playing on repeat in the back of her mind.

As soon as she climbed into the back of the Uber, she pulled out her phone and fired off a quick text to Emily: *"I asked him his last name and he totally blew me off lol."*

Emily's reply came instantly: *"Fuck it, that's him! I'm coming by this evening after work."*

That was all Nelly needed to hear. The rest of her day practically flew by. For the first time in what felt like forever, her energy stayed high-vibrant and focused.

*

The sun beamed gently over Highland Park, casting a yellow hue across the winding paths as Lisa and Emily strolled side by side, their footsteps light against the pavement. The morning air was crisp but warming fast, kissed with the early scent of dew evaporating from the grass. A soft breeze rolled through the trees, rustling their spring green leaves and carrying the faint sounds of laughter, music, and sneakers rhythmically hitting the trail.

Joggers passed by in steady strides—some with earbuds in, others chatting with partners or walking their dogs. A couple pushed a stroller, the baby's giggles blending into the atmosphere. Emily looked Lisa up and down, squinting slightly, as if she were trying to read between the lines of her expression. Something about her was off—more than off, rattled. Her usual composure was cracked at the edges.

"So, did you have a chance to talk to Rod?" Emily asked gently.

Lisa sighed, massaging her temples as if the pressure there could be wrung out like water. "Yep. I talked to him. I even made a few calls. Turns out the whole golden shower thing? Not even true," she said, eyes rolling. "Plum is such an asshole. Anything for a story. My God. Don't they care about getting sued?" Cyclists coasted along the curved lanes as Emily remained quiet, letting her vent.

"But the marriage," Lisa continued, her voice dipping lower. "That part? That part was true. And I don't know when they're planning to drop that story—today, tomorrow, who knows. My office is staying on top of it, but still…" She trailed off. "Did anything come up in the reports? That trip, his charges? I mean, how did Plum get this before us?"

Nearby, the water glistened like polished glass under the sun's caress, rippling gently with every breath of wind. Ducks drifted lazily across the surface, occasionally dipping beneath or flapping their wings in a lazy stretch. It was the picture-perfect scene—an ideal setting for a walk that felt like both a break from reality and a quiet return to it, but the more Lisa spoke, the more worried Emily became, shaking her head no. "No. We only go by 30-day analytics. It wouldn't have shown up this month. So honestly, if Plum hadn't said anything, we wouldn't know now either. Sort of fate, I guess."

Lisa stopped walking for a moment, staring ahead at nothing in particular. The sunlight was shifting now, afternoon creeping in, softening the shadows along the path as the park began to mellow. Joggers thinned; the air turned still.

"He's my biggest client, Em. Because of the pandemic we lost seventy-five percent of our accounts. Some could no longer afford it; some were too scared to spend the money…we still haven't fully recovered. You know I had to pivot into entertainment, and even now, the stars are a dying breed. Getting a brand deal for anyone who isn't chronically online entertaining followers is like…it's nearly impossible. If we lose him…I might as well shut down my business."

"But you aren't going to lose him…" Emily sympathized.

"He won't pay for our services if his money starts drying up, Em. I mean, why would he? We get him the money that your firm manages. If there's nothing to manage, then, we're screwed." The weight in her voice was palpable, dragging behind her like a shadow. Their morning walk had slowly, almost imperceptibly, turned into something else—a reckoning dressed in sunlight. Emily looked at her friend, reassuring her. "We'll figure something out, I promise."

By 5:30 PM, Nelly arrived home via Uber, stepping out to see Emily already perched on the mini-curb at the front of the entrance, arms crossed but smiling, her laptop bag in hand.

"Um, I need a key. Lisa's coming later, by the way." Nelly, too happy to be home and still riding the high of the day, nodded as she pulled out her keys.

"Okay, cool! What do you plan on doing about him?" she asked, tilting her head towards the hallway stairs as she opened the door to her loft. The moment she stepped inside, a warm, sweet aroma wrapped around them—hints of vanilla, sandalwood, maybe a touch of cinnamon.

"Oh my gosh, I love that scent!" Emily said, pausing to take in the cozy, creative energy of the space. They poured themselves glasses of wine, laughter, and chatter filling the room as they caught up. Nelly lit candles and began clearing her workspace to start a new painting—her ritual before diving into creativity. Meanwhile, Emily flipped open her laptop on the bench beneath the large windows, casually scrolling. But curiosity had a way of creeping in.

She typed slowly, deliberately.

KENNETH SUNDWALL.

The name hovered in the search bar for a moment. Then she hit enter. The screen lit up instantly, flooding with images of him. Her jaw dropped as she scrolled through the results and mountains of headlines. The articles, the red-carpet shots, the event appearances—he looked like a man who walked off the cover of a fashion editorial, sharp.

"Nelly...you're sure this is the man living upstairs?" she asked, barely able to believe it.

Janelle nearly spilled her wine, rushing to sit beside her, eyes wide.

"Yes," she confirmed, breathless. "Isn't he perfect?"

Emily nodded, stunned. "Hmm, he's alright. He ain't *perfect*. Morris Chestnut is *perfect*." But the deeper they scrolled, the more tangled it got. Article after article popped up, many with the names Noel-Lee Kwon-Sundwall and Nathanial threaded through the headlines—murmurs of business, scandal, rumors, old flame drama.

"Uh uh, nope," Nelly said quickly, waving her hand. "Search the Mars lady. That's what you call mind blown!" Intrigued, Emily typed it in: **MARS TAYLOR**. But nothing came up. Just images of the planets and academic essays. "Oh, that's so weird. Maybe that's not her real name," Janelle sighed, sitting back. "But she's a goddess. Empress energy for sure."

Emily's eyes sparkled. "I need to see more pictures of Noel."

She typed: **NOEL LEE KWON**.

"Oh…she's a bad bitch," Emily whispered, eyes locked on the screen. "Ha, ha, no wonder she had Manhattan in a frenzy. You and her kind of favor…"

The room fell quiet as they stared.

"Hmm, no. I'm Black, Black…she's mixed, no?"

"Yeah, I mean, the last name is a dead giveaway. Blasian, I think. But you guys favor…to me, at least. Seems like Kenneth has good taste."

"Girl, you need to see Mars!" At that moment, with their wine glasses frozen midair, they were just two women caught in the orbit of a world far glossier, messier, and more glamorous than they'd ever expected to be this close to.

Just then, Emily's eyes lit up, and she whipped her head around like a switch had flipped.

"I have an idea," she said, voice low and charged.

"What is it?" Nelly asked, already wary.

"Maybe you can get close to him, or even date him. Make him take you to some of the hot spots he frequents in town—and while you're out with him, just invite me to come. I'll come in and close the deal." Emily was smiling now, like the scheme was already unfolding in her mind.

"Date a married man? I mean, he's already cheating on his wife, and you want me…to…" Nelly asked, staring at her like she'd grown another head. She had to rest her wine glass down on a coaster on the kitchen counter.

"Oh, Nelle, no, no-please, this whole thing about him being married—"

"What? Are we not supposed to care? We literally just sat here and googled his wife," Janelle cut in, her voice rising with disbelief. She was appalled, stunned, shocked—and, if she was being honest, deeply insulted.

"I would hope you'd think more of me than that."

Emily sat in silence for a moment, her smile fading. Then, in a softer, more desperate tone, she tried again: "Janelle…you could have your gallery ten times over with the money I'd make from this account. All of your art—" she motioned around the room, her eyes sweeping over the canvases and sketches, "hanging in your very own space, where you host other artists like yourself. No social media crap. Just raw talent. Real eyes on your work." She looked at her friend pleadingly, a glimmer of ambition—and desperation—behind every word.

Seconds later, as if perfectly timed by fate or mischief, the buzzer rang—Lisa had arrived. Always the embodiment of grace and composure, Lisa stood outside the building holding a bouquet of fresh-cut flowers in one arm and a chilled bottle of white wine in the other. Professionally dressed, arriving straight from her office, she was a woman of class and stature. The kind to never show up to a friend's home empty-handed, no matter the chaos inside.

As she waited to be buzzed in, her mind wandered back to the tense meeting she'd had with her staff earlier that afternoon. The Rod situation was unraveling fast, and damage control was the only option. But nothing could have prepared her for the whirlwind of emotions she was about to step into.

The moment she stepped inside, the atmosphere shifted. It was thick, charged, electric. Tension sizzled in the air like static before a storm. And like lions pouncing on their prey, both Emily and Nelly erupted into a chaotic tangle of voices.

Emily lunged first, gesturing dramatically.

"Lisa, am I wrong? I asked Nelly to date Kenneth so I can close him on the deal, and she's offended!"

Lisa blinked, "Date a married man?" she asked flatly, chuckling at the madness. She and Emily exchanged hugs as she walked the flowers over to the kitchen, placing them into a water-filled vase.

"Exactly!!!" Nelly echoed, throwing her arms up. "Thank you for not seeing me as some whore."

Emily raised a brow, undeterred. Nelly offered Lisa a glass of wine before taking her cardigan and hanging it in the closet in the foyer.

"You're both being super dramatic and overthinking it. It's as easy as going for a slice of pizza and texting me to pull up. Just have to make sure the pizza is like $300 a slice. That would be perfect. I'd sell him on our firm so fast, I'm getting wet just thinking about it. I already have my pitch. I just need to meet the man."

"$300 pizzas? How sad," Nelly muttered.

"Wherever I meet him has to be exclusive. Luxury," Emily snapped back. "All you have to do is get him to court you at the very least. He's going to take you places you only dreamed of!"

"He isn't taking me anywhere because I'm not doing it," Nelly fired.

Lisa, trying to diffuse the flame, chimed in, calm and curious. "Aside from him being a married man, what are your other reservations?"

"It's disingenuous. I don't want to deceive him for money. That's not my style. I'd rather earn my money fair and square." Lisa and Emily exchanged a look. It was brief but said everything.

"Oh, bitch no!" Emily gasped.

Lisa laughed, drawing a puzzled look from Nelly.

"What?"

"Well," Lisa said, smirking now, "I'm looking to open a rebound contract on Roddy—for the sake of his image. That would mean hiring someone to be his girlfriend for a while…"

"Are—are you implying that I would do that?" Nelly asked, shocked.

"Whoa, whoa, whoa, listen," Lisa said quickly. "It's only seven months, and it's $10k a week. Right, Em? We can get that approved?"

Emily shrugged, not missing a beat.

"So, she's too moral to date a rich guy for a night or two, but oh pretending to be a famous actor's girlfriend is okay? What happened to not wanting to be deceitful? Instead of deceiving one man, she'll be deceiving the public—especially his fans!"

Lisa countered, "But at least she'll be making her own money. That can more than cover the art gallery, and it'll help save my business."

Nelly looked between them, disbelief settling in like fog. Were they even her friends? Just as she turned to retreat toward her bedroom, a loud thump sounded overhead. The bed slid. Muffled groans filled the space above.

Everyone froze.

Emily narrowed her eyes.

"Is that—?"

Lisa crept forward, then grinned.

"Oh, he's putting her through the mattress!" she snorted. They both burst into laughter. But Nelly wasn't laughing.

"Listen," she said flatly. "I'm definitely not doing the Roddy thing. Even pretending to be his girlfriend—dating someone who enjoys golden showers is just flat-out disgusting."

Lisa lifted a hand.

"Hold on now. In his defense, that was 100% false. We laid that accusation to bed."

Emily chimed in with a cheer, "Yep! The best of the best!"

But Nelly still wasn't moved.

"He still married a porn star. He's not Drake—something like that isn't going to just blow over for him."

Lisa grinned, knowing where to press.

"It will with someone like you on his arm. You're a fresh face, an everyday working girl—not a stripper, not a baby mama. You'll be loved by his fans. You'll be inspiring to them. They'll love you both."

Nelly scoffed.

"Right, but it is fake. Eventually we're going to 'break up' and then what? All those people will be left disappointed."

Lisa didn't flinch.

"Honey, the internet never forgets. But he's a Black man, so they will forgive. He'll still have his followers, and the checks will have already been cashed."

Nelly rounded on them both.

"Emily, why don't you date Kenneth?"

"Conflict of interest," she said without hesitation. "And before you ask about Roddy—he's my client."

"Lisa, why don't you date Kenneth?" Nelly fired.

Lisa burst into a laugh.

"I prayed that dick like that never found me. I'll take the five-inch dicks and minute men over that any day. Good God—I'd be crashing out every week!"

Emily shrieked with laughter. And just like that, the tension in the room cracked, just a bit. But the choices in front of Nelly still loomed.

CHAPTER 4.

THE CHOICE WAS OBVIOUS

Over the next few weeks, life seemed to tighten its grip on each of the women in its own way. Lisa felt the pressure mounting. The truth—unspoken but ever-present—materialized like a storm cloud over her professional rise.

Roddy, her star client and the crown jewel of her roster, continued to dominate campaigns—billboards, commercials, fragrance deals. No matter how many new names she pitched, the brands wanted him and him alone. He was the moment. But Lisa knew fame could be fleeting—and if the truth ever surfaced, it could cost her everything. Quietly, she began considering a pivot. Maybe it was time to diversify—bring on influencers, TikTok creators, the next big thing. Anything to protect herself from a potential collapse.

Emily, meanwhile, was deep in the trenches. Her once-glamorous wealth management firm now buzzed with rumors, whispers, and thinly veiled accusations. With Kenneth and Mars becoming tabloid darlings—spotted at rooftop lounges and exclusive restaurants—her frustration grew. Despite her industry ties, she couldn't get close. They had locked up their inner circle, making it nearly impossible for anyone to land the chance to pitch.

Nelly, the quietest of the three, found herself in an odd state of grace. Her company had begun layoffs—entire departments gone overnight. The energy was anxious and heavy. Still, she didn't spiral. Instead, she leaned into the quiet. She began photographing flowers, trees, and moments of stillness during her lunch breaks. She painted each night, her foyer now a gallery of soft colors and bold strokes. Somehow, while everything around her seemed to fall apart, her own little world was blooming.

With only four weeks until Janelle's thirtieth birthday, Lisa and Emily went into full planning mode. This wasn't going to be just any birthday—it was going to be a celebration of who Janelle had become: quietly brilliant, deeply talented, and finally stepping into her own. Lisa tapped into her network, pulling strings to secure a sophisticated private venue downtown—a converted loft with exposed brick walls and perfect gallery lighting.

It was equal parts chic and intimate, perfect for what they had in mind: a curated night filled with art, storytelling, and the kind of guests who could help Janelle get the attention she deserved. Art journalists, up-and-coming photographers, collectors, and even a few low-key entrepreneurs Lisa had done PR for. Emily handled the aesthetics—mood boards, menu tasting, flower samples—and made sure there would be space to display Janelle's best work.

One afternoon, Emily and Lisa sat across from one another at an Upper East Side coffee shop—Lisa's go-to for vanilla lattes and quiet, off-the-record conversations. The air inside hummed with the soft clatter of espresso machines and the mellow sway of jazz, creating the perfect backdrop for catching up. Lisa scrolled through her phone, toggling between RSVPs and her notes app, her polished nails tapping in rhythm.

The café itself was housed within what looked like a converted chapel—its stone façade, arched doorways, and intricate iron gates were a striking contrast to the modern pulse of Manhattan. The grand entrance stood open, welcoming in the spring breeze and soft sunlight, which poured across the tiled floor like a benediction. Inside, the space retained a kind of reverence—only now it was for single-origin coffee beans and almond milk foam art, not liturgy.

Outside, Emily and Lisa were among a scatter of well-dressed patrons seated at crisp white bistro tables, the sidewalk offering a front-row seat to the normalized chaos of the Upper East Side. The two women, effortlessly chic and tuned into each other's energy, leaned in close as they sipped their drinks. A breeze flirted with the hem of Emily's blazer while Lisa continued her multitasking.

Around them, a cast of locals and tourists lingered in the café's spell. The sun played through the wrought-iron arches, casting elegant shadows across linen pants and newspaper pages. A golden retriever dozed beneath a table nearby, unfazed by the movement above. A barista in a wine-colored apron floated from table to table, topping off drinks and offering practiced smiles, as if the place were a stage. But Emily disrupted their calm, she had more pressing matters to discuss.

She slammed the two glossy magazines onto the tiny café table with a force that rattled their espresso cups. The cover of *People* flashed a sun-drenched image of Mars and Kenneth looking suspiciously candid—eyes locked, hands brushing like a couple fresh in lust. On top of it, the latest issue of *She's Single* bore Noel's face, glowing and enigmatic, lips parted just slightly like she knew something the rest of them didn't.

"What am I missing?" Emily asked, her tone clipped and sharp.

Lisa stared at the covers, blinking slowly, trying to piece it together herself. "Well... looks like Mars and Kenneth are definitely together," she said, tapping the *People* cover. "And Noel is, apparently, single. But that photo of her? That's at least three years old. I remember that shoot."

Emily scoffed. "Didn't Plum say this wasn't a cover story? Or 'breaking'? So what changed? Who did Kenneth pay to make them relevant again—and why now? It just feels calculated. Like we're all being spoon-fed their romance and no one's asking why."

Lisa leaned back, arms crossed. "Have you made any headway running into him?"

Emily let out a bitter laugh. "No! I feel like a damn stalker. I've called just about everyone I know and still— nothing. They're somehow everywhere and nowhere at the same time. I even told my boss we should abandon him as a prospect. I can't keep living like this, circling him like I'm waiting to bump into him at any given time of day.

That's not professional. And let's be honest—if I do? He'll have me blackballed in seconds. Had I been a man, it would have been far easier. The opportunity would have just nicely fallen into my lap."

She paused, her voice softening. "And now Noel's on the cover of *She's Single*. Janelle didn't say a word. I called her—crickets. What is going on? Are they back? All of them? In some weird poly relationship funded by PR to stir up buzz again? It's too many questions... and not nearly enough answers."

Lisa didn't respond immediately. She just sat there, watching the people pass by the café, the sound of Upper East Side traffic rolling faintly behind them.

Janelle felt numb. Did she notice Mars and Kenneth gracing the front pages of magazines at the newsstand near her job? Absolutely. Did it sting? More than a little. The headlines were bold, the photos camp, and yet beneath it all, something felt off—fabricated, even. And so, quietly, subtly, she began to keep track.

She watched him.

At first, it was a casual observation—just noticing the time Kenneth's car would pull up to the loft, or when he jogged past her building in the early morning light. But soon, it evolved. Janelle would sit on the bench just beneath her window, her digital camera in hand, snapping him in motion: slipping into the building, stretching on the curb before a run, laughing into his phone. Every evening, she uploaded the photos onto her laptop, cataloging them by date and time. It wasn't an obsession, she told herself. It was a study. Art.

When Lisa and Emily finally came clean about the surprise birthday plans—an art event in her honor—Janelle knew exactly what she wanted to present: portraits. And not just of anyone. Of him.

The process gave her structure. Each evening, she'd sit at her easel and begin with a sketch—delicate pencil lines mapping out the angles of his jaw, the gentle slope of his brow. She worked in silence, letting memory and image guide her hand. Slowly, she layered in paint, building form through warm undertones and cold shadows. The first washes were light and tentative, like whispers on canvas, but each stroke grew bolder with time.

Layer by layer, she shaped him. The light caught in his hair. The softness around his eyes. The tension in his jawline she couldn't quite decode. She worked late into the night, refining the details, chasing something more than likeness—chasing the truth.

By the time June 4th rolled around, Nelly had already slipped a delicate cream envelope beneath Kenneth's door—an invitation to her birthday art showcase, handwritten and sealed with a touch of lavender-scented wax. She didn't know if he'd come. But part of her hoped, irrationally, that he would. That maybe he'd see what she saw—what she'd painted.

The night before the event, the gallery buzzed softly as the pieces began to arrive—her work carefully packed in delicate boxes, each one handled like fine china. Twelve portraits of Kenneth, each captured from a different moment, a different mood. Some showed him mid-stride on his jog, others caught him in stillness—lost in thought, distracted, almost vulnerable. Alongside these were four portraits of strangers she had photographed from her office window—faces she never knew but imagined stories for. Two paintings featured her closest friends, Lisa and Emily, rendered with affection and honesty. And two more were born purely from her imagination: abstract musings that merged fantasy and feeling.

As each canvas was unwrapped and hung, Janelle felt something stir in her chest—pride, anxiety, maybe even release. The space looked beautiful. Her vision had come to life. And for the first time in a long time, she felt something she hadn't allowed herself to in months—ecstatic.

June 5th, 6:30 PM. The big night had finally arrived, and Janelle made an entrance no one would forget.

She stepped into the gallery bathed in the soft, evening-hour light, wearing a show-stopping gown that shone with every movement. The dress was a liquid gold masterpiece, sculpted to her frame like it had been poured onto her. Strapless and daring, the bodice featured asymmetrical pleating that hugged her torso, drawing the eye to the structured corset beneath—a striking blend of art and architecture. The satin fabric cascaded from her hips in a smooth, floor-length silhouette that pooled elegantly around her heels, commanding the room with quiet glamour.

Her hair was parted to the side, cascading in shiny, voluminous waves down her back with just enough bounce to appear more dazzling. The look was effortless, yet refined—timeless Hollywood with a modern edge.

Her makeup was a rich, sultry bronze palette: soft smoky eyes lined in black with a touch of gold sparkle on the inner corners, full lashes that fanned with every blink, and brows sculpted to perfection. Her skin glowed—warm, dewy, kissed by a highlighter that danced along her cheekbones. On her lips, a muted rose-gold nude added softness to the entire look.

Janelle was radiant, not just because of the dress or makeup but because she was being seen for the first time—fully—as an artist, as a woman, as herself.

The big night was more than she could've dreamed of. The gallery gleamed under high ceilings and modern lighting, every detail arranged to perfection. Bold, vibrant pieces popped against crisp white walls—an explosion of color and character from every corner. Oversized canvases framed the room with personality, while playful sculptures sat on glass pedestals like trophies of imagination. A two-story layout added dimension, with guests drifting between levels, drinks in hand, taking in the world through Janelle's eyes.

An oversized flat-screen mounted near the entrance cycled through commercials from brands Lisa had successfully brought on as event sponsors—everything from boutique skincare lines to luxury perfumes. Their presence gave the evening a polished, upscale edge.

Champagne flowed like liquid gold, handed out by sharply dressed servers as laughter and chatter filled the air. Everyone had shown up in their best cocktail dresses, glistened under gallery lights, heels clicked across polished hardwood floors, and tailored suits were softened by genuine smiles.

The ladies worked the room with a beautiful charm—Lisa mingled by the portraits, Emily held court near the sculptures, and Janelle floated from guest to guest, glowing in her golden gown, embodying the very art she created.

Even her parents were there, standing arm-in-arm as they marveled at their daughter's work, voices full of pride. Her editor-in-chief, wide-eyed and impressed, whispered something to a colleague and nodded toward a particular portrait with interest. Coworkers snapped photos and offered congratulations, their awe impossible to hide.

Janelle had always painted what she felt—but tonight, she finally got to feel what it was like to be praised.

Two hours had come and gone, and the paintings were almost all sold out. As she stood on the second level, glancing downward toward the entrance, they entered—Mars and Kenneth, hand in hand, dressed in semi-matching attire. She couldn't believe her eyes.

Mars's dress was a vision of unique sophistication—a stylish, form-fitting black piece that hugged her silhouette with quiet confidence. The long sleeves added a touch of refinement, balanced by the square neckline that easily framed her collarbones.

A tailored piece, no doubt. Subtle contouring seams ran along the sides, enhancing her figure like brushstrokes on canvas. She wore a wide-brimmed black hat that cast a soft shadow over her face, adding an air of mystery and old Hollywood glamour.

Her heels clicked softly against the floor, and diamonds adorned her neck, wrists, and hands. The final punctuation in an entrance that left the room breathless.

Lisa and Emily had never seen Mars in person before, but the moment she stepped into the gallery, Emily felt it—that unmistakable aura, a magnetic pull. Mars wasn't just beautiful, she was *otherworldly*—the embodiment of goddess-level energy. She moved through the room with Kenneth beside her, both of them exuding a quiet confidence that turned heads without trying.

They sauntered around, pausing thoughtfully at each painting. Emily and Lisa watched from a distance, transfixed like hunters sizing up something wild and rare. But when the couple neared *his* section—the twelve portraits Janelle had poured her soul into—everything shifted.

From atop the staircase, Janelle saw them stop. Her heart slammed against her ribs. She couldn't breathe. The air thickened around her, and for a second, all sound seemed to drop out. She spun away quickly, forcing herself to swallow the rest of her champagne like it might wash down the lump in her throat.

Lisa clocked her reaction and, without hesitation, made her way up the stairs, casually greeting people on their descent to not draw attention. Her pace was steady, her eyes on Janelle.

Meanwhile, Emily seized the moment.

With calm poise, she approached the couple. She hadn't planned for this—hadn't even let herself imagine the chance to meet Kenneth face to face that night—but the opportunity was too potent to pass up.

"Good evening," she said, her voice smooth, her confidence sharp. "You both look ravishing tonight." She smiled with perfect composure, her eyes meeting Kenneth's for the very first time.

"Thank you," Mars said, extending her hand across Kenneth as if to move him aside.

The Manhattan Mogul stood quietly, his expression unreadable, but there was a shimmer in his eyes of an unspoken appreciation for the effort, the vulnerability, the artistry Nelly poured into his portraits. He took his time with each one, lingering longer than most. But Mars? Her feelings were far less concealed. The tightness in her jaw, the subtle flaring of her nostrils, the way her eyes narrowed ever so slightly—her disapproval was etched into every corner of her face.

Emily, still riding the high of being in the room with them, leaned in to discuss business—a small pitch, something light—but Mars wasn't having it. With every word she spoke, Mars drifted further away, her movements deliberate, like a queen distancing herself from a scene she found beneath her. And then, her voice cut through the room with delicate precision.

"We are not here to discuss business tonight."

The words were sharp but calmly delivered, the sting nestled in her tone, and the look she gave Emily—an icy stare that made her feel small. It wasn't loud. It didn't need to be. Mars's gaze alone said everything.

Emily stiffened. Her smile faltered. She turned away abruptly, her posture tense like a teenager who'd just been scolded in front of her friends. Mars, taller in heels, towered over her in both presence and attitude. Emily shrugged it off as best she could, scanning the crowd for Lisa or Janelle, anyone familiar. She disappeared into the mingling guests just as the energy in the room began to shift.

By nine o'clock, the night was beginning to wind down. Glasses were emptier, conversations quieter. A few clusters of guests said their goodbyes, voices trailing toward the exit. Then came the cake—brought out with laughter and candles, and the room erupted into song.

Janelle stood in the center, surrounded by love, light, and applause. But off in the shadows stood Mars and Kenneth—silent observers.

Later that night, quietly and without fanfare, the gallery received notice of additional purchases. The remaining six portraits of Kenneth.

No name. No message. Just an anonymous buyer. But Nelly knew exactly who it was.

Back at Emily's apartment, the magic of the night melted into soft laughter and silk pajamas. The girls had peeled off their glamorous gowns, wiped away the last traces of highlighter and foundation, and traded stilettos for fuzzy socks and bare feet.

Emily, already in her pajamas with her hair tied up, paraded around the living room reenacting Mars's icy stare with dramatic flair—chin raised, eyes narrowed, *"We are not here to talk business tonight!"* she mocked. Later on tossing back almonds like they were award show hors d'oeuvres. A flute of leftover champagne sat beside her, half-full and bubbly, adding to the chaos of glamour-meets-sleepover.

Lisa had just left, her townhouse only a few blocks away, waving them off with a yawn and promising to text when she got home. That left Emily and Janelle to fall back onto the plush couch, limbs tangled, mascara smudged, the high of the evening still lingering in their giggles.

They sang off-key to old pop songs playing softly in the background, teased each other about past crushes, and swapped theories on whether Kenneth even noticed Janelle's dress.

"Welcome to the Dirty Thirty Club, kid!" Emily announced dramatically, raising her champagne glass in a toast before nearly spilling it on a throw pillow.

Janelle laughed so hard she had to clutch her stomach. She felt lighter than she had in weeks—loved, safe, and a little drunk. She had a wonderful life, with wonderful friends, and she was just taking it all in.

The next morning was slow and heavy. Nelly had taken the day off in anticipation of the hangover that now clung to her like a second skin. Her heels were tossed somewhere in the foyer, her clutch abandoned by the door, and all she wanted was the familiar comfort of her own bed. After a long, steamy shower that washed away the glitter, perfume, and memories of the night before, she wrapped herself in her plush robe, towel twisted tightly around her damp curls.

She was seconds away from crawling under the covers when a knock came at the door.

Groaning, she shuffled over, barefoot, her head still in a haze. She didn't bother with the peephole. Curiosity hadn't caught up to caution just yet.

When she opened it, her breath caught.

It was him—Kenneth—standing there, chest rising and falling as he'd just sprinted the last few blocks. His brows were furrowed, jaw clenched, but his eyes… his eyes told her everything—the choice was obvious.

She didn't think. She didn't speak.

On instinct, she rose onto her toes, lips brushing his. The kiss was soft for only a second before he gripped the back of her head and deepened it, stepping inside like a storm breaking down the door.

Kenneth was all command—unfastening the towel from her hair, letting it fall with a quiet splash on the floor. Her robe came next, parting to reveal her bare skin, and she didn't stop him. She didn't want to.

She tugged at his shirt while their mouths stayed locked in rhythm, his sneakers off in seconds. And then he lifted her—strong, sure, like he'd done it a thousand times before—and carried her, unspoken, to the place he knew she needed to be.

No words. No hesitation.

Just heat, breath, and the long-awaited breaking point.

CHAPTER 5.

WHAT DO YOU WANT?

As the day slipped by in soft, honey-colored waves of afternoon light, Janelle remained wrapped in her sheets, her body still humming from the morning. The air in her apartment was quiet—too quiet—but her mind replayed everything, every breath, every touch, every stolen second between them.

I love him, she thought, eyes fixed on the ceiling as images flooded her mind.

The way his tongue had moved with meticulousness, gliding down her neck, teasing her skin before finding its place at her chest, where his hands gripped and molded her breasts like he'd studied her body in a past life. There was no hesitation—only instinct. She remembered the way he moved between her legs, like a man on a mission, skilled and unrelenting. Somehow, somewhere in between her gasps and his groans, he'd slid on a condom seamlessly, without breaking rhythm—no awkward pause, just flow.

It felt unreal. Like a dream.

And yet, the scent of him still lingered faintly on her pillow.

But every time she let her thoughts settle into the sweetness of what had just happened, reality crept in: Noel-Lee. The wife. Mars. The woman upstairs. The woman he lived with. The one Janelle might hear later that night, echoing through the ceiling, laughing or worse—moaning.

The idea twisted in her stomach.

Still, she wanted him. Now. Again. The need for him was beginning to cloud logic and blur lines. She ordered food she wouldn't touch, put on music she barely heard, and tried to journal, though her words quickly turned into his name and fragments of the morning.

He'd left his number in her phone—simple, subtle, casual—but the digits stared back at her like a dare.

She didn't text. She couldn't.

It would feel like surrender. Like chasing. Like wanting too much.

So instead, she pulled the blankets over her bare body, tucked her knees to her chest, and closed her eyes—if only to see him again.

For four days, Nelly threw herself into the art of distraction. The weather was too beautiful not to take advantage of, so after work, she'd head straight to the park with her sketchpad and paints in tow. She found a quiet bench beneath a cherry blossom tree, where the petals rained down like confetti while she captured strangers in soft, colorful strokes. It was peaceful. Grounding. But still, not enough to silence the ache.

At home, she kept busy. Her fridge was now stocked like a Pinterest post—neatly stacked fruit, labeled containers, and even a new herbal tea she'd been meaning to try. She scrubbed her baseboards until they shined, wiped down the cabinets, and completely rearranged her closet by color, category, and mood. It was obsessive, but effective.

She even set her phone to Do Not Disturb. Not because she didn't want to hear from him, but to convince herself she wasn't waiting to. The truth? Every time she "just happened" to check her emails or scroll through messages, it was always Emily or Lisa. No *him*.

Her friends were trying to align their schedules for a catch-up, group text lighting up with half-committed brunch plans and "what days work for y'all?" And while she adored them, Nelly was secretly desperate for it to happen soon. She needed their voices, their laughter, their tough love. Some things—especially things like this— could never be spilled over the phone.

By the second Saturday in June, the sun was already high in the sky, its heat making Central Park a smoldering mix of bustling visitors and sprawling green lawns. The air was thick with the scent of warm earth and the distant honking of city traffic. It was like a game of survival out there— finding an area clean enough to sit on, one that wouldn't be snagged by another group within seconds. But somehow, Nelly did it. She secured a spot. She needed this conversation, needed to release whatever was coiling inside her like a tightly wound spring, ready to snap.

Her skin felt like it was melting, coated with layers of dissatisfaction and dread. Desperation clung to her, heavier than the June heat, and the silence that had lingered between her and Kenneth felt like a weight she couldn't shake. He hadn't said a word to her. Not one. The tension was unbearable.

As the three women settled onto the blanket covering the grass, Emily dove into unpacking the picnic basket, her movements quick and efficient, while Lisa expertly helped lay out the charcuterie board, arranging the cheeses, olives, and prosciutto like she was creating a masterpiece. It was packed to the brim—corner to corner. The red wine, dark and rich, beamed in the sunlight. A $28,000 1947 Cheval Blanc, a gift from Roddy, its opulence undeniable.

The chatter between Emily and Lisa drifted over Nelly's head like a wave she couldn't quite catch. Their words seemed distant, almost meaningless to her, as her mind buzzed with her own chaotic thoughts. The world around her blurred as she tried to piece together the feelings bubbling inside her, until, without thinking, she blurted it out.

"Kenneth and I slept together."

The words sliced through the air, heavy and undeniable. Immediately, everything stopped. Emily and Lisa froze, their conversations dying on their lips. Slowly, they both turned toward Nelly, their eyes wide, searching her face for some clue, some explanation.

The laughter that escaped Emily's lips was a mix of disbelief and amusement as she slowly repositioned herself, her movements deliberate. She let out a deep breath. "Okay, I'm not mad," she said, clearly trying to find humor in the situation.

"Mad?" Lisa asked, her brow furrowing in confusion.

"Yeah, I asked her to date the man, not fuck him," Emily continued, her voice dripping with mock sarcasm.

"And then it was, 'Oh my God, he's married!'" she added, imitating Nelly's tone.

Nelly rolled her eyes and crossed her arms over her chest, visibly frustrated. She turned toward Lisa, who was sitting next to her and sighed. "I don't know how it happened, okay? It was the morning after the party. I mean, now I guess we're dating."

"No, sweetheart, you think a Manhattan royal boy is gonna court you after he bangs? It doesn't work like that with these rich boys. They get in, taste it, and dip," Emily confirmed, her voice unwavering.

Nelly's gaze turned cool as she shot back, "I'm your best friend, why wouldn't you think I'm the exception to the rule?"

Emily didn't miss a beat, replying, "Because, honey, you're not. Unless he wants to flex some cash and say he dated you, but that only works if you're famous and he's got something to gain from it. Men are selfish."

"I think you're just mad because it happened, but didn't happen how you wanted it to," Nelly fired back, leaning in slightly, challenging Emily's cynicism.

"What!" Emily's voice rose in shock, her face scrunching in disbelief. "You slept with him. He used you. That's it. My feelings aside, it doesn't change the truth." Her tone was sharp, and the air around them felt heavier.

Lisa, who had been quietly observing the tension between her friends, finally intervened. "Okay, okay, you guys—don't do this," she said, trying to break the growing tension. "It's him. The asshole is the problem. He's collecting Bad Bitches like infinity stones," she added with a chuckle, attempting to lighten the mood.

"Oh my gosh," she said, pausing and looking around. "Has he stopped sleeping with that girl?"

Nelly's voice dropped to a near whisper as she leaned back on her palms. "I don't know, but I haven't heard them above my head at all since he and I..." Her words trailed off, and she looked down, feeling a mix of confusion, regret, and something else that she couldn't quite pinpoint.

"Damn, that's crazy. Well, maybe he does want something," Lisa mused, raising an eyebrow as she tried to understand the situation.

Emily rolled her eyes, clearly frustrated.

"Why are you so mad about this? When we go on dates, I can still call you and you can do your thing. It's not that big of a deal."

"He doesn't respect you," Emily shot back, her voice firm. "That fantasy you have, that now you two are gonna be this new power couple in NYC, it isn't going to happen. I never said anything about sleeping with him."

"Maybe she wanted him. You sound jealous!" she sniped.

"Fuck you, Nelle. I'm leaving," Emily spat, her tone cold as she stood abruptly. "Lisa, don't follow me."

Lisa watched as Emily stormed off, her frustration palpable. "She's so childish sometimes," she muttered under her breath. Nelly, still processing the tension in the air, sighed. "I mean, let's get real here. What has he been saying, and how do you feel?"

"He hasn't said anything," Nelly replied, her voice soft but uncertain. "I haven't heard from him."

Lisa's eyes widened in disbelief. "I beg your pardon? It's been over a week and you haven't heard from him? Oh, Nelle, come on."

Nelly leaned forward, her arms folded across her chest as she tried to make sense of the situation. "What do you want me to say? Maybe he's busy, maybe he's trying to figure out how to break up with Mars. They haven't been having sex, which is a clear sign that he's still into me."

Nelly felt a knot tighten in her stomach. She was trying to convince herself, but deep down, she wondered if she was just holding onto false hope.

That afternoon, their picnic ended rather abruptly, and as Lisa and Nelly packed up the remnants of their light lunch, Lisa's mind wandered. She felt a pang in her chest— Janelle just wanted love, even if it came from the wrong person. Maybe that was the most human thing about her. Without much thought, Lisa reached out and wrapped her arms around her friend. Janelle stiffened for only a moment before leaning in. She hadn't expected it, but that kind of embrace—the wordless kind—was exactly what she needed.

About an hour later, Lisa arrived home, her townhouse only a short walk from Emily's place. Nestled on a picturesque Upper East Side block, her home was a vision of quiet grandeur. The limestone facade rose proudly, crowned with tall windows dressed with wrought iron flower boxes overflowing with cascading green. Two black doors with intricate ironwork welcomed guests, flanked by perfectly trimmed topiaries.

Inside, the townhouse was an elegant blend of old-world charm and modern artful boldness. The entry opened into a luminous parlor with soaring coffered ceilings, crowned with neoclassical rosettes. Light streamed in from large rear windows, dancing off the pale walls and the intricate herringbone-patterned hardwood floors. A massive artwork of a panda adorned one wall—whimsical, yet powerful—beside mid-century armchairs and a curved cream settee that softened the otherwise crisp geometry of the space.

The kitchen was a blend of sophistication and function, with matte white cabinetry reaching the ceiling, glass-paneled doors revealing an immaculate organization within. The black stone island grounded the brightness, and a pair of oversized pendant lights cast a warm glow over polished marble counters and stainless appliances. Toward the back, a sunny breakfast nook peeked out onto the garden, soft green curtains fluttering gently in the breeze.

Her bathroom was like stepping into a Parisian spa—completely wrapped in soft veined marble, with golden fixtures and a round window that let in soft, diffused light. Even the mirror seemed to glow, flanked by vintage-style sconces.

Upstairs, Lisa's bedroom was calm and layered in understated luxury. Books lined the built-in shelves near her bed, and soft white drapes framed tall windows that opened to views of the treetops outside. The fireplace remained untouched since winter, but the ornate mantel added a lived-in elegance. There was something so grounding about this space—it was thoughtful, a little romantic, and completely hers.

Lisa dropped her bag by the entry table and sank into her sofa. The silence wrapped around her like a blanket.

As nightfall slowly cast its shadow over the neighborhood, Lisa moved about her townhouse with quiet purpose. The lights were dimmed, a scented candle flickered near the window, and the aroma of sage and cedar drifted through the air. She and Brent had planned a cozy night in—just a simple dinner and a movie before bed. But while she waited for him to return from the wine shop, her mind kept tugging at the earlier events of the day.

Something about Janelle's vulnerability stayed with her. And something about Emily's swift departure hadn't sat right either. So Lisa picked up her phone, dialed Emily's number, and after three rings, she picked up.

Emily sounded casual, slightly distracted, as she coaxed her cat, Midnight, into eating before she melted into the sofa with a glass of cabernet and the latest episode of her favorite legal drama.

Lisa didn't waste time. "Just checking on you," she said. "I can't believe you left like that."

Emily let out a scoff, sharp and unbothered. "Of course I did. Love Nelle, but I can't feed her delusions. I know these men—especially the rich ones. They don't play by the same rules. Believe me, I've been there. San Francisco was messy, but New York? It's chess played with blood diamonds."

Lisa sighed, curling into her armchair. "Yes, but what's to stop you from making your pitch? The plan can still proceed, right?"

"No, girl," Emily replied, her voice edged with the kind of wisdom earned through rejection. "You should know better than anyone—this circle runs on relationships and introductions. You don't want to be tethered to the easy hookup."

"Jesus, Em…"

"What? It's true. She's giving fan. First—wait, let me grab my wine—first she paints the man like he's some mysterious muse, watching him jog and scroll his damn phone, then she invites him to her birthday where he shows up with the woman he's fucking every night just above her head. And now she sleeps with him?" A pause, then a sardonic laugh. "I don't know Mars from a can of paint, but I'd bet my savings that woman is a tough bitch."

Lisa blinked. "You think the mistress, the one he just cheated on with Nelle, is tough?"

"I think she's strategic," Emily shot back. "If she proposed a pitch from a trusted name, he'd listen. But Nelle? Bringing me? It's laughable. Doesn't matter if I have a Harvard MBA and a Rolodex thicker than a dictionary. The introduction might've been salvageable, but the relationship? It's fucked."

Just then, Brenton's voice called softly from the kitchen, "Baby, you want ice?"

Emily heard it. "Who's that?" she teased, the edge in her voice mellowing.

"Now, now," Lisa grinned, settling deeper into her chair.

"Don't be shy. You got your little boo there. Cute," Emily chuckled. "Alright, unwind. I love you. Sleep on what I said, and we'll regroup tomorrow, okay?"

Lisa's voice softened. "Okay. Love you too. Good night."

The call ended, and Lisa sat for a moment, the screen still glowing in her hand. She looked up just as Brent entered the room, ice-clinking in two short glasses. A new scene was beginning.

That night, sleep refused to claim Nelle.

No matter how tightly she wrapped herself in the covers, how many meditative breaths she took, or how much she tossed from one side to the other, her mind betrayed her. Again and again, flashes of that morning with Kenneth slipped in: the way he gripped her, the sound of his voice in her ear, the feel of him moving inside her. Her body remembered too well—every inch of her tingled, her thighs clenching as her core throbbed with longing.

Frustrated, she rolled over to face her phone, thumb hovering over his contact. She wanted to text him. She wanted to *ask*—what this was, where they stood, and more importantly, if he was still tangled up with Mars. But just before her message could fly into the void, doubt snuck in.

What if Mars saw it?

The idea paralyzed her. No, she had to be smart. She had to know he was alone.

With a sigh and a flick of her wrist, she tossed her covers back and pulled on a pair of Crocs, black leggings, and a loose crop top. Her hair was a wild mess shoved into a high ponytail, the kind you only wear when you don't care who sees you—or when you're hoping only one specific person *will.*

The building was quiet, thick with that eerie stillness late nights tend to bring. A single dim lamp glowed in the corner of the hallway, casting long shadows on the walls. As she padded softly up the stairs, her pulse quickened. The closer she got to Kenneth's door, the more her body betrayed her again—anticipation bubbling in her chest, her palms damp with nerves.

Light leaked from the bottom of his door. He was home. She inched closer, straining to hear anything from inside—and that's when it happened.

SLAM.

The front entrance downstairs clattered shut so loudly it startled her, and in her shock, she missed a step—stumbling forward with a quiet gasp, heart now racing for a different reason.

"Oh fuck!" Nelly blurted out, louder than she meant to—her voice cracking through the dim hallway.

Mars's silhouette glided toward her like something out of a nightmare, her stride sharp. She didn't say a word.

Didn't have to.

Nelly's throat dried up. Her mind scrambled for an excuse, any excuse.

"I, um...my stove," she stammered, panic hitching every word. "It wasn't lighting and—I just—thought maybe..."

But even as the words spilled from her mouth, she knew they didn't make sense. Not even a little. Mars stopped just inches away, eyes trained on her like a predator surveying its prey. Then, without breaking eye contact, she slipped off her heels one by one, collected her keys, and turned the lock with a soft *click*.

Nelly's heart dropped.

As the door creaked open, she instinctively peeked past Mars's shoulder. No sign of Kenneth. No voices. Just shadows. She didn't know whether to walk away or linger—unsure which would look more suspicious. But it didn't matter.

Mars stepped inside, then slammed the door shut behind her.

The sound reverberated down the hall, and Nelly flinched, nearly leaping out of her skin. Her breath caught, chest rising and falling like she'd just run a marathon. It was too late now—whatever innocence she thought she had left vanished at that moment.

Retreating quickly but quietly, she made her way back down the stairs and into the sanctuary of her apartment, shutting her own door with trembling hands. Her heart still thudded violently in her chest.

She didn't bother undressing. She reached for the bottle of allergy pills on her nightstand and downed three without a second thought, not because of any sniffle, but in hopes they'd knock her out.

And they did. Just enough to silence the night and all it had taken from her.

By morning, the faint sound of sniffling seeped through the walls like a whisper of sorrow, barely audible but impossible to ignore. Down below, Nelly lay restless, her body betraying her with every twitch and flutter. Kenneth drifted in and out of her thoughts like smoke, leaving behind traces of heat and hunger. The scent of his cologne still clung to her memory—warm, rich, intoxicating. She licked her lips absentmindedly, recalling the salt of his skin, the press of his body, and the electricity that still danced across her nerves.

She was *still* smitten. Utterly. Shamefully. The thought of him and Mars unraveling—splintering apart upstairs—drew a wicked little smirk to her lips. Somewhere in the corner of her heart, she knew it was wrong. But the temptation, the thrill of possibility, made it hard to care.

Above her, Mars stood in the dim light of morning, arms crossed over her chest as silent tears streaked down her cheeks. Her eyes stayed fixed on him—on Kenneth—his bare chest rising and falling in a steady rhythm as he slept, unaware. The soft glow of dawn crept in through the curtains, casting gold across the room that felt anything but warm.

She knew. She knew he had been with someone else. She could feel it in her bones, see it in the way he no longer reached for her at night. Her heart ached, raw and heavy. Quietly, she stepped back, inching away from the bed with light movements, the sheets barely rustling. She made her way to the walk-in closet, her fingers trembling as she began to gather a few of her things—maybe not everything, but enough. Enough to say she was ready to go… if she really had the strength.

He didn't say it, but he felt her pulling away—like a tide receding quietly, powerfully. And once she disappeared from view, Kenneth sat up in bed, his body heavy with the weight of everything unspoken. He moved up the winding black metal staircase to the bathroom on the second floor, washed his face, dressed quickly, and returned downstairs. The silence that greeted him was sharp—cutting through the air like glass. Then, her voice, brittle and breaking:

"I'm going back to Seattle in the morning."

He chuckled dryly, not turning to face her. "Of course you are. I'm not surprised."

"You're such a bastard. Don't act like this is my fault," she snapped, her voice low but venomous.

He stood at the fridge, back still turned, pulling out eggs, bacon, and toast like it was any other day. "Me? Mars, man—shut the fuck up," he muttered.

She grew wild with anger, eyes darting for something—anything—to throw, to smash, to use as an outlet for the pain swelling inside her. She lunged past him, but before she could do anything reckless, he grabbed her—stopping her mid-motion. Her silk robe swirled around her like a storm cloud, hair cascading around her flushed, tear-streaked face. She was disheveled and devastatingly beautiful. Kenneth looked at her like a man stranded at sea—desperate, aching, unsure whether he wanted to be saved or drown.

He kissed her. Soft at first, then greedy. His hands moved between her thighs, needing to feel her, to remember.

Tears poured freely down her face as she whispered, voice cracking, "You kissed her like this, didn't you?"

"Yo! What the fuck do you want from me?" he shouted, jerking away, anger and guilt burning behind his eyes.

Her hand flew across his cheek, the slap echoing through the loft. He didn't respond. He didn't flinch. Instead, he turned away—until he felt her wrap her arms around him from behind, clinging to him like a ghost of the girl she used to be.

"I'm sorry," she sobbed. "Why would you do that?" Her fists pounded against his back, desperate, broken, love bleeding into rage.

And still, he said nothing.

Biting his lip, Kenneth turned on instinct, grabbing her trembling hands and pinning them gently but firmly against the wall. His mouth found hers, breath hot, body burning with the fire of unresolved desire. He hoisted her effortlessly, her legs wrapping around his waist as if they belonged there. She whimpered through the tears, "I can't do this…" but her fingers told another story, sliding down the thin straps of her lingerie and guiding him closer, pressing her lips against his, lost in the dangerous kind of love—the kind that consumes.

He kissed her neck, his hands exploring as if he were trying to memorize every inch of her. They moved together in a rhythm born of tension, heartbreak, and heat—but then, she pushed him back, the internal war rising too loud to ignore.

Frustrated, Kenneth spun and punched the wall, the thud loud and sharp. Downstairs, Nelly shot upright in bed, her eyes darting to the ceiling toward her kitchen, pulse racing as muffled chaos shook the air.

Above, Kenneth's voice was different now—deeper, menacing, cracked.

"What do you want?" he demanded, chest heaving.

Mars stood barefoot, shaking, her robe clinging to her like a silk wound.

"I don't know..." she whispered, voice barely there.

"No, no, no—that's not an answer," he growled. "What do you want, huh? I have to leave my wife. I can't touch anyone else. We can't even sleep in the room upstairs because Noel and I used to be there. I need to parade you around town—the very city where I built my fucking name—and what the fuck do you have to give me back? You can't even leave that fat nigga alone! What. Do. You. Want?"

"Stop screaming at me," she snapped through her tears.

"So tell me!" he barked, voice cracking with pain.

"I want you... I do," she said, her breath trembling. "I love you."

In a flash, he rushed her again, cupping her face with both hands, pressing his forehead against hers, lips softening.

"So leave him, Marsha. Please," he begged, voice breaking into a whisper.

More tears. A storm of them.

"I can't..." she cried. "I can't, and you know that. I'm scared of what he'll do to you, to us! But I love you so much."

Kenneth stepped back like her words burned him. His jaw clenched.

"Oh, nah," he said coldly. "Get out. Don't wait until morning. Get your shit and get the fuck out. I want you gone by the time I get back."

And with that, he disappeared upstairs, leaving her standing in the wreckage of everything they'd just undone.

An hour later, dressed and ready for the day, Nelly's ears perked up at the sound of Kenneth storming out of his apartment. Her heart skipped. *They must've argued,* she thought, a small, satisfied smile curling at her lips. Her patience, she believed, was finally paying off. She slipped her phone off Do Not Disturb, propped it up, and began making breakfast. The cool morning breeze drifted in through a cracked window—*this day might actually be good,* she mused.

Then came the sharp *click-click* of heels descending the stairs. Mars. Her driver was outside, pacing impatiently beside the car as he waited to collect her bags. From her bedroom window, Nelly watched, coffee in hand, her curiosity undeniable.

Even defeated, Mars looked polished. She wore a pair of high-waisted beige linen pants and a matching crop top that clung to her sculpted figure. Her straightened hair flowed smoothly to the small of her back.

In a moment of nerve and impulse, Nelly stepped outside, pretending to take out the trash just to get closer. Maybe even apologize.

As she opened the door, Mars stood just a few feet away, still as a statue.

"I hope you're okay..." Nelly stammered.

Mars turned, stunned—eyes wide with disbelief, as though the audacity of the moment knocked the wind out of her.

"Why are you speaking to me?"

"No, no. I just heard a thud—like someone hit something. I just... I just wanted to make sure you're okay."

Mars tilted her head ever so slightly, studying her with a look so cold, it could freeze boiling water.

"You're not fooling me... or anyone," she said, voice like velvet with razor edges. "You think you've tasted the sweat of a man who's going to worship you, spoil you, adore you like some precious little sugar baby?"

Nelly's mouth parted slightly, but no words came.

"It won't happen. And I feel sorry for you," Mars continued, clicking her teeth. "All those pitiful, cheap paintings..." she shook her head, amused. "My oh my, you must really be in love with *my* man. But no worries, I bought them. Sent them where they belong."

Her words were quiet, but they hit like bricks—measured and final.

"Because I can assure you," she added, inching closer now, her eyes steady, "he doesn't even see you. And he never will."

Without another glance, she turned on her heel—cool, untouched, and impossibly composed—leaving Nelly holding nothing but her trash and an ache she hadn't yet figured out how to name.

CHAPTER 6.

MISSED CALL

The trash bag hit the ground with a thud, forgotten. Janelle stormed back into her apartment, her breath ragged, her hands shaking. Anger burned beneath her skin, pulsing hotter than her tears, which streamed freely now, carving paths down her cheeks. Her heart pounded, her vision blurred as she snatched her phone from the counter, fingers trembling as she hit the phone icon on his contact.

Ring.

Ring.

Then—static.

Her breath caught.

"I'm sorry, the number you have dialed is not in service. Please check the number and dial again."

She froze.

A second passed. Then another.

And suddenly, the weight of it all slammed into her chest.

"No—no, no, no," she whispered, voice cracking.

Then came the scream. Raw, guttural, almost inhuman. It clawed its way out of her like grief breaking the sound barrier. Her phone dropped from her hand, clattering against the hardwood floor. She stood there, body trembling, heartbreak radiating from her like heat off scorched earth—utterly alone with the sound of her own devastation echoing off the walls.

Nelly was unraveling.

To some, she was being dramatic—overreacting, even. To others, maybe just a hopeless romantic caught chasing affection in places it never truly lived. But whatever the opinion, the ache in her chest was real. She couldn't bear to face the world—let alone her friends. The lights in her loft stayed dimmed, casting long shadows that matched her mood. A glass of wine became her comfort, and old *Love Island* episodes played on loop, a pitiful distraction from her heartbreak saga.

Two days slipped by. She called out of work, retreating into solitude, though her ears never rested. Every footstep above her—Kenneth's—kept her tethered. At least it wasn't the rhythmic creaking of sex anymore. That silence, as bitter as it was, became her strange consolation.

In the daylight, she fled. Renting Citi Bikes, coasting down wide city streets, pretending she was someone else for an hour or two. The skyline, the breeze, and the buzz of Manhattan gave her back pieces of herself. But as soon as she returned and heard his footsteps echo above—he was there, and she was still invisible—rage swelled in her chest all over again.

Until one evening, still dressed from work, her face flushed from the heat of her commute and her pent-up feelings, she snapped. Enough was enough. She wasn't a doormat. She wasn't some fling he could forget. Shame, embarrassment, and fear burned in her gut, but she swallowed them all.

Head held high, Nelly climbed the stairs.

She was going to look the monster upstairs dead in the eyes and demand the one thing he'd never offered her: the truth.

She knocked firmly at first, then softer as nerves crept in. The confidence that had carried her up the stairs began to crack. Her heart pounded so violently it felt like it might echo through the hallway. Just as she considered turning around, there he was.

Kenneth.

Barefoot, shirtless, wearing only a pair of low-slung jeans. His chest was carved like marble, his skin warm and unique, his goatee full, clean, and gleaming like he moisturized with something expensive. Even the way he opened the door seemed choreographed—like he knew the effect he had.

"Hey, hey. What's going on with you? Come on in," he said casually, turning his back to her and gliding back toward the kitchen like this was just another Thursday.

Inside, the smell of garlic and rosemary floated through the air. He was mid-prep—roasted chicken resting beside a tray of golden, herb-crusted potatoes. The countertops were clean, ambient lighting warmed the space. It looked like a magazine spread.

"You look great!" he added with a smile that made her stomach flip.

Nelly blinked. She wasn't sure if she was floating or falling. "I—I came up to ask, you know, well, it's been like two weeks and I haven't—"

He cut her off. Not rudely, but with just enough impatience to remind her who had the upper hand. "Have a seat. You came just in time. I'm making dinner. Have you eaten?"

His voice was smooth. Almost too smooth.

"Um, no. I came from work not too long ago," she murmured, her breath catching in her throat.

"Ah, good. So I can feed you. White or red on the wine?" he asked as he moved about the kitchen with ease, a man in complete control of his space—and perhaps, of her.

Then, like some seductive ritual, he stepped onto the plush carpet in his living room, turned the dial of a vintage record player, and let Otis Redding fill the air. Soulful, slow, intoxicating.

Nelly stood frozen. Her mind begged her to confront him, demand the truth, hold him accountable. But her body—betraying her completely—throbbed with want. Between her legs, heat bloomed like wildfire. She fidgeted, suddenly unsure of why she had come.

For answers? Or for him?

With Otis crooning in the background and the setting sun spilling through the windows, Nelly settled onto a stool by the island. The air was rich with the scent of herbs, and the comforting clinks of cookware gave the evening a domestic rhythm that was almost too perfect. His apartment was similar to hers—open floor plan, minimalist touches—but grander. To the right of the kitchen was a spare bedroom, presumably the one he once shared with Mars. Her perfume still hung in the air like an unwelcome memory.

As Nelly took it all in, she couldn't help but feel like a guest inside someone else's fairytale. One that didn't belong to her.

"So, I never got to thank you for the paintings," Kenneth said, his voice softer now. "I was flattered, for real. No one's ever made me a muse before."

The sincerity in his tone disarmed her. Nelly blushed, lowering her eyes to the stem of her wine glass. "Yeah, I... I was looking for some inspiration for a while."

Without asking her preference, he poured white— delicate and modest—maybe because it reminded him of her, or maybe because it was easier than waiting for an answer. Still, what she really craved wasn't wine—it was clarity. Something stronger than Pinot could offer.

"Ah, I see," he nodded. "Well, I'm glad I could be that for you. Where'd you learn to paint like that?"

Nelly paused, registering the question as thoughtful, but part of her still wondered if this was a carefully curated distraction. A way to steer the conversation from the silence, the avoidance, the unspoken distance he had placed between them.

"My mom taught Spanish at a high school in our neighborhood. Before I even started school, she'd bring me with her, sit me in the back with brushes and paper while she taught. Didn't trust a sitter, and she didn't have the luxury of time off... so I just—created."

As she spoke, Kenneth sipped his wine, nodding, never once breaking eye contact. He glanced at the stove briefly, but his focus remained on her. It was unnerving— how present he seemed. How every question felt intentional. Meaningful.

And in that moment, she was torn.

Because even though part of her had come here for answers, another part—a quieter, more dangerous part—was beginning to melt under the warmth of his gaze.

Before she realized it, two hours had slipped by—laughter punctuated the room, the food was gone, and their conversation had flowed like old friends finding each other again. Nelly's guard had dropped entirely. How could anyone stay mad at a man like this? He was thoughtful. Domestic. Kind. That charm—so effortless—seeped into every glance, every sentence, every carefully timed smile.

As Kenneth began clearing the island, rinsing the plates, and wiping down the countertops, Nelly watched him with wine-softened eyes. The kitchen glowed in the low evening light, warm and hazy. Her logic dulled, her inhibitions drifting further from shore.

Quietly, she slid off the stool, her bare feet light on the tile as she padded across the floor toward him. The air between them shifted the moment she touched his arm, turning him to face her. He didn't resist. His body turned with ease, his eyes meeting hers—curious, unreadable, but open.

She bit her bottom lip, something electric pulsing through her. Her fingers moved with confidence, unbuttoning his jeans and then tugging down the zipper. His breath caught, but he didn't stop her. One brow arched, eyes darkening, watching her with quiet anticipation as she slowly lowered herself—knees to the floor, she took his penis into her mouth.

The tension was thick, electric, unspoken. And for that moment...the silence between them finally made sense.

They made love that night—slow, intentional, and sweeter than the last time. This time, it felt like something real. Nelly's body responded differently—her desire deeper, her pleasure more consuming. She stayed wetter longer, moaned louder, her back arching with a kind of freedom she hadn't allowed herself before. There was a rhythm between them, a synchronicity that made her feel seen, chosen.

And though thoughts of Mars flickered in the back of her mind—how she, too, had once lain in this bed— Nelly felt something Mars no longer had: *him.*

Everyone was wrong. He *did* see her. He *did* respect her. And maybe, just maybe, he was starting to love her. She wanted to believe that.

Morning came slowly. She awoke later than usual, sunlight creeping through the shades, the space next to her in bed empty but still warm. Stretching, she sat up—then panic rushed in. She scanned the room for her clothes, gathering pieces quickly, when something caught her eye: a photo on the nightstand next to her hair tie.

It was a picture of Noel.

She froze. Her breath hitched. Her fingers hovered near it but didn't touch. *Had that been there the night before? Was it always there—even when Mars lived here?* The questions hit like bricks, each heavier than the last. She couldn't remember.

A quiet panic settled in her chest. Grabbing the rest of her things, she rushed out the door, down the stairs, and into her own apartment—her heart pounding with a mix of confusion and doubt.

At work, Nelly smiled from ear to ear, her energy radiant and impossible to ignore. She breezed through her emails, replies swift and cheerful, and her workflow was seamless—articles written with ease, meetings scheduled like clockwork. It was as if something inside her had been reset, and recharged.

Feeling more like herself than she had in weeks, she finally opened the group chat. Typing out a single sad face emoji followed by, *"Are you still mad at me, Em?"* she hit send, unsure of what to expect. Almost instantly, Emily replied: *"Oh! She speaks. Where the hell have you been?"*

Nelly laughed, her fingers flying over the keyboard as the girls caught up, jokes and gifs flying. It felt good—normal.

By the end of the conversation, she made plans to head to Emily's after work. *"Food and drinks on me,"* she promised. And for the first time in a while, she actually meant it.

It felt like Nelly had stepped into a new timeline—lighter, shinier, with fewer burdens on her shoulders and more joy in her chest. After work, she and Lisa arrived at Emily's place, where the usual fussing and food-fueled girl talk filled the air, but the moment they sat down, something felt... different. The energy had shifted, and it was hard to ignore the glow radiating off their friend.

"Something's going on here..." Lisa said, squinting at Nelly with suspicion.

They were all still half-stuffed into their business attire, tugging at pencil skirts and unbuttoning the top buttons of their blouses, trying to get comfortable. Emily leaned in too, eyes narrowed. "Yeah, you're buying food, supplying wine, and you haven't stopped laughing since you got here…"

Nelly gave a sheepish grin, hands up in a *don't attack me* gesture. "Well... I didn't want to say anything over the phone, but Kenneth and I are doing good." Her voice was light, floating. She twirled her fingers in the air as if to say, *no big deal*—but it clearly was.

The room fell quiet.

"Oh, come on, guys," Nelly groaned.

Lisa was the first to speak. "The last time you messaged the group chat, it was to say he gave you the wrong number. And now... you're saying y'all are back on?"

Emily stayed quiet—arms crossed, eyes fixed, studying Nelly like a subject in a case study. She didn't need to speak; her silence said plenty.

"Look," Nelly began defensively, "maybe he did that as a joke or something. Or maybe it was to get me to come upstairs—because I finally did—and we had an amazing night."

Lisa blinked. "Amazing night...you slept with that man again?"

"It was more than just sex."

"But didn't his girlfriend, Nelle—didn't she just leave him? So you guys... in *that* apartment… where *she* lived?"

"Don't do that," Nelly snapped, exhaling hard. "Why can't you just be happy for me? Emily, you'll get your chance to pitch him soon. He's clearly into me now. We had dinner and, good conversation. I mean, he's going to start planning dates."

"I don't—I don't understand," Lisa said, glancing at Emily, desperate for backup. But Emily stayed mute, watching like a therapist waiting for a breakthrough. Lisa pushed on.

"You work for a women's relationship magazine. If someone wrote in with this exact story, what advice would you give them?"

"I can't believe you guys are doing this," Nelly muttered.

"We can't believe *you're* doing this," Lisa snapped back.

"We like each other. We had a good night. We're going to see where it goes. End of story."

Lisa raised a brow. "Okay. One more thing—did you even notice that your magazine had *his wife* on the cover of the spring issue?"

Nelly froze.

She inhaled sharply. "To be honest, the magazine editorial side itself is above my pay grade. I didn't know that. But actually... that's good. That means she's out of the picture for real. It's confirmation for me."

Emily finally broke her silence. "You walk into that office every day and didn't notice who the cover was?"

"No," Nelly said with forced calm. "I work in digital—online articles, YouTube, and online covers. And she wasn't on any of those. I promise you that."

The silence that followed wasn't just awkward—it was loaded like a ticking clock counting down to a choice Nelly wasn't ready to face.

The first day of summer had finally arrived, and with it came late sunsets, warmer nights, and more of Kenneth. Nelly found herself wrapped in the rhythm of their new routine—one night at her place, the next at his. It felt... cozy, like something real was forming. Eventually, she brought up the phone number situation, expecting— maybe even hoping for—an apology, some admission of guilt. Instead, Kenneth casually added the correct number to her phone and called her on the spot, flashing that same smile that always made her second-guess her intuition.

He never addressed it. And somehow, that was supposed to be enough.

Still, she stayed. She told herself they were building something, even as she began to feel the edges fray. As much as she wanted to claim him, something nagged at her: *Why haven't we gone on a single date?* The weather was beautiful, he had money—*a lot* of it—yet there were no gestures. No flowers. No random surprises. No real effort beyond sex, wine, and whatever was playing on Netflix.

It stung more than she admitted.

Meanwhile, in the group chat, things returned to normal—well, *almost*. Nelly made a conscious decision not to mention Kenneth anymore, and Emily never asked. It was like an unspoken truce had been drawn, a line neither of them dared to cross.

Instead, attention shifted.

Lisa was unraveling over Brent, who had started asking for money again, and Plum was turning up the heat, poking at her about when exactly he planned to drop *that* story. The energy in the chat was different—messy, chaotic, familiar. And yet, Nelly stayed mostly silent, her own relationship status tucked away in the background, quietly brewing questions she wasn't ready to ask aloud.

Because deep down, she knew the truth: love wasn't supposed to feel like hiding. That's what she would say to the person writing in with a story like hers.

Nelly had finally reached her limit. After weeks of back-to-back sex, wine-stained sheets, and conversations that rarely ventured past, *"What do you want to watch?"* she decided it was time. Time to see if Kenneth could show up for her in a way that actually mattered. The upcoming Miami trip for Lisa and Emily's birthdays seemed like the perfect test—fun, vibrant, and social. A chance to show him off, to *be* chosen, finally.

They were in her apartment, Kenneth comfortably sunk into her bed, a bag of chips crinkling between his fingers, leaving greasy streaks along her freshly washed sheets. Her laptop played *Love After Lockup* at full volume, casting flickers of light across the room. His phone sat facedown on the nightstand, vibrating now and then like a subtle reminder of things unspoken.

Still, she turned to him with hope stitched into her smile.

"Baby!" she beamed.

"Yeah, babe," he replied, barely glancing away from the screen as he leaned over to kiss her.

She nestled closer, voice soft and sweet, "My friends are going to Miami next month for their birthdays—Lisa's is the 11th, Emily's the 22nd. We're going from the 13th to the 20th. They're renting a yacht, booking out clubs, some celebs are going, there's going to be amazing food... We're staying at the W. I'd love for you to come with me— be my date for the week."

She kissed his neck, waiting for a spark of enthusiasm, a *yes*, anything.

But Kenneth didn't budge.

"Hmm, I don't think so, to be honest. But go and have a good time," he said flatly, still watching the screen. Then he chuckled, "The W? What do your friends do for a living?"

His tone wasn't playful—it was condescending.

Nelly's smile faltered.

Before she could respond, his phone buzzed again. This time, he picked it up, eyes squinting at the screen. The name that flashed briefly was enough to drain the blood from his face.

Her.

A missed call. The name was unmistakable.

Nelly caught her breath.

The room suddenly felt smaller. Quieter. She couldn't even hear the show anymore—just her heartbeat pounding like a warning she was finally ready to hear.

CHAPTER 7.

BROKE IN MIAMI

DAY 1: The day had arrived—August 13th, 2022, 6:39 AM. The energy was riding high as two sleek, all-black Cadillac Escalades pulled into the departure lane of New York's JFK Airport. Inside one were Emily, Nelly, and Tolly; in the other, Lisa and Brent—each crew strategically split to accommodate their mountain of luxury luggage.

Brent, 26—but to Lisa, a tad bit older—, an ex-overseas basketball player turned college basketball coach, stepped out first. He stood tall at 6'3", with a light-brown complexion. A quiet storm of a man, Brent always wore an expression that lived somewhere between confusion and calm—his brows slightly furrowed, as if he were constantly analyzing the world around him. Yet, beneath that thoughtful exterior was a sharp awareness. He was the kind of man who could spot a detail no one else noticed, who could read a room in seconds and sense when something was off before anyone else.

Even now, as he pulled their suitcases from the back of the Escalade, his eyes were scanning—clocking terminal entrances, checking traffic flow, subtly ensuring everything was as it should be. That was Brent. Quiet. Watchful. Ready.

Meanwhile, Tolly emerged from the second Escalade, a vision of effortless style. Clad in a white-on-white ensemble—loose tailored pants, a sheer pleated top, and an oversized blazer draped casually over his shoulders—he looked like he had just stepped off a runway. His dark, tousled hair framed a charming face, and a hint of scruff gave him a rugged, leading-man edge. He adjusted the gold watch on his wrist, catching the early morning light.

As Lisa spotted him, her eyes lit up. But it was Tolly who caught sight of her first, and in an instant, Lisa was running toward him, heels clicking against the pavement, arms outstretched.

The trip hadn't officially begun, but the scene felt like something out of a movie—beautiful people, a luxurious getaway, and a story that was just beginning to unfold.

As they all gathered near the curb, luggage stacked and rolling beside them, the excitement of the trip was momentarily overshadowed by a sudden chill—not just from the morning air, but from Brent's unexpected request. While Nelly was already making her way inside the terminal, Lisa stood beside Emily and Tolly, mid-conversation, until Brent gently tapped her elbow.

"Babe, you got your credit card?" he asked, voice low.

Lisa leaned in, frowning. "Huh?"

"Credit card—to pay for the tickets," he repeated, still quiet.

Lisa blinked. "What do you mean? You sent me the confirmation a month ago. You bought them already. First class. I have the window seat," she said, smiling, trying to laugh it off.

Brent shifted, rubbing the back of his neck. "Nah… I needed to get the money back for those. Listen, just grab the tickets—first class, window seat, same thing. When my next check comes, I'll give the money back to you."

She stared at him, her smile dropping like a stone. "Are you serious?" she asked, voice barely above a whisper.

Both Emily and Tolly, still within earshot, pretended not to hear a thing. They busied themselves with adjusting their carry-ons and mumbling about TSA lines, deliberately avoiding eye contact.

Lisa's jaw clenched. Her voice came through her teeth, tight and sharp. "Do you know how much those tickets are going to cost me?"

Brent looked away, shrugging. "I mean... it's just for now. I got you."

But Lisa didn't respond. She just stood there before snapping back to reality.

"Okay!" Lisa clapped her hands loudly, masking her frustration with a dazzling smile. "Let's go!" she said with a cheerfulness that felt just a bit too forced.

Inside, her stomach twisted. The ticket charge—$3,469.87—flashed on her banking app like a slap to the face. Her smile faltered for a moment.

Emily's text buzzed on her phone: *"You okay?"* She stared at the screen for a beat, then typed back a simple: *"Yeah. Just processing."*

At least the hotel was covered. Between her and Emily, they'd already taken care of the three private suites, and two personal drivers had been secured for the duration of the trip. That gave Lisa some small comfort, knowing she could settle into luxury without another surprise.

And as the group stepped outside into the warm caress of the Miami breeze, with palm trees swaying gently overhead, something shifted. The air felt magnetic. South Beach was buzzing with life—sunlight bouncing off vintage convertibles, the buzz of ocean waves meeting the bass of music floating from beachfront cafés, laughter echoing from roller skaters gliding past in colorful bikinis and shades. The magic of Miami made everything feel possible again.

Lisa, high off the rhythm of it all, leaped over to Brent and kissed him on the cheek. Maybe this wouldn't ruin her birthday after all. She was here to celebrate, not sulk.

When they pulled up to the W South Beach, the group disbanded, each heading to their own private oasis.

Lisa stepped into her suite and was instantly stunned.

The space was a flawless blend of class and edge. A white spiral staircase curled upward like a sculpture, catching the light that poured in through the floor-to-ceiling glass doors leading out to the turquoise ocean. Her bed—crisp, white, and plush—sat beneath a towering mirror headboard, flanked by expensive black lamps and nightstands that added a moody contrast to the open, airy vibe. A semi-transparent divider of floating navy and white blocks added a modern touch, partially separating the sleeping space from the living area beyond.

Soft globe pendant lights flamed like sunset clouds in the corner, casting a warm hue over a glossy black kitchenette. Beyond the room's clean white tile and minimalist furniture, the balcony opened to an unobstructed view of South Beach's famed shoreline. Blue met blue—sky to sea—as far as the eye could see.

Lisa tossed her bag onto the bed and exhaled. Now *this* was birthday energy.

Brent, not too far behind, entered Lisa's purse to find cash to tip the baggage porter. Appalled, Lisa snatched up her purse, her smile tight, and practiced as she nodded politely at the hotel staff. Only once the door clicked shut behind him did her expression crack, the tension flooding out all at once.

"Did you seriously not come here with any money? Not even money for a tip?" she snapped, kicking off her heels with force.

Brent barely flinched, his voice frustratingly calm. "Babe, I have money—it's on my card. Chill out. Why you so loud and upset? It's your birthday, you supposed to be happy."

Lisa spun around, disbelief etched across her face. "*Happy* is me not feeling like an ATM," she shot back. "Happy is you not reaching into my purse and grabbing fifty-dollar bills like you earned them. At least ask me for permission next time before you go diving into my bag."

Her voice trembled—not from weakness, but from holding back the storm behind her eyes. The suite was beautiful, sure, but no amount of ocean views or designer lighting could smooth over the growing resentment gnawing at her celebration.

Emily had her own suite—private, contemporary, and just the way she liked it—while Tolly and Nelly shared theirs, the two already deep in conversation as they unpacked. Nelly, curled up on the edge of the bed, was getting *all* the tea about Tolly's Miami crush, someone he'd only recently started talking to on a dating app. The energy was high and playful, the view of the beach below adding to the thrill of new beginnings and well-earned vacation vibes.

With the sun climbing higher and the salty breeze calling their names, they all agreed to change and meet down in the lobby. Dinner reservations were set for 8 p.m. at *Mila*, one of South Beach's trendiest spots. Tolly, Nelly, and Emily had already handled all the arrangements for Lisa's birthday dinner, making sure every detail was on point. Still, Emily wanted to loop Brent in—if only to keep things drama-free—and figured she'd ask him about it later at the beach.

The afternoon unfolded in classic South Beach fashion: bright sun, waves crashing, and cocktails flowing like music. With reggae beats pumping through a Bluetooth speaker and the scent of sunscreen in the air, they laughed, danced, and let go. Everyone was at least a little tipsy, their worries momentarily drowned out by the ocean.

Later, with the sky warming into golden hour, Emily finally spotted Brent alone. Both of them were drenched from the water activities, hair slicked back and skin kissed by the sun. She rose from her beach towel, pretending to head for another round of drinks, and called out, "Hey, Brent!"

He turned casually, wiping the water from his face. "Yeah, hey, what's going on?"

Back on the beach, Lisa let out a slow exhale, watching Emily disappear from view. She turned to Nelly and Tolly, checking in about their secret plans for Emily's portion of the trip. A catered lunch in the hotel's private dining room was locked in, followed by a club appearance the next night—thanks to some of Lisa's industry connects. It was going to be the perfect vibe for Emily, who lived for a good party. Lisa, on the other hand, loved a cozy dinner with good conversation, and somehow, the two always found balance in their differences.

Before the trip wrapped, Lisa had one last treat planned: a spa day for all of them before their final night. It was her way of ending things on a peaceful note— massages, facials, and warm silence before heading back to the real world.

"Nothing much, things are great," Emily said, brushing wet strands of hair from her face as she stepped closer. "So, you know we have the dinner for Lisa tonight at 8 over at Mila's. I wanted to check in—see if you had anything planned. Flowers, a gift, anything you wanted to add in?"

Brent shrugged, smirking as if the idea hadn't even crossed his mind. "Oh, nah, nah, it's cool. Whatever you guys have going on is alright. We celebrated, you know— her birthday already passed. We just here for the vibe, you know?"

But Emily didn't know. Her brows lifted slightly, caught between confusion and concern. She forced a polite nod, masking her surprise.

"Oh…okay," she said, her tone trailing into something awkward. The silence that followed was loud. Emily gave a faint smile before turning to head back to the group, unsure if Brent's laid-back attitude came from cluelessness or carelessness. Either way, she knew she'd have to hold it down for Lisa tonight.

As she headed back to the beach, Emily took a quick look at Nelly, playfully saying, "I see why Lisa was so patient with you."

Nelly lifted her sunglasses, eyes squinting in the sun. "Uh, uh, Tolly told me her boyfriend is a bum, don't bring that over here. That man was a choice."

By 7:15 PM, everyone was dressed, again meeting in the lobby where their cars were already parked, waiting patiently. Nelly and Tolly stood out like a power duo pulled from the pages of a high-fashion editorial.

Nelly wore a triple-layered black suit, complete with a waistcoat and long tuxedo coat. Her asymmetric waves and gold jewelry added a nice edge to the clean lines of her menswear-inspired look.

Tolly, on the other hand, was sharp in a crisp, all-white tailored ensemble with a longline blazer and statement diamonds—ring-heavy fingers, layered chains, and icy shades. The duo looked like a flipped chessboard: expertly contrasted, perfectly in sync.

Emily kept it refined and modern, walking that delicate line between edgy and classic. She wore high-waisted, wide-leg cream trousers paired with a sleeveless structured coat that flowed behind her like a cape. A sheer panel top gave a touch of softness under all that architectural tailoring, and silver platform heels caught the light with each step.

Lisa and Brent channeled vintage Hollywood glam with a twist. Lisa's look was feathered, fabulous, and unapologetically feminine—a white lace bodice with sheer sleeves, intricate detailing, and ostrich-feather cuffs. A dramatic high slit revealed sky-high white platforms and a glimpse of shorts underneath, balancing elegance with a bit of power.

Brent stood beside her effortlessly dapper in a black tuxedo with satin lapels, crisp white shirt, and a classic black bow tie. Clean, polished, and standing like a man who knows his woman is the main event.

That night, the dinner went off without a hitch. Laughter echoed off the walls of Mila's dimly lit rooftop as the table shimmered with gourmet plates, each one more decadent than the last. Glasses clinked, cocktails were poured without hesitation, and the warmth of celebration hung in the air. The table was a picture of abundance—truffle sushi rolls, seared scallops, wagyu skewers, and champagne flutes lined with condensation.

Midway through dessert, Emily and Nelly rose from their seats with a sparkle in their eyes, surprising Lisa with two beautifully wrapped gifts. First, Emily handed her a Cartier rose gold bracelet. Then Nelly followed with a plush abcDNA Luminous Velvet Throw, unbelievably soft to the touch. Lisa's eyes welled with tears. She covered her mouth, completely overwhelmed, and whispered a choked, "Thank you," before blowing out the candles atop her birthday cake.

Brent, sitting beside her, leaned back and motioned for the waitress with two fingers. "Another Jack and Coke," he said casually, as if untouched by the emotion around him.

Tolly, never one to be outdone, proudly handed Lisa a glossy Larroudé gift bag. "If it's one thing I know you love, girl, it's some good bed slippers," he grinned. "Those feet don't touch no floors, okay?" He snapped his fingers with dramatic flair, causing the whole table to erupt in laughter.

Everyone, except Nelly and Brent.

She hadn't heard from Kenneth all day. Not a "good morning," not a "what's the vibe tonight?"—nothing. While Tolly's words about slippers got a chuckle out of the group, Nelly's mind had drifted elsewhere. Kenneth's slippers. The sound of them dragging across her hardwood floors. The way he always seemed so at home, even when giving so little.

Quietly, she excused herself, stepping out to the hallway with her phone in hand. She dialed. It rang once, then straight to voicemail. Her stomach dropped, a tight knot forming in her chest as her heartbeat picked up.

When she returned to the table, something had shifted. Her smile was gone, her posture guarded. The music, the food, the laughter—it all faded into background noise. She sat down, staring into her untouched cocktail.

She wanted to go home.

DAY 2: The next day was all about recovery. In their twenties, they would've bounced back with a greasy breakfast and a laugh. But now, being thirty and up, hangovers hit differently. Heavier. Slower. Except for Tolly, who was somehow immune to it all. While everyone else was curled under blankets and nursing sparkling water, he had plans. Noon sharp, he threw on his sunglasses and headed out to meet his dating app crush. Lunch on the boardwalk and a show in the evening—it was giving spontaneous rom-com energy.

Emily, ever the mom-friend of the crew, tried to talk him out of it when he went to her suite for some perfume.

"You don't even know him, Tol. Can't it wait?" But he came prepared. Shared his location. Promised hourly check-ins. And to his credit, he kept his word. Every hour. On the dot.

Brent and Lisa spent most of the morning wrapped up in each other. But something was off with her—he could feel it in the way she held him.

"Babe," she started, voice soft but edged with something real, "how come you didn't get me anything for my birthday? Even in front of my friends?"

Brent blinked, caught off guard. "I can get you something anytime. Why does it have to be this week? I thought we were just catching a vibe. No pressure."

Lisa sat up a bit, disappointment lingering behind her eyes. "I mean, yeah, but we knew about this trip for *months*, and even the bill. You asked the waitress to give you your bill and yours alone. You couldn't even pay for my food."

He sighed, running a hand over his dark Caesar with waves. "Your friend told me earlier she already took care of all that. And I knew if they were paying for you, they definitely weren't paying for me. So that's why I did that. But if it bothered you, I'm sorry."

Lisa nodded slowly, letting the silence stretch before replying.

"Well… I don't want to pay for anything today. No drinks. No food. Are you okay with that?"

Brent chuckled, trying to lighten the mood. "Yeah, I got it. Baby, don't worry, okay? It's all cool."

But Lisa didn't laugh. Not this time.

That day, the crew scattered across Miami, each on their own version of escape.

Brent made good on his word. Planning out simple moments and free activities. He mapped out murals in Wynwood, they strolled through public parks, and when they got hungry, it was pizza slices from a walk-up window and fries shared under palm trees.

It wasn't much, but to Lisa, it was more than enough. She didn't love him for what he could buy her—she loved him for the peace he brought her. Brent was steady. He didn't raise his voice, didn't play mind games. With him, love didn't feel like a guessing game—it felt like home.

Emily, on the other hand, was reaching her breaking point. Nelly had been locked into her phone all day. Even at dinner—a trendy spot on the strip with a live DJ and a waitlist longer than the menu—Nelly barely looked up. Her eyes flickered across the screen like it was feeding her oxygen.

"You even know the name of the place we're in?" Emily asked, her tone laced with sarcasm.

Nelly didn't even blink. "Emily, please. Don't start with me. Not now, please."

Emily leaned in, pushing. "Why are you super-glued to that phone?"

"We promised not to talk about him."

"I'll be your Lisa tonight. Not Emily. Go ahead, lay it on me. What's going on?"

Nelly paused, skeptical. "You're Lisa?"

"Yep. Judge-free zone over here."

With that, Nelly sighed, finally setting her phone down. "Alright... Kenneth hasn't called. Not once. Not even to check on me."

But before Emily could rein it in, she burst into laughter, her mink lashes wet from tears. It wasn't mocking—more like disbelief, like "girl, not *him* again." Still, it hit wrong.

Frustrated and humiliated, Nelly hopped off the stool, tossed a crumpled $20 on the table, covering her half-drunk Bud Light and barely touched fries, and started to walk out.

"Oh no, no! I am so sorry!" Emily called after her, rushing to catch up, hands apologetic in the air. But the damage had already cracked through the evening, loud and messy, just like their friendship could be sometimes.

DAY 3: Hit different.

The sun was still shining, the plans were still in motion, but Nelly—Nelly was spiraling. She hadn't slept much, hadn't eaten much either, just glued to her screen like it held the answers to her sanity.

Tolly had had enough.

"Sweetheart, I'm saying this with love—but please stop. This is starting to border on infatuation." He stood near the balcony doors, watching her pace the room, her thumb moving faster than her thoughts.

Voicemail after voicemail. Text after text. And when that didn't work, she turned to Instagram—even though Kenneth didn't have an account. Still, she went full detective, Googling names of friends, exes, coworkers, even the tattoo artist he mentioned once, trying to find someone, *anyone* who might've tagged him in something. A background cameo. A story highlight. A shadow. Anything.

But there was *nothing*.

He had vanished.

Like a ghost.

Tolly walked over, calm but firm. "Listen, we have to be downstairs in a few for Yardbird. I need you to give me the phone, honey." His voice soft, nurturing.

But she clutched it tighter, like it was her last lifeline. "No! Why would I do that? I'm not obsessed—I'm confused. Why is he blowing me off? Maybe I did something...said something wrong..."

She scrolled up again. Back to **Day 1**. The beginning of this trip. A sea of blue bubbles—*delivered*, never read. Not a single reply. Just silence where a voice used to be.

And Tolly could only watch, wishing he could pull her out of that rabbit hole she didn't even realize she was in.

CHAPTER 8.

WRONG CONTACT

The girls chose Yardbird Southern Table & Bar for lunch—a stylish, upscale spot tucked into a bright white art deco-style building on a palm-lined corner in Miami. Its modern signage curved across the exterior like a quiet invitation. Inside, the vibe was warm and inviting, with rustic wooden beams lining the ceiling, exposed brick walls, and soft lights spilled over polished wooden tables. The bar was fully stocked, a refined centerpiece wrapped in gray stone with shelves of colorful bottles rising behind it like a rainbow of temptation.

Laughter danced between clinking glasses and the casual scrape of barstools as they all leaned in close, enjoying the rich, Southern-inspired dishes and sweet cocktails. But Nelly kept breaking away from the conversation—her phone in hand, eyes flickering with uncertainty. She slipped away again, muttering something about bad reception. Her friends tried not to notice, but the dim light near the entrance and the moody shadows by the bar couldn't hide the way she anxiously tapped her screen. Yardbird was alive with energy and Southern charm, but Nelly? She was somewhere else entirely.

"Is she alright?" Lisa asked, her voice low as she leaned toward Emily.

Emily blinked, thrown off. Lisa's concern caught her off guard, "Lisa, I say this with love. You have enough going on."

That hit.

Emily had been drinking steadily all day—nothing too wild, just enough to keep her buzzed and upbeat. Honestly, it was doing wonders for her mood. Tolly, ever composed, kept the table grounded. He talked about his date night with a leisurely calm, while Brent, clearly overstimulated, abruptly got up mid-convo to take a call.

Moments later, Lisa's phone buzzed. A Zelle request for payment. $244.00 requested from Brent. The memo: *covering the meal, babe*. Emily, seated beside her, caught a glimpse. Her eyes widened, lips parted in disbelief, but Tolly—across from them—kept talking, unfazed.

Meanwhile, Nelly, off in her own corner, was visibly shaken. Her fingers swiped nonstop through Instagram, having scrolled through what looked like *thousands* of profiles. Seven thousand, by her count. Her whole body trembled.

It was, in short, a bizarre afternoon.

When Nelly returned to the table, she couldn't even fake composure. She mumbled something and left. Emily, on her fourth martini, felt like she was floating. She couldn't manage a serious face if she tried—even as Nelly wiped tears from her cheeks. Lisa took charge, flagging down the server and promising to handle the bill. Tolly looped his arm into Emily's and helped her stand.

"Oh my gosh, no, girl. Are you sure?!" Emily slurred.

Tolly offered to Zelle Lisa, but she waved him off.

"You guys go on—we'll catch up," she said with a reassuring smile.

Brent reappeared as they walked off, still glued to his phone. Lisa signed the check and slid a crisp cash tip beneath the receipt. Brent was grinning like a teenager—clearly thrilled by whatever was on his screen.

"Baby, you good?" he asked, barely looking up. "I'm going to LIV tonight, alright?"

Lisa didn't answer. She was already walking away, trying to catch up with the only part of the day that felt real—her friends.

They had finally made it to the beach and were now straddling jet skis like seasoned pros. What was a trip to Miami without this? The sun was high, the water glittering like crushed diamonds, and laughter echoed across the waves as they raced one another with reckless joy. Emily let out a high-pitched scream as Tolly swerved close, splashing her with a wave. Nelly, after hours of scrolling through her phone, finally gave in to the moment—setting it down and joining them in the water, her curls springing with every dip and dive.

They took turns snapping photos—sun-kissed and dripping, posing on the jet skis like magazine covers in motion. A group of men pretending to be bartenders floated by on inflatable coolers, handing out questionable shots in plastic cups. No one asked what was in them. They just cheered and tossed them back, the ocean spinning slightly greater with each one.

For once, the world felt light.

Two hours later, sun-soaked and waterlogged, they headed back to their rooms. Sleep came easily—some collapsed on the bed, others wrapped in towels, sprawled across couches, still laughing between yawns. It was one of those golden afternoons that demanded nothing and gave everything.

But by evening, the mood shifted.

Lisa stirred at the sound of men's voices echoing from Brent's speakerphone. He was on a call, boasting to someone about having a private driver lined up for the night, promising no one would have to lift a finger for transportation. Lisa sat up slowly, her face creased in quiet annoyance. Her eyes flicked toward her phone—7:41 PM.

She exhaled. Hard.

Her breathing, shallow and sharp, didn't go unnoticed. Brent peeked out from the bathroom, the steam from his shower curling behind him like a flicker. From his angle, he could see the edge of their bed—Lisa curled in a quiet storm, face lit only by her phone screen.

"Baby," he whispered, muting his friends on speaker. "We can take the cars tonight, right? Drivers won't mind?"

Lisa didn't answer. Instead, her thumbs flew across the screen. Ten angry face emojis dropped into the group chat like landmines. Seconds later, a ding. It was Emily: *"What happened?"*

Lisa's reply was instant: *"He's going to LIV and asking to use the drivers!"*

Another message popped up.

"Ugh! Are you going to let him take them?"

Emily knew she had just as much pull to say no.

Before she could answer, Brent reappeared, towel slung over one shoulder, brushing waves from his hair like he was already halfway to the club.

"Babe, they're gonna be here in about ten minutes. Some of my boys from high school and their friends. I'll let you know so we can go down and meet them, alright?"

Lisa forced a smile, lips tight. "Okay."

Inside, she was raging. A part of her wanted to be generous—he should go out, enjoy himself, they hadn't made plans. But the other part...the bigger part...felt hollow. Forgotten. How could he be this excited about LIV and still not have acknowledged her birthday? Not even a card. Not even a cheap candle from Walgreens.

She felt like background noise to his vacation.

"Babe," he called again, more urgently this time. "We *can* use the drivers, right?"

Lisa didn't hesitate.

She lied.

"Emily said no."

As the lie left her lips, guilt twisted in Lisa's chest like a slow-turning blade. She barely had time to process it before Brent's energy shifted.

"Man...she's mad wack for that. Old stuck-up ass," he muttered, sucking his teeth as the bathroom door slammed shut behind him. Seconds later, his phone buzzed—he was already calling someone else.

Lisa stood in silence for a beat, then reached for her outfit—a cropped top, soft shorts, calf-length socks, and her trusty Crocs. Her movements were robotic, a mix of instinct and needing to not be in that room anymore. She walked the long hallway of the hotel until she stood at Emily's suite. A quick knock and the door swung open.

Inside, Tolly and Nelly were curled up on the plush couch, wide-eyed like kids caught whispering secrets.

Lisa laughed, hands on her hips.

"Don't stop talking about me now! Keep going!"

Nelly grinned, phone still in hand, but her focus was locked. The screen glowed with a paused Instagram Story. A woman. Passenger seat. Wind in her hair. And a man's hand on the wheel, fingers laced with hers.

Nelly squinted, zoomed in.

The complexion. The nail beds. The faint scar on the wrist. She *knew* that hand. Kenneth.

With the urgency of a woman on the brink, she downloaded the video using a sketchy site that swarmed her browser with ads. The moment the file hit her phone, she forwarded it to him with one caption: "Is this why you haven't been answering my calls?"

Silence.

She stood abruptly, pacing toward the balcony where the warm Miami wind licked at her skin. The city lights flickered like stars scattered across the shoreline. Her breathing was heavy.

Inside, Lisa poured vodka into a glass with more aggression than necessary, mixing it with whatever juice she found in the minibar.

"I've never seen him like this," she vented, swirling the drink. "It's like… since we got here, he became a totally different person."

There was something sharp in her voice. A sadness too tired to cry and a disappointment too proud to say it aloud. The kind of pain only your closest friends could see through.

After minutes of silence, no reply, no read receipt—just digital nothing—Nelly reopened the video, her fingers trembling slightly. She tapped through the girl's profile, relentless now. Stories, highlights, reels… she didn't care if she'd be seen in the views. Pride was a luxury. She needed answers.

Each flick of her thumb was another jab to the chest. The woman's life was out in the open: brunches, rooftops, group shots in moody lighting. Then, she froze. A Boomerang. Blurred motion and flashing lights. The girl was tucked beneath the arm of a man. Not just any man— a man whose silhouette, fade, and presence looked *far too familiar.*

Nelly's breath caught. She zoomed in until the image pixelated into nonsense, but the damage was done. The location: "Meatpacking District."

Her knees buckled.

Her stomach turned.

A slow, creeping nausea crawled up her throat, turning lunch into a live wire.

Without a word, she rushed inside, hand clamped over her mouth as the first dry heave hit her chest. She barely made it to the bathroom before vomiting, her body convulsing with betrayal.

From the living room, Lisa, Emily, and Tolly all looked toward the closed door in shock, the only sound now the running faucet and a weak cough.

Then Lisa's phone buzzed. A text.

Brent: *"Friends are here, babe, lobby. Come meet them and bring Emily so she can meet my boy."*

Lisa passed her phone to Emily, the message from Brent still glowing on the screen. She let out a sigh and collapsed onto the couch, sinking into the cushions with no desire to move—let alone play hostess to a group of men she'd never met.

But Emily was already in motion, two drinks in and all adrenaline.

"Come on!" she grinned, tugging at Lisa's arm like a kid begging for a sleepover. "You're already doing it for the plot, but that shit just got thicker if he wants me to meet his friend." She twirled, arms wide. "Lisa, we're in Miami!"

Lisa rolled her eyes but cracked a smile. "What about Nelle?" she asked, half-hoping that would delay their departure.

From the bathroom, Janelle shouted through the door, "I'm fine! You guys go ahead."

But she wasn't fine. Her voice betrayed her. Embarrassment clung to her like sweat, and her eyes still burned from tears. She just needed space to collect herself alone.

Downstairs, Emily practically skipped into the hotel lounge like a girl headed to her first crush's locker. The entrance buzzed with music, low lighting, and the thrum of nightlife anticipation. Near the doorway stood four men, all different races, dressed in the Miami male starter pack: jeans, tees, caps, sneakers.

One peeled away from the group, confident and cool. He made a beeline for Lisa.

"I don't know how we've never met before," he said, flashing a grin. "I'm Malik. It's nice to meet you."

Lisa offered a small smile, still unsure of the moment. But his charm was warm, not forced. She returned it.

"It's nice to meet you, too," she said, glancing toward Brent, who was too busy dap'ing up one of his boys to notice. "And... yeah, I don't know either."

Her words held weight, but for the first time all day, they weren't laced with frustration—just curiosity. Maybe this night wasn't going where she thought. Maybe the plot *really* had just thickened.

"And this must be the gorgeous Emily," Malik said, lifting her hand like royalty and pressing a kiss to the back of it. His friends burst into light-hearted laughter, clearly amused by his smooth delivery.

They were all young—mid-twenties at most, still in their party-boy prime. Lisa clocked it immediately and couldn't help but wonder: *What was Brent doing around these guys?* The age gap was starting to feel more apparent, like an itch under her skin she couldn't quite scratch. But she said nothing. Instead, she sat, sipping her drink, letting the buzz of conversation and easy laughter cushion the moment.

"So," Malik leaned in, clearly the ringleader, "why aren't you ladies coming out with us tonight?"

Lisa opened her mouth, but Emily beat her to it, ever the quick wit. "I don't know. We didn't get the invite," she teased, throwing a flirty glance in Malik's direction.

"What!" Malik gasped dramatically. "That's wild." He turned to Brent, who was fully immersed in a side conversation, barely acknowledging Lisa's presence despite being the one who asked her to come downstairs in the first place.

"Aye man!" Malik called out. "Come here real quick. It's your lady's birthday week. Why they not coming out with us?"

Brent barely looked over. "Oh...they cool. It's cool."

Lisa didn't bother responding. The air had shifted. Her posture stiffened as Malik, undeterred, turned back to her and Emily with a wide grin. "Well, *I* think y'all should come to LIV tonight. It'll be fun—bottle service, DJs, vibes."

Just then, Lisa's phone vibrated on her lap. A text from Brent flashed across the screen:

"NO MALIK, THEY CAN'T COME."

She stared at it for a beat, her lips parting slightly, then glanced up at Emily, who raised a brow. Lisa held her gaze for a second, then turned toward Malik with a sarcastic smile.

"No Malik, they can't come!" she announced, her tone too sweet to be genuine.

Malik blinked, caught off guard. "What?" he turned to Brent, confusion clouding his face.

Brent stood frozen, jaw tightening as Lisa met his eyes with a look that said *gotcha*.

"Wrong contact," she added with a smile that didn't reach her eyes. Then she took a slow sip of her drink, her silence louder than any outburst.

Emily stood up, smoothing her dress as the mood shifted completely. Lisa followed, her movements steady. As they turned to leave, Brent stepped back toward the far end of the room, distancing himself as if afraid of what might come next.

His eyes were locked on Lisa—searching, maybe pleading—but she couldn't read him anymore. Was he ashamed? Embarrassed? Too proud to say anything? Too cowardly? It didn't matter.

By the time the elevator doors closed behind them, Lisa had already made up her mind.

That night, in silence and with a calm that surprised even herself, Lisa packed up the last of her things from their suite. Her perfume bottles, hair products, two swimsuits drying on the edge of the tub, and a pair of heels she hadn't gotten to wear. She zipped it all up and rolled her suitcase across the polished floor to Emily's room— her new safe space.

Brent went out to LIV.

And Lisa? She didn't cry, didn't scroll, didn't second-guess. She lay back against the pillows in Emily's suite, her best friend asleep beside her, and stared at the ceiling.

She had no intention of ever speaking to him again.

CHAPTER 9.

EMILY'S

CELEBRATION

DAY 4: 2:49 AM. The halls were silent, save for the uneven footsteps of Brent drunkenly weaving his way through them. The overhead lights cast long shadows on the walls as he passed the suite he once shared with Lisa without so much as a glance. He knew exactly where she'd be now.

Emily's room.

He called. He texted. He sent voice messages— slurred apologies, drawn-out explanations, pleas. All of them met with silence. Rejection.

Now standing outside the suite, he knocked. Lightly at first. Then again. Then again. His knuckles thudded against the door with the uncoordinated rhythm of a troubled man. Eventually, he leaned his weight against it, letting his voice drop into a whisper. "Lisa..." he breathed. "Lisa, please."

Inside, the night was still. Upstairs in the spare room, Lisa slept undisturbed, but Emily stirred at the sound. She blinked through the darkness, ears tuned to the knocking, the muffled voice. Quietly, she climbed from bed and tiptoed to Lisa, shaking her gently.

"I think Brent is at the door," she murmured.

Lisa sighed, eyes still closed. "Okay. I'm so sorry he woke you."

"It's okay," Emily replied softly, already settling back under the covers.

Lisa slid from the bed and wrapped a robe around her body. Barefoot, she moved down the spiral staircase slowly, the chill of the night seeping into her skin. At the bottom, she spotted the extra hotel key resting on the counter, picked it up, and padded to the door.

She opened it.

There he was—on the ground, his back against the wall, legs outstretched, eyes heavy but focused on her like she was the only thing left anchoring him to earth.

"Lisa…" he said again, but this time, it was almost a whimper.

Her arms crossed tightly against her chest, Lisa stared him down, disbelief written all over her face.

"What do you want?" she asked, voice low, but sharp enough to cut through his drunken haze.

He looked at her—eyes glassy, shoulders slumped, guilt seeping out of him like sweat.

"I want to tell you I'm sorry. I'm really sorry."

She wanted to believe him. She really did. Because despite everything, she cared for him a lot. But her heart was raw. Still stinging.

"Why would you embarrass me like that?" she asked, the crack in her voice betraying her composure.

And then, like the liquor was working as a truth serum, the words tumbled from his lips, no filter, no hesitation: "I knew I was going to be flirting with girls."

The sentence hit her like a gut punch. Her breath hitched. One single tear betrayed her strength and slid down her cheek.

"Well, thanks for being honest," she said, voice tight, trying to keep it together.

"Anything else?"

As if on cue, his wallet slipped from his pocket, spilling onto the floor—his ID, loose change, crumpled dollar bills—a mess, just like him.

Lisa crouched down to gather it all up, trying to keep things from spiraling further. But then her eyes caught something that made her freeze:

Date of Birth: May 2, 1996.

She blinked.

Audibly gasped.

"You lied about your age?" she demanded, holding the ID like a receipt for all the nonsense she had endured. "You told me you were twenty-nine!"

"Wha—hmm." He could barely respond, swaying, incoherent, lost in the haze of bad decisions and too much liquor.

He needed a bed.

And Lisa?

She needed to be done.

That morning, before her friends stirred awake, Lisa laced up her sneakers and slipped off to the gym. No more sex meant she needed a new outlet—something that gave her the same rush, the same release.

Slim thick and comfortably a size 8, she set her sights on a new goal: drop down to a size 6. Not out of vanity, but control. Re-centering. She needed to pour all that emotion somewhere, and this was it.

As the sun climbed and her phone lit up with messages from the girls, she wrapped up her workout, grabbed a protein bar, lemon-infused water, and headed back upstairs to Emily's suite—the new headquarters. Quietly, everyone had migrated there. What started as a layover room turned into a final destination. Lisa's suite was now left to Brent. And the third? Ignored the majority of the day and night. Tolly had taken the sofa bed, and Nelle, the foot of the queen-sized bed alongside Emily.

As she entered, she heard Nelly's voice—raised, breaking from the bathroom.

"How are you feeling, babes?" Emily asked, pretending not to hear the meltdown happening just a few feet away.

Lisa shrugged, dropping her bag. "I'm alright. Who's she yelling at?"

"Voicenotes," Tolly chimed in, shaking his head.

From the bathroom, Nelly's voice cracked through the space. "I keep calling and calling and texting and you're with some bitch! You could've just left me alone. You treat me like shit—we don't go anywhere—and now you're out here laid up with some next bitch in bed!"

Lisa blinked slowly, her eyes catching Emily's, silently pleading for her to step in. But Emily just raised a brow. She wasn't going to stop it. Tolly, on the other hand, took the reins.

"Nelle, sweetheart," he said, knocking gently, "we have to find a resolution here. Talk to me. Tell me what's going on—in your heart." He pointed to his chest, calm and intentional.

Upstairs, Emily followed Lisa, who was already stepping out of her gym clothes.

"What happened this morning?" Emily asked as she turned on the shower, steam already curling into the air.

"He said he didn't want us to go...because he'd be flirting with girls," Lisa said, stepping under the water, her voice echoing through the cracked bathroom door. "Oh—and get this—he's actually 26. Not 29."

Emily's jaw dropped. "What the fuck! He sounds like one of those washed-up dudes who peaked in high school. You're so good to him, Lisa. Patient as hell. He just wants to party and blow through money. There's no future there."

Lisa wiped water from her face. "Mind you, he got a DUI before I met him. He can't even drive. I'm the one driving us everywhere."

Emily snorted. "You are Lisa *the* McAdams. Public Relations final boss. And you let that degenerate knock you off your rockers?"

Lisa sighed. "I guess I was just...vulnerable. Khalil and I argued a lot. We were always trying to be right. Then Brent came along, and he was patient and such a good listener. We never argued. I never even saw him angry. It felt like...peace."

"I get that," Emily nodded. "But as your friend—hell, your sister—I'm telling you: it's time to move on. Forgive him or don't, but don't hold on to the negativity. Appreciate the good parts, yeah—but don't lose sight of the bigger picture. The whole thing just isn't for you."

Downstairs, Tolly's intervention with Nelly was finally beginning to work.

"What made you believe you two were an item, Nelly?" he asked softly.

Nelly looked down at her phone, her voice almost a whisper now. "The more I think about it…the more I realize—I don't even have an answer for you."

With their love lives officially on pause, the crew pressed forward, keeping to the trip's original schedule. Parasailing in the morning, a sun-soaked beach party in the afternoon, a private lunch hosted by the hotel staff, volleyball with strangers-turned-friends, and drinks flowing like the ocean tide. Emily, knowing she'd be guzzling cocktails the next day for her birthday blowout at the club, opted for a break from alcohol. Instead, she toted around a full gallon of water, sipping it slowly, the plastic jug almost comical against her glam beachwear.

Lisa, meanwhile, was on the phone—working, of course—confirming last-minute details with the club promoter. Everything had to be flawless: the DJ's setlist, her client guest list, and even Roddy Richardson's appearance, which she was especially excited about. She couldn't wait for him to meet her girls, to witness the life she had built outside of PR.

Surprisingly, with every confirmation text and green light, she felt a strange but welcome wave of relief—Brent wasn't part of this. Not anymore. No awkwardness, no emotional weight tugging her down. Just freedom. Fun.

And in that freedom, Lisa and Emily rediscovered each other. They talked and talked, filling in the blanks of their lives—the parts they'd skipped over or hadn't had time to unpack. Old memories came flooding back, along with new layers of laughter. It was like finding a hidden chapter in a favorite book.

The sun dipped low over the water, casting the sand in shades of gold, and for the first time in days, everything just felt...right. It was the perfect day.

DAY 5: Emily's big day had finally arrived, and she was practically glowing with excitement. It was her birthday celebration day and she was ready to celebrate it the way she deserved—loud, bold, and unforgettable. Nelle and Tolly had already darted off to their suite to freshen up, prepping for the group's pre-celebration brunch. Emily kept it casual but cute, slinging her ever-present gallon of water over her arm like a designer bag. "My liver should be ready for the madness tonight," she joked, sipping dramatically as they walked to their drivers.

Lisa, dressed effortlessly chic, had one hand on her phone—though not by choice. It was blowing up with messages and missed calls from Brent. He clearly assumed she only needed a day to cool off and would now be open to talk. But he assumed wrong. There were texts from unknown numbers, No Caller ID spam, and even desperate shots sent through those shady TextNow accounts.

Lisa showed the group, amused and mildly annoyed.

"Look at this," she said, handing her phone to Emily.

"Girl, block and delete!" Emily said.

Tolly laughed, "He's texting like he's trying to get a job back."

"Well, considering I was paying for damn near everything, yes!" Lisa laughed.

Even Nelle, still navigating her own emotional maze, nodded. "Radio silence is the only language men like that understand."

Tolly beamed over to her. "Now ma'am," he said, eyes over his shades.

Lisa agreed. She wasn't going to break her peace for someone who didn't respect her.

But Nelle... Nelle had a new idea brewing—one she instinctively kept to herself. It lingered in her mind like a little secret, curling behind her lips in a smile no one caught.

As they arrived at Nikki Beach, the hostess greeted them with champagne flutes and sun-kissed smiles, ushering their party of four to a prime table by the sand. Laughter, light bites, and flirtatious energy flowed naturally as afternoon melted into early evening. The food was perfect, and the vibes were immaculate.

It was the calm before the storm—and it was bliss.

After a long, luxurious nap, the crew was back up and brimming with excitement. The energy was electric—tonight was *the* night. Emily's birthday celebration at E11EVEN Miami was finally here, and it felt like something straight out of a movie. Downstairs, sleek black cars waited like loyal chariots, engines humming low, ready to whisk them off into the glittering Miami night.

Brent had been calling nonstop, flooding her inbox with texts that wavered between calm persistence and polished desperation.

We need to talk. I've apologized and I'm ready to do the right thing. I would love it if you could forgive me.

He was measured. Too measured. That scary kind of calm that made Lisa pause. She wanted to believe him—wanted to believe that maybe, just maybe, he meant it. But something about the timing felt off. Too precise. Too clean.

Deep down, she couldn't shake the feeling that Brent didn't want her back—he wanted back *in*. Into her world. Her circles. Her clout.

E11EVEN wasn't your average nightclub—it was exclusive, intimidating, and borderline impossible to access without connections. And Lisa? She was *on the list*. Not just that—she was VIP. Reserved tables, comped bottles, and a DJ shoutout. A portion of the night was carved out to honor her best friend, Emily. That kind of pull doesn't come from popularity—it comes from respect, from credibility.

Brent knew that. And Lisa knew *he* knew that.

So while he pressed on, trying to secure a last-minute spot in her world again, she slipped her phone into her purse and walked confidently toward the waiting elevator, her friends trailing behind, laughing, flawless, and unbothered.

Tonight was about Emily.

About joy.

About moving forward.

And Brent? He just *can't come.*

That night, Tolly stepped with a loud confidence, his outfit striking a balance between casual charm and tailored precision. He had chosen a crisp white Lueq shirt that hugged his upper body, the simplicity of it drawing attention without effort. His grey trousers were immaculately fitted, each step revealing their careful tailoring. Beige suede loafers with tassels softened the look, and over one arm, he carried a tan jacket, casually draped but chosen with care. He maneuvered like someone who understood style without needing to speak of it—polished and entirely composed.

Lisa turned the street into a runway. She wore a textured black turtleneck tucked into a high-slit leather skirt, its fringe slicing the air with each step. Over it, she draped a long black coat that flowed behind her like a cape. Her gloved hands held a bold yellow clutch—an unexpected splash of brightness in her monochrome ensemble. With pointed heels and large sunglasses, she looked like she belonged to another era.

Nelle had the night wrapped around her like silk. Her top—a sheer black lace bralette—left little to the imagination, while her high-waisted black jeans with long fringe hems brought movement to every sway of her hips. She accessorized with a wide Gucci belt cinched at the waist, dark cat-eye sunglasses, and a pair of So Kate's that clung to her feet. The glow of streetlights danced on her skin as she leaned against the open car door.

Emily had slipped into a form-fitting long-sleeve top, the fabric smooth and matte, save for the voluminous satin bow that cascaded from her shoulder like armor. Her trousers hugged her curves, and she walked in black stilettos with signature red soles—each step a quiet proclamation. A structured black handbag hung from her fingers, and behind dark sunglasses, she watched the world bend to her will.

Upon their arrival, there was no line, no waiting—just instant access through the rear entrance, where a velvet rope was lifted and the night opened up like a dream. They were escorted to the largest air conditioned section of the venue, tucked high enough for privacy yet visible enough to make a statement. For one night, they were royalty.

As the hours passed, the energy swelled. More and more celebrities flowed in—actors, rappers, athletes—all veering toward their section. Each one greeted Emily with a kiss on the cheek and discreetly slid crisp bills into her hand, the kind of gesture reserved for women celebrated in full. Roddy arrived flanked by four other high-profile actors, all of them ready to spend. Bottles popped, sparklers flew, and the section turned into a glittering shrine of celebration.

Emily was told her night was on them—and it was. Everything from the premium drinks to the surprise desserts that appeared out of nowhere. The music was loud and perfect, each song better than the last. Guests crowded the rope line, holding up phones, asking to take pictures with them. Some begged just to be photographed near the group.

And there was the photographer for the evening, weaving in and out of the haze of lights and laughter, capturing every dazzling moment—proof that this wasn't just a night out. It was *the* night. One they would all remember.

The longer they danced, the more the world seemed to melt away. It was just them—the music, the lights, the liquor buzzing through their veins. Laughter burst between bass drops, and the energy on the floor was magnetic. Emily was in her element, Lisa glowing effortlessly, and Nelle, drunk on rhythm and rum, swayed with reckless abandon.

Across the room, Roddy couldn't take his eyes off Nelle. His gaze was intense, lingering too long to be casual, and Tolly noticed. He leaned in, half-laughing over the music: "Girl! I think Roddy has a thing for you!"

But Nelle, far too drunk to filter her thoughts, waved a dismissive hand.

"He don't like girls like me. He's married to a white porn star!" She giggled, stumbling slightly on her heels.

Tolly stopped laughing.

The words hit different.

He blinked at her, processing, then quickly ducked away to a quieter corner of the club. Phone in hand, fingers flying, he searched every blog, tabloid site, and gossip page he could think of. Nothing. No recent news, no wedding photos, not even a scandal. But something about the way she said it... confident, careless—it didn't sound made-up.

So, he took it a step further. If it were real, there would be a record.

Public records.

And sure enough, after a few clicks and a growing sense of disbelief, there it was—clear as day:

A Marriage Certificate between Roderick "Roddy" Richardson and Nicole Dixon, aka NikkiThaThickest.

Tolly's eyes widened. He had struck *gold*. Real tea. And Nelle?

She danced on, completely unaware she'd just set off a chain reaction.

Pushing through the sea of sweaty bodies and flashing lights, Tolly sang along to every word the DJ spun, high off the thrill of discovery. His eyes scanned the dance floor until they landed on Lisa, still swaying to the beat with a cocktail in hand. He didn't waste time—he grabbed her wrist and tugged her toward the ladies' room corridor, dodging stumbling partygoers along the way.

Before Lisa could ask what was going on, he shoved his phone in her face. She blinked, squinting through her haze of alcohol, until the words came into focus.

Her breath caught.

"Wh—what?" she gasped, her voice cracking with panic. Heart racing, she snatched her phone from her clutch, fumbling past the swarm of missed calls and texts from Brent. Ignoring them, she opened her browser and typed Roddy Richardson's name.

Nothing.

No headlines. No wedding posts. No TMZ.

She looked up, alarmed.

"Did TMZ run the story?" she shouted over the bass.

Tolly shrugged with all cool confidence.

"No! Nelle spilled. Lisa, this is tea! I have to run it on my YouTube channel!"

Lisa's eyes widened, her buzz quickly wearing off. "What? No. No! This could ruin him! If TMZ didn't touch it, why do you think you should?"

She laughed nervously, trying to steady her breathing. But Tolly didn't flinch.

"I run a gossip channel, Lisa. You know that. It's my job to report the tea. So what, just because I'm not TMZ, I don't get to break a story first? Girl, come on. You're my friend. Why would you keep this from me?"

Her face hardened.

"Because Roddy is my client! If this gets out, he could lose every endorsement he has. Do you even understand the implications? Plum has been sitting on this story for months. You don't just blast something you know nothing about!"

Tolly's smile disappeared. His tone turned sharp. "Oh, fuck you. It doesn't work that way, honey."

Lisa stepped forward, eyes blazing.

"Tolly, I'm warning you—if you run with this, I will do damage control. And if you're in the way, you're getting caught in the crosshairs. Sit this one out."

"Oh, and what are you gonna do, huh?"

"We'll sue for defamation—" she began, her tone cold and calculated.

"You won't win, bitch, because it's true!" he snapped, his words laced with venom.

She didn't flinch. Instead, she took a step closer, the corner of her lip twitching with disdain.

"It's not about winning," she said calmly. "You're just some YouTuber. We can afford to drag this out in court until you have mere pennies to your name. You won't even be able to afford the lawyers."

He scoffed and turned on his heel. "Bring it on."

And with that, he was gone.

Lisa stood there, fists clenched, teeth gritted.

Her rage boiled over.

She stomped her heel against the tiled floor, over and over again. "Fuck! FUCK!" she screamed, the music swallowing her cries.

Her night, her plans—spiraling.

And she knew this was only the beginning.

Thankfully, the night was winding down and the chaos, at least momentarily, began to settle. Emily, too drunk to keep her eyes open, had to be taken back to the hotel. Lisa, still fuming, stormed out of the club, pushing past the velvet ropes with fire in her step. She flagged down one of their cars and barked instructions to the valet— Tolly could catch the other ride. She was furious, yes, but not heartless enough to leave him stranded in the Miami streets.

Nelle trailed behind, arms overflowing with Emily's birthday haul—gift bags, envelopes stuffed with cash, and a few trinkets from partygoers they barely knew. Inside the car, Lisa sat forward, pounding water like it was medicine, willing the alcohol to leave her system. She had work to do.

"Take us to the nearest McDonald's, please," she ordered the driver. Moments later, they were rolling through the drive-thru, Lisa rattling off a list of burgers, fries, and chicken nuggets like a woman on a mission. The food came quickly, and she tore into it with the same urgency. No time for grace—just survival.

Back at the hotel, she kicked off her shoes and slung them in one hand while hoisting Emily up with the other, half-carrying her down the hallway.

"Lisaaaa," Emily slurred with a dreamy smile, eyes half-closed. "What's the matter baby, you look so angry!"

Lisa gave a tight laugh, brushing her hair from her face. "Oh, nothing, hun. Let's get you upstairs."

Once inside the suite, it was game on.

Lisa's mind switched gears. The moment Emily was safely tucked in and Nelle was busy organizing the gifts, Lisa pulled out her laptop and started typing. Whatever Tolly was planning to leak, she had to stay ahead of it. The night might've been over, but the damage control had just begun.

An hour later, as Emily lay peacefully in bed, tucked away in the soft pajamas they'd gently changed her into, Nelle sat up, unable to rest. Guilt gnawed at her. She glanced over at Lisa, who was hunched over her laptop, eyes wild with focus, fingers still flying across the keyboard as she sent email after email. Judges. Social media CEOs. Cameramen from the party. Anyone who could help her get Tolly blackballed from every platform he dared to touch.

Nelle broke the silence, voice low and heavy with remorse. "This is all over what I said to Tolly? I swear, Lisa, the second the words left my mouth, I regretted it."

But Lisa barely looked up. She was too deep in crisis mode, rage and loyalty pulsing through her. Then, Nelle said something that made her pause.

"I have to face reality. Kenneth isn't for me. I know I fucked up tonight, so if you still want me for the Roddy thing... I'll do it."

Lisa's fingers stilled, her gaze finally lifting. But she didn't jump on the offer. She needed to be sure. They were all still floating somewhere between mild intoxication and reality.

"I know you think I'm still drunk," Nelle said, standing up and demonstrating a wobbly but committed show of balance—bending down to touch her toes, then walking backward in a straight-ish line.

"But I ate. I'm not. I'm coherent... mostly. I'll do it. I can pretend to be Roddy's girlfriend, and you don't even have to pay me. I'll do it for free."

Lisa let out a long, exasperated sigh, running her hands over her face. "Nelle... I can't let you do that. And I promise, I'm not mad at you."

But Nelle pressed on, her voice cracking into a laugh through the tears forming in her eyes. "I want to do it. Maybe it'll help distract me, you know? Lisa, I'm down bad, girl. I downloaded the TextNow app just to call Kenneth from a fake number. I'm desperate. I'm begging—put me on the mission."

Lisa stared at her, caught somewhere between pity and amusement. Then suddenly, they were both laughing—laughing until they slid down to the carpet, backs pressed against the wall like teenagers hiding from their feelings.

"Are you sure?" Lisa asked, watching her closely.

"Yep," Nelle replied, smiling through the chaos. And just like that, Lisa *the* McAdams was ready to go to war.

CHAPTER 10.

WHAT'S YOUR
PRICE?

DAY 6: Although they weren't staying at the hotel, Lisa had arranged an exclusive morning escape at The Ritz-Carlton Spa, South Beach, and it was nothing short of a dream. The moment they arrived, the atmosphere shifted—serene, sophisticated, and utterly isolated. Thanks to Lisa's connection with publicist Mariella Sanchez, the spa was theirs and theirs alone for the morning. No crowds, no distractions, just a peaceful retreat mapped out to perfection.

Inside, the spa's reception area exuded understated class—dark marble floors, soft lighting, and minimalist touches welcomed them with calming energy. The muted tones and modern wood finishes added to the sophisticated ambiance, immediately setting the tone for rest and renewal.

They began their indulgent morning in the outdoor jacuzzi, nestled between tropical palms and tucked into a tranquil corner of the spa. The warm, bubbling water was the perfect contrast to their chilled mimosas, and the sun filtered in just right.

The ladies later moved into the nail and salon area, a beautifully designed space that was airy yet intimate. The geometric flooring in soft beige, white, and black played with light, and the warm, neutral palette made everything feel fresh and luxurious. From plush chairs to custom shelves lined with premium products, every detail was intentional.

Irony hung in the air like the citrus-scented mist from the eucalyptus steam room. In a space designed for inner peace and pampered stillness, Lisa was anything but. While Emily and Nelle reclined with cucumber water and sugar scrubs, Lisa toggled between calls, texts, and verbal rundowns with military precision. She was deep in crisis management mode, running point on Nelle's fast-tracked transition into anonymity and tailored visibility—a delicate balance only someone like Lisa could pull off.

Her voice barely rose above a whisper, but the intensity was palpable. She fired off questions to Nelle like a litigator cross-examining a witness. Every word, every tweet, every past affiliation—all under review. This wasn't just a spa day; it was a war room wrapped in terry cloth robes and rose-gold pedi basins.

She explained the rules of the arrangement: $280,000 as a payout for Nelle's involvement because this wasn't charity. This was a job. A calculated move in a game of optics, perception, and cold, hard PR. First order of business? Disappear. Not entirely, just enough to control the narrative. Every social media platform was deleted or wiped clean except for Instagram and Twitter, the only two Lisa deemed strategically useful. Once Nelle handed over her passwords, Lisa's team got to work like digital ghosts. Posts vanished. History erased. Her old life? Effectively archived.

Nelle had officially resigned from her job, too. A clean, professional letter now sat in her editor's inbox—ghostwritten and dispatched by Lisa's assistant without Nelle ever lifting a finger. She was untethered, yet not free. Not yet.

Sitting through her pedicure, Nelle scrolled through Twitter. Her stomach twisted when she saw the trending threads. Tolly was already getting started:

"The Miami curse strikes, and this time it's hot!"

"Hey guys, my YouTube might get taken down, but just know that I have the hottest tea in entertainment right now! Roddy Richardson TEA! Make sure to subscribe to my Patreon so you don't miss it when I get back!"

The replies were chaotic. Thousands of retweets. Mentions spiraling out of control. And still, Lisa insisted Nelle remain silent. It was as if Lisa were managing her too—not just Roddy.

Then, as if channeling every crisis manager from Olivia Pope to Harvey Specter, Lisa sprang into legal action. She was now on the phone with a judge and county court clerk, demanding that the documents be sealed.

"Shelly, I can wire you $30,000 right now. We're handling the divorce, so think of this as a premature step."

A pause.

"Amazing—let me get the details."

She typed ferociously into the notes app on her second phone before turning to mouth to the girls: "Anyone can be bought."

Nelle, cool behind oversized shades, raised a quiet but valid concern.

"But won't people just find it suspicious that the court documents are sealed and then… realize it might be true?"

Lisa, never missing a beat, muted her call and turned to Nelle with a sly smirk.

"That's the beauty of this business. People are nosy and entitled enough to want your business, but far too lazy to fact-check any of it. That's why false news spreads faster than a lawyer on a retainer."

Just then, a ding.

Laura (Assistant): "Hey Lisa, this Tolly guy is tweeting like mad. Roddy's already lost around 2,000 followers on IG. Twitter remains steady, though."

Lisa's eyes lit up. The moment to strike had arrived. Emily could see the tensing in her shoulders, so she chimed in.

"Hey! Why don't we leave tomorrow? I can have my boss send his jet. This way, you get ahead of Tolly. He won't record anything until he's back in his home studio."

Lisa felt the weight lift from her chest.

"Yesssss let's do it!"

The next morning, by 6 AM sharp, the battlefield had shifted—from Miami to the skies. And Lisa, ever the tactician, was already three moves ahead.

Touching down in New York City, the reality of home hit harder than the heat radiating off the tarmac. Lisa's driver, already stationed and waiting, sprang into action, helping the ladies shove their luggage into the sleek black town car.

The bags piled on like a game of Tetris, every inch of space accounted for. Cramped but grateful, the trio collapsed into the backseat, the Miami sun still fresh on their skin.

First stop: Emily's place.

Warm hugs were exchanged, the kind that lingered after a trip that would be talked about for months. Lisa barely looked up from her phone, her fingers firing off text after text, calls rolling in one after the other.

In the far corner of the car, Nelle sat quietly, her mind spinning—not just from exhaustion, but from everything left unsaid with Kenneth. Her eyes drooped, her body heavy, hoping for a nap on the way home. But then—

"Laura is meeting you at the Loft, okay?" Lisa said suddenly, breaking the silence. "She's bringing some boxes and stuff to help you pack."

"Pack?" Nelle echoed, confused, blinking away the haze.

"Yep. We've got a condo set up for you in Lincoln Square. It's on Broadway. I know you'll want your painting supplies and whatever else, but I haven't found a moving company to handle my request since it's so last-minute. But believe me, I will."

Nelle sat upright, alert now. "And once... once I'm there... then what?"

"You can take the rest of the day," Lisa said, scrolling. "Some paps will be there later in the evening to catch you going in and out of the building. Just to give the illusion that you and Roddy have been together for a while. You know—living together."

"Live together?" Nelle repeated, wide-eyed.

"No, no. You won't *actually* be living together. Roddy already lives in the building. But once the press starts seeing you both coming and going, it'll make headlines. It'll sell. It'll look like you've been a couple for some time now."

Nelle felt her stomach drop. So this was it. The illusion. The life behind the glam. Behind the paparazzi. Behind the followers and the filters.

Was anything in this world real?

As the car glided into the heart of the Meatpacking District, the energy shifted—high-end boutiques, cobblestone streets, and the buzz of city life wrapped around them like static. Up ahead, Laura's car came into view, parked slightly crooked at the curb, hazard lights blinking.

Laura—heavyset, warm-toned, with flushed cheeks and soft blue eyes framed by a messy bun—waved as they approached. Dressed in a cropped hoodie and leggings, she had the easygoing vibe of someone who preferred loungewear to labels.

Lisa and Nelle stepped out into the morning haze, exchanging a final hug that felt more like a goodbye than a see-you-later.

"Laura, I'll be at the office!" Lisa called out, already stepping back into her car. "Call me if you guys need anything."

And just like that, she was gone.

"Hey girl," she smiled, helping Nelle with her luggage. "Welcome back."

As Janelle stepped inside, the familiar scent of the building wrapped around her—old paint, and faint incense from *his* apartment. It triggered something deep. Her eyes watered unexpectedly. This was supposed to be a cinematic moment. A grand gesture. A man making it right.

She imagined Kenneth flinging open his door, calling her name, rushing to her, apologizing with his whole heart and arms wide open. But there was no movement. Just stillness. And then—a sharp, piercing cry cut through the quiet.

A child.

Nelle froze, chest tightening, forehead glistening with sudden sweat. Her hands trembled at her sides. Her breath grew shallow. "Did you hear that?" she asked, voice thin.

Laura, cheerful but confused, tilted her head and paused. "Hmm. Hear what?"

"The child," Nelle whispered, eyes scanning the ceiling.

As if on cue, the little girl's cries rang out again, louder this time, echoing down the stairwell.

"Ohhh, yeah," Laura grinned, brushing it off. "Sounds like it's coming from upstairs. So cute."

But Nelle didn't smile.

There was nothing cute about it. Her mind raced, unraveling quickly as she climbed the stairs to his loft, the weight of unanswered texts and a broken connection heavy on her shoulders. Her heart beat like a war drum. She wasn't sure what she would find—or what version of herself would walk away once she did.

But she was leaving now anyway.

What did she have to lose?

TWO DAYS EARLIER: The shift from the crisp, misty breeze of Seattle to the thick, sweltering heat of a New York City summer was jarring—something Noel hadn't quite prepared for. As the private jet coasted down the tarmac, she remained seated, staring out the window, lost in thought. Just a few years ago, this city was her playground. Late nights with friends, luxury galas, rooftop brunches. Now, everything had changed. She was a mother. A wife. And she was back with a mission: get her man back.

When the door to the jet opened, Noel emerged like a vision—striking, poised, untouchable.

She stepped down the aircraft stairs with grace, her posture tall and commanding. Her outfit was pristine: an off-white off-the-shoulder top that hugged her lower collarbones and wrapped elegantly around her bust, paired with high-waisted tailored pants that flared subtly at the ankle, elongating her already statuesque frame. The gold accents—a belt cinched at the waist, stacked bangles on each wrist, oversized rings—added an air of regality. Her strappy heels caught the sunlight with every step, adding a delicate glint beneath her powerful presence.

Her hair, now cut into a chic, cropped pixie, framed her face in soft waves. It was a bold change from the long, loose curls she used to rock, but one that made her cheekbones pop and her almond-shaped eyes seem even more intense. Her makeup was minimal but flawless, accentuating her natural beauty—high cheekbones, golden-toned lids, a soft nude lip, and brows that sat like sharp commas over a gaze full of quiet fire.

Trailing just behind her was her nanny, cradling a sleepy child against her shoulder, shaded beneath a wide-brimmed sun hat. Together, they moved toward the black Escalade waiting just beyond the tarmac.

Noel didn't hesitate.

She walked like someone who had unfinished business.

Because she did.

Everything about her was different now—her look, her energy, her aura. She was no longer the girl who let things fall apart without a fight.

She had come back to reclaim what was hers.

The loft wasn't quite how Noel remembered it. Somehow, it felt bigger—emptier, even—but there was no mistaking it. This was the place they had called home. *Her* and Kenneth. Where laughter once echoed and Sunday mornings lingered into afternoon. Now, it was still. Tidy. A little too perfect.

Kenneth stood near the entryway, arms crossed with the controlled stillness of a man holding back a storm. On the outside, he was calm—polished in his usual composed manner—but inside, he was on fire. His wife, his Noel, was finally here. And she looked... different. Beautiful, yes. But changed. Sharper. Stronger. And more distant than he'd expected.

Their greetings were brief. A courteous nod to Maribel, the nanny, who offered a kind smile before setting about her duties. Noel said nothing as she slowly wandered into the open-plan living space, running her fingers along the edge of a marble countertop, the corner of a bookshelf. Touchstones of a life that used to be hers.

Noticing his daughter begin to stir, Kenneth gently reached down to her on the couch, lifting his litte girl into his arms with an ease born of familiarity. Suzume Sundwall was the perfect blend of them both. "Hi Daddy," she blinked up at him with sleepy eyes before nestling into his chest.

Behind him, Maribel and the driver quietly unloaded the car, their soft movements grounding the space with a rhythm of normalcy.

Kenneth turned back toward Noel, watching as she stood in the middle of the room, eyes slowly scanning—searching, almost—as if she were hoping to find something, or *someone*, still lingering in the air.

She didn't speak. Instead, she slipped off her heels one by one and set them neatly beside the couch. Then came the jewelry—her gold bangles, rings, earrings—all carefully removed like armor.

He wanted to ask how she was. If she'd been okay. But instead, he held his breath and hoped.

Hoped they could talk.

Hoped they could be civil.

The loft felt like a glass box—wide open and exposed. No doors, no corners to hide in. Just air, light, and years of history trapped in every crevice. Maribel sensed the tension without a word. She cleared her throat gently, her eyes flicking to Suzume, then to Noel, then to Kenneth.

"I'll take her to the park," she offered softly.

Kenneth, grateful for her intuition, nodded and pulled a crisp string of hundred-dollar bills from his wallet, handing them to her. "Have lunch. Take your time."

With a knowing glance, Maribel took Suzume, gathered her things, and disappeared down the stairs. The sound of the car door closing below left a vacuum behind, one filled only by the heavy silence between Noel and Kenneth.

Their eyes met.

"I didn't come to argue," she said, her voice low but steady.

"I don't want to fight with you, Noel," he replied, his gaze never leaving hers.

He wanted nothing more than to close the distance between them. To fold her into his arms and pretend like none of it happened. But he knew better. It was too soon, too raw. He was in love with two women—yes—but only one could cut him to his core, silence his ego, and bring him to his knees without lifting a finger. It was her. It had always been her.

"When were you planning on coming home?" she asked, searching him.

Kenneth's voice was soft, almost a whisper. "As soon as you told me to... I would have come."

Noel inhaled deeply, her chest rising with the weight of it all. "It was all so very hard on me. The pandemic... the postpartum... I didn't..." She paused, gathering her thoughts like scattered puzzle pieces. "I didn't know how to talk to you. I didn't know how to express what I was feeling without sounding controlling... or just angry all the time. Like you could never do anything right."

It came out rehearsed, but it was honest. She'd practiced this in her head for months.

Kenneth nodded, his expression unreadable. "I can take accountability. Being locked in the house with an infant... yeah. That messes with your head. I could've done more. I *should've* done more. I should've been better for you. I think we just... both broke at the same time."

The room went still again.

"Are we gonna talk about her?" Noel asked, her voice cracking as tears welled in her eyes.

Kenneth looked away. A sigh left his body like he'd been holding it in for years. He made his way to the minibar, grabbed a tumbler, and poured a glass of whiskey, neat. The clink of the bottle hitting glass echoed between them.

Did he want to talk about her? No.

Did he need to, for them to begin to heal? Yes.

He turned, drink in hand. "What do you want to know?"

Noel entered the conversation armed with the tools her therapist had given her: Be still. Be honest. Listen to understand, not to respond. But no amount of emotional preparation could brace her for the shrapnel of truth Kenneth unleashed.

At first, she held steady—nodding, breathing through the ache in her chest—but as the details of his affair spilled into the open, something inside her broke loose. Her composure cracked. She erupted.

The loft, once quiet and charged with unspoken tension, now echoed with raised voices and sharp profanity. Emotions flew like shrapnel—blame, pain, disbelief—all jagged and unrelenting.

Kenneth's confession cut deeper than she expected. Not just the affair, but the duration of it. The timing. Mars had been with him after Noel had asked him to leave their Seattle home. After the tears. After the silence. After she'd believed they were merely taking some time apart. Another woman had been there—*in her place*.

She felt sick.

Noel was his wife. The mother of his child. She had bled privately while the world speculated publicly. Her face plastered across magazines, tabloids whispering about her disappearance from events, her absence in the city. Still, she'd said nothing. She held the truth close, protected it. Protected *him*.

But Mars? She had never made it to those headlines. Noel had no idea they were parading around like a couple, careless and unbothered. And now, everything was unraveling. The betrayal wasn't just personal—it was *public*.

The shame, the embarrassment, the scrutiny—it loomed heavy on her shoulders.

She wanted to leave.

She *needed* to leave.

But her legs wouldn't move.

Kenneth knew better. If there was even a sliver of hope to salvage what they had—what they'd built—he had to strip himself of every lie, every half-truth, and lay the full mess of it on the table. Honesty was the only way forward. And so, trembling at the edge of consequence, he confessed. Even about Nelle.

"Listen," he continued, voice low and rough, "she's just some innocent girl. Nothing came of that, and nothing was ever going to come of that. She's a nice girl, and I fucked up. Alright?"

Noel blinked, stunned. Then she laughed—a sharp, bitter laugh that twisted through the room like a blade.

"Fucked up?" she repeated, a cruel smirk curling on her lips. Her hands trembled, her voice quivering in fury. "You fucked your neighbor?"

Her words cracked like thunder. The disbelief, the disgust—it poured from her in waves.

"What are you—some sex addict now? Where are your morals? Where's the respect for yourself?" She stepped forward, eyes blazing. "Why does every bitch with a pulse get to say she's had a turn with my husband!?"

Her voice broke at the end, emotion catching in her throat like glass.

Kenneth said nothing—he couldn't. The shame weighed heavily on his chest, dragging his gaze to the floor. He knew there was no defense. No excuse strong enough to soften the blow of his betrayal. All he could do now was stand in the wreckage he caused, hoping—praying—that the woman he loved would still see something worth saving.

PRESENT DAY: Nelle knocked with a confidence she didn't truly feel—her knuckles firm against the steel door, her breath shaky. She told herself to stand tall, to keep her composure, to be ready for whatever came next. But as the locks unlatched one by one, her resolve began to crumble.

And then the door opened.

There she stood.

Noel.

A vision of effortless beauty, her frame slender yet toned, partially concealed beneath a cropped white tee and black nylon biker shorts. Her skin glowed under the sun's jealous gaze seeping through the bare windows, and her sneakers, designer and spotless, added a quiet punctuation to her casual luxury. But it wasn't the clothes that arrested Nelle—it was the rings.

On Noel's left hand gleamed an engagement ring and wedding band so brilliant they practically blinded her. The diamond, massive and radiant, sat like a crown, surrounded by a halo of smaller, flawless stones. The band, a perfect eternity loop of platinum and pavé diamonds, glittered with every flicker of movement. It wasn't just jewelry—it was legacy, status, devotion.

"Hello, how can I help you?" Noel asked politely, voice sharp and composed, though her expression held the cool distance of someone who already knew the answer.

Nelle's mind scrambled. The images of Noel from Google flashed before her like an old film reel. But this version of her was different. Her hair was shorter now. More controlled. More intentional.

"I'm—I'm Janelle. Is—"

Before she could finish, Noel cut her off. "Nice to meet you. I'm Mrs. Noel Sundwall. I hope you have a great rest of your day."

Behind her, boxes were stacked neatly in the living room—evidence of a move. Of an ending. Or maybe a beginning. Nelle's eyes widened. He was leaving.

Before she could say anything more, the door closed—softly but firmly. A second time, she was shut out.

Laura, watching from downstairs, stood stunned. Her mouth parted, but no words came. She felt bad for Nelle—really bad. Because what just happened? That wasn't rejection. That was obliteration.

Lisa had not yet been home. It was Friday, which meant the streets of Lower Manhattan pulsed with the usual buzz—horns blaring, heels tapping, and food carts crowding the corners. But inside her PR firm, hidden just off Pier 26 at Hudson River Park, time seemed to slow.

Her office was a masterclass in modern minimalism and subtle luxury. The open-concept space breathed with light from wall-to-wall windows, softened by warm neutrals and polished concrete floors. Modern pendant lights hung like statements from the exposed ceiling, casting a soft light on the mix of contemporary furniture and vibrant abstract art lining the walls.

Clusters of low-profile leather sofas and cozy accent chairs created inviting nooks for impromptu meetings or quiet reflection. Lush green plants dotted the space, bringing in a touch of nature to counter the industrial chic. A long communal table stretched near the far end, surrounded by ergonomic chairs—ideal for brainstorming sessions or post-client debriefs over espresso.

At the center, the front desk, elegant and understated, welcomed guests beneath a glowing sign that simply read: *Branndet PR.* This was Lisa's domain. A place where brands were built, reputations managed, and image was everything. And today, with her hair slicked into a perfect bun and coffee in hand, Lisa was ready to handle it all before the weekend officially began.

Moments later, Roddy entered, his presence impossible to ignore. Lisa's secretary greeted him with a warm smile before quickly buzzing her on the intercom.

"Send him back," Lisa's voice rang out.

Roderick "Roddy" Richardson, just twenty-seven, had become a household name almost by accident. Cast as the understudy for Emmett Till in a high school play at Fordham High School for the Arts, fate intervened on opening night when the lead actor fell sick. Roddy stepped in and delivered a performance so moving that it brought the house to tears—and caught the eye of a casting agent in the audience.

That moment sparked a career filled with highs and hurdles. Though Roddy found himself frequently cast in roles rooted in generational trauma—slavery films, flashback sequences, and historical dramas—he craved more. Deeper, fuller portrayals. Stories that made space for joy, love, and modern Black life. It wasn't until Lisa stepped in that his narrative began to shift. Her pitch landed him a breakout role in a Tyler Perry film as the charming love interest to a powerful single mother. The public took notice, and so did Hollywood.

Now, Roddy walked into Lisa's office with the cool confidence of a man who'd earned his place, yet still carried the quiet fire of someone who remembered his humble beginnings.

He wore a light grey oversized hoodie with a dramatic, structured hood pulled just above his brow, giving him an effortlessly stylish, almost mysterious air. Underneath, a textured black top peeked out—clean, minimal, but high-quality fabric. His tan trousers were slightly tapered, hugging his frame in all the right ways, and were detailed with black side stripes that added a modern edge.

A pair of black combat boots grounded the look, perfectly paired with leather wrist cuffs and layered silver chains around his neck.

"Miss Lisa, how are you doing?" Roddy's voice filled the room with its deep, bass-heavy resonance—a voice that demanded attention, even as his tone remained respectful. He was always a gentleman, never brash, even when frustration simmered beneath his calm surface.

"I'm good. Have a seat! I really appreciate you dropping by. I know this is short notice."

"Yeah. I mean, it's life, I guess," Roddy replied, easing into the chair adjacent to her desk. He sat with his legs apart, arms folded across his chest—a body language that spoke of both defense and fatigue. Then, without wasting time, he got to the point. "So, I take it you're not too fond of my wife."

Lisa's expression didn't flinch. "Roderick, listen, it's not me. It's the film execs, the investors, the—the brands, the fans—"

"Why is it like that, though?" he pushed, brows drawing together. "Why do I have to live my life to appease a bunch of strangers or fans who will never, ever be in the same room as me? I don't know who they marry or date. Why is it their business who I choose to be with?"

"I agree. I do," Lisa said gently. "But you know with this new wave of social media and technology, it's like... to really stand out with the public and be marketable on a global scale, you need those numbers. We need their support. Casting directors are now being forced to look at social media accounts to determine who they're going to cast in their films to help offset marketing costs."

Roddy scoffed, the irritation bubbling up in his tone. "But why? It's not like that extra money is going to *us*. So what difference does it make? I don't feel like I can be myself, and that's crazy. I don't owe Black women an explanation on why I choose to date a white woman."

Lisa simply shook her head, saying nothing for a moment. She listened.

"They're all so damn sensitive. Like me for my *art*, for the hard work I put into every role I'm given. Not the woman I'm sleeping with at night."

"I get your perspective," she said. "But again, this generation is all about relatability. Social media's changed everything. Parasocial relationships are out of control. Everyone feels like a star now, and when they follow you, they think that gives them a seat at your table. That little unfollow button? It holds a lot of power."

"Bullshit," Roddy snapped, standing.

His movements were sharp, deliberate. "I want to see them memorize lines, commit to method acting, and work 24-hour shifts in the freezing cold. But instead, I'm being reduced to a caricature—'go here,' 'say this,' 'don't upset these people,' 'only like *these* people.' Like what the fuck? Why should anyone have to live like that? Most Black women don't even like me anyway! I'm 5'6, barely got muscles, and they think I'm 'too nice.' I can't tell you how many times I got friend-zoned."

"I get you, I do," Lisa said, voice soft with understanding. "And I'm sorry. But think of it this way—

in a few years, you can retire, and all of this will be behind you."

"If I don't go broke first."

"Emily is a genius. You're not going to go broke," she replied with a deep sigh. "But let's talk about this contract, okay?"

Roddy gave a low hum of reluctance.

"We have a young lady for you—Janelle. She's an everyday girl, from cubicle to red carpet. The kind your fanbase will fall in love with."

"But what about my wife?" he asked, eyes narrowing. "I have to keep her a secret? That's fucked up, for real. How's she supposed to take that?"

"She married you. She knows what comes with the territory."

He exhaled, jaw clenched. "I guess. How long is this fake relationship thing?"

"Seven months. You do appearances, get seen going in and out of the condo together, we stage the date nights, plant the paparazzi—keep the narrative going just long enough for whatever Tolly or Plum from *TMZ* puts out to blow over. People will forget in due time."

Roddy sat back down, the weight of it all pressing into his shoulders. "Yeah, but even then... I still can't love who I want to out loud."

Lisa didn't miss a beat. "If she's white? No. And—this isn't just about the color of her skin, Roddy. She's a porn star. Not OnlyFans level. Like, full on—RedTube, Pornhub…"

"What? So, we're judging people on how they make their money now?"

"Me? No. But the people who write your checks? Yes. And they're judging hard. They can find your replacement in two to three business days. We don't want to give them any reason not to work with you."

An hour after their exchange, Roddy had come around. His resistance had melted into reluctant agreement, and he promised to share the plan with his new wife—hoping, praying, that she'd understand and comply.

Lisa, meanwhile, returned from lunch feeling the weight of another victory, no matter how bittersweet. She barely had time to set her bag down when the phone on her desk rang—sharp and abrupt. With her secretary out for the afternoon, Lisa instinctively picked it up.

"Oh, to what do I owe this honor? She answers on the first ring," came the unmistakable voice of Plum—cunning, and sarcastic.

Lisa sighed, instantly regretting it. "What is it, Plum?"

"Listen, Lisa, I like you. But I've been thinking a lot about leaving journalism. And, I don't know if you've noticed, but Tolly's doing your boy dirty over on Twitter."

"I'm handling Tolly," Lisa shot back. "He thinks he's Tasha fucking K."

"Oh, is that right?" Plum's voice dripped with amusement. "Maybe. But eventually, he'll want his story corroborated—and I noticed those court documents are sealed now. The thing is, I still have a copy."

Lisa felt the shift instantly. The real reason for the call was about to surface.

"So, I was thinking," Plum continued, his tone suddenly lighter, almost wistful, "I'm getting tired.

Journalism doesn't pay like it used to. Social media killed the thrill. Kenneth was buying up a lot of media real estate, which made your story irrelevant for a while, but now, it's trending again. And truth be told, I want nothing more than to leave this behind."

"Is that right?" Lisa said coldly.

"Yes. Yes, I have a lot of respect for you," Plum added, sweetening the edge of his ask.

Lisa's patience thinned. "Plum, enough. What's your price for the certificate?"

"My price?" Plum echoed, pretending to be surprised. "Well, I've always wanted to disappear. A little island escape. So I'll take a quarter mil, and this story disappears with me. You'll never hear about it again, and your golden boy's reputation will be safe."

Lisa blinked. "A quarter, as in a quarter of a million dollars?"

"You can afford it. I *know* for a fact Roddy can."

There was a beat of silence.

Then, firmly, Lisa ended the call. "Goodbye, Plum. Do what you want."

She hung up. It wasn't the first time someone tried to leverage secrets for money.

CHAPTER 11.

LIGHTS, CAMERA, ACTION!

The next few days passed like an artistic dream, a surreal haze of planning, staging, and coordination. Then came the moment of truth—Lisa brought Roddy and Nelle together for their official introduction. The atmosphere was soft and cordial, short-lived discomfort masked by practiced smiles and warm greetings.

Roddy's eyes lingered the moment he saw her again. It had been a little over a week since Miami, but now, under the afternoon sun, Janelle looked even more beautiful. The sunlight poured in behind her, casting a subtle halo over her curls.

"Roderick, this is Janelle. Janelle, this is Roderick aka Roddy," Lisa said, her tone neutral but expectant.

Nelle smiled graciously and extended her hand. Roddy took it, bringing it to his lips with a playful kiss. "The pleasure is mine. It's nice to properly meet you... I mean, you're going to be my girlfriend now," he said, laughing nervously.

The room joined in the laughter, letting the ice crack and melt.

"Alright, so, we've got a lot to go over!" Lisa clapped, shifting them back to business mode. And from that point on, it was full speed ahead.

Evenings were devoted to Nelle's new condo, a luxury haven tucked away from the public eye. Lisa and Emily helped her furnish it, picking out candles, wall art, and plush throws. Though Nelle was barred from ever posting anything from inside, she found peace there—a sanctuary wrapped in opulence and secrets.

It didn't take long for her to open up to her closest friends about Kenneth and Noel. At first, she hesitated, nervous about how it would all land. But once she spilled, her friends barely flinched. They had already guessed that the "breakup" was either strategic or temporary. Regardless, Nelle assured Lisa she was fully committed to the arrangement. No hesitation. No second-guessing.

Meanwhile, Emily saw her own opportunity to make things right with Mr. Sundwall. Quietly and diligently, she started planting seeds.

Lisa went to war in the background. She pulled every string, called in every favor, and got Nelle and Roddy on every major VIP list in the city. She tipped off the paparazzi herself and even paid a few to leak staged images and write-ups directly to *TMZ*.

So, when Tolly finally dropped his "bombshell" video, the damage was already undercut. The narrative had been spun, re-spun, and layered in sugar. There were already reels of content showing Roddy and Nelle hand-in-hand, entering and exiting the condo.

But the final nail in Tolly's coffin came from Miami: Emily's party. Promoters, influencers, and photographers had all shared candid moments—laughing, dancing, drinks in hand. Pictures that showed Roddy with his arm around a Black girl named Janelle. And that, by all accounts, was now the truth.

Janelle's new life was dazzling—glam squad on speed dial, a stylist rotating designer looks through her closet, and a weekly cleaning crew that left her condo spotless and smelling like bergamot and roses. She was living the kind of life she used to only glimpse through glossy magazine pages at *She's Single*, but beneath the organized calm, anxiety churned.

Some days were golden—filled with painting, coffee by the window, and PR packages stacked to the ceiling. Other days were clouded with doubt. She missed the steady rhythm of a real job, a life with structure. The fear of becoming too comfortable in this world, of losing herself in the image she was paid to project, began to creep in.

Then came another deposit.

Her phone buzzed one morning with a notification: $40,386.17. Her account had never seen that kind of number before. It was all hers—every last cent. She thought about handbags, luxury brands, and a new car. But she stopped herself. Instead, she reminisced about the small gallery near The Sky building—a space she'd long admired. After a quick inquiry, the owner quoted her $20,000 a month with a $10,000 deposit. It was steep, but suddenly within reach. The dream of owning her own gallery wasn't so distant anymore—it was real. Tangible. And that made her even more obedient.

She played the role to perfection. She showed up on time. She smiled, flirted, and initiated kisses with Roddy in public. She let him hold her waist and caress her behind for the cameras. They were Hollywood's newest *It Couple*. Fans gave them couple names—#Relle and #JayRod floated to the top of the trend pile. Everyone was buying what they were selling.

By the seventh week, brands were lining up. Lisa's inbox overflowed. Nelle could make $3,000 just to post about weight-loss gummies. She wanted to decline—she'd never been a big social media person—but the money kept growing. With each new check, each luxe PR package, her resistance dissolved. Her follower count surged, and her wardrobe evolved to match. She was becoming the girl on screen.

Eight weeks in, and the rhythm was seamless. As the weather started to feel more like fall, Nelle adorned the condo with her original paintings—one every week. Her art captured the energy of her new life, each brushstroke a confession of quiet chaos. With the Bozeman Bons Awards on the horizon, she felt alive, inspired. The world was watching—and for the first time, she welcomed it.

But elsewhere, the shine was beginning to tarnish.

The day before the awards, Roddy burst into Lisa's office, his face a thundercloud. Laura tried to stop him at reception, but he shoved past, unannounced.

Lisa, mid-call, held up a finger. "We're closing this deal!" she mouthed, grinning. But Roddy didn't smile back.

The moment she hung up, he exploded.

"Thanks for ruining my life!"

Lisa froze.

"Nicole is leaving me!"

Her mouth parted slightly. "Leaving?"

"YES!" His voice cracked. "All this press. Me groping some girl in public, kissing her—it's everywhere! My marriage is in shambles. She's pregnant and insecure, and I'm begging her not to read the comments under my posts!"

Lisa stood, smoothing her blouse. "Okay, I hear you. I'll talk to Nicole. I'll fix this—"

"Fix? Why can't we just end this?"

Lisa's tone sharpened. "Because we can't end this. Not before award season. And especially not before the Golden Globes. We don't even know if you'll be nominated for 'Borderline'. If you get a nomination, you need Janelle on your arm. And Valentine's Day—imagine the engagement, the clicks, the reach!"

Roddy stared at her in disbelief. "Is that all you care about? Money?!"

He stepped back, eyes glassy with frustration. "My wife is pregnant... and she's leaving me. Either you fix this, or I end it myself."

Without waiting for a reply, he stormed out. Lisa remained behind her desk, stunned, his final words echoing through the lobby:

"I can't believe I let you talk me into this!"

Lisa barely flinched; she didn't have the bandwidth to worry about his crumbling marriage—not when the world was watching. She had built something powerful, and no porn star was going to undo it. Roddy's star was hotter than ever, and thanks to her, doors were flying open. Every week brought fresh offers, new clients, and elite brands scrambling to land on her roster and his Instagram page. Lisa was no longer just a publicist—she was *the* publicist in New York. If you wanted your name to matter, you went to Lisa.

Later that afternoon, she took a rare moment to unwind. She and Emily had agreed to meet in her office for a much-needed girl chat. Lisa ordered Caribbean vegan dishes—plant-based jerk chicken, rice and peas, callaloo patties, and fresh sorrel. As she finalized a contract on her laptop, Laura peeked in:

"Emily's here!"

Lisa stood, checking her blouse—the buttons had a sneaky way of unexpectedly popping open—just as Emily walked in, doing a playful spin in head-to-toe Chanel.

"Is that the new pastel Chanel collection?" Lisa beamed, embracing her.

"The very one," Emily grinned, showing off her designer ensemble. "Chanel from my hair clip to the soles of my feet."

They moved to the round table at the rear of the office, plates steaming and laughter easy. It felt good to pause, even for a moment.

"Do tell!" Lisa said, ready for tea.

In between bites, Emily dropped the bomb she'd been sitting on for months.

"I closed on Sundwall."

Lisa nearly fell out of her chair.

"Oh my *GOD*—Emily! That's huge. Details, now!"

Emily leaned in, eyes gleaming.

"Girl, I had to do some real work. Called around in Seattle until I got through to his office. I told a little white lie—said I was invited to the party by Nelle's PR. Left our personal ties out of it completely. And he listened."

Lisa's face betrayed a flicker of disappointment—just a flash.

But Emily wasn't done.

"His wealth is insane. Healthcare, weaponry, and tobacco. Just in dividends? Over three million dollars a year. Real estate everywhere. Tech startups with 15.5% ROI. Oil stocks. He said he wanted to start small, see how I manage. Gave me only his NY portfolio to handle—about $12 million. Nothing for his LA or Seattle properties, though."

Lisa grinned widely. "Listen, a win is a win. I'm so proud of you!"

Emily blushed. "Thank you!"

Lisa stood, walking over to her desk. "Speaking of clients. Aaron Anderson—MLB. Just signed him to a two-year retainer. Told him about your firm."

She handed over the card, and Emily clutched it like gold.

"Girl. Thank you! That's major—and congrats! I saw him trending last week. This rebound contract is putting you on fire."

Lisa shrugged, but she couldn't hide her satisfaction. "It's been a season."

"Aww," Emily smiled. "As for Mr. Anderson, I'll call him before I leave the office for the day."

Then Lisa tilted her head.

"Are you gonna tell Nelle about Kenneth?"

Emily's tone turned serious.

"No."

A beat passed.

"Well... maybe. I'll have to eventually. I'll be flying to Seattle once a month, but she's in such a good place right now. Happier. Focused. Her skin's glowing, Pilates has her snatched—she's thriving."

They both laughed. For a moment, everything felt light again.

Until Lisa's phone rang.

Her usual instinct was to answer with her polished signature:

"This is Lisa."

But she paused.

She looked down and froze.

The name on the screen made her stomach drop.

It was Brent.

She ignored it. Lisa didn't hate Brent, but she had been so wrapped up in her life that she didn't really have time to process their ending—and to be honest, she didn't care to.

The next day came quickly: another big night in New York among Hollywood's elite. The BBA honored celebrities not just for talent, but for cultural impact, risk-taking, and reinvention across entertainment, fashion, business, and activism. Roddy needed to rub elbows, make introductions, and land himself opportunities to be seen as a humanitarian.

Inside the limo, Lisa couldn't keep her eyes off Nelle, winking at her and basking in her beauty. Nelle wore a show-stopping ombré tea-length gown, starting in a deep, sparkling ruby red at the top and fading into a soft blush pink near the hem. The entire dress shimmered under the light with intricate crystal embellishments, catching every angle like she was dipped in stardust. Her hair was swept up into a regal bun, elongating her neck and giving her an almost heavenly flare. She was stunning. Over the past few months, she and Lisa had grown even closer, but tonight, she looked untouchable.

Roddy remained quiet. Something was brewing inside of him.

Once the car came to a halt and they all prepared to exit, the carpet was already full—paparazzi pressing against the velvet ropes, workers, fans, security swarming the perimeter. Roddy pushed his way out first, the driver too slow to reach the handle in time. As Nelle tried to follow behind him, he inadvertently slammed the car door shut—her right ankle caught in the frame.

She let out a sharp wail.

Lisa plunged back into the car to reach her. Her ankle was beet red, already swelling.

Roddy kept walking—waving at fans, signing autographs, taking pictures, fully unbothered.

"I'm so sorry. How is it feeling?" Lisa asked, panic in her voice, the driver now pushing his head into the cabin to inquire about the injury.

"It's alright," Nelle lied. The pain was pulsing like a heartbeat, but she didn't want to mess up the night. Gritting her teeth, she pushed herself not to limp. But Roddy was steps ahead, and she needed to move quickly to catch up, her face wincing from the pain. The moment—her crushed ankle, her forced smile—was captured by fans and photographers alike.

Lisa was worried.

Once the night wrapped, she declined every invitation to the after-parties. The video had spread like wildfire. Instead, she headed straight to her office, where she, Nelle, Laura, Roddy, his security, and a few agency photographers gathered.

She was livid.

"You need to put out a statement," she said to Roddy, refusing to look him in the eye. "People are flooding the comments, and here come the conspiracy theorists. Once The Shaderoom gets a hold of this? The comments will be brutal."

"Who cares?" Roddy said, a bottle of Don Julio in hand.

"I don't know what's gotten into you lately, but you have to get it together," she snapped. "People think you're abusing her. Physically. You'll lose everything. No studio or brand will touch you if they think you're a woman-beater."

Lisa was over the back and forth. "Laura, let's get a statement typed up. He apologizes. These actions were heinous—"

"I mean, how was I supposed to know she was coming out on my side?" he interjected.

"Where else did you think she was going to come out? Into oncoming traffic? We've never deviated from the plan. It's always been your side."

Lisa stood, furious. "Post the statement. Nelle, we'll get something written for you, too. At approximately 11:48

PM, you'll post a photo of you both laying in bed, just before sleep. A kiss on the forehead, and we'll caption it."

They regrouped at Roddy's condo to stage the shot. Everything was structured—down to the lingerie she'd wear, how her curls would fall, her hand resting on his chest, the soft intimacy of a forehead kiss. Four images later, they had the right one posted. Nelle left shortly after, returning to her own place.

As she reached the door to head home herself, Lisa looked back at him:

"You have the Calvin Klein campaign shoot tomorrow, 6 AM sharp. The driver will be downstairs." Roddy was left alone with his thoughts.

The next day, as if like clockwork, Lisa checked on Nelle as soon as she woke in the morning. But what she heard was anything but great.

"I barely slept. It was throbbing all night. I think I'm going to go to the emergency room later today."

Lisa couldn't believe her ears.

"No, no, I'll have a physician make a house call."

"House call?" Nelle asked, confused.

Lisa chuckled. "Yeah, Nelle. You're famous now— you can't just walk into a hospital. The doctors come to you. I'll get on it and let you know once I'm on my way, all right?"

Nelle sat upright in her bed, the sunlight streaming in through three grand bay windows. The bedroom, draped in rich floral wallpaper and warm creams, looked like something out of Architectural Digest. A rare black writing desk sat under the windows, a soft blush of peonies resting in a vase, and mirrors lined the wardrobe doors, multiplying the morning light across the room.

From her bed, Nelle could see into the living room through wide double doors, where velvet and silk met carved wood in a masterclass of taste. Moss-green walls hugged the space, adorned with gilded sconces and modern art. Just beyond, the sitting room flickered with the soft glow of a fireplace framed by a golden-paneled wall.

And then there was the kitchen. High ceilings soared above a dramatic chandelier, casting delicate shadows over a dark wood island crowned with a small bouquet of tulips. Cabinets stretched to the ceiling, a rolling ladder tucked to one side for graceful access. At the same time, pristine subway tile and stainless-steel finishes offered the kind of refinement that came with serious money—or serious fame.

"Okay," she said, her voice soft.

Yeah, house calls made sense now.

After a quick visit and a gentle but thorough exam, Doctor Aruna confirmed what Nelle suspected—a grade two sprained ankle. Nothing too serious, but enough to keep her off her feet for a few days. She scribbled out a prescription for a small dose of Oxycodone and handed it over, along with some sample packs. Nelle took one pill with a sigh of relief, sinking back into the plush bedding, her gaze trailing over the mirrored wardrobe doors that caught fragments of the room's ornate wallpaper.

But before Lisa could even walk the doctor to the front door, her phone buzzed aggressively. She glanced down at the screen. "Calvin Klein's team. Great."

She answered with the same energy she used to put out fires.

"What now?" she snapped. Her brows furrowed, eyes narrowing. "He did what?" A pause. "Of course he did." She ended the call with a sharp tap, then stood upright and rolled her eyes so hard they almost stuck.

"Roddy," she hissed through clenched teeth.

Still packing up her bag, Doctor Aruna looked up with a light smile. "Oh, yes. How's he feeling?" she asked cheerfully.

Lisa blinked. "Feeling?"

Nelle tilted her head, too.

"Yes," the doctor went on casually. "He gave me a call last night. Said he was having trouble sleeping. I dropped off some Ambien."

Lisa's jaw dropped. Her voice pitched up instantly. "Ambien?!" she practically shouted. "Why the hell would you give him something so strong? What happened to melatonin gummies, or hell, warm milk and cinnamon?! He has work! He's a celebrity!"

Doctor Aruna gave a mild shrug, utterly unbothered. "He said it was urgent."

Nelle, still nestled in the sea of velvet throw pillows and linen sheets, blinked slowly. Her ankle did feel better, but she couldn't help glancing between them, completely lost in the chaos.

"What even is going on today?" she mumbled, sinking deeper into her blanket as Lisa stormed out of the room, already dialing Roddy.

"Nelle, I love you. Call you later," she shouted.

"Love you too," Nelle shouted back.

CHAPTER 12.

THE ARTIST

As the day went on, Nelle did the unthinkable. She popped another oxy, her body aching but her spirit refusing to bend. The shower that followed felt like a luxury spa in a Swiss villa. She exhaled, long and heavy, letting the heat seep into her bones. Then, with newfound clarity, she slipped into a soft wrap dress, tied her curls up, and made her way into Midtown.

What she didn't expect were the strangers—wide-eyed and whispering, phones at the ready. People stopped her on the street, asking for photos like she was someone. She played the part, smiled, and let them take their shots.

Emily agreed to meet her at the gallery. *Her* gallery. Nelle had done it. A signed 12-month lease. First month and security deposit paid in full.

"I did it!" Nelle squealed as Emily arrived, arms stretched open wide, her voice echoing through the empty space.

The gallery was raw and alive. It had old exposed brick on one wall—rugged and real—while the other three were smooth, white, and waiting to be claimed. Tall factory-style windows let in soft beams of afternoon sun that dappled across the polished concrete floors. There was an open loft above, accessible by a slim iron staircase—perfect for an office or reading nook. The scent of potential hung in the air.

"I love how we're all watching our dreams unfold right before our eyes!" Emily beamed.

Nelle was on another planet. She spun like a child, yelling just to hear her voice bounce back to her. She pranced through the gallery, pointing out spots to repaint, areas to redesign.

"Oh! Do you think we should have a paint party?"

Emily blinked. "We? Paint party? You mean a fake invitation to come and do extensive manual labor?"

"Yes!" Nelle grinned. "I just sank thirty grand into today. I can't afford to hire professionals to come and paint the space, too!"

Emily gave her the look. The look that said, *girl, no.* But Nelle kept smiling, trying to sell the desperation.

"I'll pay for the painters. That'll be my gallery gift to you," Emily declared. "And don't you eva—and I do mean evaaaa—ask me to do no ish like that again!"

Nelle laughed so hard she almost cried. "I love you! Thank you!"

In that empty gallery, two friends stood shoulder to shoulder, basking in the warmth of new beginnings. For the first time in their lives, everything felt like it was finally aligning. No chaos. No catch. Just magic.

Across town, chaos was the moment.

Lisa was putting out yet another Roddy-related fire. She arrived at the CK set where she found him slouched, incoherent, hands flailing like a drowning man. He was dehydrated, drowsy, and borderline unconscious. She jumped into damage control.

"He's got a back injury," she lied smoothly. "He just needs rest."

The studio wasn't happy, but Roddy was too valuable now. Too *hot* to risk recasting. They agreed to reschedule—but only after Lisa agreed to cover the day's losses. Another financial hit. Another dip into Roddy's growing fortune.

She shot Emily a quick text, her thumbs flying: *"Unprofessional. Embarrassing. I can't keep doing this."* But deep down, she understood. Roddy was supporting nearly everyone in his orbit. He was young, rich, and running on fumes. He didn't know how to say no, and he didn't have anyone telling him to slow down.

He wasn't just an indie darling anymore. He was being circled by the big leagues. More multi-million-dollar pictures. Global exposure. A single bad headline could ruin it all.

Back at his condo, Lisa snuck Roddy in through the back with help from her driver. His limbs were heavy, his head drooping. She got him inside and spotted Reggie, his live-in chef.

"Reggie, oh my God, thank goodness you're here. Please help me get him to his room."

Reggie didn't hesitate. He moved with purpose, slipping off his gloves and apron, as if this wasn't his first time. Together, they did the one-two-three lift, straightened Roddy's posture, and half-carried him up the winding staircase to the master suite.

Lisa didn't follow. She stayed downstairs, stewing in quiet anger. Concern. Fatigue.

When Reggie returned and saw her still there, his face registered mild surprise.

He didn't realize this time that she wasn't leaving until she got some answers.

"How long has this been going on?"

Reggie peeled on a fresh set of black gloves with a slow, deliberate motion, then re-fastened his apron, eyes narrowed, jaw locked. The kitchen had fallen silent, save for the hum of the Sub-Zero fridge and the quiet boiling of a pot left unattended.

"Has what been going on?" he asked, his voice calm but laced with challenge.

Lisa folded her arms, stepping forward. "His behavior. This isn't like him. This isn't normal. Is he on drugs? I need to know."

Reggie stared at her, unreadable. "Why?"

A beat passed.

"What's your problem?"

"I don't have a problem. *You* have a problem."

And with that, she knew.

The wall was up. She wouldn't get past it that day— not with Reggie. His deflection, his nonchalance—it wasn't ignorance. It was allegiance.

Lisa turned and left, her heels echoing sharply against the marble floor before hitting the pavement outside. The afternoon air kissed her face with just enough sting to keep her grounded. She didn't want the car. She needed wind, space—truth.

Her phone buzzed in her palm, the caller ID flashing a name she didn't want to see: Bree Lopez.

Lisa answered anyway. "This is Lisa."

"It's Bree."

It was always civil—barely—but never warm. Bree Lopez, talent agent to the stars, was the one woman Lisa had no patience for. Their rivalry had grown teeth. Bree's clients were defecting, one by one, trading her dated strategies for Lisa's results-driven precision.

"Are you aware of what's going on with Roddy?" Lisa asked, her voice clipped.

"I am."

She paused.

"Okay... and? What is it? Why is everyone so tight-lipped?"

"No one's tight-lipped. We just see right through you," Bree replied, venom sweetening her voice. "You're working this poor kid to the bone to fund your and your friends' lifestyles. Flying him here and there for commercials, campaigns, auditions... he's exhausted. And frankly? Unappreciated. Paying that girl over two hundred grand is insane. Meanwhile, his mother's ill, and his wife's trying to threaten child support for a fetus and alimony to help retire her deep throat."

Lisa's spine straightened like steel. Her voice cut clean. "First of all, let me stop you right there. Those rates are industry standard. This isn't new. If you didn't sit on your fat ass all day staring out your window waiting for your phone to ring, maybe you'd know sometimes you have to pull strings behind the scenes. See, your hunger for results doesn't compare to mine because as long as your husband's salary puts food on your table, it's fuck the talent, right?"

Silence.

Then: "Goodbye, Lisa. We'll discuss this another day."

Click.

Lisa exhaled hard, her jaw clenched so tight her teeth hurt. She unlocked her phone, fingers moving fast.

Text to Nelle: *"Can you meet me at the office? It's urgent."*

Across the city, Nelle and Emily were just finishing an early dinner, their laughter still lingering like perfume in the air when Nelle's screen lit up.

The main office area was a warzone of ambition—phones ringing off the hook, Laura juggling two lines at once, her voice tight but steady as she placed callers on hold with polite urgency. Interns darted between desks with folders in hand, while copywriters clacked away at keyboards and advertising directors exchanged sharp-tongued ideas near the glass wall. A public affairs assistant nearly dropped a stack of media kits, catching them just in time to avoid a domino of chaos.

And then Lisa walked in.

Like gravity had shifted, the room realigned. Her team swarmed her like she was the main course at Thanksgiving dinner—urgent questions, outstretched clipboards, budget approvals waved in her face. She nodded, signed, gave quick approvals, and slipped past them like a ghost desperate to breathe.

Inside her office, the door clicked shut and the buzz dulled into a muffled buzz.

Lisa moved straight to the cabinet in the corner, pulled out a bottle of top-shelf tequila, and poured herself a generous glass. The first sip burned, but not enough. She took a deeper gulp, feeling the warmth spread across her chest like armor. She lowered herself into her chair, elbows on her desk, and for a moment... she let herself feel.

Brent crossed her mind like an uninvited memory. She saw the softness of his eyes, the way his voice lowered when he was concerned. She shook her head sharply, almost physically rejecting the thought. *Not now.* She blamed the feeling on the stress. On exhaustion. On the tequila.

Then the door opened.

Nelle walked in with a lightness Lisa envied. But the moment she stepped inside, her eyes flickered with concern. Lisa had already finished her first glass and was mentally on her way to pouring a second.

"Hey, are you alright?" Nelle asked, voice laced with skepticism.

"Yeah," Lisa said, too quickly. She changed the subject. "How's your ankle?"

"Oh, it's good. I barely feel anything. The oxy did me good!" Nelle beamed. "I have some amazing news!" Her voice turned sing-song, playful.

Lisa raised a brow. "Oh? What's going on?"

"I put the money down on my storefront for the gallery!" Nelle jumped in place, her excitement practically radiating. "Got the keys today!"

In that instant, Lisa's stress fell away like a dropped coat. Her problems paused. She stood up and hugged her friend tightly, knowing what this meant. *Really* knowing.

"Oh Nelle, that's so good. Congratulations!!!" Lisa said, her smile wide, real, and warm. "I can't wait to see the pieces. So what are you thinking? Is it going to be just your work, or are you showcasing other indie artists too? Promo ideas? What's the vibe? Do you want a shot of tequila?" She laughed, the first time all day it felt natural.

"Hell yes!" Nelle agreed, grinning.

As Lisa poured her a glass, Nelle began mapping out her vision, talking through color palettes and breaking from the tired all-white gallery aesthetic. She wanted accent walls, vibrancy, something with personality. Lisa listened closely, nodding and encouraging every beat—even glancing down at her phone only sparingly.

"But yeah," Nelle said after a breath. "I think it's going to be great."

Then her voice softened. She reached across the desk, her fingers gently curling around Lisa's hand.

"I did have a small favor to ask…"

Lisa tilted her head, intrigued.

"Would you mind doing my PR?" Nelle asked, her tone hopeful but earnest. "Like you did for my birthday, but bigger. More grand. You know, especially for the opening."

Lisa laughed, her head tilting back slightly as the sound filled the room with warmth.

"Of course I'll do your PR!"

Nelle shot up from her seat, practically vibrating with joy. She tossed back the rest of her tequila, wincing just slightly, and skipped over to the mini bar to pour herself another. This moment had to be celebrated—loudly and with liquor.

"Ahh! I love you!" she exclaimed. "And don't worry, I definitely plan on paying you. I don't want any handouts. What's your fee?"

Lisa chuckled again, but the laugh stalled when she caught Nelle's face. She was dead serious.

"My fees?" Lisa blinked. "Nelle… it's okay."

"No, no," Nelle insisted, lifting her glass and waving it for emphasis. "Lay it on me. What am I looking at so I can budget?"

Lisa sighed, amused but obliging. "Alright. My base retainer is $29,000 a month, and my billables are about $475 an hour, for 30 hours a month, depending on the industry."

The tequila hit Nelle's throat at the exact wrong moment. She choked, eyes bulging slightly, doing her best to suppress the cough that desperately wanted to erupt. Her cheeks turned red, not from the alcohol but from the utter disbelief that followed. She forced it down, lips pressed tight, determined not to ruin Lisa's Persian white rug or her dignity.

Tears pricked at the corners of her eyes—not from emotion, but from the sheer violence of the swallow.

"On second thought," she gasped out, still recovering, "thank you so much. You know I hate asking you or Em for anything, but the money's practically already spent from this contract. I mean, between the contractors, the permits, and the light fixtures…"

Lisa's expression shifted—less amused now, more… guarded. "Speaking of the contract," she cut in gently, "we're going to be taking a little break from that."

Nelle blinked. "What? Why?"

"Roddy isn't feeling too well," Lisa said, carefully choosing her words. "We have to prioritize his mental health."

Nelle's face softened instantly. "Oh no! I'm sorry to hear that. Is there anything I can do?"

"Well…" Lisa trailed, then took a slow sip of her drink. "Just be a friend. I think he enjoys talking to you. The rapport you two have… I'm sure it helps."

"Rapport?" Nelle asked, confused. "Roddy and I haven't spoken outside of our schedule."

Lisa's brow furrowed as she let out a nervous, dry laugh. "How is that possible?"

"Well," Nelle began, uncertain, "I was treating it like a job. You said it was a job."

"Sure, yes, but…" Lisa stood, reaching for the tequila again. "He's still a person. What about the dinners? You've gone to dinners."

"Right, but once the photographers get their shots— us kissing or holding hands—we just part ways. We don't really talk during those. We mostly just stare at the menu and pretend to laugh at bad jokes. I thought that's what you wanted."

Lisa handed Nelle a refill as she processed the weight of that truth. She took a breath, then calmly explained how she had hoped Nelle would at least try to form a platonic connection with Roddy—something sincere. He didn't need just another expense. He needed someone real.

Nelle listened closely, suddenly feeling a pang of guilt twist in her chest. She hadn't known Roddy was struggling, not like that. And now she wondered if her distance had made it worse. She sipped her drink quietly, absorbing the shift in tone, knowing something about their arrangement had just changed—and maybe, for the better.

The next few days were spent rescheduling Roddy's packed itinerary—auditions, appearances, fittings, and brand collaborations were all pushed back. He was asked to rest. No, *ordered* to. And Lisa didn't mind one bit. The break gave her room to breathe, finally catching up on overdue invoicing and redirecting her sharp focus toward landing high-value deals for both her new and legacy clients.

Meanwhile, Emily was finally getting around to her long-postponed meeting with Mr. Aaron Anderson.

Aaron was the kind of man who made first impressions count—tall, poised, and always appearing three steps ahead of the conversation. With rich brown skin, a perfectly lined beard, and thoughtful eyes that gave the impression he'd already read the fine print, Aaron had the demeanor of someone who never rushed but somehow was never late. He wore a navy cardigan with red-and-white stripe detailing, the clean lines and fit suggesting a quiet luxury. Underneath, a crisp white tee kept things grounded, casual even, but intentional. Hands in his pockets, posture relaxed, he exuded calm confidence, the kind that came from always knowing your value.

Emily, sharp as ever, took note. She stood in the modern office, caught mid-conversation on the phone. Her expression was serious and focused, hinting that the call may be intense or important. Dressed in a fitted black top paired with high-waisted pinstripe trousers, her long, voluminous curls were moisturized to perfection.

"Okay, no problem, Mr. Long. I will have Carrie send those right over," she said, hovering the phone over the receiver as if to hang up.

"Let me guess? Your favorite color is pink?" Aaron asked, his smile against his complexion was the definition of flawless.

Emily blushed, her cheeks blooming like the soft rose tones that surrounded her office. "Well, I am kind of a girly girl," she said with a warm smile, extending her hand across the desk. The fifteenth-floor view of the High Line glimmered behind her, soft light spilling through the expansive windows of The Spiral building. Every detail of her office—blush-pink walls, velvet seating, and flourishing greenery—was made to feel personal.

Outside, curved glass walls encased private conference pods, while natural light spilled through floor-to-ceiling windows, illuminating snake plants hidden neatly in terra-cotta planters. The open floor plan gave way to cozy alcoves adorned with pastel seating, vertical white slats, and cascading greenery.

Aaron took her hand, kissed the back of it gently, warmly—his eyes lingering a moment longer than necessary. The pink chair she offered him made him pause, as if surprised by its bold femininity. Still, he sank into it, watching her as she moved, gathering documents and notes she'd spent days compiling.

"So, Mr. Anderson. Batting leader with a .375..." she said, her tone teasing yet informed.

He raised a brow. "Oh, you know the game, or just enough to make me *think* you know the game?"

Emily looked up briefly, her expression unreadable. "I don't know baseball. I know money. I know investments. I know growth opportunities. But before I could know all of that, I had to know who stands to benefit from what I know. Otherwise, what use would it be?"

Aaron clicked his teeth, amused and intrigued. "No, no. Don't talk like that. I have some knowledge of my own. For instance... I know a five-star Michelin restaurant overlooking crystal waters in Santorini. You can see straight to the bottom."

She blushed again—this time, uncertain. "Is that your other area of expertise?" she asked, flirtation lacing her words.

"Not particularly. Only enough to want one woman to benefit from what I just so happen to know."

"*Mr. Anderson,*" she replied, imitating the iconic line from *The Matrix,* "If I didn't know better, I'd say you were asking me on a date."

"Is that a problem?"

"For me? No. For this firm and its policies? Yes."

Without pause, he reached into his cardigan pocket and pulled out his phone case—a leather fold with compartments stuffed with cards, cash, and a blank check. Unfolding it, he leaned forward, snagged one of her pink pens, and chuckled. "You tell me the amount you earn from closing me today... and I'll give it to you."

Emily laughed, amused by his confidence. "I've seen what I could find of your financials..."

"Yes, what you *could* find. So what's the number?"

"A one-year retainer?"

"Make it two."

She did the math quickly.

Two years. 10% commission. After the firm's cut, her take-home would be just under $1.3 million. But her voice betrayed none of it. "Twenty shy of a million," she lied.

His brow lifted. "Dang, you ain't do no research." They both laughed. The air between them relaxed, electric.

"Is that the final number, Ms. Harrington?"

She nodded, biting her lip bashfully.

He had done his research.

A minute later, Aaron scribbled the amount without hesitation, laid the check gently on her desk, and said, "My number's on the check as well. I hope to hear from you."

Then he stood, straightened his cardigan, and left, leaving her staring after him—half in disbelief, half in awe.

CHAPTER 13.

BREAKFAST IS

SERVED

It was still unreasonably warm for the end of October—sunlight casting long, amber-colored fingers through the leaves of Central Park, brushing them in manners of orange, yellow, and fading green. Though none of them knew it yet, this afternoon would be one of the last times they'd all gather like this—just them, without the pressures of work, love, or responsibility calling them elsewhere.

Emily, Lisa, and Nelle had agreed to meet for lunch beneath the changing trees. As Nelle's taxi rolled past the building of her old job, she didn't feel a trace of longing. No nostalgia. No regret. She didn't miss the coworkers, the deadlines, or even the bylines. What she loved now was freedom—her own rhythm, her own time.

Lisa had just started to find her footing again after taking in her sister's dog, Korri—a sprightly five-year-old Shih Tzu with big eyes and a diva's energy. The transition from fabulous New Yorker to full-time pet parent was softened by the help of her doganny, Eliana, a stern but loving Ukrainian woman who handled Korri's meals, baths, and long city walks. The nickname had been coined by Lisa's sister, Leilani—equal parts tease and truth.

Lisa and Nelle arrived first, staking out a bench with just enough shade and breeze. Moments later, Emily emerged, following her GPS, smiling the second she spotted them. She picked up her pace, arms already opening wide as she neared. Hugs, laughter, and the usual flurry of "you look amazing" circled among them like wind.

"I bring news," Emily said, eyes gleaming. She reached into her designer handbag and pulled out two envelopes. "This one's for you, madam," she said, handing Lisa hers. "And this one... is for you," handing Nelle the other.

They exchanged puzzled glances. There were no birthdays, no bachelorettes. Cautiously, they opened the envelopes.

Lisa gasped—inside was a check for $400,000. Nelle's hands trembled as she read her own: $90,000.

"What is this?" Lisa whispered, stunned.

Nelle was speechless. Emotion overwhelmed her as she leapt up from the bench, tears rushing down her face.

"Aaron," Emily said, her voice light but proud. "I didn't even sign him, but he paid me anyway. Lisa, he was your recommendation. Nelle—consider this your grand opening gift."

Lisa blinked. "Wait… he just gave you that kind of money?"

"Sure did," Emily said, grinning. "And we're going to Greece next Friday."

"Greece?" Lisa and Nelle shouted in unison.

"Oh, so this is serious?" Lisa teased.

"As serious as it's going to get. I don't plan on letting him go anywhere," Emily replied, confidence dripping from every syllable.

The park felt different—almost magical. The kind of moment that feels suspended in time. Nelle looked at her friends, her life, and thought to herself, *Gosh, life is good.*

Later that evening, Lisa returned to her office, trailed by Eliana and a freshly groomed Korri. The scent of lavender and rosemary hung in the air as Eliana moved to the kitchen, already preparing the dog's evening meal with quiet competence.

Lisa walked to the bar, poured herself a drink over ice, and began reviewing ad budgets—her usual routine—when Roddy appeared in the doorway.

"Hey, Miss Lisa," he said, fidgeting slightly.

She looked up, surprised but happy. "Oh hey! How are you feeling? Rested?"

"Yep. Ready to get back to work. Back on socials. You know, the usual." But Lisa could tell he wasn't.

"Roddy, talk to me," she said gently, setting her drink down. "How are things with Nicole? The baby?"

He shifted, unsure. "Things are cool," he muttered, but his voice betrayed him.

"They're not cool," she said, eyes soft. "Do you need to tell me something?"

He sighed, defeated. "She's back at the CT house full time. She's starting to show... changed the locks. I can't go there anymore."

Lisa nodded, walking toward him with a smile full of comfort. "Then I'll visit her."

Roddy sat with his shoulders slumped, eyes low, and voice heavy. "I don't know. I've tried everything," he confessed. "I told her I want to be there for her and the baby. My mom's not feeling too well, and I even offered to take her to Pennsylvania. No paps, no pressure. Just us. But she's not hearing it. She wants nothing to do with me."

Lisa listened, the weight of his pain settling between them. "You both loved each other at some point," she said gently. "So I'm going to see her and hopefully get this all straightened out. Alright?"

She pivoted, shifting the energy.

"In the meantime," she continued, "you and John Legend are set to co-host the October Fall Fest in Tribeca. Keep your schedule tight. Your masterclass interview is coming up—it's straightforward, just talk through your prep, how you get into character, that kind of thing. We finally got confirmation on the Maddox role—it went to Jonathan Majors. But, don't worry, I'm going to get some more stuff lined up. GQ magazine shoot is confirmed for November 9th, and Nelle will be on-site with you."

Roddy perked up slightly. "She's doing the cover with me?"

Lisa shook her head. "They asked, but I declined. You two have a niche fanbase, yes. But we want the spotlight to remain on *you* and you alone. This moment is yours."

Roddy gave a slow nod, understanding. A few moments later, he stood, thanked her quietly, and decided to head back to his condo—alone with his thoughts and the ache of something slipping through his fingers.

Before the door even closed, Lisa was texting.

"Nelle, Roddy is heading back home. Please try and spend some time together."

Nelle read the message, paused, then typed back:

"Of course!"

And just like that, another page turned.

At home in her sun-drenched condo, Nelle stood barefoot in front of her latest work-in-progress, a striking canvas she had titled *Thunder Rolls*. The piece, bathed in dramatic browns, soft yellow hues, and whispery green tones, stretched across the whitewashed canvas, commanding attention even in its incomplete state.

Around her, light filtered in, dancing across the surfaces—her paints, brushes, and scattered 3D modeling tools. Though the composition wasn't finished, the artwork pulsed with energy, as if it had its own breath, its own storm waiting to break.

Nelle stared at it, heart tugged by something she couldn't quite articulate—an ache, a message, a whisper from the universe. She had big plans for this one. It would be her first step into 3D expression. A piece that didn't just hang on the wall, but reached into space, into *you*. She had even ordered sculpting materials and textured mediums, now lying in open boxes beside her bed. But lately, her creativity felt like a faucet that wouldn't fully turn off— she'd jump from one idea to the next, rarely finishing before a new inspiration pulled her elsewhere. Still, she always returned. She gave herself grace for the messiness of her process. The art was speaking to her. She just needed to listen.

Across town, a different scene was unfolding.

Lisa's black SUV pulled up to Roddy's Greenwich property, a futuristic structure nestled behind well-manicured hedges. Inside, Nicole lounged in the living room surrounded by her glam team, laughing as an episode of *The Real Housewives of Beverly Hills* played on the flat screen. Lisa approached the front door, heels clicking softly on the stone path. She knocked once—lightly, respectfully—then paused as she heard a rustle from the nearby bushes. Probably landscaping, she reasoned.

But something didn't feel right.

She knocked again, more assertively this time.

The door swung open. Nicole appeared in a satin robe, eyebrows raised in curiosity.

And then—

Click.

The sound was unmistakable.

A camera shutter.

Lisa's eyes darted toward the bushes. But, inevitably, she ignored it and glanced down at her phone—no news alerts, no surprise headlines. Still, the hairs on the back of her neck stood up. Someone was watching. She could feel it. Nicole stood in the doorway, heavily pregnant—eight months along, and glowing in the way only a woman nearing the end of pregnancy could be. Her belly edged into the doorway, but her energy made it clear: Lisa would not be stepping inside.

"What are you doing here?" Nicole asked, her voice sharp, eyes hard. Lisa stayed rooted on the stoop, posture composed, but her mind racing. Something about the rustle in the bushes, her driver's disinterest as he clipped his fingernails—none of it sat right. She had been followed. She was sure of it.

"I don't want any issues," Lisa said quietly, voice low and calm. "We need to talk. About Roddy. And the baby."

Nicole scoffed. "Roddy didn't want to be a husband, let alone a father. If he did, he wouldn't have hidden me like I was some dirty little secret."

"Nicole, this is the business," Lisa replied, choosing her words carefully. "He didn't hide you. He does love you. But you know how this works. He's building a career— one with momentum. With endorsements, films, and fans. The world we live in isn't kind to everyone."

"You mean pornstars," Nicole snapped.

"I mean, people who choose to live differently. That doesn't make you less than. But we had to be cautious, protect the image." Lisa's tone was firm, but not cruel. "This is about longevity."

Nicole's voice cracked. "He was cheating on me. With that girl."

"Janelle?" Lisa laughed, shaking her head. "No, absolutely not. I know her. Trust me—there was no sex, no romance, not even a text thread. They were working. They don't even like each other enough to have a conversation."

Nicole's arms folded across her belly, her expression skeptical. "You wouldn't say that if you saw what I saw. The pictures. The captions. It looked real."

Lisa gave a half-smile, not without empathy. "That just means I'm really, really good at my job."

A pause lingered between them—tense, unyielding.

"Look," Lisa said finally, softening. "Think about what I said. Call me if you need anything. I'll let Roderick know we spoke... and that he can come by."

Nicole nodded once, lips tight. The door shut gently behind her.

Back at Roddy's high-rise condo, the mood couldn't have been more different.

Nelle stepped into the foyer and immediately felt her shoulders relax. The sound of Duke Ellington & John Coltrane's *In A Sentimental Mood* drifting from hidden speakers gave the air a luxurious ease. She inhaled— jasmine, tobacco, leather. A mood.

Roddy met her at the staircase, a vision in a black-and-gold Versace robe, cigar in hand, a boyish grin tucked beneath his chiseled jawline.

"I had no idea you were coming down," he said, eyes lighting up.

Nelle smiled, noticing the colorful stains embedded under her fingernails. "I needed a break from painting. This place is... really nice."

"Reggie cooked earlier," he said, motioning toward the kitchen. "I can fix you a plate if you're hungry."

"Sure," she replied, a faint smile curling her lips. She wasn't there for anything more than support—but even she had to admit, the way he looked under that chandelier light? Dangerous.

Nelle wandered the space. She had only seen it mostly at night, bathed in cold light for staged photoshoots or quick meetings before retreating upstairs to her unit on the eighth floor. But now, with time on her hands and the buzz of quiet curiosity in her chest, she was finally able to take it all in.

The place was stunning—large and unapologetically masculine. A three-bedroom, two-bathroom condo carved in concrete elegance. Every inch of it felt curated, though Roddy had nothing to do with it.

The bedroom was moody and minimal, swathed in greys and browns like storm clouds pressed into linen. An abstract piece hung above the bed—wild, chaotic strokes in white like whispered secrets no one could quite decode. The headboard stretched the width of the wall, soft yet commanding. The view, even from here, caught a slice of the skyline, low and hazy.

The main living area was even more impressive at night. Floor-to-ceiling windows framed the city's glittering sprawl, while black marble and dark wood grounded the space quietly. A sculptural light fixture hovered over a long dining table like a halo with attitude. The artwork throughout leaned modern and obscure, but one piece stopped her cold—Jean-Michel Basquiat's *Hollywood Africans* hung above the fireplace.

"Oh my God, is this real?" she turned to him.

Roddy shrugged, casually. "Yep. One of a kind."

He wasn't into art. Hell, he didn't even know who designed the condo. Someone told him where he'd live, handed him a key, and he moved in. Still, he wanted to impress her. So he lied.

As he poured her a glass of whiskey—neat, of course—he opened cabinet after cabinet in search of plates, growing visibly frustrated at not knowing where anything was in his own home.

"So, I'm going to be honest," Roddy admitted, standing awkwardly near the oversized kitchen island. "I have no idea where anything is... Reggie usually handles everything in this area. He's off for the night, probably somewhere in the back of the house. I can order in, if you'd like."

Nelle glanced at the warm spread sitting untouched behind him—steamed vegetables, roasted potatoes, perfectly grilled salmon—all cooked with the kind of precision you don't get from takeout. Her brows furrowed just slightly, the thought of wasting food tugging at her.

"Oh no, it's fine," she said gently, stepping forward. "Let's just find what we need. I'll help."

With her there, the search turned swift. In less than a minute, the cabinets gave up their secrets—white porcelain dishes stacked neatly, lavish silverware tucked into velvet-lined drawers.

She rinsed her hands under the cool water, sleeves rolled back, skin glowing under the soft pendant lights. "I've got it from here," she said with a smile, brushing a curl from her cheek. He gave a nod and settled into the barstool at the island, watching her move with quiet admiration.

She spoke as she worked. Her voice had rhythm—light, airy, grounded in warmth. She talked about her apartment upstairs, the way the morning light hit her balcony just right, and at her loft, the Haitian and Trinidadian spices that filled the air when her mother visited. She told stories about her time as an undergrad, her childhood, and the chaos of having two older brothers who always fought over the remote. And how she would use tracing paper to draw the cartoon characters on their TV screens. She could never just *watch* something, she had to draw it.

Roddy didn't say much. He couldn't. He was... caught. Not by her looks—he'd always known she was beautiful—but by the ease in her presence. The way she filled the room without trying.

"So, you're into art?" he asked, more to keep her talking than anything else.

At that, her eyes lit up. She turned toward him, drying her hands on a linen cloth. "God, yes. I practically lived at art school," she began, launching into a passionate monologue about impressionism, the fluid rebellion of contemporary Black artists, her love for Basquiat, and the gallery in SoHo that always had new gems tucked in the back if you knew who to ask.

Roddy nodded along, though the words blended into a blur. Four minutes in, he was visibly bored—but he stayed locked in, forcing himself to listen. Not because he cared about brush strokes or texture, but because *she* did. And maybe that was enough for now.

They talked for what felt like hours, slipping deeper into comfort with every sip of whiskey. The conversation meandered—through childhood memories, embarrassing moments, favorite movies, and half-formed dreams. Between their laughter and long pauses, they each went back for seconds of Reggie's meal, the kind of food that sticks with you not just for the taste, but the warmth it carries.

Nelle could feel her inhibitions softening, unraveling gently like the slow descent of her eyelids. The edges of the evening blurred—the sound of their laughter bouncing off the walls in slow, echoing waves.

Then, he asked, "Can I ask you something?"

She raised a brow, amused. "Of course—we've been asking each other questions all night."

"Are you single?"

It caught her off guard. Not because the question was bold, but because of its simplicity. It struck her as almost ironic, considering the world already believed they were a couple. She laughed, maybe a bit too hard, and for a moment, it was all just... theater. A beautifully scripted show for everyone else.

"I am," she said with a bright, gleaming smile.

But in the seconds that followed, that smile faltered—just slightly. A flicker in her eyes betrayed her as a thought passed through her mind. Kenneth. The way things ended. Or maybe, the way they never really began.

"Oh, that smile," Roddy said gently. "Where'd it go? Bad breakup?"

She hesitated. "Well... we weren't together. It's a long story." She brushed it off, trying not to sound affected. "I've moved on. And so has he."

"Oh, moved on with me?" Roddy teased, smirking. "I'm joking."

She looked at the time. 1:27 AM. The whiskey had settled into her limbs, and her body felt light. She stood.

"I should go," she said softly.

He rose with her, offering to walk her home. She declined, gently but firmly. The night had been warm, and full, and maybe a little too easy. She needed to be alone with her thoughts and her slightly spinning head.

Still, he watched her from the doorway as she walked toward the elevator, her steps steady but unhurried.

"Hey," he called out. "That dinner invitation's still open."

She turned just as the elevator dinged, her eyes catching his one last time.

"Okay," she said, smiling—this time, without hesitation.

The morning sunlight spilled softly through the blinds across Nelle's comforter. She stirred gently, eyelids fluttering open to a quiet, peaceful stillness. Surprisingly, she felt... good. No pounding headache, no sour stomach. Just clarity. She chalked it up to the top-shelf whiskey and maybe the company, too.

Stretching languidly, she reached for her phone, thumb hovering over her notifications. Nothing from Lisa. Odd, but not alarming. She figured she'd catch up with her later. The plan for the day was slow and simple—grab a matcha from her favorite café, and head to the gallery to test out paint strips against the walls. A creative cleanse. She pulled on a pair of loose jeans, tied her hair up, and hummed softly to herself as she got ready. The night before already felt distant.

But on the other side of the city, peace was a luxury Lisa didn't get to keep.

The sharp buzz of her phone sliced through the haze of sleep. Groggy, she blinked at the screen, the name "Plum" lighting up. A new message. She tapped it open with a yawn still clinging to her chest.

"Breakfast is served."

Attached were four images.

Her breath caught. Each one more damning than the last—Lisa and Nicole, unmistakable, standing outside Roddy's Connecticut home. The angle was discreet, the timing... intentional.

Her heart thudded against her ribs, sleep falling away in an instant. A coldness spread through her chest. She sat up straight in bed, mouth parted but silent, eyes darting across the images, her fingers trembling.

CHAPTER 14.

REGINALD RUIZ

Lisa moved on autopilot. She ignored the message for now—she couldn't face it yet. Instead, she thumbed open her contacts and tapped Emily's name, the dial tone humming in her ear as she stumbled into the bathroom, nearly tripping over her own feet. Korri danced around her excitedly, tail wagging, eyes full of mischief and morning energy.

For a moment, Lisa paused.

She bent down, let the puppy lick her cheek, her fingers stroking soft fur. Just one brief moment of joy before chaos resumed. She couldn't afford to neglect Korri—not when everything else felt so unsteady.

The call finally connected. Emily sounded groggy, but alarmed by the urgency in Lisa's voice and texts. She promised she'd be in her office before 9 AM. Lisa exhaled a shaky breath, stepping into the shower as warm water coursed down her back. The day was spiraling before it had even begun.

What Lisa didn't know—what Emily hadn't yet said—was that she had news of her own. A quiet discovery tucked away in financial records: Roddy had spent over $600,000 on gambling just the month before. Emily hadn't told anyone, unsure of whether it was worth the panic. It was his money, after all. Still… something about it felt off.

Meanwhile, Midtown was wide awake.

Horns blared, feet pounded pavement, and coffee cups steamed. But Nelle, fresh-faced and light-hearted, was enjoying the rhythm of her morning—matcha in hand, gallery-bound, sunglasses perched delicately on her nose.

Then came the interruption.

"What a strange surprise," a voice said behind her.

She turned.

He was tall, stylish, effortlessly composed—someone who looked like he belonged on the cover of *Bon Appétit*.

Reginald Ruiz, known to many as Reggie is a grounded man in his early 40s. He has a rich, warm complexion with olive undertones. His hair is thick, dark, and tightly curled—cut short at the sides and slightly longer on top, giving him a polished but rugged edge. A full, salt-and-pepper beard frames his strong jawline, adding a distinguished charm to his presence.

Despite the morning breeze, he wears a denim button-down shirt, slightly unbuttoned at the top to reveal a silver chain resting against his chest. The rolled-up sleeves show off muscular forearms and a sturdy black watch on his wrist, hinting at both strength and functionality.

His expression is serious yet thoughtful, like someone who's seen things, lived through stories, and still manages to look forward with purpose. Reggie carries himself like a man who knows exactly who he is.

Nelle blinked, confused for a beat. Had they met? Was he about to ask for a photo?

Then he smiled, pressing a hand across his chest with a mix of charm and humility. "I'm Reggie Ruiz. Roddy's chef. You were at the condo last night."

Her face lit up with sudden recognition. "Oh my gosh—hi!" she said, quickly juggling her drink and bag to free her hand. "I'm surprised you recognized me!"

Reggie chuckled. "I mean, you're a bit famous—and you're dating my boss. So, of course, I'd recognize you."

They stood in the middle of a bustling Midtown sidewalk, laughing like old friends, while the city rushed around them—some pedestrians sneaking photos.

"Where are you headed?" he asked politely, his tone easy and unbothered, like someone used to asking questions without second-guessing himself. His Whole Foods trip was clearly on pause now, curiosity winning out over groceries.

Caught off guard, Nelle hesitated. She was heading to the gallery—*her* gallery—but the place was still under wraps, known only to a small circle of friends and her parents. Still, lying didn't sit well with her. She smiled lightly, tucking a strand of hair behind her ear. "Um... I'm heading to a space not too far, a few blocks up, across from the Sky building."

"Oh nice," he grinned. "I'd love to join you. I'm not doing much."

There was something warm and genuine about him, his energy easygoing and unthreatening. Nelle could tell it wasn't a line—just honest curiosity. So she agreed.

They walked the short distance together, chatting casually about the weather, city traffic, and of course, Roddy. When they arrived, Nelle fumbled through her bag for the keys, trying to shake the nerves she didn't know she had.

"Oh, this place is empty. You own it?" Reggie asked, his eyes scanning the facade with admiration.

Nelle nodded, slowly, still getting used to the sound of that herself.

"Ahhh," he said, stepping inside as the door creaked open. "This is an amazing space!" He strolled around, glancing back at her with an approving smile as she flicked on the lights.

"What are you going to put in here?" he asked, curiosity glowing on his face.

"An art gallery," she replied, her lips curling into a soft, proud smile.

"You're an artist?"

"Yes," she said, and in that moment, with the sun filtering through dusty windows and the walls still bare, she felt it more deeply than ever.

"Ahhh, I see. Very nice! Well, looks like this place could use a good cleaning. I will help you," Reggie offered, flashing a grin that was as charming as it was unexpected. His Dominican accent rolled out fast, smooth, and lighthearted, with a playfulness that made Nelle laugh before she could protest.

Within minutes, they were armed with Windex, brooms, cloths, and a mop and bucket like a scene out of a feel-good movie. Side by side, they got to work. The place echoed with the sound of scrubbing, light conversation, and the occasional laugh as dust danced through the morning light.

As they cleaned, Nelle found herself talking—again—about her love for art and how she'd found her way to it. It was a familiar story by now, having just told Roddy the night before, but Reggie's curiosity made it feel new again.

"What about you?" she asked, glancing at him over her shoulder between streaks on the storefront window.

"Me?" he said, eyes lighting up as he leaned on the mop handle. Reggie was a man of many words, animated and expressive, talking with his hands in a way that made even the most mundane story feel like an adventure.

"I'm from the Dominican Republic. Came to America when I was just four years old. My mother—ah, my mother could cook like you wouldn't believe. She had a little food stand in our village, sold empanadas, tamales, you name it. And she hustled—she did everything there. Anything to make money."

Nelle listened, smiling as he spoke. There was something comforting about his story—raw, real, and familiar. Like him, it felt grounded and full of life.

Reggie felt like the kind of person you'd known forever—easy, open, and without pretense. There were no awkward silences, no trying to impress. Just two people, sharing space and conversation, the air warm with the kind of comfort that rarely comes from strangers.

"Do you have kids?" Nelle asked casually, wiping down a shelf.

"I do," he said, a quiet pride lighting his face. "A seventeen-year-old daughter, Rayneli. I was married—eighteen years. My ex-wife and I had great memories. Been divorced now about five years." He paused, his voice softening with reflection. "She's a wonderful woman. I was in this place in my life, trying to figure out myself and money, so I wasn't home. She said, well… might as well be alone if I'm going to feel alone."

Nelle nodded gently, sensing the honesty in his words. "Ohh. I mean… did you always live with Roddy?"

Reggie laughed, shaking his head. "Oh no, no. I've been a personal chef for almost twenty years. In between, I bought real estate all over Manhattan—a house out in Long Island, too." He leaned against the counter, cloth in hand, his tone proud but never boastful. "Roddy is my first younger client. Everyone else was, ahhh, your football coaches, your basketball agents—a little older."

She raised her brows, impressed.

"I ended up living with Roddy because he asked," he went on with a shrug. "And I said, hey, why not? The money's good. I live good. And I take care of my whole family back home."

There it was again—that grounded sense of loyalty, of purpose.

"Oh," Nelle nodded, her voice light, testing the waters. "Earlier, you called me his girlfriend, or implied," she laughed softly, brushing a loose curl from her cheek.

Reggie paused mid-wipe, the cloth in his hand still as he turned to look at her. His expression was steady, unreadable for a beat, before softening with a knowing gaze.

"I know all about your role in his life," he said, calm, composed, a trace of humor in his tone. "This is not a new practice—I was merely teasing."

There was something in the way he said it that made her stomach flutter. A quiet declaration that he saw her clearly, and perhaps, saw something more. She bit her lip, trying not to grin too much. In a way, she'd brought it up just so he'd know—she was available. And yes, she was attracted to him.

"Oh," she smiled, letting her guard down just a bit more.

Reggie set the cloth aside and leaned against the counter, folding his arms. "Roderick is a good kid. A bit troubled, but he needs someone close to him. Someone to help him, guide him, and, uh, give him a sense of security," he said, his tone shifting into something more serious. "Otherwise, those friends? No good. I've seen it all in this business."

His eyes darkened a shade with memory. "It's one of the reasons I go from client to client. You see a 300-pound athlete beating on his 120-pound girlfriend, and morally, I cannot stay. I have a daughter. I wouldn't want that for my child."

Nelle felt a pang in her chest. Not just from the weight of his words, but from the conviction behind them. He wasn't just a man who talked—he stood for something.

"Roddy is not a womanizer," Reggie added. "He is simple, but troubled."

And somehow, in that quiet moment between brooms and Windex, she saw Reggie in full—thoughtful, principled, and unexpectedly gentle.

With a slight pause in the air, Reggie grinned and said, "Lunch is on me, okay!"

"Only if you cook it," Nelle shot back without missing a beat.

He laughed, full and genuine. "Where would I cook it?" he teased, looking around the raw, unfinished space. "You got a kitchen in here I don't know about?"

They both broke into hysterical laughter, the kind that left your cheeks sore and your stomach fluttering. For Nelle, it had been a long time since she'd smiled that hard, really smiled.

She felt light, caught in the ease of his presence. Her eyes lingered on him as he moved around the gallery space, wiping his hands on his jeans and grinning like they'd been friends for years.

She was glad he was there.

Shockingly, Lisa and Emily arrived at the office building at the same time, Emily clutching a hot cup of coffee like armor against the chaos of the morning. They exchanged quick, tight-lipped smiles before making their way upstairs. As they stepped into the main area, Laura greeted them with a troubled smile—an expression that lingered a second too long, hinting at something more. But Lisa didn't have the energy to ask. She offered a polite "Good morning," and continued toward her office, Emily trailing behind her.

Once inside, Lisa grabbed the remote and raised the blinds, letting the soft morning light stream in, washing over the clean lines of her desk and the tension in the room.

"Why does it feel like when one good thing happens, 700 bad things happen right after?" Emily asked, her voice low, tired.

Lisa paused, her eyes on the skyline. "I don't know. But it's really starting to weigh on me. I feel like I'm anxious 24/7."

Emily didn't know how to respond. The look in Lisa's eyes unsettled her—distant, restless, almost resigned. As Lisa reached for the office phone and dialed, Emily watched her, a knot forming in her stomach. The call went on speaker, the line barely rang once before it was picked up.

"I'll wire the quarter million by noon," Lisa said without hesitation.

Emily's eyes widened in disbelief. She reached for the phone and quickly hit mute.

"What? You're sending him money? Why? Roddy's money?" she whispered sharply.

Lisa didn't answer right away. Her jaw was tight, her fingers trembling slightly as she stared ahead. Unmuting the phone, they heard Plum's voice on the other end, calm, amused—even smug.

"Now Lisa," he said, chuckling, "you and I both know… yesterday's price is not today's price."

"You had me followed. That's stalking. That's illegal," Lisa snapped, her voice low but sharp with fury.

"Perhaps," Plum replied coolly. "But involving law enforcement only means that the images come out. Either way, I want this to go away as much as you do. I'll hand over everything I have—for one million."

Both Lisa and Emily audibly gasped, the weight of the demand crashing down like a brick through glass.

"No fucking way!" Emily barked, unable to hold back.

"Oh, Emily, you're here," Plum said smoothly, a mocking lilt to his tone. "I should have known. You two are glued at the hip."

He continued, unbothered. "Anyway, that's a fair amount. Roddy was up for Kang in a Marvel movie. He's got big eyes on him. All I'm asking for is a slice of the pie before he even makes it to that other side. Once Coogler gets a hold of him, his checks will be too large to even count."

A beat passed, the silence heavy.

"So really... what's a million dollars?"

Emily slammed the mute button again and leaned toward Lisa, her voice urgent and low. "Roddy is gambling his money away. Six hundred thousand in expenses at the casino last month. He can't afford this bribe—and Nelle, and glam, and travel... and *you*."

Lisa's eyes widened in disbelief. "I'm sorry, what?"

"I didn't want to say anything," Emily replied, almost breathless, "but his gambling is increasing month after month. At first, it was a normal amount, maybe even stress-related. But last month? He went completely overboard."

Lisa leaned back in her chair, overwhelmed. "But we can't have those images out. If things were bad before—when he married that girl—this? This will destroy him. People will think he cheated on Nelle. And this is all right after the ankle incident."

Emily nodded grimly. "One million is a lot. A lump sum like that could ruin him. Maybe if we negotiate payments, it's doable. But this... this will set him back tremendously."

Just then, the phone crackled back to life.

"Hellooooo!!" Plum blared through the speaker, his voice dripping with false cheer. "Ladies, I hope you're not wasting time trying to talk yourselves out of this. Tick-tock!"

Lisa had to think fast—and she did. Without missing a beat, she scribbled a message onto a sticky note and slid it across the desk to Emily: "Call Nelle. Now." Then, turning her attention back to the call, she steadied her voice.

"I'll have Emily wire the money," she said smoothly, a lie she knew she'd retract the moment the line went dead. Without waiting for a response, she hung up.

Turning to Emily, she exhaled sharply. "Nicole may still take him for child support even after this mess, so I don't want him to go bankrupt in a year. We need a Plan B. We'll get him to pull a Kevin Hart."

Emily blinked, thrown. "A Kevin Hart?"

Lisa nodded, her mind racing. "Admit to cheating and say he's taking full responsibility for the baby. The public will roast him, sure—but it's better than this. Better than a million-dollar bribe and a career-crippling scandal. We manage the narrative before it leaks. Crisis control."

And just like that, they were in motion—phones out, texts firing, damage control underway. The clock was ticking, but Lisa was determined to protect Roddy... even if that meant breaking him first.

By noon, the wheels were already turning.

Emily and Lisa had spoken to attorneys, working swiftly to file a motion to dissolve Roddy and Nicole's marriage—sealed documents, airtight confidentiality. Damage control was in full effect. Meanwhile, across town, Nelle and Reggie were mid-floor, cross-legged on a drop cloth, sharing a greasy pizza and letting their laughter bounce off the gallery walls.

When her phone rang, Nelle hesitated before answering. She didn't need to hear a word to know something was wrong. The tension seeped through the line, heavy and urgent.

Lisa launched in, her voice low but authoritative. She explained it all like a strategist: Roddy would post a video—filmed from his car or bedroom, intimate and raw. In it, he'd appear devastated, tears welling, voice cracking, confessing to the truth: he'd gotten a porn star pregnant. He'd call it a mistake. Reckless. Unforgivable. The fans would eat it up.

Nelle's role? Silence. No posts, no public statements. Her silence would become her power. The public would defend her, uplift her, and protect her. Lisa promised that within 24 hours, Roddy would issue a follow-up statement—one crafted with care—expressing his deep regret and unwavering determination to keep his relationship intact.

"The ball is in your court," Lisa said. "But silence is strategy."

And then came the kicker: Plum's photos would leak, and once Nicole's identity hit the web, the internet would devour her. Lisa was banking on public outrage. The perfect storm. Roddy was hesitant. "I can't do this to her…she's pregnant."

"She doesn't love you, Roderick," Lisa countered flatly. "She wanted money. This is how we fight back."

Emily sat at the edge of it all—watching, listening, calculating. And when the plan was finalized and the script was rehearsed, Roddy hit "send."

The video was posted.

Within minutes, the internet was in flames.

Comments surged by the second, and hashtags like #RoddyExposed, #PrayForJanelle, and #NicoleTheSideChick dominated trending lists. Notifications bombarded Nelle's phone until it froze completely, buzzing with the force of a cultural earthquake. Reggie, peering over her shoulder, read the flood of headlines pouring in from *TMZ*, *CNN*, *Variety*, *People Magazine*, and even *She's Single Magazine*, which made a point to mention Janelle as a former employee, looping her full circle into the media frenzy.

In under an hour, "Janelle" and "Roddy" shot into Google's top five most searched terms worldwide. Everyone was watching. Everyone had something to say.

Nicole, meanwhile, went on a full-out offensive—posting stories, tweets, livestreams, anything to claw her way out of the side-chick narrative. But it was too late. The tide had turned. Her attempts to spin the truth fell flat. She was already cast in the role of homewrecker, and no PR team could save her from it. Roddy, as expected, was weathering the storm better. The public leaned toward him—always did. Lisa knew that. It was a harsh reality, but a real one: the man is forgiven. The woman is expected to survive the fallout, hold her head up, and move on.

Those were the rules. Lisa didn't write them. She just played the game.

And Janelle? Her follower count exploded—20,000 new fans and rising. Some came to show support, others to lurk, to dissect. Yes, people were outraged that Roddy cheated—and with a white porn star at that—but if he cried loud enough, said he loved Janelle enough, they were more than willing to look past it.

All he had to do now was play the part of the broken man desperate to do better. And so far, the audience was buying every second of it.

Nelle and Reggie sat in the gallery, their eyes locked on their glowing phone screens as the world unraveled around them. They hadn't spoken in minutes, both too consumed by the headlines, the comments, the endless scroll of speculation.

Outside, people began to gather—first just a few curious faces, then a small crowd. Passersby pressed up to the window, whispering, pointing, phones raised to snap quick photos. The energy shifted.

Then it happened.

"She's cheating, too!" someone shouted from the sidewalk, loud enough to slice through the glass. The words echoed through the space like a slap. Reggie's head jerked up, eyes narrowing. Nelle didn't move—just swallowed hard, her phone still in hand.

Whispers morphed into murmurs. Stares sharpened. It didn't matter if it was true or not. It had started. The public was already writing her chapter.

CHAPTER 15.

THE TRUTH IS A LIE

The emails were relentless—brand after brand flooding Lisa's inbox, each one both urgent and demanding. They needed clarity, control, and answers. But Lisa, sharp as ever, fired off rapid responses like a machine. She reassured, reframed, and repositioned the scandal as "under control." Even if it wasn't. A quick calculation in her head told her the truth—none of it compared to the million Roddy would've had to pay Plum. Damage control was always cheaper than blackmail.

Meanwhile, Nelle tried calling her.

Once. Twice. No answer.

Lisa was too busy. Too locked in. Too sure she had it all handled.

But everything changed in an instant.

Back at the gallery, Reggie helped Nelle to her feet. She was frozen, stunned, and breathless—just as a glass bottle came crashing through the front window. Shards exploded like fireworks.

"Cheaters!" a woman screamed from the sidewalk.

Janelle's heart thundered in her chest. Panic gripped her lungs. Reggie didn't hesitate—he pulled her by the hand, guiding her swiftly to the back exit. They burst through it into the alleyway, ducking into the shadows until they surfaced on a quieter street. He flagged down a yellow taxi, shielding her from the curious eyes starting to linger.

Inside Lisa's office, her and Emily's phones buzzed nonstop. They ignored them, thinking it was just more alerts from the earlier chaos. But they were wrong.

By the time they checked, TMZ had already updated their headline: "Caught Cheating? Was This Ever a Real Relationship?"—with a photo of Janelle and Reggie fleeing the gallery together.

And that... was the tipping point.

Lisa finally got through. After what felt like an eternity of redials and failed connections, Nelle picked up—her voice trembling, tears slipping down her cheeks. She'd reset her phone so many times just to make it work, her hands shaking with every attempt. The world was crumbling around her, and this call felt like the only thing keeping her tethered.

"Go to my house," Lisa said firmly. "Not the office. Emily and I will meet you there."

There was no time to waste.

Hanging up, Lisa was already dialing again—this time, the police. Her voice was crisp, unwavering. She reported the incident at Nelle's gallery with precision, demanding immediate action and insisting that the woman caught in the TMZ photo be arrested for vandalism.

"This was a targeted attack," she said. "And I want her prosecuted to the fullest extent of the law."

It was a race against the clock—not just to keep Nelle safe, but to take back the narrative before it slipped even further out of their control.

Arriving at Lisa's townhouse felt like reaching shelter after a storm. The tension in the room was palpable, but relief flooded her chest the moment she saw Nelle walk through the door, safe, though shaken. Reggie, however, wasn't holding back.

"I knew it was you behind this," he said, his voice sharp, accusing.

"Me?" Lisa asked, genuinely caught off guard.

"Yes, you're playing with people's lives like this is a game of Barbie," he snapped. "And Roddy is the most stressed I've ever seen him."

Lisa's patience thinned. "You mean the richest you've ever seen him. According to his financials, you got a raise months ago—and you weren't complaining then."

Reggie's face twisted.

"Money is money! It's frequency. It's energy. All money isn't good money. She was almost hurt. What if I wasn't there?"

"She would've been fine!" Lisa barked back. "Those people reacted the way they did because you were there! Speaking of which, why were you two together anyway?"

"Excuse me?" he stepped forward. "Are we pawns or people?"

"Okay, enough," Emily cut in, stepping between them like a shield.

Reggie's voice simmered down, but his words landed hard. "All of these publicists are the same—cutthroat, mean, entitled. You don't see people, Lisa. You see dollar signs. And no matter what, you have to control a narrative." He let out a bitter laugh. "This is how people get hurt. You're playing with everyone's emotions—the ones on this side and the people watching from the outside. Where is your conscience? Forget damage control... you people need conscience control."

Lisa didn't respond. Not at first. His words sank in like stones dropped in water, rippling through her thoughts. This was supposed to be an easy job—take someone ordinary, make them extraordinary through press, headlines, and clever PR maneuvers. But at what cost? How far was she willing to go to protect a brand? Where was her line?

Her eyes drifted to Nelle, curled on the couch, visibly shaken. Meanwhile, Reggie had stepped into the other room, trying to explain himself to whoever was on the other end of his call—probably someone who saw his face plastered across TMZ's homepage.

Lisa's phone buzzed again. No word from Roddy. She swallowed her pride.

"Reggie," she called softly, "I can't get through to Roderick. Can you please call him?"

He didn't respond right away, but she could tell he heard her.

Eliana moved quietly through the space, offering water and snacks, her presence warm and grounding. Upstairs, Korri slept soundly in the serenity of a nursery filled with lullabies and lavender mist from a humidifier. For a moment, peace tried to settle over the confusion.

Emily gathered her things. "I have to go into the office, but I'll be back later tonight," she promised, squeezing Lisa's shoulder gently before heading out.

The house was full, yet the silence was the loudest thing in the room.

It was in the polished stillness of the lobby that Emily first saw him—Brenton—sitting with his head low, hands clasped tightly, as if trying to squeeze courage out of his skin. The sight of him here, in this building, felt off. Out of place. Her firm handled high-net-worth portfolios, hedge fund strategy, and generational wealth. Brent's history, though charismatic, was nowhere near this world.

Still, she approached, uncertain what to say... or why he'd come.

"Hey," she offered, gently pushing through the glass doors.

Startled, Brent rose quickly, smoothing his pants and adjusting his shirt. "Hey, can I talk to you for a minute?" he asked, voice calm but urgent.

"Um, sure," Emily replied with polite surprise. "Let me ask my assistant to postpone some of my calls."

She led him down to her office, where he sank into one of the plush pink chairs while she offered him water. He declined. And then the reason for his visit spilled out.

"I hope you don't mind, I found you on LinkedIn since you and Lisa don't use Instagram... It's just—I know Lisa is still mad at me. I don't care if she's moved on or if she's seeing someone else. I just need to talk to her."

Emily laughed softly, easing the tension. "Well, after thirty, Instagram kind of stops being the place to connect.

We talk to people in real life now," she joked. "And no, not someone else... a dog. Lisa got a dog."

Brent's face relaxed, a trace of hope crossing his features.

Emily stood firm, arms crossed and heart steady, as Brenton laid it all out—his regrets, his intentions, and his plea for another chance.

"Listen," Emily said, her voice measured. "You seem like a good guy. But Lisa was hurt. And I don't want to be the one who brings you back around only for her to go through that again. She has a lot going on right now. Maybe... now just isn't the time."

Brenton nodded, sighing. "I know. I saw the blogs. Everyone's talking about this Roddy Richardson guy."

There was no bitterness in his tone—just weariness. Regret.

"I made some mistakes. No denying that. I thought I could still live a certain lifestyle and just... shield her from it. Like, keep her in this separate bubble."

Emily furrowed her brow. "That's selfish. You know that, right?"

"You're right," he said without flinching. "And I take full accountability. I have to choose now, and I choose her. I don't want to be out or chasing a scene anymore. I want to come home to her—only her. The truth is, I've felt that way for a while. I just didn't think she'd walk away."

Emily let out a dry laugh. "Do we know the same Lisa? She's strict. She doesn't play."

"I know," he grinned. "I thought I was the exception to the rule. She's intimidating as hell, but that's exactly what I love most about her."

And then, just when Emily thought the conversation had reached its dramatic peak, Brenton pulled a receipt from his pocket.

"I bought her an engagement ring," he said softly.

Emily blinked, thrown. "Engagement? Brenton, please. I don't need to see that receipt. Baby steps, okay? I don't even know if she wants to talk to you, let alone marry you."

She softened, just slightly. "Look, from the moment I met Lisa, I never got domesticated wife and mother vibes. So, unless you're okay with that, don't waste her time. Or yours. That's my sister for real."

"I completely understand," he said. "Just help a brother out."

After a long pause, Emily finally nodded. "Okay. But I'm going to tell her we talked. And that you'll probably be around this Saturday when we go to lunch, so she's not blindsided."

"If she's not open to it," Brenton added quickly, "I'll back off. No pressure. I mean it."

And with that, they reached an agreement. Emily remained skeptical, fiercely protective of her friend, but she knew this wasn't her call.

Roddy was unraveling. His social media, once a haven of fan love and admiration, had become a war zone. The comments under his posts were brutal—calling him a sellout, a hypocrite, a disgrace—not just for cheating, but for getting a white pornstar pregnant while in a high-profile relationship with a beloved Black woman. Laura had no choice but to mute or limit interactions across his platforms.

Meanwhile, Plum was scrambling for relevancy. He reached out to Tolly in desperation, hoping to film a joint YouTube video exposing their "truth," complete with timestamps and receipts proving Nicole and Roddy were married. But no one was biting. The fans weren't buying it. It was as if Lisa had managed to hypnotize the public—her strategic manipulation so precise that it erased every other account. Facts were irrelevant now. Emotion ruled. And the court of public opinion had spoken.

Plum was running out of options. Fast.

Lisa, too, could see the tide was shifting—but she knew how to stay ahead. The only way to keep Nelle from being pulled under was to make her look like the victim once again. It pained her to do it, but she needed Nelle to cooperate. A sidewalk shoot—sad, shaken, tears in her eyes. The paparazzi would be tipped off in advance, camera-ready to capture every frame of her grief. Lisa was already dialing the photographers, giving them a time and location.

Nelle didn't argue. She couldn't. Not with the money tied to the contract. Not with her future on the line. She had to play along—had to be the heartbroken girl America wanted to root for. This wasn't about truth anymore. It was about selling the perfect story.

By mid-afternoon, the carefully staged photos of Nelle looking heartbroken and vulnerable hit the internet—and just as Lisa predicted, the public rallied behind her. The sympathy poured in, especially from women who saw themselves in her pain. Her follower count surged by the thousands, and comment sections turned into digital support groups. Nelle was now not just a public figure—she was a symbol of grace under fire.

Ironically, one of the first emails to land in Lisa's inbox came from *She's Single Magazine*, Nelle's former employer. They offered $25,000 for an exclusive cover shoot and story—a poetic full-circle moment. But Lisa, ever the strategist, declined. The goal was not to break up the relationship. If they played this right, Nelle and Roddy would come out stronger—or at least more profitable.

Then came the real jackpot: *People Magazine* reached out. $200,000 for the cover and a multi-page centerfold spread, complete with a sit-down interview. Lisa didn't hesitate. She accepted immediately.

The plan? Coach Nelle to perfection. She would speak her truth—but a carefully crafted one. She would allude to forgiveness, to "working through things," and most importantly, to not leaving Roddy. It was risky, but the reward was too great to pass up. The narrative was shifting, and Lisa had her hands on the wheel.

There was little time to prep. Hair, makeup, wardrobe, media training—it all had to be done in a matter of hours. But that was the business. Timing was everything. And in the chaos of scandal, opportunity always knocked. Lisa just made sure she was the one answering the door.

Nelle's deals had come just in time. While Roddy lost two major endorsements, she picked up two of her own—enough to balance the books and keep their shared brand afloat. Lisa viewed it as a win: a pivot, not a loss. But for Roddy, it felt like a gut punch.

He was footing the bill for the entire operation—Lisa's team, the crisis management, even Nelle's growing visibility—yet he was no longer the focal point. The narrative had shifted and left him on the sidelines, a supporting character in a scandal with his name on it. The worst part? The woman he was supposed to be pretending to love was becoming more famous by the minute… and he was starting to feel like the fraud in the equation.

By the time Reggie arrived at Roddy's condo, the damage was already done. Roddy was sprawled across the couch, eyes glassy, caught somewhere between the calming haze of mushrooms, the sting of three tequila shots, and the numb clarity of perfectly aligned lines of cocaine on the glass coffee table.

"Ohh! The man I wanted to see," Roddy said, a crooked grin sliding across his face.

Reggie sighed, dropping his keys. "What is this, man? Why are you doing this?"

Roddy leaned back, his voice slow and slurred. "How was she?"

"Who?"

"The woman I'm paying to be my girlfriend."

Reggie bristled. "I don't know what you're talking about. I was being a friend. Nothing happened. We cleaned, we ate pizza… and then a brick came flying through the window."

Roddy let out a dry laugh. "I like her, you know… like… even if she is being paid to like me back. I like her."

The confession hung in the air, heavy and raw.

"Then you should be honest with her—and with Lisa," Reggie said, his tone calm but firm. "So they can stop putting on this show and doing more harm than good. At least if the connection is genuine, then all of this can come to an end, and you can both live in your truth."

There was a slight pang in his chest as he spoke. He wasn't sure when it happened, but somewhere along the line, he'd started to like her too. Not in the way Roddy did—maybe not even in a way that mattered—but enough for it to sting. Still, Reggie knew his role. He wasn't the man in the spotlight, and he had no intention of overstepping into territory that wasn't his.

"You're right, Reggie. I think I'm going to do it," Roddy mumbled, slurred and slow.

But he didn't move. His body gave out before his words could catch up. His arms went limp, and within seconds, he was out cold, drifting into a deep, heavy sleep on the couch, his mind probably miles away from the chaos he'd helped ignite.

Just then, Reggie's phone buzzed. A text lit up the screen:

Nelle: *"They want me to do an interview with People…"*

He stared at it for a moment, then locked the screen. No reply. No explanation. Respectfully, he ignored it—choosing, in that quiet moment, to preserve his peace, his career, and his boundaries over a woman caught in a whirlwind none of them had asked for.

With Roddy asleep and the world still spinning outside, Reggie turned toward the kitchen. He rolled up his sleeves and got to work preparing dinner for the night.

Within just two days, Nelle found herself seated across from the host of *People Magazine*, cameras rolling and eyes fixed on her every word. The studio buzzed with energy—the steady hum of production equipment, the soft shuffle of stylists and assistants, the distant echo of someone yelling "quiet on set!" It was overwhelming, yet electric. Like stepping into a new dimension where the rules were different and *she* was the center of it all.

Lisa and Laura followed close behind, heels clicking against the polished floor, clipboards in hand and pens moving furiously as they took note of everything—every cue, every quote, every look that could make headlines. Though the interview wouldn't air for another week, the stakes felt immediate. The cover shoot was scheduled for later that evening, but already, Nelle could feel the weight of the moment. This wasn't just press. This was a transformation.

For the first time in her life, she was being pampered—editorial style. A glam team circled her like clockwork, brushing, pinning, and powdering. She sat still, watching her reflection shift into something polished, effortless, iconic. And she liked it. God, she *liked* it. The feeling was intoxicating—better than any high, more seductive than any man's attention. It wasn't about vanity. It was about being seen. Being valued. Being told in a thousand subtle ways that she mattered.

As she sat in the chair, sipping cucumber water from a glass tumbler with her name taped to the bottom, Nelle began to understand. This was the reason people clung to fame like oxygen. Why actors kept chasing roles between heartbreaks. Why singers stuck it out even after the charts forgot their names. This pedestal—this fragile, glittering world of light and luxury—was addictive. And letting go? That was the hardest part of all.

Janelle was no actress, but in that chair, under the bright lights and watchful eyes of what would soon be millions, she performed the role of a lifetime. Tears welled and fell on cue—not forced, not theatrical, but graceful, genuine, devastatingly timed. Where other entertainers strained to produce emotion, hers flowed naturally, beautifully, without hesitation. She didn't flinch at the tough questions either. After all, the truth had long been replaced with fiction. But she knew how to weave a believable one—drawing from the last raw ache she could recall.

Kenneth.

She channeled what she felt watching his wife open the door. The sound of Mars slamming it shut in her face. The way Kenneth had once lifted her in his arms, carried her inside like a promise, laid her down like she mattered. Those memories weren't meant for this stage, but she summoned them—threading them through her answers, stitching together heartbreak and hope. It worked. Her story landed. She was no villain. Just a regular woman who found love in the most unexpected way—with someone she believed wanted the same things she did: stability, honesty, a future.

She didn't pretend to be perfect. She didn't have to. That was Lisa's genius—the blurred lines between performance and reality. Even when asked about the ankle incident, she leaned into the narrative. *It was an accident,* she said, steady and convincing, as she invited viewers into the supposed quiet corners of their private life. Vulnerability became her armor.

And the people around them bought it.

It was the perfect interview.

The host praised her composure, her courage. And then came the final question: *How do you move forward with Roddy now that he's going to be a father?*

Nelle didn't blink. "The baby is innocent," she said, voice soft but steadfast. "And that baby deserves to have its father. No matter what Roddy and I may go through, I will never rob that child of having the relationship he deserves with the man who I know loves him and will do anything to be the best role model for him going forward."

Cue applause. Cue admiration. Cue redemption.

She walked off that set not as a scandal, but as a woman the world could root for.

Before the day came to a close, Lisa made sure Roddy was on a flight to Alaska, headed to the set of a film he'd signed onto over a year ago—long before the drama, the headlines, and the TMZ ambushes. Scandal or not, the studio wouldn't let him go, and frankly, Lisa wouldn't let them try. He needed the distraction, the distance, and most of all, the discipline that came with being on set. It was the perfect opportunity to let the fire cool while the People interview simmered in the background, waiting for its November 4th release.

With the spotlight momentarily shifting, Lisa shifted gears too. She arranged for 24/7 security to patrol Nelle's gallery, a necessary precaution after the vandalism and threats. But more than protection, it gave Nelle the space to breathe. To feel. To be. Lisa recommended she use the downtime to focus on herself—meditating, journaling, healing. This was the quiet before the next storm, and Lisa knew better than anyone how rare and crucial that stillness could be.

For the first time in days, the world wasn't pulling Nelle in a hundred directions. There were no surprise paparazzi, no staged meet-cutes, no chaotic back-and-forths. Just a woman, some silence, and a brush in her hand—preparing to reclaim control, one stroke at a time.

By Saturday afternoon, Lisa couldn't bring herself to get out of bed. The exhaustion from the whirlwind week had finally caught up to her. She had made plans to meet Emily for lunch, but with a soft chuckle and zero guilt, she called her best friend to confirm her cancellation text.

"I know we have lunch today, but I can't do it," she said, voice slightly hoarse as she buried deeper beneath the duvet. Korri, her tiny furball of a dog, curled up beside her on the California king, both of them tucked away in the cocoon of plush blankets while the central air kept the room perfectly chilled.

"I don't blame you," Emily replied, casually feeding her cat while scanning Netflix for a feel-good rom-com. Aaron was coming over later, and until then, she was soaking up the peace and quiet. "By the way, I had a little surprise planned for you today."

Lisa perked up slightly, squeaking a toy to distract Korri. "Surprise?"

"Yeah. Brenton stopped by my office a few days ago. Said he wanted my help getting you to talk to him. I figured if we did lunch, I'd casually bring him along... but since you bailed, I told him never mind. He misses you."

Lisa rolled her eyes so hard it was audible. "Hmm. He went through all that trouble, you'd think it actually meant something. Men these days... how do you trust them?"

Emily sighed, now on the couch. "I don't know. But let's not forget—he didn't even make an effort for your birthday. And you know how I feel about that. Mess up anything else, but my birthday? Hell no."

"You're right."

"And girl... he said he got a ring."

Lisa paused, blinking slowly. "A ring?"

"Yeah," Emily said, dramatically lowering her voice. "An engagement ring."

Silence.

Lisa sat up in bed. "From the vending machine?"

Emily let out a loud shriek of laughter. "Lisa!"

And just like that, the weight of the week melted into giggles and inside jokes, the two of them laughing like teenagers on a sleepover. Sometimes, a friend who gets it is better than any apology or ring, especially one possibly bought next to a pack of gum.

Across town, that night, a quiet sadness began to settle over Janelle like a fog she couldn't shake. It was that aching kind of déjà vu—being ignored, left in limbo, feelings caught somewhere between hope and reality. Reggie hadn't called, hadn't texted, not even a simple "hello." And while she could admit they had only met once—briefly at that—something about his energy lingered. It wasn't just his looks, though those didn't hurt. It was the way he carried himself—wise, measured, masculine in every sense. There was stability in him, a groundedness she found herself yearning for more than she expected.

Still, she tried not to take it personal. Maybe he was busy. Maybe he was over it. Or maybe he, like so many others before him, didn't think she was worth the follow-up.

Draped in an oversized sweatshirt that hung just past her fingertips and UGG boots she typically only wore around the house, Nelle pulled her hair into a neat bun and quietly made her way downstairs to Roddy's condo. It wasn't clear what she was looking for—comfort, conversation, or just a break from the noise in her head—but she needed somewhere to be that wasn't her own silence.

CHAPTER 16.

ARE YOU SURE...?

Janelle knocked softly on the door, smiling politely as neighbors passed by, dressed to the nines for a Saturday night out. It was a surreal feeling—outdoors, she was beginning to feel like someone, a name people whispered and stared at. But inside, among the other residents, she was just another face in the hallway. A soft "hi" here, a head nod there. No flashing cameras. No pedestal. Just Janelle.

The door unlatched, creaking open just enough for Reggie's hand to reach out and gently take hers. She stepped inside slowly, her eyes sweeping over the familiar space as he ushered her in. She didn't want to come off too eager. "So... how are things going?"

"I know, I know. You're wondering why I haven't called," he said, beating her to it.

Her heart fluttered a little. A man who didn't deflect or gaslight. Who didn't wait for her to break the tension—he just owned it.

"Well, yes," she said honestly. "Did I do something wrong?"

"No," he replied quickly, his voice low and assuring. His pajamas brushed the hardwood floor, and his white V-neck clung gently to his broad chest, exposing just enough chest hair to make her curious. His left arm was a mural of tattoos—strong, detailed, masculine.

"I, uh… I didn't want to overstep my boundaries," he continued, eyes softening. "You are, after all, a contracted partner."

She tilted her head, her brow raised in disbelief. "What does that even mean? That doesn't change the fact that I'm single. I can date—and be with—whoever I want."

His gaze darkened with something unspoken, something warm. He half-smirked, leaning slightly toward her. "Is that so?"

"Yes," she said again, her voice dropping slightly, teasing.

He smiled. "Have you eaten?"

"I had a salad earlier... and some salmon over vegetables from the sushi spot downstairs."

"So I can't feed you?" he asked, playful, moving toward the open-concept kitchen.

"Not food," she flirted, a sly grin playing on her lips.

Reggie's laugh was low and knowing as he reached for two glasses and a chilled bottle of Veuve Clicquot Yellow Label from the bar. He led her to the balcony, sliding the doors open to let in the crisp October breeze. The city lights sparkled below them as the wind danced around her oversized sweatshirt. The night, it seemed, was just getting started.

The balcony stretched generously along the condo's edge, offering an unobstructed view of towering high-rises and the bustling city below. Iron railings framed the space, modish and simple, while clusters of vibrant greenery and potted florals added warmth to the modern aesthetic. Two contemporary white cushioned chairs sat facing each other around a round, low-profile black table.

Her mind was made up—no wine, no dinner, no small talk. Just desire. For the first time in a long while, she felt completely free. Desired. Confident. As if something inside her had finally awakened. She reached for his hands, placing them at her waist as she gently lifted the hem of her sweaterdress, revealing the soft blush of her pastel thong. His eyes followed every curve with quiet hunger before he leaned in, his lips finding the warmth of her neck.

The breeze from the balcony swept around them, cool against her skin, but his arms were her shelter—firm, protective, wrapped around her like a vow. His kiss was intentional, slow, the kind that knew exactly what it was doing. Her breath caught in her throat as he touched her, expertly, like he'd anticipated her responses. Her body melted into his, legs trembling, breath stuttering. The panties between her legs were soaked as he massaged her clitoris gently.

Without hesitation, he lifted her—smoothly—her legs instinctively curling around him as he carried her inside. With a quiet thud, the glass doors slid shut, sealing the moment in privacy. He eased her down onto the couch, his eyes never leaving hers as he settled between her thighs, licking her vagina masterfully. Skilled, diligent—suckling as though he were an expert. His hands gripping her thighs, her hands gripping his, and there were no signs of him stopping or slowing down. She was rolling, twisting, her body contorting to every inch of his tongue.

She moaned.

Moments later, her body trembled with release, her legs twitching as waves of pleasure rippled through her. A soft moan escaped her lips as she lay breathless, overwhelmed, her warmth lingering between them. Reggie hovered close, his lips brushing against hers before trailing to her ear. One hand gently cradled her throat, not to restrain—but to hold, to anchor her in the intensity of the moment.

"Are you sure you want to do this?" he whispered, his voice low, seductive, and sincere.

Her eyes fluttered shut, lips parted as if pulled by a force beyond logic. "Yes," she whispered, almost a plea. "Please."

Without another word, he swept her up into his arms, their mouths meeting in a kiss that deepened with every step. He moved with confidence, navigating the space like it was second nature, as if every hallway had been rehearsed, every moment fated. The bedroom welcomed them in shadows and soft light.

What followed was slow, intense, unforgettable. Reggie loved on her with intention—every touch, every thrust, purposeful. Janelle had never experienced anything like it. In his arms, she wasn't just wanted—she was worshipped.

Monday morning, Janelle returned home with a quiet glow that only came from feeling truly seen. After a weekend wrapped in Reggie's oversized tees, bare-skinned under borrowed sweats, and wrapped up in hours of unfiltered conversation and uninterrupted passion, she felt lighter. More grounded. The kind of clarity that doesn't need explanation. During breakfast, he was calling her *his lady*—and she didn't flinch. No hesitation. Reggie was steady, direct, and refreshingly transparent. With him, there were no games, no decoding mixed signals. She could ask him anything, and he'd answer without flinching. For the first time in a long time, love didn't feel like a guessing game. It felt safe. Real.

After showering and slipping into something fresh, Janelle made her way to Lisa's office. It had been a while since she'd popped in without a text or call, but this time felt different. She was glowing, and she knew it.

Inside, Lisa stood at her desk, fingers grazing the petals of a stunning bouquet. The card sticking out read, *From Brenton Pryce. Baby, I miss you and I'm sorry.* The gesture was elegant, the flowers a masterclass in apology. But Lisa didn't fold—not yet. She needed space to heal, to find her footing again.

Janelle walked in with her usual warmth. "Hi!" she beamed, greeting everyone in the office with cheerful hellos and breezy smiles.

"Hey!! How are things?" Lisa shot out, barely skipping a beat. "Did they fix the window at the space? And security's still there, right?"

"Yes to everything," Nelle grinned, settling into the chair across from her. "I came for the schedule."

Lisa, mid-email, glanced over. "Well, aren't you perky!"

"I am," Nelle said, eyes flicking to the flowers. "And who are those from?"

Lisa sighed. "Brenton."

"Ahhh."

With the smallest smirk, Lisa pushed her laptop aside. "Laura has your schedule. Since things are cooling down and the *People* interview drops Friday, I want you to fly out to Alaska for a few days. Just to keep the buzz alive. Some casual posts, let folks know you and Roddy are still in the same orbit."

Nelle nodded. "Where am I staying?"

"With Roddy."

Nelle straightened. "Really?"

"Yes. Big suite. Separate sides. It's no biggie," Lisa said, brushing it off like it was nothing. "Oh, and heads up—Thanksgiving. You'll be in PA with Roddy's family for a quick shoot, then you can come home to your folks. I think Emily is putting together a Friendsgiving too, for you to meet Aaron."

Nelle gave a polite smile, though her mind instantly flashed to Reggie. Things were still new, but she didn't want to lock down any holiday plans until she talked to him. For now, she played it cool. "When do I leave for Alaska?"

"Tomorrow morning," Lisa replied.

Nelle's jaw dropped. "Tomorrow?!"

"I know, I know—it's tight. But it'll be quick. You'll be back before you know it."

On her way out, Nelle pulled Lisa in for a quick hug, then tapped away on her phone, updating Reggie. He understood, even if he was reluctant.

By 4 AM Tuesday, Nelle was gliding across the tarmac in a sleek black Cadillac Escalade, its headlights cutting through the darkness like whispers of something grand waiting just ahead. The SUV rolled to a gentle stop beside a gleaming white-and-gold jet, its polished surface catching the first flickers of pre-dawn light. Her breath caught. It was stunning—bigger and more extravagant than Emily's boss's jet, with a quiet authority that made her wonder, *Just how much is Roddy worth?*

She stepped out in a cozy grey tracksuit, hoodie pulled up over her head, dark shades hiding the sleepy glaze in her eyes, and crisp sneakers grounding her against the surreal moment. Equipped with minimal luggage and understated confidence, she climbed the small staircase and stepped into the main cabin.

It was more than she expected.

A plush bed was already laid out for her in the heart of the space, flanked by a tray of warm coffee, fresh-cut fruit, and delicate snacks. Everything she didn't ask for, but somehow needed. It was a quiet welcome, rich with thoughtfulness. Nelle smiled to herself—this was new.

As the plane lifted off toward Fairbanks, the sky outside transformed into strokes of amber and cotton-candy pink. She melted into the seat by the window, knees curled, eyes tracing the shifting horizon. The beauty of it all left her breathless.

But not even the jet's luxury or the sunrise above the clouds could distract her for long.

Two hours in, her thoughts began drifting back to Reggie. His touch. His laugh. The way he looked at her was like she was already everything. She was floating thousands of feet in the air, headed toward another man, and yet— her heart was tethered to someone else.

The contradiction gripped her chest.

Eventually, she let the thought of him cradle her. She leaned into the silence, letting her eyes close, the hum of the engine a lullaby. And somewhere between where she was and where she was going, Nelle surrendered to sleep.

The cabin of the jet was warm, cradling her in comfort until the door creaked open and a gust of icy air rushed in like a reminder: she wasn't in the city anymore. Alaska greeted her at a crisp 34 degrees, a sharp and sudden drop her body was not prepared for. She shivered slightly, instinctively pulling her hoodie tighter until the pilot and co-pilot stepped forward, offering her a thick coat and wool scarf. "Thank you," she said, slipping them on with gratitude.

Then came the moment—stepping outside.

The cold bit at her cheeks and danced down her neck, but her eyes were too captivated to flinch. This place was... spectacular. Towering evergreens dusted in snow, a sky so open it felt infinite, and a hush in the air that felt sacred. She turned in place, slowly, a soft grin tugging at the corners of her lips. *How did I get here?*

Just a few months ago, she was hunched over a desk at a job that drained her soul, typing articles that no one would remember. Now she was flying private, wrapped in designer warmth, landing in a secluded corner of Alaska, and waiting to be picked up by a fleet of black trucks flanked by a full security detail.

She wasn't just existing anymore. She was *somebody*.

And in that clarity, she felt something deep and bittersweet. *Everyone in the world deserves to feel this at least once,* she thought.

She climbed into the backseat of the SUV, the heater already humming to life, and tucked herself into the corner like she was curling into a secret. She checked her phone—low bars, but enough for a quick message:

"Made it safely."

Within seconds, the group chat came alive.

Lisa: *"Yay!! Love you! Bundle up!"*

Emily: *"Make sure you see the Northern Lights!"*

Nelle smiled, her fingers lingering over the screen, before glancing out the frosted window as the driver received their directions.

Wherever this road was leading… she was ready.

Perched on the sloped shoulder of a wooded Alaskan hillside, the house stood like a watchful guardian, silently surveying the endless tapestry of forested valleys below. From its vantage point, the land spilled out in layers—soft ridges draped in green, laced with silver ribbons of water glinting under a restless, ever-changing sky.

Inside, light poured through wide windows like a living thing, warming the air and lending every corner a golden hush. The bedroom was especially breathtaking—panoramic glass framed a living canvas that shifted with the hours, from fog-kissed dawns to fire-orange sunsets that seemed to burn along the horizon. On clear days, the clouds pressed so close they might've been reached with a stretch of the hand.

The wraparound deck offered its own kind of magic: deep wicker chairs with plush cushions, perfect for sipping coffee or wine, sharing secrets, or saying nothing at all. The air was scented with pine and birch, carried gently on a breeze that hummed with birdsong and the occasional far-off stir of wildlife—maybe a fox, maybe a moose. Everything about the space was intentional. Peaceful. Isolated. Private.

From above, the house looked modest—silver-roofed and nestled beneath a canopy of trees, almost shy among a scattering of other remote dwellings. But inside, it told a different story. Luxury met wilderness. And although Roddy was nowhere in sight, the house buzzed with inaudible motion. Nelle was greeted by the house manager: a petite, brown-skinned woman with a sharp Kris Jenner bob, dressed in all black save for a pair of soft leather flats. Her presence was firm but warm, her voice clipped yet polite as she showed Nelle to her suite.

The cold that awaited outside was quickly forgotten. Inside, the heat was a balm—soft, radiant, and so complete that Nelle barely felt the shift in temperature. She walked through the space with a quiet sense of awe, phone in hand, snapping photos as instructed. She uploaded them to her Instagram profile with casual captions: a steaming cup of coffee, the moody skyline, the luxurious interior with snowy woods just beyond the glass. Subtle.

It didn't take long before the internet connected the dots. Blogs began reposting. Fans and followers filled the comments under her posts with reactions ranging from celebratory to cynical.

"I know that's right, girl. Stand by your man!"

"I can't believe she's staying with him after *everything*."

"Black women love them some struggle love."

And then, under that:

"He isn't broke, so there's no struggle. Just love."

Nelle read the notifications in silence, her phone buzzing steadily in her palm as she sat near the window. Her legs tucked beneath her, the wild Alaskan landscape stretching out before her like a painted myth. She didn't respond. She didn't need to.

As Nelle unzipped her suitcase and began laying out neatly folded clothes onto the ornate, pinewood dresser, the soft creak of the bedroom door startled her. Angela— the sharp, all-black-wearing house manager with the Kris Jenner cut—popped her head in without warning.

"Do you have your schedule?" she asked briskly.

Nelle blinked. "Hmm… no."

Without missing a beat, Angela slipped inside, iPad in hand, her fingers already scrolling. "Okay, let's go through it. Tonight, we're doing a candlelight dinner. Very soft, very moody. We've got photographers flying in to capture moments of you and Roderick together—intimate, natural, not too posed. But that's for later. Glam is setting up downstairs now."

Nelle stood still, trying to mentally process every word.

"Tomorrow, you'll be on set with Roddy. Just some behind-the-scenes stuff. Think casual, effortless, like you're just visiting. Off-guard candids are key—laugh a little, maybe look unsure in a couple of frames. The public loves a good *Is she back with him or not?* vibe. Makes you relatable. Keeps 'em guessing."

Angela kept talking as she paced slowly across the room, eyes never leaving the iPad screen.

"He shoots for 8 to 14 hours most days, so if you want, you can go shopping. He usually leaves a card or has one sent up. Thursday's the big one—he's off. Northern Lights date night. Very romantic. Very viral. Any questions?"

Nelle, trying to catch up with the storm of logistics, shook her head gently. "Uh, no."

Just then, a cheer erupted from downstairs—the unmistakable sound of celebration. Angela paused, finally glancing up from her screen. "Oh, and I'm Angela, by the way."

Nelle smiled, lips curling in that careful way she'd mastered for this new chapter of her life. "Nice to meet you. My name is Janelle."

A voice floated up from the living room, high with excitement: "He got the role! He's playing Irving in *The Yellow Brownstone!*"

Angela raised her eyebrows and flashed Nelle a look that said it all: Welcome to our world.

Once the coast was clear, Janelle sat on the edge of the bed, legs swinging softly as she pulled out her phone and dialed Reggie. It rang twice before going to voicemail.

"Hey," she said gently, her voice quiet, almost uncertain. "I just wanted to hear your voice… I made it. It's beautiful here. Cold, but beautiful. I miss you already." She paused, letting the silence linger before adding, "Call me when you can."

She ended the call and set her phone face down on the nightstand. A gentle hush fell over the room, interrupted only by the distant sound of laughter echoing from downstairs and the constant movement of people through the house—doors opening, heels clicking, coffee brewing. Everyone seemed busy, performing productivity like it was part of a scene being directed somewhere just out of view.

But Janelle didn't mind. The chaos felt far away from the peaceful bubble of her room. The view from her window was magnetic—Alaskan hillsides stretching endlessly. It was a living painting, too beautiful to leave untouched.

She walked to her bag and pulled out her sketchpad, the edges worn, corners slightly curled from travel. Curling up near the window, she opened to a fresh page and began sketching with a soft pencil. Her hand moved slowly at first, lines forming the strong silhouette of the trees in the distance, their spiky limbs etched with careful detail. She captured the dips and rises of the land, the flow of the distant river like a ribbon gliding between valleys.

The clouds above were more challenging—pillowy and light, yet heavy in their presence. She shaded them gently, letting the contrast build in soft layers. She drew the way the light touched the snow, how it sparkled in some places and melted in others, revealing patches of earthy green and stone. It was calming, the movement of her hand, the quiet rhythm of creating something from observation. Just pencil and paper, and a moment that belonged entirely to her.

Evening crept in quietly, faster than Janelle had anticipated. The sun dipped behind the Alaskan hills, and then came the sound—that voice. Deep, familiar, warm. It sent an involuntary chill down her spine.

Roddy.

He knocked softly at her door, and she quickly paused her game of Tetris, the blocks frozen mid-fall.

"Come in," she said, her tone composed, legs crossed neatly on the edge of the bed.

He entered, his face lighting up the moment their eyes met. "Hey, beautiful," he said, the corners of his lips curving into a smile that felt both charming and nervous. He looked younger like this—unguarded.

"Hi," she replied, rising to greet him with a brief hug. It was warm, but distant, more polite than passionate.

Roddy was still in costume, fresh off set. A period piece, no doubt—he wore a weathered sheriff's uniform, complete with a leather holster at his hip and dust smeared across his boots. Even in character, he seemed softened in her presence, almost boyish. There was something about Janelle that made him shy, made his usual bravado fall away. He shifted from foot to foot, then finally said, "I'm so glad you're here. We finally get to have that dinner I promised you."

He gave a gentle nod, glancing down the hall. "I'm going to shower and get myself together. Angela's going to bring you something to wear. I'll meet you downstairs in a bit, okay?"

Janelle gave a soft smile, the kind that didn't reach her eyes. "Okay."

He lingered a moment, then turned and left, the scent of set makeup and pine clinging faintly in the air behind him.

Moments later, Angela entered like clockwork, arms draped in a black gown that glimmered subtly under the light. "Here you are," she said, holding it up for Janelle's approval. Not that it was really a question.

Behind her, glam poured in—a stylist, a makeup artist, a hair girl with hot tools already buzzing to life. Janelle barely had time to blink. She stood, wordless, letting them peel away her casual layers and drape her in something more cinematic.

She had no say, no opinion, just stillness. A body being shaped and molded into a picture-perfect muse. While Roddy was in his room, hoping to connect, Janelle was upstairs becoming the version of herself that the world expected to see.

An hour later, the house was quiet—eerily so. The stylists, the manager, the assistant with the earpiece constantly buzzing—gone. All of them staying in nearby hotels, scattered throughout the frozen town like chess pieces removed from the board. But not her. She was staying with him.

When Lisa first mentioned the arrangement, it hadn't seemed like a big deal. She'd shrugged it off, too busy being swept up in the chaos to give it much thought. But now, standing at the top of the stairs in this unfamiliar home, silence settling over the wooden beams like a blanket of snow, a knot began to form in her stomach.

She didn't know Roddy like that. Not *really*. Not well enough to be alone with him overnight, not without a camera crew or someone just down the hall. And though her thoughts trembled with uncertainty, her exterior didn't betray her. Outside, she was flawless—dazzling. The black gown clung to her like a liquid shadow, hugging every curve, the fabric catching fire in the low light whenever she moved.

Downstairs, Roddy waited.

He stood by the fireplace, one arm resting casually along the mantle, the other cradling a glass of cognac. The flames flickered and danced beside him, casting amber across the lines of his face. The oversized window next to him framed a view so pristine it looked almost surreal—trees dusted in frost, the tiny twinkle of outdoor lights, and the distant rustle of nocturnal animals navigating the snow.

He turned slightly when he heard her heels touch the floorboards. She was the picture of poise, elegance in motion. But beneath it all, her heart beat too fast, and her thoughts spiraled quietly: *What happens next?*

Dinner was spread out like a scene from a film—warm dishes lined the length of the long wooden table, steam curling into the air, and tall candles flickering in the center, their flames swaying in rhythm with the gentle draft that rolled through the room. Roddy, ever the charmer, smiled as he took the back of Nelle's hand and pressed a soft kiss against her skin.

"After you," he said, pulling out her chair with a grace that almost made her forget how tense she felt.

The lighting was low and intimate.

Outside, the sounds of the Alaskan wilderness continued to murmur—a rustle of branches, the far-off hoot of an owl. Inside, it was quiet. So quiet that Nelle could hear her heartbeat, steady but fast. Roddy moved through the space like he'd lived there his whole life, far more confidently than that night in his condo.

Trying to soften the quiet, she asked, "How long do you have to stay out here?"

"Twenty-one days," he said, pouring water into her glass. "But I'll be home before Thanksgiving, which is good. I know Lisa said you'd be, um, meeting my family. What do you think about that?"

Nelle froze for a second, her mind racing to catch up. She hadn't thought about that—not even for a second. In fact, she hadn't planned on being there more than five minutes.

"I'm not sure," she said, carefully. "Um… my family wanted me home for the holidays."

"Oh, nice," he nodded, undeterred. "We can go together if you want. Maybe an hour or two with my family, then we head to yours."

He spoke like this was real. Like they were real.

Nelle blinked. "Oh…" she whispered, caught off guard by his forwardness. "I didn't really think to tell my parents about this…you know…"

"Oh, nah, I get it," he replied quickly, a touch of embarrassment creeping into his smile as he began sharing out the dishes between them. "Well, I just wanted to make sure I did everything right this time."

He laughed, light and genuine, gesturing around the house. "I know where everything is, so you don't have to lift a finger. Think of this as a nice vacation."

Nelle smiled softly, watching him. And for a moment, just a flicker, she forgot the lines between pretend and reality.

The night unraveled with an unexpected ease— smooth, warm, almost too natural. Over dessert, they laughed more than either of them anticipated. Roderick had been on his absolute best behavior. No lingering touches, no suggestive glances, no attempts at closing the space between them. He was measured, respectful even. And for that, Nelle felt grateful.

Now seated in front of the crackling fireplace, a half-empty glass of wine in her hand, she turned to him and asked softly, "Do you ever get lonely in this profession?"

"I do," he admitted, not missing a beat. "I don't know who to trust. The people around me aren't friends, they're employees—people I have to treat like friends just to keep some sense of normal. No one wants to be around someone like me unless they're getting something out of it. Especially when they know they can... you know?"

"But doesn't that blur the lines of professionalism and pleasure?" she asked, eyes narrowed slightly, genuinely curious.

"It does," he said, with a heavy exhale. "And then I become the bad guy. The one who has to scold the very people I encouraged to believe we were... friends, in some way. I take it for what it is. I don't get angry—I just accept it. If I have to fire someone for not doing their job because they got too comfortable, well… I own that. I apologize. And I move on. Try to do better next time."

He looked at her, and then, really looked at her. The firelight flickered across his face, softening the edges, illuminating the quiet admiration in his eyes.

"You're really beautiful, you know that?"

Nelle blushed, a small smile tugging at her lips. "Oh… thank you. And you're very handsome."

She paused, the moment suspended in the air like a breath not yet released. Then, with a soft sigh, she stood. "I think I'm going to head to bed. I've been up since 3 AM."

Roddy sprang to his feet, almost too quickly. "Yeah, of course. That makes sense. Did you want me to walk you up?"

"Oh no, it's okay," she said gently, already backing away. "I'm just going to shower and doze off. But thank you for dinner. And for the conversation."

He nodded, lingering where he stood, watching her walk away.

And she felt it—his gaze, the weight of unspoken things resting on her shoulders. Each step upstairs felt heavier than the last. Guilt tugged at her ribs as she climbed, invisible fingers pulling her back into the reality of what this all was.

What am I doing? she thought, shutting the door behind her. *What am I really doing?*

The next morning passed quickly.

Reggie finally called, but the conversation felt distant—his voice competing with the jarring sounds of power drills, shouting men, and the clatter of construction in the background. It caught Janelle off guard, making her realize just how far she felt from anything familiar. She missed home. Each hour she spent in this surreal arrangement chipped away at her enthusiasm, leaving a hollow ache behind.

However, visiting Roddy on set felt like stepping into a parallel universe—one meticulously crafted, yet entirely artificial. Elaborate props, bustling crew members, towering camera rigs, and actors in full period costume moved about with seamless coordination. It was a world built on illusion, but somehow, when the cameras rolled, it all felt real. That was the magic of it.

She caught Roddy's eye in between takes, and he smiled—warm, familiar. She walked over to him and gave him a light hug, his costume slightly stiff beneath her touch. Then, just as quickly, he was gone again, slipping into character with practiced ease.

Janelle stood back and watched. His delivery was sharp, emotionally grounded. His body language, voice, expressions—it was like a switch had been flipped. One moment, he was Roddy. The next, he was someone entirely different. It was mesmerizing.

What impressed her most was his focus. He not only knew his lines, but the lines of his co-stars too, gently whispering cues or offering an understanding nod when someone fumbled. There was no arrogance in his guidance, only the quiet confidence of someone who had mastered his craft.

And now, she understood. She understood the applause, the admiration, the obsession. Roderick didn't just act—he transformed. This world was where he thrived. This was his truth. On set, he wasn't just another actor—he was a legend in the making. A force. A man with purpose. And watching him in his element, Janelle felt something shift within her. Maybe, just maybe, she wasn't seeing the role anymore… she was finally seeing the man.

They started off making silly videos for social media—inside jokes, trending dances, playful back-and-forth banter. It was supposed to be content, promotional fluff. But somewhere between the laughs and the filters, something shifted. The line between fiction and reality began to grow legs. Janelle's smile, once calculated and camera-ready, became something else entirely. It was genuine. Soft. Unforced. She was actually having fun.

In his trailer, they rapped old-school songs with offbeat confidence, cracking up when they missed lines or lost rhythm. They shared lunch like old friends, elbows brushing, conversations flowing without pressure or performance. And when it was time for her to leave him to his work, she found herself lingering—not because she had to, but because she wanted to.

Back on set, she pulled out her sketchpad. The world around her faded as her pencil danced across the page. She captured Roderick in motion—each look, each subtle shift in energy. Her drawings held layers: sharp lines for his intensity, soft smudges for his vulnerability, shadow work for his range.

She didn't just sketch him as an actor. She captured him as a man, in all his moods and transformations. It was raw, expressive, and remarkably alive. Inspiration like this only came once, maybe twice, in a lifetime—and she wasn't about to waste it.

By the time shooting wrapped that evening, the entire crew gathered under a large white tent. The mood was warm, celebratory. Fold-out tables were stacked with food, laughter echoing from every direction. They swapped stories, toasted to past films, and reminisced about the journey that brought them all here.

Janelle found herself nestled beside Roderick as though she belonged there. Without realizing it, she'd slipped into his embrace, her back to his chest, her body naturally settling between his legs. His arms curled around her without hesitation—protective, intimate. There was nothing performative about it. It just… was.

As the voices around her softened into background noise, Janelle leaned her head back against his shoulder, eyes fluttering closed. And in the quiet comfort of that moment, surrounded by strangers who felt like family, she let herself rest—drifting off to sleep wrapped in something that felt dangerously close to real.

CHAPTER 17.

NORTHERN

LIGHTS

The day had been perfectly planned—today was the day they'd chase the Northern Lights. Janelle could hardly contain her excitement. She woke up early, meticulously deleting old photos and videos from her phone, clearing space to capture every second of what she hoped would be an unforgettable experience. Her sketchpad was packed, along with a fresh set of Derwent colored pencils. She was ready for the scenery, for the magic, for whatever this adventure would bring.

The drive from Fairbanks to Chena Hot Springs was nothing short of breathtaking. Snow-capped mountains stretched across the horizon, the open road slicing through a winter wonderland. Roderick and his crew filled the van with light conversation, their warmth and kindness making Nelle feel completely at ease. They were thoughtful, respectful, and above all, made sure she was always included.

With each turn of the winding roads, Nelle snapped photos and shot videos, sharing moments that didn't feel like work—they felt like joy. There were multiple scenic stops, and each one felt like stepping into a postcard. The photographers who traveled with them clicked away with their professional cameras, capturing intimate moments in crisp 4K: Nelle gazing at the sky with wonder, her hand in Roderick's, the two laughing in the snow.

In real time, the team downloaded images to their laptops, swiftly editing and uploading to Getty Images and Twitter. The buzz was immediate. Lisa texted them both play-by-play updates of the media frenzy.

"You're trending. #Relle is BACK!"

It was surreal. The internet was alive with speculation, celebration, and fan edits. Nelle watched it all unfold from the backseat of the van, her phone lighting up with likes, reposts, and DMs. It was as if the world had been waiting for this—to see them together again. But unlike before, this time felt different. This time, it felt like she wasn't just part of a story. She was illustrating it.

The day had already felt like something out of a '90s love story—nostalgic, slow-burning, impossibly romantic. And by 3:30 PM, as the sky began to dim, they were tucked away beneath the soft hush of winter, settling into a quiet corner of the campsite. Roderick and Janelle sat together under the gentle slope of a canvas tent, warmed by a small portable heater powered by the van parked nearby. Around them, others dotted the snow-covered landscape—his team, a few brave fans, influencers filming content in hushed excitement, and camera crews from Bravo and Hulu capturing ambient B-roll, pretending not to eavesdrop.

Despite the buzz of bodies and cameras, their little tent felt like a secret. A moment stolen from the chaos. Roddy's arm draped gently around Nelle's shoulders, pulling her just a bit closer. The temperature was dropping, their breaths becoming visible wisps in the fading light, but it didn't matter. The air was charged with anticipation.

Then, it began.

At first, it was just a faint glow. A ribbon of pale green light teased the edge of the horizon. Slowly, gracefully, it began to stretch, expanding across the sky like a living, breathing thing. Nelle gasped softly as waves of emerald, lavender, and icy blue shimmered and danced above them, bending and curling like brushstrokes across a cosmic canvas.

It was otherworldly—no photo or video could ever do it justice. The lights flickered like silk in the wind, their movement fluid and hypnotic. Time stood still. The hush that fell over the campsite was sacred. Even the influencers put their phones down for a moment, caught in the spell.

Nelle leaned into Roderick, her cheek brushing his shoulder, her eyes wide with wonder. The aurora felt like it was reaching just for them, a private show stitched into the sky. It wasn't just beautiful—it was overwhelming. Like the universe had paused to remind them of something ancient and eternal.

He looked down at her, watching her face glow beneath the lights, her eyes reflecting green and violet. And in that instant, nothing else mattered—not the fans, not the cameras, not the "make-believe." It was just the two of them, wrapped in warmth beneath a sky full of magic.

His heart raced with anticipation, louder than the whispers of wind brushing against the tent. *"Do it now. Now is your chance,"* the voice inside him urged. So he listened.

With a tender touch, he lifted his hand, placing an index finger just beneath her chin. Gently, deliberately, he tilted her face toward his. Their lips hovered—so close they could feel each other's breath, their mouths perfectly aligned. Behind them, the Northern Lights burned bright, casting a surreal glow around their silhouettes. It was cinematic, divine—a moment designed for a kiss.

Their eyes locked.

Her breath caught.

But just as the world leaned in… she pulled away.

Nelle's heart clenched in her chest. Embarrassment. Guilt. Panic. It all hit her at once. She could barely look at him. She didn't mean to reject him—not cruelly, not publicly—but something inside her wouldn't let her cross that line. Not now. Maybe not ever. Her heart just wasn't there.

Roddy stayed frozen, hand suspended in the air, lips parted in confusion. The soft light from the aurora painted his face in streaks of green and purple, but all Nelle saw was the hurt in his eyes. He didn't speak, didn't move. He knew better than to follow her. He let her go.

She turned and walked quickly, eyes stinging, chest aching. Each step back to the van felt like a betrayal. *What did I just do?* she thought. She couldn't shake the feeling that she'd broken something precious. Not just the moment, but maybe something deeper.

Curling into the corner of the van, she wiped her eyes and stared out into the dark, glowing sky. The only way forward now was the truth. Painful or not. Honest or not. It was all she had left.

The ride back to the house was cloaked in silence, heavy and suffocating. Roderick didn't say a word, and neither did anyone else in the van. The tension was palpable, thick enough to choke on, and everyone instinctively respected it. Janelle sat pressed against the window, her face turned away, letting the tears fall quietly. No dramatic sobs—just silent streams of guilt and confusion.

She felt awful.

Back at the house, the warmth of the interior did little to soothe her. She packed in silence, folding her clothes with slow, heavy hands. Her flight was in the morning, and all she could think about was home. Distance. Clarity. Escape.

The night stretched ahead, and she knew—without question—that they'd be alone. Everyone else kept their distance, pretending not to notice what had happened. But she could feel the shift in the air, the way glances lingered too long or didn't land at all.

Roderick was downstairs, sitting by the fireplace. He looked calm—too calm. His glass half full, the amber swirl of whiskey catching the flames.

She approached him slowly, out of her snow suit now—just leggings and a top. Her hair was in a high ponytail, swaying gently with each step. She felt exposed, small, and uncertain.

"I'm sorry," she whispered.

He didn't look at her right away, just lifted his brows slightly, as if her voice barely registered.

"It's cool," he said, his tone low and distant.

"I think you're a great guy... I just... I didn't come into this with the intention... of... um..."

"...being with me." He finished it for her with a short, bitter laugh. "It's cool."

The ice clinked as he swirled the drink in his hand, staring into it like it held the answers.

"I'm used to it. Respect to you, though. For real. Most women would've just pretended. Stayed for the perks, the clout. Pretend like they care while they build their little exit plans."

She swallowed hard.

"I don't know what your plans are after this, Janelle. But I respect the honesty. Staying for security versus staying for me? That's a big difference. You chose to walk away. That says something."

He paused, his voice lower now. "Then they say, 'he don't date Black women.' And I do—I try. Black women are my first choice. But where do we go when we're not chosen? When we're not even considered? Nobody talks about that."

"Don't do that," she said, shaking her head. "I'm one woman. I don't represent everyone you've ever dated."

He gave a dry chuckle. "Yeah. Janelle. The exception. Out of the many. And because I don't treat women like Future, because I don't play that toxic role... I get boxed out. Dismissed. Ignored."

He looked deeply into her for the first time, directly. "And let me guess... we can just be friends, right?"

"I would love that," she said, voice small but sincere.

He let out a long, exhausted sigh. "It's cool, Janelle. Honestly. The car will be here for you at six. I hope you have a safe trip home."

And just like that, he got up, bottle and glass in hand, and walked upstairs. She listened as the soft click of his bedroom door echoed down the hallway.

Janelle stood frozen, staring into the flickering fire, her chest giving the illusion of it rising and falling. The only sound in the room was the pop of burning wood—until she finally exhaled the breath she didn't know she was holding.

Back at the condo, Janelle could hardly focus. The weight of her choices settled heavily in her chest like wet cement. Rejecting America's golden boy while secretly carrying on a forbidden relationship under his roof. Guilt gnawed at her, relentless and raw. She wanted to disappear.

Before she could even process it, her phone rang—Lisa. The timing was cruel, but perfect.

In her office, Lisa was drowning in the commotion.

Her voicemail flooded with Roddy's rage, each message louder and more insistent than the last. He wasn't just angry—he was out for blood.

With Janelle dodging her calls, Lisa had no choice but to push forward. It was Friday morning, and the office buzzed with its usual hum, but Lisa moved differently—a tension in her shoulders, a storm in her chest. On her way in, she snatched a copy of *People* Magazine from the newsstand downstairs. Janelle graced the cover, radiant and composed, a national moment.

For a fleeting second, pride softened Lisa's nerves. She flipped through the pages, smiling at the powerful spread. The digital files rolled in simultaneously, ready for printing and archiving in the thick portfolio that lined the back of her office. It should have been a moment of celebration, but it turned into a crisis.

"Lisa!" Roddy's voice boomed through the speaker.

She froze. "Did you see the images I emailed you?"

"Fuck the images. I want her fired. Come up with something—she came here, I ended things. Make it go in my favor. I want this over with. I don't want to keep paying this girl."

Lisa blinked, stunned. "Wait, what? What happened? There are so many pictures—you guys look like you're having such a good time."

"That's not important. I have to go. Clip the contract and send me a statement or something to post on my Instagram."

Click. The line went dead.

Lisa remained seated, staring at the phone, her hands trembling just slightly. The magazine in her lap now felt like a bomb. The pages were glossy and beautiful, but none of it mattered.

Janelle sat on the edge of her bed, shoulders hunched, phone vibrating relentlessly beside her. Lisa was calling again. And this time, there would be no dodging. With a clenched jaw and fists tight in her lap, she finally answered, her voice barely above a whisper.

"Hello?" she said, damp curls dripping onto her bare shoulders.

A rush of city traffic bled through the speaker, followed by Lisa's unmistakable roar: "What the fuck happened in Alaska?"

Janelle froze. Where was her best friend?

"Lisa? Please… calm down."

"I *am* calm. This is me, *calm*," Lisa snapped, voice full of fire.

Desperate to defend herself, Janelle blurted out the truth: "Roddy tried to kiss me, and I didn't kiss him back!"

The silence that followed was deafening. And then, Lisa's rage shifted.

"What? Why would he do that?"

With a deep exhale, Janelle felt understood. Like an anchor had lifted off her shoulders, she paused, her voice shaking with emotion.

"I don't know. I—I felt horrible. I didn't come into this for that…"

To her surprise, Lisa agreed.

Furious, yes—but no longer at her.

"I'll call you back," Lisa said, voice low and burning with a new purpose.

Click.

Janelle was left staring at her phone, unsure if things had just fallen apart—or started to fall into place.

Millions were at stake—and Lisa didn't lose. Not in business. Not in this game. With steady fingers and a racing heart, she flipped through her contacts and landed on the one man who could shift the tide: Jerry, from The Hollywood Foreign Press Association.

"Jerry!" she said, trying to keep it together, though the panic in her voice bled through.

"Hey there, lovely," he replied with the calm of someone enjoying their morning toast.

"Jerry, I need a huge favor."

"Oh, Lisa. You're my girl. But you don't sound too good... what's going on?"

"It's Roderick..."

His tone changed instantly. "Listen, he's a great actor, great kid—but he's up against Majors in the press, and Majors is coming out on top. That *Loki* performance is causing waves. He didn't get the nom."

"I figured, believe me. I saw it coming. But that's why I'm calling. I'm not asking for him to win—just the nomination."

There was a beat of silence on the other end.

"At the Globes? That's a huge ask; he won't win, and you know it. He's up against Austin Butler and Hugh Jackman. He's not even eligible for a nomination. You want me to put him in that category? Seriously?"

"Jerry, I'm begging you. I know the studio didn't back it, but I will. Personally."

"You'll fund the nomination... not the win?"

"I mean, look at who you just mentioned. If he wins, it won't even seem real. But a nomination? That's believable. That gives us leverage."

Another pause.

"Hmm, I don't know. He didn't even come up in conversation among the committee."

"Jerry, I know. But we have way better scripts coming down the pipeline. More endorsements. More followers. It's all coming together."

He sighed. "I'll get him on for half."

Lisa exhaled, calculating instantly. "Perfect. I'll wire the money this afternoon. Just text me the details."

To Lisa, it was a small investment for a massive return. A nomination could elevate Roddy's industry clout overnight, allowing him to demand more from the studios—and giving her the perfect excuse to raise her rates.

Nelle's contract? Just pennies in a bucket now.

As she hung up, a new campaign confirmation lit up her screen—one she'd been hesitating on. Over a quarter million dollars. Just like that, the decision was made. Roddy would have to play along. Because in Lisa's world, compliance wasn't optional—especially when the money started talking.

As much as she missed him—craved him, even—Nelle couldn't bring herself to climb out of bed. The world outside felt too loud, too demanding. Beneath the sheets, she found her only refuge. Reggie, ever attuned to her, could hear the sadness in her voice when they spoke. She didn't need to ask—he knew. And so, quietly, he came to her.

With a plate of her favorite food in hand, he stepped into her condo, cautious, respectful of her space, her spirit. He had a surprise tucked away—a gift he'd planned—but something told him now wasn't the time.

From beneath the comforter, she heard the door close and felt her guard begin to melt. She hadn't even seen him yet, but already, her heart softened at the thought of his presence. Reggie placed the food in the fridge, then moved toward her, his eyes catching her reflection in the mirror. She lay facing away, hips peeking out from beneath the blanket.

Without a word, he undressed down to his boxers, climbing gently onto the bed. She shifted, giving him space. And in the stillness of the morning, with the city slowly waking beneath them, he wrapped his arms around her.

He smelled of fresh soap and warmth.

She kissed the inside of his forearm, a silent thank you. He brushed her hair from her face, revealing soft, worn features. Pressing a kiss to her cheek, he held her close.

In that quiet, intimate moment, no words were needed. The ache remained—but now, so did the comfort. Together, they drifted back into sleep.

CHAPTER 18.

FRIENDSGIVING

Across the web, the interview ignited like wildfire—over 940,000 views in just eight hours. Screenshots flooded social media, comments surged, and everyone had an opinion. But as the sun dipped below the skyline and Lisa's office began to empty, filled with tired goodbyes and flickering exit signs, she remained seated, unmoved.

The day had gone smoother than expected, despite a few hiccups. She'd managed to get Roddy on the phone, and though he didn't like what he heard, though he raged, accused, and resented her for the control she held, he complied. He had no choice.

The nomination, the press, the arrival on the carpet with Janelle at his side... it was all part of the design. It wasn't just about career control—it was a rebrand, a resurrection. And come December 9th, when the names were announced, his would sit beside legends: Hugh Jackman, Jeremy Pope, and Brendan Fraser. Even if he hadn't earned it, the perception would be that he belonged.

With the buzz of her office dimming, Lisa leaned back in her chair, the weight of the day finally easing. She sipped her drink, its chill matching the cold calm in her heart. Emily was off somewhere with Aaron, and Janelle was now ghosting her texts. But none of that mattered now.

This was the moment she'd been waiting for.

She reached for her phone and dialed.

Finally.

"Hi," she said, her voice soft, smooth—like velvet over steel.

Meanwhile, Nelle and Reggie lay tangled beneath linen sheets, bare and breathless. Her fingers traced lazy circles through the soft curls on his chest, her heart quietly thudding with words she hadn't yet said—but soon would. She was in love. Deeply. Dangerously.

"Lisa says I have to go to PA for Thanksgiving," she murmured, her voice muffled by his shoulder.

"Is that so?" he replied, arm draped securely around her.

"Yes," she said, lifting her gaze to meet his.

Reggie nodded thoughtfully. "My daughter is usually with me for the holiday. My mother and sisters fly in from the DR. I'd love for you to meet them. Come to the Long Island house. Choose the car you want."

A smile crept onto her lips. "I'd love that, honestly. To meet your family." She paused, thinking aloud. "In PA, I don't think I'll be there long. Then I'll see my parents. Maybe I can get to Long Island in the evening… around seven?"

He chuckled. "That's a busy schedule. I don't want you overworked and exhausted." He snuggled her closer, pressing a kiss to her forehead. "We'll figure it out."

Then, her phone buzzed—a reminder text.

It was from Lisa earlier that day: *The People interview is on YouTube.*

Nelle sighed, unbothered, but showed Reggie anyway. His eyes brightened with pride.

"Let's watch it," he said, practically bouncing.

With a smirk and a roll of her eyes, Nelle opened the YouTube app and played the interview. There she was—dolled up, composed, magnetic. Reggie moved back and forth from the kitchen, plating dinner and peeking over to catch glimpses of her on-screen.

"I did really good in this," she said, laughter spilling out, a little stunned by her own performance.

Reggie returned to her side, the food warming behind them. She kissed him—slow, certain, hungry. What started as affection unfurled into something deeper. Their bodies found each other again, the air thick with tenderness.

In the background, her voice rang out from the screen: *"I love Roddy. Our relationship will overcome this."*

And yet, here she was—breathless, undone, wrapped in a man who wasn't him.

The perfect lie told in pixels.

The perfect truth lived in the flesh.

The next day, Lisa was back in her element—high heels clicking across the office floor, coffee in hand, eyes scanning through her inbox with ease. Her favorite trick? Scheduled emails. She could be lounging oceanside or stuck in London traffic on vacation, and somewhere, someone was receiving a perfectly-timed message from her desk like clockwork. Power in automation.

But today, her high came from more than productivity. She'd spent the entire night on the phone with Brenton, navigating their complicated history, untangling their feelings. No titles. No pressure. Just a beginning—imperfect but honest. And that, to Lisa, was progress.

About an hour into her morning, Aaron called. She'd texted him earlier to check in on his placements, and in classic Aaron fashion, he didn't wait—he showed up. His driver pulled up within fifteen minutes, quick as ever.

Lisa's face lit up when he stepped inside. "You smell lovely," she grinned, hugging him warmly.

"Thank you, thank you," he smiled back, settling into the chair across from her. "How are you doing?"

"I'm well, thank you. So, you've got the *TIME* cover coming up, and then *GQ*, January issue. You excited?"

"Honestly, I am. Still adjusting to this whole celebrity thing. Before, it was just *'play the game'*, do a few interviews on the field, and maybe a licensed brand collab. But now? Man, there's so much money to be made. Magazine covers are paying me to be on them, brands cutting checks for single posts. Your negotiations? On point."

Lisa laughed. "Thank you!"

"But," Aaron added, leaning forward, "I did want to talk to you about something else…"

Lisa raised a brow, intrigued. "Of course. What's up?"

"Emily. Your friend…"

Lisa blinked. "How'd you know we were friends-friends, not just business casual?"

"She told me. Said you recommended me. First date and all."

"College," Lisa nodded, a nostalgic smile forming. "We go way back."

Aaron grinned. "So you weren't gonna tell me she was your girl like that? You know I'm out here—no wife, no kids, a damn catch. And you didn't think to hook us up? You just sent her my card?"

Lisa burst out laughing. "I'm not a matchmaker, I'm a moneymaker! And so is she. It made sense."

"Well, apparently it did," Aaron chuckled. "Because now, we're pretty serious. And I'm thinking... around the holidays... I want to pop the question. Need to get a ring, and who better to help me?"

Lisa froze, a tear nearly forming. "Oh my God. *My* Emily?"

"Yeah," he nodded, soft and sure. "I knew from the moment I met her. She's light. Smart. Playful. Her whole office is pink—did you know that?"

Lisa laughed. "Of course. I helped her decorate it."

Aaron laughed too, eyes bright. "Ya'll wild. But seriously? I want to spend my life making her happy. Not sometimes. *Every* day. That laugh and that smile she got, precious."

Lisa pouted, her voice catching. "Awww. Of course I'll help you find the ring!"

As the morning blurred into afternoon, laughter echoing in the office like old music, elsewhere, Nelle and Reggie slipped into Midtown—unaware of the engagement brewing, or how love was quietly blossoming all around them.

Reggie was nervous, the kind of nervous that made his palms sweat even in the cool breeze of the early afternoon. The seasons were shifting, autumn creeping in with its bite and breath, and he made sure Nelle dressed warmly before flagging down a taxi. She'd barely returned to the gallery since the window incident, only trusting the quiet updates about repairs. The thought of facing it again made her stomach turn.

Security was still posted out front, stiff in posture and tone. To Nelle, it was overkill—protection that felt more like a spotlight. What was once her sacred creative space was now slowly becoming a tourist trap, Instagrammed and hashtagged into something she hadn't intended. What hurt most was how quickly the world could take something intimate and turn it into a spectacle.

But today was different.

As they stepped out of the cab, Reggie paid the driver and added a generous tip, nerves fluttering behind his smile. Nelle glanced up, immediately clocking the curtains drawn across the gallery windows. That was new. Her brows furrowed, suspicion blooming.

She turned to him. "Why are the windows covered?"

Reggie grinned softly, the nerves still there but dressed in calm. "Close your eyes," he said.

Before she could protest, he pulled the spare key from his pocket—the one he'd secretly duplicated from her keychain weeks ago.

Nelle's storefront had undergone a loving transformation—one that could only come from passion and intentionality. What was once a stark, sterile expanse of white, now breathed with new life. The walls that had stood bare and indifferent were now layered with deep, warm hues: Olive, Arabica, Caramel, and Crema—tones that whispered intimacy, depth, and story.

The exposed brick running down one side was refined with a smooth polish, contrasted by pristine white walls that would let each piece of art speak freely. Off-white moldings and more expressive colors were layered proudly below striking glass sculptures in the color cinnabar, adding dimension and movement to the space. Every corner designed to feel lived in and alive.

Reggie didn't just restore the gallery—he restored Nelle's spirit. This wasn't just a space for showing work anymore. It was hers. A sanctuary reborn. A place where art didn't have to fight to be felt.

The tears welled in her eyes as she stepped past it all, her fingertips gliding softly along the newly painted walls—warm and familiar, like an embrace. Her nails, olive-toned and almond-shaped, blended seamlessly with the hues around her, as if they'd been chosen by fate, not fashion. It was all too perfect. Too intimate. She let the tears fall freely, unafraid this time, as Reggie's voice floated in from behind her like a gentle hum.

"When you went to Alaska, I called in some favors and we got to work," he said, almost bashfully. "I know you mentioned these colors when we were cleaning… so I just made a mental note of everything."

But his words became a distant echo, lost in the heartbeat of the space around her. She ascended the stairs slowly, reverently, noticing how even the steps had been seen to—repainted, buffed, and polished until they shined with care. The railings were repaired, some even replaced. Every detail whispered: *You were remembered.*

Turning back, her eyes found him, and the weight of it all—the love, the restoration, the quiet devotion—

crashed over her. She stepped toward him, tears streaming, hands gently cupping his face. Standing on her toes to meet his lips, she breathed the words that had lived quietly in her chest until now:

"I love you."

"I love you, too," he said.

As the days grew shorter and the leaves turned gold, crimson, and amber, the girls found themselves wrapped in the silent thrill of new love and late-night laughter. There was something soft about this season—something that made it easy to fall into the arms of someone who made you feel seen. But while joy bloomed in private corners, tension brewed just beneath the surface.

Roddy remained on set, consumed by his work, only resurfacing for his GQ cover shoot on November 9th. Nelle showed up, of course—physically present, poised as ever—but mentally, she was miles away. What had once been a platonic relationship had now morphed into quiet disdain. Their work had soured into something cold, bitter. They hadn't officially revisited things, but somewhere along the way, they had silently become enemies. He couldn't look at her without the sting of rejection prickling his pride.

She hadn't told him or Lisa about Reggie.

She couldn't.

The fallout would be explosive. So, she fed them breadcrumbs, keeping them in the loop just enough to avoid suspicion when it came to her whereabouts. But Reggie knew. He knew she was tiptoeing around them. And he hated it.

Reggie wasn't a boy—he was a man. And in his world, love wasn't something to be hidden or denied. He was done playing games, tired of being the secret in someone else's story. He wanted her, fully. Openly. And he was willing to pay the price—literally. He offered to buy her out of her contract, to give her freedom from the tangled obligations she no longer wanted.

Yet, she declined.

But with every headline, every tagged photo, every whisper online, he felt himself shrinking into the background. A ghost. A bystander. As if loving her made him a villain. He didn't even have social media, but his daughter did. And with Thanksgiving around the corner, the idea that she might scroll across Nelle's face and piece together a manufactured truth—that her father was some careless paramour—left him unsettled. He wanted to do this right.

In the days leading up to Thanksgiving, the group chat was ablaze—buzzing with spicy, emoji-laced messages and playful debates about the latest plot twist: Lisa and Brenton were unofficially back together. After a rollercoaster of ups and downs, they had recommitted to one another, and Lisa wasn't shy about letting everyone know.

But not everyone was thrilled.

Emily remained skeptical, many of her replies laced with passive judgment. She still didn't trust Brenton—never had—and deep down, she hoped Lisa would catch feelings for one of Aaron's friends at the Friendsgiving she was hosting. Brenton, conveniently, wasn't on the guest list. To Emily, this was strategy. To Lisa, it felt messy.

Lisa defended her man like her life depended on it. "He's different now," she argued in voice notes and texts. "He's got a new job. He listens. He shows up. It's not like before." Money wasn't a sore spot anymore, and for the first time in a long time, she genuinely felt cared for.

Janelle, watching the drama unfold from the sidelines, kept her opinions measured in the chat, but privately, she was fuming. She texted Emily outside the thread, calling her out. "It's wrong," she wrote. "If Lisa says he makes her happy, why can't that be enough?" But the message wasn't just about Lisa and Brenton. It was about her.

Janelle was projecting, deeply. What she really wanted was the space to share her own love story, without judgment. To be met with the same compassion and grace she was now advocating for Lisa. Because loving someone openly, in a world that loves to pick sides, takes courage.

But Emily didn't care. Her stance was firm. She didn't want any of her friends settling—especially not for men who, in her eyes, weren't operating on the same level. Dating down felt like betrayal. Not just of self-worth, but of the collective standard they'd worked so hard to uphold. To her, it screamed imbalance, a silent invitation for future heartbreak. But to keep the peace, she complied.

"Fine," Emily typed, clearly begrudging. "Brenton can come. But Lisa, as my friend, just know—I invited Ryan. And I hope you aren't closed off to the possibility of meeting new people."

Lisa let out a deep, weary sigh. "Mmhm," she replied. Not a yes. Not a no. Just a space-filling syllable meant to end the conversation without starting a new one.

However, the chat pinged a little longer, everyone chiming in with final confirmations about dishes, drinks, and outfits. Everyone except Nelle.

Her phone was on Do Not Disturb, lying face down on the bathroom counter while the cold water crashed over her like punishment. Her relationship with Reggie was a secret, and the secrecy was starting to eat at her. It wasn't fair. Not to him, not to her.

She knew she'd need to touch base with Lisa soon to finalize plans for Thanksgiving, but the thought alone drained her. The pressure to pretend, to manage schedules, to exist in this fabricated version of reality—she was over it. As the water ran icy down her spine, Nelle counted the days. The contract's end couldn't come soon enough.

November 20th arrived before anyone was truly ready for it. In New York, the air had shifted—not quite the biting cold of winter yet, but the kind of crisp chill that made scarves and gloves necessary. The trees that still clung to their leaves burned brightly in shades of amber and deep, smoky red, their beauty fading a little more with each gust of wind. Holiday lights had begun to sprout up across storefronts and brownstones, but it all felt a little different this year—softer, more cautious.

After the long, heavy years of COVID, the city was just beginning to breathe again. Streets bustled, but many still wore masks tucked around their chins or pulled tightly over their faces. It wasn't the loud, chaotic New York of old holiday cheer, but a newer version of it, one trying to stitch itself back together. People clung to the traditions they missed, eager for any glimpse of normalcy, even if it was a little battered, a little bruised. Just gathering, just seeing each other, felt like a victory.

Inside the condo, Janelle threw herself into her work, yet again, lost in the rhythms of painting, sculpting, and shaping her dreams into something tangible. After seeing the finished space Reggie unveiled, she had barely seen her friends. There was no plan B if this didn't work. No safety net. She could never, and would never, return to corporate. This was her one shot, and she knew it.

That evening, Emily's Friendsgiving loomed, the invitation's stern "8 PM sharp" replaying in her mind. Janelle's brushes continued to beat the canvas, frantic and alive, when her phone rang. Lisa.

Janelle wiped her hands on an old cloth before answering, but for the first time in a long time, she hesitated, reluctant to pull herself out of the little world she was fighting so hard to build.

"Hey there!" Lisa chirped, her voice bright and eager, missing the closeness she and Janelle once shared. "You've been quiet. You barely talk to us in the group chat."

Janelle exhaled softly, her voice low. "Yeah, sorry. Just have a lot going on."

"I can imagine," Lisa said warmly, determined to lift her friend's spirits. "Well, we have everything set for your big opening in a few weeks!" she added, waiting for the excitement to spark, but Janelle stayed quiet, her energy weighed down by something heavier, something unsaid.

"Are you okay?" Lisa finally asked, the concern threading clearly through her words.

"Yeah, I'm fine," Janelle lied, her voice a brittle shield. In truth, she felt like the outsider among them, adrift. The looming thought of spending the holiday with a stranger's family gnawed at her relentlessly, a parasite feeding on her uncertainty.

Lisa, sensing her friend needed some light, continued, "I have some more good news. Roderick is going to PA by himself, so I was thinking...if you wanted...we could go see your parents and then have a mini celebration together."

Janelle froze, her heart thudding in her chest. The smile she tried to suppress fought its way to her lips. Spending the holiday with Reggie—and meeting his daughter—meant more to her than anything right now. Their relationship was deepening fast.

"Oh my gosh, Lisa, that's such good news! And I would love to, but..." she trailed off, the truth sitting on the edge of her tongue, desperate to be shared. She wanted to tell Lisa everything about the man who made her feel alive again, but she couldn't. Not yet. "I don't see my parents often," she said instead, "so I'm going to just stay by them for the weekend. I hope you don't mind."

Lisa's smile could be heard through the phone, warm and understanding, even if she didn't know the full story. "Of course not," she said gently. "I just want you to be happy."

Lisa and Janelle began making their way to Emily's just as the sun disappeared from the sky, casting a soft indigo hue over the city. The car ride to her place had been silent—uncomfortably so. Lisa couldn't help but steal glances at Nelle, noticing how different she looked tonight. Rejuvenated. More confident. There was a quiet certainty about her now, even though she barely spoke. Her aura had shifted in a way Lisa couldn't quite explain, but she admired it nonetheless.

Despite having defended Brenton to her friends in the past, Lisa had made the quiet decision to leave him out of Friendsgiving this year. Deep down, she knew he might not be the man for her. He had apologized, made attempts at reconciliation, but his efforts felt hollow, overshadowed by broken promises and a communication style that left her feeling unseen, once again. It was as if winning her back had been his goal, not keeping her. Once he felt he'd succeeded, he drifted back into his familiar, comfortable indifference.

Maybe, Lisa thought, being open-minded wasn't such a bad idea. Maybe meeting Ryan wouldn't be the worst thing after all.

At approximately 7:30 PM, Janelle and Lisa stepped elegantly from the town car that came to a slow stop on East 75th Street in front of Emily's apartment. The evening murmured with a chill in the air.

Janelle stunned in a red, glittering mini dress that hugged her petite frame, the plunging neckline daring yet graceful. Her hair was styled elegantly and simply, parted cleanly down the middle and pulled back to spotlight her bold red lip and delicate gold jewelry. Strappy black heels added the perfect finish, elongating her legs and making her presence all the more striking.

Lisa, by contrast, exuded effortless cool. She wore an oversized beige suit, the relaxed drawstring trousers pooling stylishly over sharp pointed-toe heels. A fitted cropped tank underneath showed off her toned midriff, bringing a sporty, modern twist to the otherwise classic silhouette. The jet-black sheen of her bob caught the light as she stepped easily beside her best friend.

Inside, Emily's dining room was perfect, setting the stage for an unforgettable Friendsgiving. The space was wrapped in soft, muted tones, with a grand alabaster chandelier hanging overhead, casting a gentle light across the room and creating a cozy, friendly atmosphere.

At the center of it all sat a rich, polished wood dining table, dressed impeccably for the occasion. Crystal-clear glassware and fine china were neatly arranged atop crisp white linens, while tall silver candlesticks with slender white candles added height and a classic, romantic touch. A lush bouquet of fresh white roses and ranunculus served as the centerpiece, bringing softness and a touch of organic beauty to the otherwise tailored setting.

Around the table, plush taupe chairs invited guests to sit and stay awhile, their cushioned seats promising comfort through long conversations and second helpings. A large mirror along the back wall reflected the flickering candlelight, doubling the room's inviting glow and giving the illusion of endless detail.

Every aspect spoke of quiet sophistication—from the understated abstract art on the walls to the delicate orchids placed thoughtfully along the console.

The wait staff moved quickly, but quietly, ushering Lisa and Nelle toward the back of the apartment after gracefully taking their coats. Always one to anticipate the finer details, Lisa had earlier arranged for a delivery of decadent desserts and a few bottles of the city's finest red wine, ensuring the evening would unfold with just the right touch of indulgence. She was pleasantly surprised to find that a few guests had already arrived.

In the dining room stood Marian, a poised young woman cradling a glass of champagne, her smile warm and inviting. Lisa had heard plenty about the talented Juilliard professor and felt a spark of excitement at the prospect of meeting her.

"Good evening," she said, extending her right hand. "I'm Lisa McAdams."

Meanwhile, Janelle drifted naturally toward the rear of the space, her heels in hand to move quietly through the plush hallways. She tapped lightly on Emily's bedroom door before easing it open to find Emily mid-change, slipping into a breathtaking ivory Celine gown.

The dress naturally clung to her figure—a corseted waistline accentuated her curves, while a soft draping detail and slightly flared hemline gave her an ethereal air. One shoulder was adorned with an intricate rosette, the other with a long, flowing scarf that added a dramatic flourish.

Emily's room was a whirlwind of fabric and shoes, evidence of a frantic search for the perfect look. Music pulsed through the apartment—familiar notes that stirred old memories Janelle thought she had long buried. For a brief moment, the thought of Kenneth pierced her focus, but she shook it off, determined not to let the past bleed into tonight.

"You look nice!" Janelle said warmly, stepping inside with a bright, supportive smile, bringing a sense of calm to the storm of nerves Emily tried hard to mask.

Meanwhile, in the softly lit dining room, Marian, Lisa, and Sabine gathered by the tall windows, their frames softened by sweeping emery linen drapes.

"Of course, we know who you are. You're New York's PR final boss," Marian teased with an easy smile, shaking Lisa's hand firmly before gesturing to her wife, Sabine King-Signature. "Emily speaks so highly of you! This is my wife, Sabine."

"Likewise," Lisa replied, her smile warm and genuine. "I mean, Marian Signature—the tenured theater professor. Your work speaks for itself. I love how you capture African American history through storytelling. It's captivating, inviting, and such a fresh take. I'm a huge fan of your work."

Marian offered a soft, gracious smile, her voice smooth but rich with depth. "Ah, thank you so much. That means a lot."

At the same time, tucked away at the rear of the apartment, Emily paced in her bedroom, the hem of her satin gown brushing against scattered heels and dresses on the floor. Janelle sat cross-legged at the edge of the bed, idly flicking a pair of silver stilettos back and forth with her toes.

"Why do you look so sad?" Emily asked, pausing mid-stride.

"I'm not sad!" Janelle insisted a little too quickly.

"You've been quiet..." Emily pointed out, studying her carefully.

Janelle hesitated, her voice dropping to a whisper. "If I tell you something, can you promise not to tell Lisa?"

Emily shot her a skeptical look, her eyes blinking fast. "Is there a time limit on the secret?"

"What do you mean?"

"Are you eventually going to tell Lisa yourself? I don't want to keep something from her forever."

"I mean, yeah, eventually. I just feel bad right now, you know?"

Emily gave a small shrug, turning back to her vanity where she rushed to curl a few loose strands of hair and dab on a light layer of makeup—not that she needed it; her beauty shone effortlessly. "Well, spill."

Janelle took a breath, her voice hushed. "I'm in a relationship with Roddy's chef, Reginald."

Emily froze, catching Janelle's reflection in the vanity mirror, her expression flashing from shock to intrigue in an instant.

"How the hell did that happen?" Emily burst out laughing, genuinely caught off guard. It wasn't that she cared Janelle was in a relationship—far from it. It was her pattern that made Emily's head spin.

"Em, please don't be a jerk," Janelle groaned, tugging at the hem of her dress.

"I'm not," Emily said, still chuckling. "But seriously, how did that happen?"

Janelle sighed, bracing herself. "Lisa told me to try and build rapport with Roddy, and...in the process, I happened to—"

"Fall on the dick of his chef? Got it," Emily teased, tapping the compact of blush against her cheek with a few light, playful taps of her manicured nails.

"Why is everything a joke to you?" Janelle snapped, half-laughing despite herself.

"No," Emily grinned, lowering her blush. "I'm just...flabbergasted by you. So, now what?"

Janelle's shoulders slumped. "Well, you know Lisa agreed to do my gallery opening and...I want Reggie there with me. Emily, he built that space with me. He did the carpentry, the electrical work, the painting, the fixtures—everything. He's been by my side through all of it. I feel terrible not including him."

Emily nodded slowly, her smile softening. "So, invite him..."

But mid-sentence, realization flickered across her face. Her mouth clamped shut. Her brows furrowed.

"Oh wait, no—you can't. The press..." she trailed off, her voice dropping as the implications set in. Their eyes locked for a beat, understanding passing between them just as the door creaked open.

Lisa breezed into the room, her excitement electric. "You know THE Marian Signature?" she asked, her grin wide, completely oblivious to the serious conversation she'd interrupted.

"Yep, her dad signed with our firm a few years ago," Emily said casually, wrapping up her makeup routine. "But it's her sister, Nova, that's the big fish. I need to sign her. Just haven't had a chance to lock her down yet—and according to Marian, they don't have the best relationship. You know how it is. But her haircare line? It's so good...and profitable."

Lisa nodded, half-listening, her eyes flickering with curiosity. They continued chatting, their conversation weaving effortlessly between business and admiration. Meanwhile, Janelle, feeling the familiar sting of exclusion, smiled politely and slipped away.

She padded down the softly lit hallway, passing the dining room where Marian and Sabine now sat deep in discussion, their heads bowed together over a cellular phone filled with notes about their theater documentary. Janelle paused, introduced herself with a warm, brief smile, before making her way to the sideboard.

Grabbing a goblet, she poured herself a generous glass of wine, the rich red liquid swirling as she exhaled quietly. Just as she brought the glass to her lips, the front door opened—the sharp creak followed by the thud of heavy footsteps.

Aaron and Ryan. Their laughter and deep voices filled the entryway, carrying through the polished space like a wave.

Without hesitation, Janelle tossed back the entire glass, the burn warming her chest almost instantly. She poured another, feeling the eyes of the wait staff graze her with unspoken judgment, their silent observations clinging to her skin.

The chatter around her only seemed to rise in volume, the energy in the room shifting. Lisa and Emily finally emerged from the rear hallway, still engrossed in animated conversation. But then Emily's eyes drifted across the room—and in a heartbeat, she locked eyes on him.

But before she could rush forward and embrace Aaron, her eyes drifted lower—catching sight of the man standing beside him. He was undeniably handsome, with sharp features and a cool, relaxed swagger, but what struck her most was his stature. He stood no taller than 5'6", a sharp contrast to the towering presence of Aaron, who was easily 6'4".

Despite the difference, the smaller man carried himself with a self-assurance that filled the room, exuding the magnetic confidence usually reserved for men twice his height. His smile was easy, charming even, but standing side-by-side with Aaron, the contrast was impossible to ignore.

Emily, catching the slight falter in Lisa's expression, spun on her heel to face her with a warning glint in her eye. "Don't be mean," she hissed through gritted teeth, barely moving her lips, before quickly turning and disappearing into Aaron's waiting arms.

Left to play hostess, Lisa offered a tightly controlled smile as Ryan stepped forward, extending his hand. She and Emily both instinctively glanced down as they shook hands, the awkwardness of the height difference palpable between them.

"Uh, Nelle," Lisa called out, her voice a little higher than usual as she turned her head, desperate for an excuse to slip away. "Come meet someone!"

The evening unfolded into a beautiful, if chaotic, symphony of flavors and endless laughter. Emily's dining room glowed warmly under the white light, the four-course meal a stunning display of sophistication—from roasted squash bisque to decadent chocolate tarts. Between mouthfuls of food and bouts of mirth, however, Lisa found herself trapped in a slow-burning nightmare.

Ryan, blissfully unaware, continued to pepper her with conversation, laboring under the delusion that she might be interested in him. She was not. In fact, as she sipped her wine, raising her glass more often than anyone else at the table, Lisa found herself secretly wishing she had just invited Brenton. He wasn't perfect, far from it, but at least he was her type. That, she realized bitterly, mattered far more to her right now than being cornered by a short king proudly showing off his collection of Donald Duck memorabilia.

"When I was a kid, I loved Donald Duck," Ryan shared, animatedly scrolling through photos on his phone. "He reminded me of my dad when he got mad—just miserable and short-tempered. But deep down, good guy. Family man."

Lisa smiled thinly, feeling her soul leave her body for a moment. She subtly waved her empty glass toward the waitstaff, signaling for yet another refill, while Janelle, seated beside her, hid her amusement behind a small, knowing smile.

Beneath the table, Janelle's phone buzzed incessantly with messages from Reggie, their flirtatious back-and-forth providing a welcome distraction from the evening's social awkwardness. She knew it was rude, but the temptation was impossible to resist.

Seated in a wide, circular layout, no one could hide— each person visible to the next under the golden wash of candlelight, the night somehow managing to be both intimate and excruciatingly revealing.

As the evening wound down and the last bites of dessert disappeared, Aaron rose from his seat, gently clinking his champagne glass with the side of his fork. The lively chatter that had filled the dining room quickly hushed, all eyes turning toward him. Emily sat just beneath him, her cheeks flushed from the wine, a wide, beaming smile stretched across her face. She was utterly smitten, unable to look at him without feeling that familiar, dizzying warmth in her chest.

Just as she wondered what he could possibly have to say, the waitstaff approached, one of them holding out a phone. On the screen was a FaceTime call—and there, her mother, Tippy, smiled brightly back at her. Emily's heart flipped in her chest, her eyes already welling with emotion.

"Hi, Mom," she said, her voice cracking slightly as a tear slipped free.

"Oh, honey! Hi!" Tippy cried out, her voice trembling with excitement.

Emily glanced around, confused and overwhelmed, her gaze shifting back to Aaron just as he began to speak.

"Emily Harrington," Aaron said, his voice steady and full of reverence. "It feels like destiny, because ever since the moment I met you, I haven't been able to imagine a life without you. Not for a second."

Around the room, Marian and Sabine clutched one another tenderly, exchanging a soft, knowing kiss, their memories of love blooming afresh. Lisa and Janelle leaned in, their eyes wide, their hearts pounding in anticipation— Janelle finally sliding her phone away to give the moment her full attention.

"You have a smile and a spirit that's electric, hypnotic, mesmerizing," Aaron continued, emotion thick in his voice. "It's unlike anything I've ever known. Your laughter, your light—it's contagious, baby. And I want to spend the rest of my life making sure you never stop smiling, every night before bed, every morning we wake up together."

With a smooth, deliberate motion, Aaron pulled out a small velvet box, opening it to reveal a breathtaking solitaire engagement ring—an 8.5-carat cushion-cut diamond that glittered fiercely under the chandelier's soft light. Lowering himself onto one knee, his posture regal and sure, he looked up at her with nothing but devotion in his eyes.

"Emily Harrington," he said, voice rich and unwavering, "will you marry me?"

The room seemed to hold its collective breath.

Emily turned toward the screen, her mother watching with teary eyes, then back at Aaron, tears now streaming freely down her face. Her lips trembled as she gasped out the word, her heart so full she thought it might burst: "Yes," she cried, her voice breaking with happiness.

As if on cue, the room erupted into laughter, cheers, and a symphony of congratulations. Emily, overcome with emotion, ran toward Lisa and Janelle, hastily sliding chairs out of her way as she made a beeline for her friends. Her hands trembled with excitement as she held them out, desperate to steady herself enough to proudly show off the dazzling ring.

"He did good," Emily laughed breathlessly, the sparkle of the diamond drawing gasps of admiration.

"He sure did!" Lisa winked, grinning widely. Their eyes locked for a brief, tender moment, and Emily, moved beyond words, leaned in to embrace her.

"I love you," she whispered into Lisa's ear, her voice soft and full of gratitude. She knew—without a doubt—that Lisa's hand had been involved, helping Aaron pick the perfect ring. She had seen right into Emily's heart and made sure her dreams were captured in that perfect stone.

Janelle quickly wrapped her arms around them, and for a few precious seconds, the three women stood there—laughing, crying, holding on to one another as if they could preserve the moment forever.

Emily made her rounds next, floating from chair to chair, her smile never dimming as she showed off her ring to everyone. She even held her hand up to her mother through the phone, beaming proudly as Tippy laughed and cried on the other end.

In a quiet moment, unnoticed by the rest of the room, Emily tilted her head toward the ceiling, her eyes glistening through tears.

"I love you, Auntie Vern," she whispered, sending her love into the heavens, wishing more than anything that her grandaunt could have been there to witness this unforgettable night. And as the evening wore on, the laughter, and the love spoke of new beginnings, sealing the night into memory—a night that ended as beautifully as it had begun.

CHAPTER 19.

YOU'VE BEEN

SERVED

Janelle slipped quietly into her condo, the soft click of the door behind her barely stirring the peaceful air inside. She was surprised—and touched—to find Reggie already fast asleep in her bed, his broad chest rising and falling in a slow, steady rhythm. Moving with care, she showered quickly, then changed into something light and chic, tying her hair into a messy bun atop her head.

Still feeling the heady buzz from the night's celebrations, she poured herself another glass of wine, unwilling to let the feeling fade. As she sipped, her eyes wandered back to Reggie, sprawled across her bed with the sheets carelessly draped over him. The scene before her wasn't just intimate; it was art.

In Janelle's world, everything was a masterpiece waiting to be captured—and tonight, Reggie was her subject.

Carefully, she moved a blank canvas from the center of the living room to the threshold of the bedroom, setting it up with a small light just above her easel. She perched herself on a stool, her bare toes curling around the rung for balance. The moonlight poured in through the windows, stretching its silvery touch across Reggie's body, illuminating the lines of his muscles, the quiet strength in his hands, the way the sheet kissed his hips just so— suggestive, but respectful of his slumber.

Janelle's pencil moved instinctively, guided by something deeper than sight. Every line she drew seemed to pull her closer to him, not just physically, but spiritually. She captured the softness of his mouth in sleep, the tension still lingering in his brow, the gentle vulnerability of a man who trusted her enough to fall apart in her space.

Stroke after stroke, she fell a little further in love with him, with the moment, with the silent story they were creating together. The night was hushed, sacred, and utterly theirs.

Day after day, it was as if life had suddenly picked up speed, and each of them was being pulled along different currents. Lisa and Emily were now deep in the throes of wedding planning, spending their afternoons flipping through bridal books, pinning swatches of fabric to corkboards, and daydreaming about floral arrangements and first dances. It had become their whole world—a world Janelle could only orbit from the outside.

For Nelle, life was moving at a different pace. She was focused, head down, pushing through the final stretch of her contract, determined to honor her commitments even as impatience nipped at her heels. Her gallery opening was just around the corner, the holidays loomed heavily on the calendar, and although she sometimes felt like she was drowning under the weight of it all, she kept her struggles to herself. She didn't want to burden her friends with worries they wouldn't understand—not now, not when everything for them was so joyful.

So she carried on.

When Thanksgiving arrived, she slipped away to Harlem, where the comfort of family wrapped around her like a worn, beloved quilt. The laughter of cousins, the warm embraces of aunts and uncles, and the teasing from nieces and nephews filled the house with life. Even though some of the younger ones were far more intrigued by her now-public relationship with a movie star, her parents treated her just the same as they always had: lovingly, simply, without any fanfare.

One of her brothers eventually arrived with his wife and their two tiny children, both too young to recognize her beyond a friendly face willing to play. Nelly didn't mind. She got down on the floor with them, laughing, chasing, and letting the noise and commotion of family life wash over her, a sweet reminder that some parts of her world remained beautifully unchanged.

As the evening began to wind down, she hugged her parents tightly, kissed her little nieces and nephews goodbye, and slipped out into the cool November night, feeling both grateful and heavy-hearted all at once.

The sleek black car Reggie sent for her was nothing short of perfection—immaculate, gleaming, and luxurious, a symbol of how far she had come. As she settled into the plush leather seats, the group chat buzzed to life, Emily flooding it with sweet photos of her with her mother, Tippy, and Aaron's smiling family. Lisa, too, seemed wrapped in happiness, spending her day with Brenton, visiting his parents before making their way to hers down in The Bronx.

Janelle sipped her complimentary champagne quietly, letting the soft hum of the road beneath her stir her thoughts. The ride to Long Island felt like a ribbon of calm unwinding before her. Her heart felt full, stretched wide with gratitude, but also quietly aware: she wasn't the same girl who once lived in the loft, scared of her own voice and too timid to demand the respect she deserved. That version of her had quietly died somewhere along the way.

Now, she craved a life that mirrored her growth—one built on stability, connection, and a deep, spiritual bond not just with a partner, but with herself. As the city lights gave way to the suburban sprawl of Long Island, Janelle couldn't help but look ahead. With Emily now engaged and building a new future, she found herself daring to dream: in a perfect world, maybe one day, she too would stand as a wife, a mother, rooted, radiant, and entirely her own.

As the town car eased through the towering iron gate, a gentle beeping accompanied the entry of a secret code. Embedded street lights flickered to life across the winding road ahead—the pavement itself seemed to shimmer, an almost cinematic entrance that whispered wealth. Nelle sat upright, her eyes wide as the vehicle curved through dense trees and manicured gardens.

It took another three minutes just to reach the house. And when they finally pulled up, her breath caught in her throat. The home unfolded before her like something from a modernist dream: a massive, angular structure clad in warm cedar wood, with dramatic, sloped rooflines that rose and dipped like frozen waves. Huge geometric windows caught the last of the sunset, their clean frames slicing through the wood like art.

Reggie stepped out to greet her, his expensive tracksuit fitting him perfectly, his scent rich and intoxicating—an irresistible mix that made Janelle melt into his embrace a little longer than usual. She had missed him, missed this feeling of being wrapped in something that felt like home. "Come on baby, everyone's inside," he said warmly, nodding to his driver to park and come in from the cold.

Inside, the house felt even larger. Towering stone walls anchored a sprawling living room with minimalist furniture—low, plush seating in soft creams and whites, punctuated by matte black accents and abstract art. Above, a wood-paneled ceiling stretched steeply upward, pierced with skylights that bathed everything in natural light. A fireplace, carved into a massive gray stone wall, crackled softly, grounding the otherwise airy space.

The moment she crossed the threshold, Janelle was hit with a wave of warmth and the delicious aroma of Dominican dishes. Spanish filled the air, woven into the rhythm of children laughing and running through the halls. It was a vibrant contrast to the polished, quiet dinners she was used to in the city. Here, life happened loudly, joyfully.

In one corner, a group of men crowded around a pool table, cigars in hand, their laughter deep and hearty. In another, a sea of children tumbled and played. The kitchen was alive with energy—older women cooking, swapping stories, cleaning dishes without missing a beat, while the TV blared hits from Bad Bunny and Shakira.

As they made their way into the living room, an elderly woman approached them, her smile wide and full of love.

"Ella es hermosa, hijo," she said, her eyes twinkling.

"Gracias, mamá," Reggie beamed, pride heavy in his voice.

The woman's expression shifted to concern as she asked, "¿Comió ella?"

Reggie turned to Janelle, laughing lightly, "She's asking if you ate."

Janelle couldn't help but chuckle, sensing immediately that feeding people was a love language in this family. She shook her head and assured his mother she was fine, thanking her warmly for her kindness.

Reggie then introduced her to everyone, including his daughter, who barely looked up from her phone, too busy scrolling TikTok and vibing to music through her headphones. Janelle didn't take it personally—she remembered being that age, too.

Beyond the main living area, Janelle caught a glimpse of something she hadn't expected: a full-sized indoor pool. The pool room was lined with the same pale wood as the exterior, and arched windows soared nearly to the ceiling, framing the forest outside like living paintings. Lounge chairs and an understated marble-topped bar lined one side of the water. The entire room smelled faintly of chlorine and cedar—clean, sharp, and expensive.

That night, Janelle felt free. Free to love, to create, to exist without fear or reservation. Reggie's family wrapped her in their warmth, pulling her into the center of the room to teach her how to dance the merengue. She stumbled and laughed, letting the music guide her until her feet ached and her cheeks hurt from smiling.

Once the younger children were tucked into bed, the atmosphere shifted—more lively, more sensual. The liquor flowed easily, loosening tongues and softening inhibitions as the adults gathered in the grand, open living space downstairs. The house was so large that the noise of their laughter, music, and celebration never reached the sleeping wings upstairs.

They played card games, told jokes, and traded old stories about Reggie that made everyone howl with laughter. His aunts and uncles produced childhood photos—Reggie as a chubby little boy, grinning widely with arms full of food, always sharing his lunch or sneaking bites for his friends. It came as no surprise to anyone that he grew up with a passion for cooking and was generous and good with money. His family remembering fondly how he always found a way to stretch a dollar without ever being stingy.

Janelle listened, soaking it all in, her heart growing softer with every word spoken about him. Her eyelids grew heavier the longer she sat there, the alcohol a slow, sweet burn through her veins.

She stole a glance at him across the room—laughing, easy, utterly in his element—and in that moment, she knew: she was ready for him.

Nelle was living in her own world now—unapologetically, beautifully. But even in the middle of her newfound joy, a gnawing feeling remained: she knew that until she came clean with Lisa, a wall would continue to stand between them. She couldn't take it anymore. The happiness bubbling inside her, the pride she felt in how far she had come, needed to be shared, discussed, and celebrated with the people who mattered most.

With the Golden Globe nominations set to be announced in just a day, she decided the time was now. She needed her friends in her corner. Knowing that Emily and Lisa had been alternating office visits to help plan Emily's wedding, and that today was Lisa's day, she sent a quick message to the group chat: *"Stopping by today."*

Her message was met with heart-eye emojis and Emily's playful, *"Okay, stranger!"* A laugh bubbled out of her, but underneath it, there was guilt, too. She had pulled away, unintentionally, just as big milestones were happening for Emily and Lisa—Emily's engagement, Lisa's second chance at love. She felt selfish.

Wanting to make it right, Janelle volunteered to bring lunch, choosing hearty Caribbean vegan dishes from a spot they all loved. It was a small gesture, but it came from the heart—her way of saying, *I'm here. I never stopped loving you.*

That afternoon inside Lisa's office, Emily waited patiently, large bridal books slapped open across the table, a highlighter tucked behind one ear. Lisa sat at her desk, her posture rigid.

"Yo, does it matter to you at all that I'm unhappy?" Roddy's voice crackled through the speaker.

Lisa sighed, her fingers drumming lightly on the desk. "Of course it does. I know these past few months have been hard on you. But we have to stay the course. The nominations come out tomorrow and we need to put on a brave face. We have everything set up to record you and Nelle on the jet, to capture your first reaction to being nominated."

"Fuck that, Lisa! Fuck her! I'll do the jet, but I wanna be with my boys. With my people!"

Lisa's jaw tightened. "No. It doesn't work that way. Because you couldn't fuck her, you wanted to fire her, and now you want to miss this moment too? I gave you Thanksgiving. Even though posts of you and her being with your parents would have been great for PR, you didn't want that. So no, we're not compromising this one."

There was a beat of silence before Roddy's voice exploded again. "Yo, I try to have so much respect for you, but you have no idea how upset you make me. You work for me."

Lisa remained unnerved, calm as a surgeon. "So, fire me," she said coolly. "If you think your career is going to stand a chance without me, pull the plug. I dare you at this point. You sound high almost every time we talk. You're becoming harder and harder to manage. Bree and Leon have already quit. It's just me. I'm all you've got."

"Bree wasn't doing shit anyway."

"She wasn't," Lisa agreed, her voice razor-sharp. "But having her name attached to you on your IMDB page looked good. It was impactful."

Across the table, Emily pretended to flip through the bridal books, but her eyes occasionally lifted to Lisa, sensing the fire brewing behind her friend's calm exterior.

Mid-conversation, Janelle entered the office, her arms weighed down with takeout bags. She flashed a bright smile at Emily, who quickly hopped up to help her.

Together, they cleared the table, pushing aside the massive bridal books and magazines to make room for their impromptu feast. The scent of Caribbean spices quickly filled the small space, a welcome distraction from the tension thick in the air.

Across the room, Lisa remained locked in a fierce phone call with Roddy, her voice clipped but composed.

"Roderick, I have no idea what to tell you," she said, her patience clearly thinning. "We're almost at the finish line—just a few more weeks. Then you can declare yourself a single man, and we'll spin it. Hell, the richer you get, the better it'll look that you're unattached."

There was a pause before Roddy snapped back, bitterness lacing his words. "Being single doesn't matter because I won't be with a Black woman."

Lisa didn't even flinch. "Listen, Roderick, whatever floats your boat. If you want to marry a bunch of white women or have a whole harem of them, who cares at this point? It sounds to me like you're giving up."

"I ain't giving up! I just want my life to be my fucking life!" he shouted, his voice cutting sharply through the room before the call abruptly ended.

Lisa clicked the receiver without a word, the tension hanging heavy for a moment before she turned her focus back to the girls, as if nothing had happened at all. She glanced over at Janelle, flashing her a bright, almost forced smile. "Did you get my email? We have the jet set up for tomorrow, for the Golden Globe nominations," she said.

Janelle nodded quickly, her nerves stirring beneath the surface. It was the second week of December, and it felt as if something had shifted in the air—like time was speeding up, pushing everything toward an inevitable moment she could no longer delay.

As the girls caught up, with Emily animatedly discussing flower arrangements and potential venues, Janelle felt the pressure mount. Her heart beating rapidly with the need to get the words off of her chest—after all, how bad could it really be?

"I have a boyfriend," she blurted out.

The room froze. Lisa and Emily exchanged a brief, wide-eyed glance before Emily's jaw dropped slightly, realizing the fire she sensed was no longer brewing; it arrived.

Lisa shrugged it off at first, casual. "Okay, I mean, that's not a big deal. Is that why Roddy's losing his mind?" she asked, stabbing at her jerk tofu salad with her fork.

"No, he doesn't know," Janelle admitted.

"Oh," Lisa said, her tone shifting slightly, more guarded now. "Well, a boyfriend isn't a problem, as long as he knows you have a job to do right now."

Janelle took a deep, shaky gulp. "No, he doesn't know because... it's Reggie," she whispered.

The moment the words left her lips, she realized how unprepared she truly was. Lisa froze, mid-bite, staring at her. "As in... the chef? Roddy's chef? The guy from the gallery?"

Janelle nodded quickly. "Yes, but at that time nothing was happening!" she defended.

Emily quietly slid back into her seat, picking at her food, trying to stay neutral but watching intently as the situation unraveled.

"Janelle, fuck!" Lisa exploded, slamming her fork down. "Roderick is already so vulnerable and falling apart. The last thing he needs is to hear that the girl he likes is sleeping with his chef!"

"It's not just sex," Janelle said firmly. "I've met his daughter. His family. It's serious. And that's why I'm telling you."

Lisa pressed a hand to her forehead, trying to steady the migraine threatening to break through. But Janelle wasn't done—might as well rip the bandage off completely.

"I know you're planning the gallery opening, and I know the contract isn't up until Valentine's Day," Janelle continued. "But I'd really like Reggie to be my date for the event. He's done so much for me, Lisa. I can't just pretend he's not a part of my life."

Lisa's heart raced. The walls of the office seemed to be closing in.

"Please... stop," Lisa said, voice shaking. She pushed herself up from her chair, needing space, needing air.

Emily jumped to her feet, ready to follow, but Lisa turned sharply at the door, her voice low and strained, "Don't... don't follow me, please."

Emily turned to Janelle, confusion written all over her face. "Why would you do that?" she asked quietly, her voice heavy with disappointment.

"I had to, Em," Janelle said, her own voice trembling. "I'm in love with Reggie. I don't want to hide him anymore. When we first set the date for the opening, I had no idea any of this would happen. I can't just pretend he doesn't exist."

Emily shook her head, struggling to understand. "But with the press already thinking you were cheating with him once... it's messy, Nelle. Complicated. That was already handled—the magazine interview, the statements. Lisa cleaned it up. I just... I don't get it."

"I know," Janelle whispered, feeling her throat tighten. "I don't either. I just... I feel like I have to do the right thing. I have to live honestly."

Emily's frustration broke through. "But she's worked so hard on this. Lisa got you four major brand deals, Nelle. Four. They're sponsoring the opening, basing it all on your momentum—on the timing, the potential sales, the exposure. Journalists are flying in, photographers are booked... What do you expect everyone to do now? Risk it all for one man?"

Janelle blinked back tears, her hands twisting in her lap. She knew Emily wasn't wrong. She knew she had dropped a grenade into the middle of everything they'd built. All she wanted was her life back—her life, simple and real, without the puppet strings pulling her every move. But she also knew the damage had already been done.

The next day, Lisa still wasn't ready to face Janelle. She had spent the night venting to Brent, unraveling every knot of frustration inside her. If there was one thing Brent was good at, it was listening—really listening. His eyes stayed locked on her, his body language patient and open, taking in every word so that when he spoke, his advice wasn't just comforting—it was grounded, sensible, exactly what she needed. Lisa had always loved that about him, and even during their time apart, she found herself missing it. Brent didn't just hear her; he understood her.

Meanwhile, the energy across the city was tense. The Golden Globe nominations were just hours away, set to be announced by Mayan Lopez and Selenis Leyva at 8:15 PM. Time dragged, stretching the day into an unbearable marathon of nerves and waiting.

Across town, Roddy and Reggie sat in Roddy's condo, trying to pass the hours. But their conversations kept slipping into dangerous territory—Roddy, laced with bitterness, couldn't resist throwing jabs at Nelle. Reggie, though the anger simmered beneath his calm exterior, stayed silent, watchful, determined not to take the bait.

It felt as if the whole world had been put on pause, all of them suspended in the same breathless moment, waiting for the one thing that could finally set them free—or break them completely.

Janelle spent the morning and early afternoon completely immersed in her art, a sense of unexpected relief washing over her. Despite the chaos that could have been unraveling around her, she remained unfazed. Her truth was out in the open, and she had enough trust in Lisa to handle whatever came next. With steady hands, she focused on her work, particularly the piece of Reggie sleeping. She added delicate shades of light, letting the colors swirl and dance together, all while smooth jazz played softly in the background, filling the silence of her creative space.

Every now and then, she would glance at her phone, checking for new tags and random follows on social media. But for the most part, the blogs seemed consumed by one thing: the anticipation of the upcoming nominations announcement.

As the clock neared five, Laura's voice buzzed through the intercom, calmly informing Janelle that the car was downstairs, ready to take her to the tarmac. Janelle followed the instructions without hesitation, but a small, unfamiliar pang tugged at her chest. The instructions hadn't come from Lisa, and for the first time...ever, she feared for the future of their friendship.

Hours later, Janelle stepped onto the jet, immediately overwhelmed by the swarm of photographers, interns, journalists, and unfamiliar faces that crowded around her. The atmosphere was awkward, forced, like they were all playing a role in a staged scene designed to give the illusion of mid-flight. Photos were being taken, captions written, all for the sake of creating a narrative that wasn't quite true.

As she made her way past security and towards the cabin, a familiar scent hit her, sharp and unmistakable—it was his. Her heart skipped a beat as her eyes scanned the room, searching for him, a mix of anxiety and anger bubbling up within her. She couldn't believe it. They had been in constant communication all day, yet not once did he mention that he'd be on the jet with them.

Her gaze drifted to the entrance as Lisa boarded, her notepad in hand, with Laura trailing closely behind. They took their seats, following the unspoken rules of the charade. But something about the moment felt wrong. Her eyes kept scanning until they landed on Roddy. Calmly, without a care in the world, he was laying out lines of coke on a nearby surface, using a hundred-dollar bill to snort it.

Lisa sat adjacent to Janelle, the silence between them palpable. No words were exchanged, even when Janelle tried to speak, reaching out to her best friend. But Lisa was entirely absorbed in her work, her focus deliberate and cold.

Frustrated and uneasy, Janelle found herself forced to relocate by an intern. She took a seat next to Roddy, the space between them unnervingly close. Behind them, Reggie settled into his seat. Janelle could feel his presence before she even turned—she knew that unmistakable scent. But she kept her eyes forward, determined not to acknowledge it. Yet, her body betrayed her, every nerve alive with the familiar stirrings of desire. Her vagina throbbed, her pulse quickened, and she could hear his breathing, steady and close, wrapping her in an overwhelming sense of intimacy.

Her hair was styled in loose curls, but the strange woman adjusting her makeup made her feel like a stranger in her skin. No one—no one—was explaining what was happening, and the disorientation was starting to consume her. Even Lisa, her closest ally, had turned her back, absorbed in her own world.

Janelle's chest tightened with the urge to scream, to grab Reggie and walk away from the mayhem. But something held her back, a quiet, persistent voice telling her that the consequences would be too severe, that walking away wasn't an option—at least, not yet. The situation was slipping out of her control, and with every passing second, she felt more and more like a pawn in a game she had knowingly signed up for.

Between the coke, the shrooms, and the alcohol, it was honestly a miracle that Roddy was even coherent. Within just ten minutes of settling into their positions, he was indulging in it all—popping pills, snorting lines, taking swigs from a bottle. The mix of substances seemed to fuel him, leaving him oddly hyper, but also dangerously disoriented.

At exactly 8 P.M., the small television on board the jet flickered to life. It wasn't much, but it was enough to set the tone for the evening. Lisa's voice broke through the haze of the moment, calm and directive. "Hold hands," she instructed, her eyes scanning the group for compliance. "Smile. Kiss his cheek. Make prayer hands." The commands came swiftly, rehearsed, almost robotic. It was all staged, every action choreographed to fit the perfect narrative she was creating. And somehow, it all fell into place.

Video after video was uploaded to social media, and the audience lapped it up. Comments flooded in, eager to contribute to the carefully crafted story. "#teamrelle. He deserves the nomination!" one comment read, followed by another, "Glad she stuck by her man, watch them elevate together. #blacklove." The illusion was seamless, and to the outside world, it was exactly what they wanted to see: a couple in love, standing strong together. But Janelle felt a gnawing unease, as though the act they were putting on was becoming something far darker than she ever anticipated.

The feeling in the air was strange, indescribable, even. They all knew it was coming, but still, there was an undeniable tension as they held their breath, waiting for the words from Mayan Lopez herself. The anticipation hung thick, as though time had slowed in the seconds before her announcement.

Reggie sat with his legs apart, a silent sentinel rather than the laid-back chef he was supposed to be. His posture was rigid, more like a bodyguard than anything else. His lips were sealed tight, his gaze fixed on the scene unfolding in front of him. Janelle was playing the part they had assigned her—kissing, touching, exchanging loving gazes. But every moment, every gesture felt wrong. These were things meant for Reggie, and yet, they were now being directed at Roddy.

But Reggie handled it all with a level of restraint that was almost eerie. He never uttered a word, his emotions never once slipping through the cracks. He remained calm, stoic, a wall of composure as the charade played out in front of him.

Lisa, ever the strategist, watched him closely, her eyes flickering between the action and his stillness. She was hoping to catch him in the frame, to somehow capture a moment that would completely extinguish any doubt in the minds of the audience—that Janelle could be anything but loyal to Roddy. Nothing would change until she decided it was time, and she wasn't ready to let that shift just yet.

The clock clicked to 8:15 P.M., its ticking the only sound that seemed to echo through the charged silence. Outside, the world had dissolved into pitch-black darkness, the night consuming everything beyond the jet's windows. Inside, however, all eyes were focused on the small screen, the air thick with anticipation.

Then, the words finally broke the stillness, spoken with careful gravity from Mayan's lips:

"...and the nominees for Best Performance by an Actor in a Motion Picture, Drama: Austin Butler ("Elvis") Brendan Fraser ("The Whale"), Hugh Jackman ("The Son"), Jeremy Pope ("The Inspection"), and... Roddy Richardson ("Borderline")."

For a split second, everything seemed to freeze. The moment hung in the air, suspended in time. It was as though the entire world was holding its breath, waiting for a reaction. And when it came, it was a mix of disbelief, excitement, and tension that was impossible to ignore.

The phones were on, cameras rolling, and the tension in the air was palpable. Roddy was in full performance mode, his rehearsed charm turned up to an unsettling level. He leaned in, his movements exaggerated, grabbing Nelle by the face with a force that felt more like ownership than affection. He kissed her aggressively, and she had no choice but to go along with it, though every inch of her body screamed in discomfort. The kiss lingered longer than expected, and Nelle fought desperately to keep her composure, her body stiff with disbelief. She was not okay—she was angry, but more than that, she was trapped in a moment that felt like a betrayal.

Reggie's fists clenched at his sides, the muscles in his arms tightening with fury. But before he could move, Laura, ever the control freak, snapped him to attention off-camera. His anger boiled just beneath the surface, but he held back, for now.

The kiss continued, and Nelle's chest tightened, the urge to cry threatening to break her. She wanted to scream, to slap him, to do something to stop the madness. But all she could do was endure, her heart racing in her chest.

It wasn't until the moment dragged on that Lisa, oblivious to the underlying malice, finally realized something was wrong. "Cut the camera!" she screamed, her voice cracking with panic. She lunged toward Roddy, but her movement was too late. Reggie, seeing red, was already in motion, his body charging toward the actor. However, Roddy was too high to fully comprehend the situation, as Reggie was intercepted by security before he could reach him.

Lisa, now frantic, pulled Roddy back by the arm, her grip tight. "What the fuck are you doing?" she snapped, her words sharp and filled with disbelief. The chaos was just beginning, but Nelle knew this moment was a line crossed—one that couldn't easily be undone.

The moment lingered in the air, heavy and thick, as everyone stood still in the aftermath. It was the raw part, the part that the world didn't get to see—those unscripted, unpolished moments that felt like the truth beneath the façade. The cameras were off, the applause had quieted, and the energy had shifted from excitement to something darker.

As the announcement ended and the others began deboarding the jet, Roddy remained seated, his eyes distant, his posture heavy. He was taking it all in, disgusted by his own actions, but there was something else there too—a twisted sense of satisfaction. His ego, bruised and battered, had felt a temporary boost. He had exacted some form of revenge on Nelle, and for the first time in what felt like forever, he felt like he had control.

Lisa, ever the orchestrator, moved swiftly to follow her friend, who had already started walking away, her steps brisk with purpose. Janelle was no longer interested in facing anyone, not now, not after what had just happened. Lisa understood, watching as she disappeared into the distance, no longer moving in response to the cold night air, but to find somewhere private to break down. Somewhere she could cry in peace.

Left alone with his thoughts, Roddy didn't follow the crowd. He needed space, to breathe, to think. As security helped him deboard the plane, Reggie trailed closely behind; he pulled out his phone and dialed Janelle's number, but it went unanswered. Her phone didn't ring through, and a nagging worry began to creep in. He had had enough of the games, enough of the charades. His mind raced with thoughts of her, of how she was coping, and if she was okay.

As Roddy's security team ushered him into the waiting vehicle, Reggie stepped aside, assuming it was just another airline worker approaching. But this man was different—someone they had never seen before. With smooth, deliberate steps, the stranger approached Roddy and, without hesitation, asked, "Are you Roderick Jesse Richardson?"

Roddy nodded, his confidence shaken, his answer unsure. "Yes."

The man didn't waste a moment, thrusting papers into his hands. "You've been served."

Reggie looked on, confused, while the security team exchanged puzzled glances. Roddy's fingers trembled as he looked down at the papers—the words on them barely registering at first. It was a summons for child support.

CHAPTER 20.

BROKEN

Reggie wanted to quit—right then, right there. The urge to walk away from it all, from Roddy, from the madness, clawed at him with every breath. But he didn't. It wasn't in his nature to abandon a man at his lowest, no matter how much anger he carried in his chest. Still, forgiveness wasn't on the table. Reggie knew he would never forget how Roddy humiliated Janelle, how he put her in such a vulnerable, powerless position. Another man had wielded control over his woman, and it left a bitter taste in his mouth. He couldn't allow that to slide.

Instead of making a scene, Reggie chose a quieter rebellion. When he arrived at the condo, he moved in silence, packing his things and leaving behind the key to the condo—short, to the point, but powerful enough that Roddy would know exactly where they stood from now on. There was no fight, no angry words exchanged—just an absence that would speak louder than anything he could have said.

Roddy, for his part, had no plans of going home that night. Still riding the wave of his spiraling emotions, he instructed his driver to take him to Nobu Downtown, seeking to numb whatever feelings he couldn't name with a crowded room, expensive drinks, and the hollow noise of meaningless conversation.

Meanwhile, back at the condo, Janelle arrived around 10:35 PM, her body exhausted and her spirit even more so. The first thing she did was turn her phone off—shutting out the world—and step into the shower. As the water rained down on her, hot and unrelenting, her mind wandered to her loft. Her sanctuary. How would she afford it if she quit early? She had nine weeks and three days left on her contract, and already, the days felt like they were dragging on an endless, miserable loop.

The math didn't add up. Over two grand a month in rent with no income would eventually catch up to her. And while delaying the opening of her gallery sounded comforting in theory, it wouldn't work in practice. She was already losing money on the space just sitting empty.

Her thoughts bounced from survival to guilt—would Reggie understand if she didn't include him in her big moment? Would her friendship with Lisa survive this betrayal and confusion? Everything felt tangled, too much to sort through.

She tilted her head back, letting the water soak her freshly washed hair, now stretched past her shoulders to the small of her back. She scrubbed and scrubbed, as if she could scrub away the doubt, the shame, the heaviness pressing down on her. For a fleeting moment, under the steady stream, the weight of the world slid off her skin—but deep down, she knew it was still waiting for her when she stepped back out.

By morning, the scandal had already taken on a life of its own. Headlines screamed across every gossip site and entertainment blog: *"Roddy Richardson's Baby Mother*

Demands Child Support—Up to $200,000 a Month!" The internet was ablaze, dissecting every detail, but Lisa remained unfazed. She knew exactly what to do.

Calm and calculated, she instructed Laura to post a carefully crafted statement to Roddy's Instagram: a humble apology where Roddy took full responsibility for his actions, promised to care for his child, and pledged to be a present, attentive father. In the message, he made sure to publicly thank his "wonderful partner, Janelle," praising her for standing by him through these hard times.

Once the post was live, Laura immediately switched to Janelle's Instagram account, liking it and reposting it to Janelle's story—solidifying the image of a united, unbreakable front. Within minutes, the wildfire of bad press had been tamed, at least on the surface. The headlines slowed, the public softened, and the damage control machine kept churning.

Across town, however, the man at the center of it all was unraveling. Roddy could barely keep his eyes open. His body felt like it was sinking into itself, legs heavy, heart pounding erratically in his chest. He stumbled across Reggie's key—a final goodbye of sorts—but barely glanced at it before tossing it into the trash without a second thought.

Still half-dazed, Roddy reached for the nearest bottle of bourbon, pouring a heavy shot and swallowing it like water. It burned going down, but he welcomed the sting. With a groan, he dragged himself back into bed. The world might have been spinning outside, but Roddy Richardson was lost in a storm all his own.

It was a crisp Saturday afternoon, and even though Janelle hadn't answered a single call or text, Lisa knew she couldn't just sit back and do nothing. Some things needed to be handled face-to-face. Determined, she made her way down Broadway, the city buzzing quietly around her. As she passed rows of brownstones, she caught glimpses of children playing in front yards—despite the nippy weather—their laughter floating through the air like music.

For a fleeting moment, Lisa allowed herself to imagine a different life—one where she, too, had a home, a yard, maybe even a family. The thought made her chest constrict with an unfamiliar ache. Almost instinctively, she grabbed her phone and shot a quick text to Brenton: *"Stay over this weekend?"*

His reply came almost instantly: *"Of course."*

Lisa tucked the phone away with a sigh. She wasn't in love with Brenton—not really. Their relationship was easy, comfortable, and a safe place to land when the loneliness crept too close. It was a situationship she managed with one foot in and one foot out, always balancing between desire and detachment. Deep down, she knew it wasn't forever. It wasn't the dream.

Sometimes, when she let her guard down, she feared she was simply afraid of being alone. But today, as she drove past the scenes of suburban bliss, she accepted her truth: she was a woman in her thirties with a fierce, demanding career and the entire world at her fingertips. The life she once pictured—hot cocoa by the window, children laughing in the front yard—felt like a different universe now. And maybe, just maybe, if she ever wanted that version of life, she'd have to settle for less than what she truly needed. That realization lingered heavily as she pulled up to Janelle's building, ready to face whatever broken pieces she might find inside.

Arriving at the door, Lisa was greeted by the calming scent of burning sage and the smooth sounds of Donald Byrd spilling softly from the speakers. She knocked lightly, hearing Nelle's footsteps approach, and within seconds, the door swung open. Janelle stood there, a small but genuine smile tugging at her lips before she pulled Lisa into a warm embrace.

"I take it you're having a good day," Lisa said, a touch of surprise in her voice.

"I am..." Janelle replied, her tone light, almost peaceful.

Stepping inside, Lisa took in the immaculate space. It was spotless—almost too spotless, as if untouched. But as she wandered further back into the condo, her breath caught. Rows and rows of paintings stacked against the walls, vibrant and raw, a testament to months of quiet creation. Each piece seemed to pulse with emotion, as if Janelle had poured every bottled-up feeling onto the canvas.

Lisa slowly slipped off her coat, draping it over a kitchen stool, her eyes wide with admiration. She moved from painting to painting, letting herself get lost in the colors, the strokes, the stories Janelle had unleashed in silence. It was the most beautiful thing Lisa had ever seen her friend create, and for the first time in a long while, she understood Janelle had been transforming.

"These are so beautiful," Lisa said, her voice soft with awe as she moved from canvas to canvas. Janelle stood nearby, a cup of hot cocoa with marshmallows nestled in her hand, watching her friend admire the work.

"I made some hot cocoa," Janelle offered with a warm smile. "Do you want some? I have whipped cream and marshmallows too."

Lisa nodded, grateful. "Thank you."

As Janelle poured cocoa into a second mug, she glanced over her shoulder. "So... I saw the Instagram post," she said casually, her tone even. "Is there anything you want me to do?"

Lisa took the mug, blowing gently at the steam before replying. "Post these," she said firmly. "Share them with the world. They deserve to see you outside of him. And you have the following now: the support. I know you were against putting your art on social media before, but... this isn't a moment you miss. You take full advantage."

Janelle considered it as she sipped her cocoa, the rich sweetness grounding her. Together, they paced through the space, discussing the various brush strokes, color choices, and emotions behind each piece. Janelle shared her plans for the gallery now that it was ready—where each painting would hang and how she envisioned the flow of the room.

As Lisa sifted deeper through the collection, her hands brushed against a familiar image—a painting of her, Emily, and Janelle together, frozen in a moment of pure happiness. A tear slipped from the corner of her eye as she looked up at her friend, emotion gripping her throat.

"Oh," Janelle said softly, almost as if she had forgotten it existed.

Seated together on the floor, surrounded by rows of paintings like old records in a music store, Lisa and Janelle talked for hours. They flipped through each piece, their laughter and nostalgia saturating the room like a favorite tune. Conversations soon turned practical, brainstorming different marketing strategies and ways Janelle could begin monetizing her social media without feeling like she was selling out.

Although skeptical at first, Janelle eventually shared her real fears with Lisa. "I don't know what I'm going to do if this fails," she admitted quietly, pulling her knees closer to her chest. "Reggie's offered to buy out my contract, but I keep thinking about it, you know? If he spends ninety thousand dollars on me... and I move past this, and everything else still goes to shit... then would I even be able to ask him for help again?"

She paused, taking a long sip of her cocoa. "That's a lot of money," she whispered.

"I get it," Lisa said, her voice softening like an older sister comforting the younger. "It's scary for anyone stepping into the unknown like this... as a creative, pouring your heart into something and just hoping it'll be enough to put food on the table and give you a better life. We all want that. But this-this is your starting point. You can't focus on failing, because if you do, that's exactly what will happen. And you're already so much further along than most. I'll tell you that."

Janelle listened, her fingers nervously tapping against her cocoa mug before voicing her next worry.

"But Valentine's Day... how do you plan on getting me out of this unscathed?" she asked, a shaky laugh slipping through. "Roddy's loved even more now—the nomination, the movie roles. I don't want the Nicole treatment."

Lisa smiled reassuringly. "I would never let that happen. You just have to trust me."

Without hesitation, Janelle set her mug down on the floor and opened her arms wide, pulling Lisa into a tight embrace. They sat there, just the two of them, the world outside forgotten. They spent the rest of the day wrapped in conversation, reminiscing about their partners, laughing about old memories, and even shedding a few tears while planning for Emily's wedding. It was a rare, quiet kind of healing neither of them realized they needed.

It was a quiet night in December, the rain tapping steadily against the windows like a soft lullaby. Inside Lisa's warm townhouse, she and Brenton stayed cocooned beneath a mountain of plush covers, the scent of rain and fresh linen filling the room. At the foot of the bed, Korri was curled up peacefully in her own little nest, the occasional twitch of her paw betraying the dreams she chased. Under the low rumble of distant thunder, Lisa and Brenton kissed and made love, the storm outside only deepening the intimacy between them.

A few blocks away, Emily and Aaron were wrapped up in their own little world inside her apartment. Wedding plans temporarily forgotten, Emily lay sprawled across him on the couch, giggling as she tossed popcorn into his mouth. "Love Jones" flickered in the background, the soft dialogue and jazz melodies weaving through their laughter, creating a cozy memory neither would soon forget.

Meanwhile, Reggie made his way back into the city after a long day. He had returned to Long Island earlier to pack a few things and prepare his home for the coming storm, ensuring everything would be in place during his absence.

At the condo, Janelle sat quietly in the darkness, her only light coming from a small lamp that illuminated the corner of the living room where her easel stood. She had moved it back to its rightful spot, in front of the large window overlooking the wild, rain-drenched trees. The shadows danced across her walls, but she welcomed their company.

There, in the stillness of the night, she continued working on her latest piece—a portrait of Reggie, peacefully sleeping in her bed—capturing the fleeting, tender moments that words could never quite explain.

The soft click of the condo door didn't startle Janelle—she had been expecting him. Even after Reggie told her he'd left Roddy his key, resigning from his position, she knew deep down he would find his way back to her. A pang of guilt stirred in her chest, but it quickly dissolved when he assured her none of it was her fault. He didn't work out of necessity, he explained, but out of boredom, craving something to pass the time until he transitioned into something more fulfilling on his own terms.

As Reggie stepped quietly into the room, Janelle could feel the weight of his gaze settle warmly on her back. She stayed focused on her painting, carefully refining the small, delicate lines of his forehead. Without a word, he came closer, his hands landing firmly but gently atop her shoulders. The strap of her camisole slipped down her arm, and instinctively, she closed her eyes, turning her head to press a kiss to his hand.

Nelle was bare, save for a pair of panties and a thin shirt, her hair softly framing her face and casting an air of mystery around her.

"Is that me?" he asked, his voice teasing and tender.

She smiled without looking up, the brush in her hand gliding lovingly across the canvas, capturing every detail of the man who stood behind her.

His hand curled gently around her neck as he lowered himself to meet her. Janelle stayed focused on the painting, but inside, she welcomed him—yearning for his touch, hoping he would slide his fingers between her parted thighs. She told herself she could multitask, could balance the art in her hands with the burning need inside her.

Reggie's fingers cradled her chin, guiding her face toward his. Their lips met in a slow, wet kiss, tongues brushing in a tender, unhurried dance. The brush in Janelle's right hand and the palette of swirling colors in her left froze midair, forgotten in the heat of the moment. Without saying a word, he gently removed them from her hands, setting them aside, his eyes locked to hers with a gravity that made her heart race.

In one fluid motion, he lifted her from the stool and pressed her against the wide windowsill, the glass trembling with the beat of the rain pounding against it, as if the storm itself was desperate to intrude on their moment. His mouth trailed kisses along her cheek, her neck, leaving a trail of fire in his wake before disappearing between her thighs.

Janelle's legs found their place over his broad shoulders, her body arching toward him instinctively. Reggie's back and arm muscles flexed with each slow, deliberate motion, his tongue working her clit in deep, rhythmic strokes that made her toes curl against the cool of his upper back.

"Oh my God."

Her breath hitched as she moaned softly, her hands pressed against his, one minute; her fingers gently threading through his hair, the next. The sensation built within her, waves of pleasure cresting until she trembled, overwhelmed by the intensity of the moment. Even as her body shook, he didn't stop, his movements steady, as if determined to push her further into ecstasy. Her mind raced, heart pounding, and just as she thought she couldn't take anymore, he released her, his touch lingering before he walked her over to the bed.

She moved with him, eager to please, watching the way his muscles tensed beneath the weight of their shared passion. The sound of her name whispered in the air, followed by the deep grip of his hands around her waist, guiding her with every movement. They were lost in each other, in a rhythm of their own that defied the world outside their room. In that moment, it was just the two of them, reckless and free, indulging in a nasty night that felt as perfect as it was forbidden.

As the weeks moved quickly, the ladies found themselves caught up in the momentum of their busy lives, each day blending into the next, with whispers of another vacation on the horizon—an all-girls trip, of course. While their friendships flourished and their personal lives seemed to fall into place, Lisa's attention remained consumed by Roddy. She had worked tirelessly to keep him grounded, keeping him focused, and, above all, out of trouble. But with the Golden Globes just two weeks away, and the event they'd all been waiting for—the night of his first-ever nomination—looming large, the weight of her responsibility was becoming harder to carry.

It was 1:17 AM when the phone rang. The name on the screen was Sam, the manager of Nobu Downtown. Lisa's heart sank as she listened to the message. Roddy was beyond drunk—so drunk that his driver had refused to take him anywhere, fearing he might be struck by the unruly star. She could feel the exhaustion creeping into her bones, but sleep was impossible now. She climbed into a black car, hoping for a smooth and uneventful resolution—no paparazzi, no accidental run-ins with journalists. Just peace.

Brenton, however, was furious. He didn't understand the unpredictability of Lisa's work, the way her career sometimes demanded sacrifices others couldn't relate to. She tried to explain, tried to make him see that her job was different. But in the quiet of the night, as she headed toward another potential disaster, the burden of her two worlds collided, and the task ahead felt more daunting than ever.

By 2:30 AM, Lisa had set Roddy up in her guest room, making sure he was comfortable enough to sleep off his drunken stupor. But just as she thought she might finally get some rest, Brenton arrived, his footsteps heavy as he entered her space. "I'm not letting you sleep alone in the house with no drunk ass dude," he sniped, his voice laced with concern. She couldn't help but smile, appreciating his protective nature. She loved him for it, even if he did drive her crazy sometimes.

"I'm not alone, Eliana is here," she quipped, trying to lighten the mood. But Brenton only side-eyed her in response, and without saying another word, he motioned for her to rest in his arms. She welcomed the comfort, letting her head fall against his chest, allowing herself to drift off, even if just for a few hours.

Day after day, Lisa found herself defending Roddy's behavior, making excuses for his lateness to photoshoots, his missed interviews, and the delays in posting his brand sponsorships. She knew he needed help—he deserved it—but no matter how hard she tried, she couldn't shoulder the weight alone. She was stretched thin, constantly trying to manage the chaos around Roddy while simultaneously neglecting her own business. The clients she once focused on were becoming secondary to his needs, and the passion she had for her work was slowly being replaced by frustration. This was not the kind of business she wanted to run, but with Roddy's behavior spiraling, she felt like she had no choice but to keep making sacrifices.

Lisa quickly found herself thinking on her feet, juggling the uproar surrounding Roddy with her other clients, including Janelle, where it made sense—especially when it came to social media posts. She wasn't in the business of giving refunds, and she wasn't about to let the situation spiral any further. So, she made other arrangements, taking on extra work to fill in the gaps.

Slowly, though, everyone seemed to be dropping away from Roddy's circle. Even Emily, once the closest person to him, was growing increasingly concerned with his reckless spending.

Roddy's gambling addiction had become more pronounced, and the consequences were starting to catch up with him. His cleaning lady hadn't been paid in weeks, his driver was beginning to voice frustrations, and his friends were all lingering in the background, waiting for their share of the spoils. Meanwhile, Roddy was hanging out with the wrong crowd—rappers who encouraged him to drink more, party more, and spend even more of his money in the clubs. His once-polished image was starting to tarnish, and if Lisa didn't know any better, she could've sworn he was actively trying to push her away, too.

It wasn't just his behavior that was spiraling; the entire world around him seemed to be collapsing, and Lisa found herself holding everything together by a thread. She didn't want to admit it, but the cracks in their business relationship were starting to show, and she feared it was only a matter of time before everything came crashing down.

In the quiet of her office, late into the evening, the city outside barely made a sound. Emily entered, accompanied by Laura, the three of them settling into their usual routine—no time for small talk, just strategy. As the last traces of daylight faded into the darkness of the night, they immediately dove into the heavy conversation at hand.

"He can't get rid of it fast enough... the money. It's like he resents you for making him richer, and he's throwing it all away," Emily remarked, taking off her coat and relaxing into her seat with a weary sigh. Laura, ever the calm one, handed both Lisa and Emily a steaming cup of tea, trying to soothe the tension in the room.

"I've done everything on socials. I try to keep it positive and light," Laura chimed in, her voice a little more upbeat but no less concerned.

Lisa, still seated behind her desk, was wrapped in the solitude of the office's dim light, her thoughts swirling. "Em," she began, her voice strained, as she rubbed her hands together, pondering her next words slowly. "I think I'm going to bill out."

Emily's eyes widened in disbelief. "What?"

"You mean, fire him as a client?" Laura confirmed, her voice low but steady.

Lisa nodded, the weight of her decision pressing on her. "Yeah, I'm burned out, and I can't keep doing this. I'm owed millions, and if he's just throwing it all away like this, I need to cut ties before he blows through what he owes me... and Nelle too." Her eyes flickered with frustration as she spoke.

Emily sighed heavily, rubbing her forehead. "I get it, I really do. But... what's he going to do without you?"

Lisa's eyes welled up, her heart heavy with the thought of leaving him. Roddy had become more than just a client; he was family, and she hated what was happening. "If the press had their way, he would've been done already. Do you know how many people I've had to pay off in the last two weeks just to keep quiet? He's out at Nobu, getting trashed in public, like it's nothing!"

"Why is he doing this?" Laura asked, her tone soft but laced with confusion.

"I don't know. When I ask him, he goes off about not being appreciated, about being taken advantage of... oh, and now he knows about Reggie and Nelle. He found that out from his so-called friends." Lisa paused, a lump in her throat.

Emily's face tightened. "But he and Nelle didn't even have anything romantic. So that shouldn't even matter."

"He liked her," Lisa said quietly.

"Felt entitled to her, you mean," Emily corrected, her voice sharp. "Typical man... they don't get their way, so they lash out and make it everyone else's problem."

Lisa shrugged, her mind spinning. "Yeah... I guess."

Emily took a deep breath before turning to the next piece of the puzzle. "Well, I'm ready when you are. Just so you're aware, because I'm not sure what the invoice is going to look like once it crosses my desk. After our firm fee is deducted, he'll be down to about $1.2 million in assets and $580,000 in liquid capital."

Lisa's jaw dropped. "What! What about the deals and the A24 film he just did in Alaska?"

Emily shrugged again. "That money hasn't come in yet, and if he continues on the path he's going now, it'll be burned through by the time it does. Studios can take years to issue payments."

"But he's union. Surely that'll come through quicker."

Emily didn't flinch. "I'm just letting you know what I know."

Lisa leaned back in her chair, her mind reeling. "The nomination was half a million. I haven't even recouped that yet, and you're saying that's all he has?" The room fell into a heavy silence. It was as though the words had been spoken, but no one knew how to move forward from here.

With her event fast approaching, Janelle was in full-on planning mode for the big night. Lisa had connected her with top-tier caterers and event planners, and she threw herself into the work with a renewed sense of purpose. Every waking moment was consumed with decisions—finalizing the details for the decorations, lighting, and even the music. Each choice felt personal, a reflection of her vision for the evening.

Luckily, Reggie had offered his help with the food. They spent countless hours together attending tastings, collaborating on dishes, and incorporating his professional expertise. It felt good, having him by her side in this way. They were a unit now, a team. Their bond had grown stronger, and for Janelle, that was more than she could have ever hoped for.

Though the date of the event hadn't changed and the familiar guilt still lingered in the back of her mind, Reggie seemed unbothered. He only cared about what was best for her, and that was enough for her to push aside any lingering doubts. As Lisa promised not to involve Roddy in the evening's events, it made everything easier to bear. Roddy would attend, walk the red carpet, snap a few photos, and then leave—his presence would be brief, a formality, nothing more.

Invitations were sent out, and the words "Save the Date" were bold and clear: *January 11th.* It was Janelle's lucky number, and she hoped that this night would be perfect, just the way she dreamed.

Lisa was already planning her exit, and she wasted no time billing Emily for Roddy's outstanding expenses, along with Nelle's. The invoice sat at the top of her inbox, heavy and glaring. Even with debts being paid down, including the money Roddy owed Reggie, his reckless behavior showed no signs of slowing. He was in full-on "expense it" mode, throwing money around carelessly, tipping wait staff $500 on a $200 dinner tab, acting like the well would never run dry.

Trying to salvage what she could, Lisa had invited Roddy to stay at her place for a while. She even enlisted Eliana's help to keep an eye on him while she was busy with work, a task Eliana agreed to without hesitation. Both Lisa and Emily knew Roddy was suffering. Therapy seemed like the obvious next step—or maybe even rehab—but the burden of getting him checked in, managing his care, and trying to save his career was too much for Lisa to bear alone. She couldn't add another impossible task to her already overwhelming to-do list.

Meanwhile, as Roddy spiraled further, his opportunities began to dry up one by one. Meetings were canceled, phone calls went unanswered, and the deals that once came in easily started to fade into silence.

It seemed that no matter how many promises Roddy made—to be a better father, to take accountability—brands were no longer lining up to associate with him. The golden boy image had tarnished beyond repair. To make matters worse, Janelle had grown distant; the proof was undeniable as fewer and fewer photos of them surfaced online. Lisa didn't dare upload any herself—there was no way to hide the exhaustion in Roddy's eyes, the heavy, dark circles that clung to them like a shadow.

He was drinking from morning until night, pausing only to snort lines with his so-called friends over FaceTime. His decline wasn't slow or subtle; it was catastrophic, a trainwreck you couldn't look away from no matter how hard you tried.

One night, while Lisa was out trying to piece together yet another broken deal, Brenton took it upon himself to cook dinner. The house was quiet, the air heavy with tension.

In the guest room just above them, the sound of furniture crashing against the floor echoed through the house. Brenton stiffened, set the spoon down, and wiped his hands on a towel before storming up the stairs. He didn't even bother knocking—just twisted the handle and pushed the door open.

The room was a mess. Lamps knocked over, sheets tangled, a chair tipped on its side. And in the middle of it all, Roddy, sitting dazed on the carpet, breathing heavily. Brenton clicked his teeth in frustration as he stepped inside.

"Man, what the hell is going on in here?" he snapped.

Roddy's eyes darted to him, wide and worried. "Nothing. I'm sorry. I was just trying to get some sleep, and I fell," he lied, voice shaky.

"Sleep?" Brenton repeated, looking around in disbelief. "Listen, man, what's really going on with you?"

Roddy hesitated, the walls he tried so hard to keep up finally cracking. "This shit is lonely, man. I... I don't have anybody," he admitted, his voice breaking under the weight of it.

"You can meet people. You can go anywhere, do anything. You got the world in your palms," Brenton reasoned, trying to talk some sense into him.

Roddy shook his head slowly. "It's not like that. It's not what it's cracked up to be. It's all work. Even when you think you're getting a break, trying to go home to something real, it's still just...work."

Brenton sighed, leaning against the doorframe. "Come on, bro. We men. Shit gets rough sometimes, but at least you got the resources to turn it around. Some dudes never make it out the hood and still find a way to make shit shake. You looking real crazy right now, man."

Roddy lowered his head, struggling to push himself off the floor. "My mom was sick. Really sick. Sent money for the funeral... but my sister said she don't want me there. Said I'm the reason ma ain't here. That I left and didn't change nothing for them."

"It ain't like that, though," Brenton said, his voice softer now.

"This acting shit," Roddy muttered, dragging himself onto the edge of the bed, "before Lisa, it didn't pay like people think. They see you on TV and swear you got it made. That you're supposed to spend everything you got on them. But it's harder than you think. I paid over two million dollars for cancer treatment, stays, medication. She wouldn't apply for no government help—said she got a boy on TV. So... I said no. Thanksgiving, man. I said no."

Brenton stood frozen by the door, his mind racing to piece together the right words, something, anything that might make it better. But before he could even open his mouth, Roddy broke down, "It's my fault!"—loud, sharp cries tearing through the room, raw and uncontrollable.

Brenton shifted awkwardly, his hands useless at his sides. He hated this feeling, hated seeing another man crumble and not knowing how to fix it. With a heavy heart, he reached for his phone and did the only thing he could think to do—he called Lisa.

When she picked up, he didn't sugarcoat it. "You need to come home," he said, his voice low and urgent.

On the other end, Lisa didn't hesitate. "I'm coming home now!" she said, and the line went dead.

Brenton pocketed his phone, glancing back at Roddy, who sat hunched over; he was broken.

CHAPTER 21.

THIS IS HER STORY

Lisa burst through the front door, her heart pounding as Brenton quickly filled her in on what Roddy had confessed. It all made sense now. In that instant, Lisa shed her publicist persona; she wasn't here to fix his image tonight. She was here to be his friend—the one thing he desperately needed.

Along with Eliana and Brenton, Lisa spent the night encouraging Roddy, helping him clean up, sitting him down with something warm to eat, and flushing the drugs he had hidden away. They rallied around him, doing everything they could to hold him together when he clearly couldn't do it himself.

Later, standing in the upstairs hallway just outside his bedroom door, the three of them quietly debated their next move.

"We should probably get him into rehab before the Globes. Christmas is in two days. It's all about Mariah Carey right now anyway. The blogs have enough content."

"You think he's in any shape to go to a televised award show that's airing live?" Brenton asked, his arms folded tight across his chest.

Lisa didn't flinch. "He doesn't have a choice."

Brenton scoffed, shaking his head. "Oh, I see what he means now... 'cause that's actually insane. Rehab means withdrawal. He'll be going through mad shit."

"I'll call Doctor Aruna in the morning," Lisa said, her voice steady, her mind made up. "See if there's something she can give him to get him through."

Christmas morning was meant to be filled with laughter and warmth, but inside Lisa's townhouse, it was anything but. Roddy, weak from the prescribed medications meant to help him detox, spent most of the day vomiting behind closed doors. The sounds were heartbreaking, but there was little more they could do. Eventually, Lisa and Brenton made a quiet decision: they needed a break, even if just for a few hours.

Living in New York offered them that escape. Restaurants were still open for the holiday, and so they went out, finding comfort in a nontraditional celebration. Over a cozy meal, they exchanged small, meaningful gifts, their spirits lifting with each passing moment. Later, they glided across The Rink at Rockefeller Center beneath the glittering Christmas tree lights, the night feeling almost magical—an unexpected silver lining to an otherwise hectic day.

Meanwhile, Janelle and Reggie headed uptown to Harlem, where Reggie was formally introduced to her family. The vibe was quieter, more intimate. Instead of festive fanfare, they gathered over hearty food and soft conversation. Though Janelle's family wasn't Spanish, her mother's fluent Spanish impressed Reggie, prompting lively exchanges across the table—until her father, smiling warmly, chimed in, "Now, now, it's English only in this house."

Far from the city, Emily and Aaron spent Christmas in Aspen, enjoying the fresh powder and the affluent world of ski resorts. Aaron's friends from the association and their wives welcomed Emily into their circle with open arms. Being a "baseball wife" had a certain ring to it—one Emily found herself liking more and more with each passing day.

During those final days in December, Roddy was beginning to feel more like himself again. He returned to his condo, seeking comfort in the familiar: marathon video game sessions, endless playlists, and a steady stream of Uber Eats deliveries. Outwardly, he seemed to be moving on, even convincing himself—and those around him— that the guilt over his mother's passing was beginning to fade. But deep down, unfamiliar and unsettling thoughts still raced through his mind, shadows he couldn't quite shake. Still, time marched forward, and so did he.

Lisa, naturally, worried about him. But once Roddy left her care, there was little else she could do. Life picked back up in small ways, and on New Year's Eve, the group was ready for a fresh start. Renting a private space inside a restaurant in Times Square, they all gathered to watch the iconic ball drop. Reggie had officially become one of them now, and Lisa welcomed it; she loved seeing how effortlessly and tenderly he adored Janelle. The two were practically inseparable, sharing stolen kisses and laughter like no one else existed.

It was freezing outside, but inside, the $4,000 splurge was worth every penny—floor-to-ceiling views of the glittering square, endless food and drinks, and, most importantly, the kind of warmth only New York's finest winter hospitality could buy. As the countdown began, surrounded by friends, laughter, and a new sense of hope, it truly felt like a new beginning.

Between the endless sex, alcohol, food, and laughter, no one was quite ready to return to the grind—but reality called, and so they all trudged back into their routines. Slowly, things started to feel semi-normal again: the office phones buzzed nonstop, media chatter returned to a steady hum, emails flooded in, and before anyone knew it, it was time for the big moment.

Janelle had been sent four breathtaking gowns to choose from for her red carpet debut beside a newly nominated Roddy Richardson, who himself received an impressive lineup of designer suits from Thom Browne, Dior, and Canali. It was surreal. For Lisa, this was a career-defining milestone—the first time she had broken a client into true mainstream success.

The energy in the office was electric. A few bottles of champagne left over from New Year's were popped open, and everyone was encouraged to indulge. It was a celebration not just for Roddy, but for all of them—proof that their hard work had paid off. In the spirit of gratitude and triumph, Lisa announced a well-earned 9% raise for everyone in the office. They deserved it. Every bit of it.

Day after day, Janelle arrived at the office studio for fittings, each one more intense than the last. Glam teams rotated in and out, trying different hairstyles, makeup looks, and dress options—it was a whirlwind unlike anything she had experienced since signing her contract. Previous red carpets had been far simpler: a dress would arrive, a glam squad would be hired, and a look would be assembled almost fluently. But this time was different.

The stakes were higher. The event was bigger. Legends would be in attendance. Eyes from all corners of the industry would be watching, judging, remembering. This wasn't just about looking good; it was about establishing herself among the greats.

Roddy was no exception. His schedule was just as packed with fittings, press sessions, and meetings with stylists and designers. And although Janelle and Roddy often passed each other in the hallways like distant coworkers, their interactions remained minimal. Cordial at best. While he occasionally offered a polite nod or a soft hello, she rarely acknowledged him at all—her focus was elsewhere, and she preferred to keep it that way.

Stepping out of the elevator the night before the Golden Globes, Janelle paused, letting the cool pulse of New York City wrap around her like an old friend. She needed this moment. The dresses she had worn over the last few days—the softest, most luxurious fabrics she had ever touched—still seemed to linger against her skin, a reminder of how far she had come. Gratitude swelled in her chest. And in just three days, she would step into the biggest event of her career, but tonight, she simply wanted to breathe it all in.

Earlier that afternoon, a truck pulled up to her condo to transport the 35 pieces she had selected for her gallery's opening night—all her own work, all originals, and each one carrying pieces of her soul. Among them was her proudest creation: her first-ever 3D sculpted art piece, a labor of love that demanded every ounce of her patience and creativity. The process had been messy, arduous, and full of doubt, but she hadn't held back—and now it was finished. Soon, it would sit in a glass case at the rear of her gallery, a testament to her perseverance and an introduction to the world of who she really was.

That night, Janelle danced. The weight of her work lifted as most of it was already transported out, leaving her condo feeling lighter, freer. The opening of her gallery had already taken the internet by storm, courtesy of Lisa, and to her surprise, the free tickets had sold out in a record-breaking thirty minutes. Over two hundred tickets—gone in an instant. Some of her followers even asked for more, a wave of support that left her overwhelmed with gratitude.

She let herself get lost in the music, letting the melodies of *"Let's Hear It for the Boy"* by Deniece Williams and *"Footloose"* by Kenny Loggins fill the room. Her hair swung in her face as she moved, feet shifting to the beat, her body gliding in a way that defied rhythm but felt completely natural. It was her moment, her joy, her expression, completely uninhibited.

Reggie entered not long after, but Janelle hadn't noticed. He simply stood in the doorway, watching her, captivated. Her movements were fluid, her hair whipping back and forth with each turn, embodying a raw, unguarded freedom. It was as if the room itself had faded away, leaving only her and the music in a private celebration of everything she had worked for.

By 5 AM, the whirlwind of preparations was finally complete. The jet was ready to take off, its interior buzzing with a mix of excitement and exhaustion. Interns, stylists, and staff shuffled onboard, the hum of quiet chatter mixing with the sound of cell phones ringing. Roddy, ever the enigma, was buried beneath a hoodie and jacket, attempting to retreat from the chaos with a quiet solitude, his eyes barely open as he slumped into his seat.

Janelle, still feeling the effects of a late night, had barely caught any sleep. The passionate hours spent in Reggie's arms had her feeling worn but content. Her eyes were heavy, the soft warmth of the private jet's cabin lulling her into a state of dreamy exhaustion. Yet, despite the fatigue, there was a sense of satisfaction—it was all going to be over…soon.

She leaned back in her seat, a soft smile playing at the corners of her lips, knowing the journey ahead would be more than just a flight. It was one step closer to another chapter in her evolving story.

The weather in Beverly Hills was a welcome contrast to New York's winter chill, with the warm sun making everyone shed at least two layers of clothing. As they arrived at the hotel, the atmosphere shifted into a relaxed mode—time to unwind, grab a bite to eat, and prepare for the evening ahead. The Golden Globes, though, were about to turn everything up a notch.

The event was nothing short of a spectacle—an extravagant celebration of the finest in film and television.

The red carpet stretched out like an electric runway, lined with rows of flashing cameras, eager reporters, and a brigade of publicists ensuring everything went off without a hitch. Celebrities stepped onto the carpet, radiating an unforced grace that commanded attention. The constant clicking of cameras created a whirr of excitement that filled the air, a rhythm that spoke to the magnitude of the night.

Publicists were everywhere, like silent directors, offering last-minute reminders and guidance. "Smile, pause for a second, angle your body towards the light," they whispered to their clients, ensuring every shot was perfect. The celebrities, seasoned pros at this glamorous dance, knew exactly how to pose—one hand casually resting at their side, the other elegantly perched on their hip. Posture straight, chin lifted, eyes locked with the lenses, and every movement calculated. Each step, each smile, designed to capture their essence and leave an impression that would last.

When Janelle and Roddy appeared together, they stole the show without even trying. Their looks were flawless, their chemistry undeniable. Janelle, in a shimmering, form-fitting gown with a train that trailed off behind her with every step, and Roddy, effortlessly sharp in a tailored suit that screamed sophistication. They moved in perfect harmony, stopping for photos, each click of the camera only enhancing the magnetic energy between them. Their presence on the carpet was captivating, drawing every eye in the room, every camera focused on their every move.

Meanwhile, Lisa stood just off to the side, capturing the moment for herself. She snapped photo after photo, knowing this was a pivotal moment—not just for Janelle's career, but for her own as well. The media frenzy around them was intensifying, and Lisa, with her camera in hand, knew she was witnessing something monumental. This was Hollywood in its most dazzling, breathtaking form, and it was all unfolding in front of her eyes.

The night was nothing short of spectacular, a flurry of excitement and energy that only the Golden Globes could bring. Fans shouted Roddy's name as they arrived closer to the venue's entrance. With one hand raised in a wave and the other wrapped around Janelle's waist, they were the picture of perfection—young, radiant, and exactly what Hollywood had been waiting for. The chemistry between them was undeniable, and as the images of their arrival flooded social media, the world took notice. Lisa's business phone buzzed uncontrollably, a constant stream of messages and calls from agents, reporters, and potential clients. The demand was overwhelming—everyone was eager to buy into the vision, the fairytale, the...con.

For a split second, Lisa wondered if firing Roddy was the right choice. She hesitated, realizing that their star power was just beginning to shine. The night was still young, and with every passing moment, their presence only grew more magnetic. Inside the venue, the atmosphere was electric. Stars in every direction, all dressed to the nines, filled the room with a sense of wonder and exclusivity.

Janelle's eyes wandered, taking in the sight of it all. There were celebrities everywhere, some of them complimenting her on her gown, others sharing a quick hug or a warm handshake. It was surreal—just a few years ago, she had only seen these faces on television. And now, they were greeting her, engaging in conversations, snapping photos together as if they were old friends. Janelle couldn't believe her life had led her here, to this very moment.

The night took an unexpected turn when Jerrod Carmichael, the host of the Golden Globes, made a lighthearted joke that caught Janelle's attention. "I'm here because I'm black," he said with a smirk, the room erupting in laughter. But for Janelle, the words hit differently. It made her sit up and take notice, the implications of the remark lingering in her mind as the evening progressed.

As the awards ceremony continued, it became clear to everyone in the room that Roddy wasn't going to win. The anticipation that had built up in him slowly fizzled out, though a part of him still held on to the faintest hope— just the slightest vision of his name flashing across the screen.

But even as the win slipped further from reach, he told himself the nomination was enough. The applause from his peers, the smiles, the nods from people he admired—it made him feel seen, appreciated, if only for a moment. But that moment faded quickly. Recognition from strangers could only fill so much.

Roddy's eyes scanned the room, looking for a connection, a sign of support, but it never came. His family silent. The woman on his arm, bought and paid for. No texts, no calls—nothing. It was as if no one cared. Not even his so-called "friends." The crowd of faces around him seemed to blur, distant and unfamiliar, like a distorted reality he couldn't quite place.

The recognition he craved was out of reach, and it left him feeling hollow, all over again. Slowly, he mentally checked out. As the evening wore on and they all made their way back to the Beverly Hills Hotel, Roddy drifted in silence, disconnected from the world around him, his mind on autopilot as the lights of the city blurred past.

Back at the hotel, the night continued with a sense of casual luxury. Everyone kicked off their shoes and made themselves comfortable in the expansive suite they'd secured for the occasion. Only two individual rooms had been booked for Janelle and Roddy, while the rest of the group gathered together in the main suite, the excitement of the night still lingering in the air. Champagne corks popped as glasses clinked, filling the space with bubbly chatter.

Lisa, ever the professional, flipped through her phone, reading aloud the list of brands that had flooded her inbox in the wake of the Golden Globes. Her voice barely masked the excitement as she rattled off the numbers. "Rick Owens—$180,000 for one Instagram post or tweet. LUEQ—$160,000 for a post and a dress for an event. Old Spice—$270,000. Irish Spring—$491,000 for a three-month campaign," she continued, the figures stacking up like a dizzying tally of success. The list didn't stop there; each brand offered substantial sums for their association with Janelle and Roddy, evidence of the influence they had garnered that night.

Janelle smiled at the figures, her eyes gleaming with the potential of it all, but there was a clear weight in her expression. She was exhausted. The sparkle from the night had begun to dim under the weight of her fatigue. She kissed Lisa on the cheek, a quiet gesture of appreciation, before excusing herself from the room. Her footsteps were soft as she exited, heading to her suite to unwind after the whirlwind of the evening, leaving behind the buzz of excitement and the promises of a future filled with opportunities.

It didn't take long for everyone to notice that something was off with Roddy. But no one wanted to be the first to say it aloud, to disrupt the celebration with their concern. So they let it linger in the air, unspoken, as they continued to toast to success. Meanwhile, Roddy had disappeared into the bathroom connected to the large suite, the door shutting behind him for what stretched into an uncomfortable amount of time—at least an hour, maybe more.

The bathroom wasn't far from the main living area, its proximity making his absence all the more noticeable. Conversations continued, phones buzzed with new opportunities, and some of the team started trickling off to bed. Still, Roddy hadn't returned. It wasn't until the room had quieted that Lisa, now half-distracted from a text she was reading, realized he hadn't reappeared. A ripple of panic stirred in her chest.

"Maybe he went to his suite?" someone offered, but no one could say for sure.

Lisa's heart quickened. She called out, her voice cutting through the late-night haze, "Roderick!" No answer. She started searching around corners, peeking onto the balcony, scanning the living area. Nothing.

When she finally made her way toward the sleeping quarters at the back of the suite, she noticed the bathroom door was shut. She knocked lightly at first, then harder when there was no response. Her hand trembled slightly as she pressed her ear to the door. Silence.

The door was locked.

"This door is locked. Does someone know how to get it open?" Lisa called out, her voice sharp with urgency. But no one answered—most of them were either half-drunk, dozing off, or simply too clueless to comprehend the situation. Frustrated, Lisa pounded on the door again, harder this time. No response.

Without wasting another second, she rushed back into the living room, motioning frantically for one of the interns to follow her. "Come on, see if you can get the door open!" she ordered, thrusting her hand toward the back hallway. At the same time, she snatched up the phone and dialed the front desk with trembling fingers, pacing in tight circles.

She dropped to her knees, peering under the bed just to be sure—she *had* to be sure. But there was nothing. If Roddy wasn't out here, he had to be in there. And silence... silence was an answer in itself.

"Hello, this is the front desk," a calm voice answered.

"Hi! We need someone to come up to the premier suite now, we need a key for the bathroom," Lisa said quickly, her words rushing out before she slammed the phone down. "See if you can jimmy the lock!" she barked at the intern, who was now fumbling nervously with the doorknob.

The energy in the room shifted instantly—no longer festive, no longer joyful. Panic set in. Lisa's tears started to fall, uncontrollable, as she called out again, her voice cracking, "Roddy!"

Moments later, a soft knock sounded at the suite door. Lisa sprinted to open it. A housekeeper stood there, slightly startled by the urgency on Lisa's face.

"Where's the key?" Lisa demanded.

The woman quickly handed it over, and Lisa didn't even wait to say thank you. She sprinted back down the hallway, her heart pounding in her ears, hands shaking so badly she fumbled twice before she could get the key into the lock. With one final breath, she turned the key and pushed the door open.

"Ohhh God!" Lisa gasped, her voice splintering into a sob as her body jolted backward. Behind her, the intern dropped to his knees, vomiting onto the pristine carpeting.

The bathroom was a vision of calm and luxury—white marble floors with gray veining, a deep built-in tub framed under a soft, striped Roman shade, natural light seeping faintly into the muted, beige-toned room. A delicate white orchid perched on the edge of the vanity, surrounded by polished chrome fixtures and neatly hung white towels, all blending into a scene that should have felt serene.

But the image was shattered.

Roddy's body lay slumped in the deep bathtub, one arm dangling limply over the side, his face tilted away, his suit soaked and wrinkled. Beside him, an empty Ambien bottle rattled quietly against the porcelain, and a bottle of champagne, a silent witness to the choice he had made. He looked almost peaceful, as if he had simply fallen asleep—but Lisa knew better.

Without thinking, she sprinted forward, slipping on the marble as she lunged toward him. "Call 911!" she shrieked at the intern, who scrambled to his feet, pale and panicked.

Lisa pulled Roddy's heavy frame out of the tub, her arms shaking violently as she cradled him on the cold floor. "I'm so sorry," she wept over and over, the words tumbling from her lips in broken cries. She tore off his soaked Dior suit jacket with trembling fingers, exposing his white button-down shirt.

Stripping away the layers, she lay him flat, her hair falling into her face, her dress bunched and wrinkled at her knees, her bare feet slipping on the wet marble.

With no hesitation, Lisa began CPR—desperate, frantic—pressing her hands hard against his chest, breathing into his mouth between gasps of her own.

"I'm so sorry," she whispered in ragged breaths, the room around them fading into a haze of sobs, sirens in the distance, and the blinding ache of helplessness.

It all unfolded in slow motion, as if the world had been dipped underwater—sounds muffled, movements blurred. The chaos of the night bled seamlessly into the pale rise of the early morning sun, casting long, forgiving beams down the hotel hallway.

Lisa sprinted alongside the EMT gurney, her hair wild, her dress soaked with sweat and tears. Her eyes, bloodshot and raw from crying, were wide with fear, locked on Roddy's unmoving body. The gurney wheels pushed across the carpet floor as paramedics barked orders, their voices urgent against the heavy, suffocating silence.

Janelle, rubbing her eyes, cracked open her hotel room door just in time to see the blur of frantic movement rush past her. For a moment, she just stood there, stunned, her mouth covered by trembling hands. Lisa's disheveled figure flashed by—a jarring, devastating sight—and reality hit Janelle like a punch to the gut.

This couldn't be happening.

Snapping out of her daze, Janelle turned on her heel, rushing back into her room. She scrambled for her phone, her keycard, and slipped on the nearest pair of slippers. Her heart hammered in her chest as she bolted out again, following the sounds of panic.

While the others crowded into the elevator, Janelle tore for the stairwell, taking the stairs two at a time. Every heartbeat, every breath, felt like it was carrying her further into a nightmare she couldn't wake up from.

OPENING NIGHT

January 11th arrived with the electric energy only New York could deliver, and Janelle rose to the moment, serving a fierce, ultra-chic all-black look with an unapologetic attitude. She was a vision of power and poise, cloaked in a dramatic, long, black textured fur coat that billowed around her like a storm. Beneath it, she kept the silhouette chic and lethal—a fitted black top tucked into high-waisted black pants that hugged her frame perfectly.

Her boots made a statement all on their own: black over-the-knee leather with pointed toes and razor-sharp stiletto heels, each step clicking with authority. Accessories were razor sharp and deliberate—a small black handbag tucked neatly under her arm, overpriced black cat-eye sunglasses perched on her nose, and minimal but impactful jewelry, including a gleaming ring and small, elegant earrings. Her hair was slicked back into a polished, low style that made the whole look feel graceful yet intentional.

She wanted to be unforgettable—to own the room without letting her fashion overshadow her work—and she struck the perfect balance.

The gallery space buzzed with life: vibrant art hung against suspended panel walls, while oversized statues stood like sentinels off to the sides. Each piece was priced between $450 and $990, and they were all hers for the taking.

To her surprise, a line wrapped around the entrance, an eager crowd waiting to get in. Lisa, though away, had anticipated the turnout and planned accordingly. Janelle couldn't help but feel impressed.

Flanked by security and with her man no more than five feet away, Janelle made her entrance, her heels slicing through the hum of conversation like a queen taking her throne. This was her moment, and she was ready.

Surrounded by a room buzzing with admiration and fresh opportunity, Janelle moved through the space like a magnet. Everywhere she turned, eyes lingered—some filled with curiosity, others with genuine respect, but all of them ready to take her seriously.

From the rear of the gallery, she caught sight of Emily and Aaron waving excitedly, their faces lit with pride and support. Janelle stood, microphones thrust in her face, reporters firing off question after question about a man she had no desire to discuss. His name, once tied to her every move, was now a shadow she was desperate to escape. Yet, somehow, despite her best efforts to move forward, her moment was being overshadowed by a person who no longer held a place in her life. It was as though the world refused to let go of an old narrative, one she had already discarded.

But enough was enough.

In that moment, Janelle decided it was time to take back her story. It was time to reclaim her narrative, to tell it on her terms—raw, real, and unregretful. The truth would no longer be obscured by the past. Her life, in all its vibrant color, was now her own to define.

Her eyes scanned the room, locking onto him. Reggie. Standing at the far side, drink in hand, silently observing the spectacle they had all created around him. The manufactured world they had built seemed to distance him, but Janelle felt no hesitation. It was her time. She would no longer be silent.

With a breath of determination, Janelle made her move. She shifted through the crowd, gracefully weaving past guests, her strides purposeful and confident. The cameras flashed, the reporters' chatter grew louder, but Janelle was undeterred. The light seemed to shift, focusing entirely on them, a spotlight that could no longer be ignored.

Reggie noticed her approach, his lips curving into a small, knowing smile. He turned towards her, the noise of the room fading into the background as their eyes locked. Without a second thought, Janelle stepped forward, closing the distance between them, and kissed him. Their tongues met in a passionate dance, a moment of connection that resonated in the stillness of the room.

A collective gasp rippled through the crowd, but it didn't matter. This was her story. No more distractions, no more shadows. Just them. Together. And in that kiss, Janelle had finally taken control.

THE END

Lisa K. Stephenson

ASIAS BRANDS

Original Music

Download/Stream Now

www.asiasfilms.com

MESSAGE THE AUTHOR

To share your thoughts and feedback, contact Lisa at
press@shessinglemag.com

Lisa K. Stephenson